SUNSET

SUNSET

The Unmaking

Raymond Sharp

Copyright © 2024 by Raymond Sharp.

Library of Congress Control Number:	2024909777
ISBN: Hardcover	979-8-3694-2219-9
Softcover	979-8-3694-2218-2
eBook	979-8-3694-2217-5

All rights reserved. No part of this book may be reproduced or transmitted in any form or by any means, electronic or mechanical, including photocopying, recording, or by any information storage and retrieval system, without permission in writing from the copyright owner.

This is a work of fiction. Names, characters, places and incidents either are the product of the author's imagination or are used fictitiously, and any resemblance to any actual persons, living or dead, events, or locales is entirely coincidental.

Any people depicted in stock imagery provided by Getty Images are models, and such images are being used for illustrative purposes only.
Certain stock imagery © Getty Images.

Print information available on the last page.

Rev. date: 12/12/2024

To order additional copies of this book, contact:
Xlibris
844-714-8691
www.Xlibris.com
Orders@Xlibris.com
849608

PROLOGUE

2008

Whoever fights monsters should see to it that in the process he does not become a monster. And when you look long into an abyss, the abyss also looks into you.

Friedrich Nietzsche

I have been here for 25 years. A lifetime for some, many lifetimes for me. As the years march unrelentingly by, I've began to view time as the Great Bully it is, there is either never enough or entirely too much. I adhere to the latter since I am sitting in a California supermax prison.

Don't misunderstand me, I'm not a convict, but a prison guard, and believe me when I tell you that going to work is just like doing time. An eight hour shift seems to stretch into ten or twelve hours, and I am constantly looking at the clock thinking it must be slow or broke or just getting even. When I was young it was not like this, my head was on a swivel and my shift was gone in the blink of an eye. It's amazing what fear can do. Believe me too, when I tell you that this environment and these people - convicts - rub off on you in some very unexpected ways, some are artificial and not pleasing, while others leave you stunned by their clarity.

As time passes, the line between guard and prisoner, good guy and bad guy, has grown evermore indistinct. The young guards speak the same slang and swagger just as boldly as the convicts, but there have been deeper changes too, which would lead some to believe that the labels should be switched. I wouldn't argue that, as I know I've changed, or has this always been the real me?

I'm not a writer. I was told by a Doctor to write down the events of what happened and this will help me come to terms with it and eventually put the incident behind me. What she doesn't know is that I have barely touched the surface. She reads the incident reports aloud and I nod and agree. I add a few embellishments because I know this makes her happy. She likes it when I squirm. If I were to tell her the whole truth, she would be the one squirming. This is why I can only give her bits and pieces, the detritus that floats just below the surface. I am in enough trouble as it is.

"Mike?"

"Mike?"

"Mr. Walker, we have to get through this. Where were you just now?" Dr. Adams asked insistently.

I've been caught slipping again. Everytime I do this she becomes suspicious that I am hiding things from her, which of course I am. What she doesn't know is that I am hiding them from myself as well. But these things, they are persistent, they 'work' their way around my guard and assult me with their strength. She doesn't know that I am fighting a battle, even if she did, I suspect that she would not care much as she is a liberal watchdog who thinks that we should coddle our prisoners or just release them outright. Not for the first time, I wonder which of us needs therapy more.

Doctor Adams is a court appointed psychologist, she is meeting with me to determine if I am mentally competent to stand trial, it seems that swinging from a light fixture at the end of a knotted sheet tends to make people mistrust your sanity. Most think I tried to kill myself to spare my family the shame and humiliation of a public trial; that seductive spectacle of a good man gone bad and I'm not going to correct them, at least, not yet.

"I am just a little tired, Doctor. It is difficult to get a good night's sleep here."

I have found that it is better to sprinkle my lies with a bit of truth than to avoid her questions, because everytime I avoid one she starts scribbling furiously in her notebook. I guess this is a form of avoidance as well, I wonder where I picked that up and immediately change course. I don't want to know the answer. "We've been through this dozens of times, Doctor. I don't know what else to tell you or what else you want to hear."

Then I cringe, because I know what she is going to say and exactly how she will say it. I dread to hear it, as the brutal bareness of the words seem to batter me, and I don't know how much longer I can hold out.

"I just want to hear the truth, Mike." She says accusingly.

2

20 Years Earlier

I get yard today. It's nothing to brag about, just a 10 x 20 concrete box with 20 foot high walls and a diamond mesh grating for a ceiling. It's enough to keep you in but not enough to keep the elements out. There is not much to do besides walk, so that's what I do.

I slowly walk circles, encircled by gray walls and covered by a gray sky. I can't tell where one ends and the other begins. But it doesn't matter, I just keep walking. As I walk, I stare at the sky and begin to grow dizzy; at least that's different. As I'm looking up I hear the seagulls cry, it's a god awful racket which tears into the silence and seems to rip the very sky. I tilt my head further back and yell, "so, you're still alive then"?

And as if in rebellious confirmation, their shrieking redoubles and echoes off the heavens. Their tenacity is a thing to behold. Suddenly it occurs to me, was the question meant for them or me? I grin, and feel like shrieking my own confirmation to heaven and hell.

I can hear D-Man's heavy footfalls behind me and know that he's going to break the silence too. I brace myself for one of his laconic statements and am not disappointed.

"Fucked up day, huh"?

I grunt in reply, as there is no answer, nor does he want one. I just hope to stretch the silence a little longer, and he obligingly complies, so I'm free to retreat once again to my thoughts.

There is a strong scent of woodsmoke floating on the air, and I know that today must be a burn day. One of those days when the city allows people to burn their shrubs, grasses, dead branches, among other things, because it's deemed safe to do so. I enjoy yard on a burn day. I notice that my walking has slowed and I almost have to fight my way through the air, as it has suddenly grown heavy, or is it possible that it is the weight of the memories it carries with it? The memories come unbidden and I can only relive them.

I am a child sitting in front of a roaring fire on a cold winter day, and I'm surrounded by those who used to love me and by those who still do, both lists are short and growing ever shorter with time. I think of those whom I still have, my mother and brother, and am thankful. The rest are dead, or maybe they never were. I can laugh at my ignorance now, but when I realized that the world did not stop and lovingly wait for me, I was shocked. Now I know that life waits for no one, neither does Death. The gulls cry again and rouse me from my dead thoughts. I look back and see D-Man doggedly cold trailing me around our little yard and grin, it's good to have a loyal friend here.

"Are you ready for a beatdown in handball?" I ask maliciously.

"You couldn't beat your way out of a wet paper bag, ol' man!" he responds in kind. I like his confidence and straightforwardness, but most of all I prize his loyalty. So we settle down to a vicious game of handball. The handball is made out of the wadded waistband of a pair of underwear. Yeah, I know, life is a freaking peach, ain't it?

I

Things were different when I started here. Guards were guards and cons were cons. Sometimes a grudging respect could develop between the two, but as far as it went was a look and a nod and the two would retreat back to the safety of their own. I liked it better when things ran this way, it was simpler. Once you get to know someone, the lines blur and the labels become less sticky.

I became a prison guard in 1983, I was 21 years old and things were black or white. I had the ignorance and arrogance of youth. I didn't know that there was a middle ground and now looking back I also realize that this is the blessing of youth; for the gray area is where the danger lies. I smile when I hear people say youth is wasted on the young, because I know it would also be wasted on the old, as we know too much to be able to enjoy it.

Prison is run by the convicts. We all play our part in the pretense that the guards run the show, but the truth is and always will be, that we only show up after the alarms go off. We are not preventers but minimizers. When the convicts want to kill someone, they do; when they want to shoot drugs or sell them, they do; of course, we throw them in the hole, but the damage is already done. The cons steal everything that is not nailed down and make weapons out of it, most times they steal the nails too. More than once have I seen a convict staggering across the yard with a rusty nail buried to the hilt in his neck. The danger the guards face is very real, although thankfully, most of their violence is directed towards each other. I would hate to think what would happen if they funneled their rage against us. It is these rare instances that refuels and reinforces the hatred between the two.

Prison gangs are like a rash; the more you itch it, the more it spreads. They and their influence are all pervasive. Life behind the walls is run solely by the rules which they impose on their members and nonmembers alike. These rules are capricious and childish, but they are enforced with such violence and brutality, that they have to be taken seriously. It's true that children can be cruel, I pray most never witness the cruelty these children are capable of. These gangs are segregated by race and this is strictly enforced. The rare white convict who runs with a black gang is instantly and viciously attacked, so most of these cons are kept off the mainline yards. It's as much for their safety as it is to save us a headache and avoid a crapload of paperwork. The strange thing about the racial segregation is that the majority of cons have no racial beliefs or feelings beyond the protection that being with their own offers, so it's a vehicle of convenience only. The gangs priorities are accumulating power and money, if race is on their list, it's down at the bottom buried in the sludge. Race is only a means used very effectively, therefore it's not taken seriously by us guards. There's one exception to this, the white supremacists. Groups such as Neo-nazi skinheads are much more racially and politically motivated and the majority drug-free. Yet, even here, numbers breed correct behavior and when isolated most revert to typical convict ways.

The yard has eight blocks, each housing over one hundred men. The blocks have two tiers, each with 32 two man cells. Needless to say, with this many convicts crammed together, it stinks and it's loud. The cells are smaller than an average washroom, but the cons soon grow used to being cooped up. They are on lockdown so much that they don't know how to act when their doors are finally opened. It's like watching a dog at the animal shelter having its cage opened, it just stands there wagging its tail, to apprehensive to step out. You wonder at its hesitancy; you wonder if maybe it's been ruined by being locked up too long; you wonder if perhaps it might be better to leave it locked up until its gone. Private thoughts are sometimes shocking.

We don't worry about cell violence too much. Although there is the occasional cell murder or assault, the bulk of all violence is saved for the yard; it's as if they prefer to perform before an audience. Stabbings, beatings, riots, they seem to horde them up and bide their time, when they are released from their cells something else seems to be released within, because they come out with a sense of having to restrain themselves, and eyeing wildly anyone who comes within arms reach. They congregate on the yard by race, staying well away from each other. They stand in groups of 10 or 12 and whisper and plot, while constantly throwing meaningful glances at the other groups. The guards congregate as well, for we are expected to fight both sides into submission after they've spent themselves on each other. At these times, the tension is so thick that it lays on your skin and sticks as if you've walked into a spiderweb. It's a rare day when we are able to run an entire yard and lock up the cons without an incident. Even these occasions are wearisome because you're wound so tight for so long that it drains you.

The general atmosphere is pregnant with a sense of waiting. Waiting for mail, waiting for food, waiting for cell doors to rack, waiting for a release date. Even the lifers are not immune from this intangible longing, this unfounded expectancy, they just know how to hide it better. The guards too wait. When your shift is over and you drive out of the front gate, it's like an oppressive weight lifting. It's not just the prison environment, but the daily act of caging other humans. Of course, most deserve to be here, but it's the odd one or two who don't belong, the ones you can imagine yourself having a beer with or a barbecue, these are the ones that take a toll, the ones you long to escape before your empathy overwhelms you.

There are consequences to working here, far beyond the harmless. People look at you strange when you tell them you're a prison guard, like you've only one rung higher than the convicts and should be watched. I actually don't mind this too much, it's my foolproof 'get out of a boring conversation scot-free card.' But the unintended ones, that's where your trouble begins. The lack of recognition, like a drunk in denial, keeps you from seeing those consequences until, in most cases, it is far too late.

When I'm standing in line at the grocery store, I catch myself constantly checking my back to make sure no one is creeping up on me. But this is a small town and these are just my neighbors. They stand well back and eye me pityingly and nod and smile. I nod and smile back and know that I've done it again, I have lived up to the talk. I wonder if I'll ever shake these habits, or have they taken too strong a hold? Most people learn trust, I have unlearned it.

As unlikely as it may be, there is a community behind these walls, a city within a city. It is complete with its own form of governance, a corrupted form no doubt, but is there any other kind. At least theirs is truthful in its intent. There are laws that govern this community, which are as honest in their brutality as they are brutally honest.

They do not tolerate rapists, child molesters, snitches. These inmates are ruthlessly murdered or savaged with a naked aggression that gives weight and credence to their laws. They are much less likely to break the law inside than outside; maybe there is something we have forgotten. Out here we make speeches laced with self-righteous indignation about protecting the defenseless - our children - but when push comes to shove we slap the offenders hand and speak of his disease and of the help he needs. I often wonder which is right in the deliverance of justice. Justice is after all, fairness, and what is fairer than an eye for an eye? If they are wrong, then are we wrong in administering the Death Penalty? Spreading Democracy from the barrel of a gun? Or are we simply guilty of teaching one truth while living another?

This community aspect mirrors the outside to other extents. The poor - those cons with no one to send them money or care packages - are looked after by their own. They are given food and hygiene items, and above all, coffee; the universal drug. This sharing acts as a cohesive force within the groups and comes with certain expectations, namely; that the recipient will be there during a race riot and that they will watch each others back. We have written rules forbidding this sharing of property; we attack the group, then the individual; isolation, divide and conquer, classic military strategy. It may seem overly dramatic to speak in terms of war, but in here it is constant war constantly. We continuously pit them against one another. So as to keep them away from us, it's not hard. I don't want to give the impression that I would like to live in a community such as this, it is too stringent, too unforgiving, for my liking. I only wish to show its honesty, not all honesty is beautiful. Those few cons who refuse to take part in this community with its herd mentality are ostracized and fair game for all.

Prison politics is the number one pastime. It is practiced with all the eagerness and naiveté of those new to the Hill. Those with the permanent grins fleshed with the expectation of reward. They wheel and deal behind the scenes and eventually end up selling out their friends; signing contracts and treaties, only to break them at the first convenient moment; starting Race Wars, shadowy motives lying shallowly under a thinly veiled guise; does this sound familiar? They learn well from their "betters".

Every incident which occurs here is due to politics; whether it is driven by revenge, fear, greed, jealousy, does not matter, the vehicle used is politics and the weapon of choice is the wagging tongue. If another con has a higher pay slot which you want to slide into, you simply fabricate a lie and release it to the rumor mill; you'll have a promotion in no time. Since politics is amoral by its definition, and life without morals is a much simpler proposition, it has found an enthusiastic and welcoming audience within these walls.

Another community aspect is productivity. The majority of cons are highly resourceful. Curiously enough, they have all the tools required to make it on the outside, yet, their reason for being here has more to do with what they lack, which are social skills and a respect for authority. They are always on the prowl or hustle, trying to turn an easy buck. They are ingrained with the get rich quick mentality, not understanding that an objects value is determined by the amount of work put into it. They engage in everything from drawing, tattooing, writing, to distilling moonshine from pruno with homemade stills. They learn crafts, making intricate picture frames and chandeliers from folded pieces of shiny paper. Typing, landscaping, cabinet construction, all these and more are learned and practiced with skill. I've seen artists who could blow your mind with the realism of their work, who could actually be something in the art world. Yet, here is where they sit and inexorably fade, and seem content with the choices they've made.

I often think, but that for one wrong decision, I could be wasting away in one of these cells, living the narrow life of a prisoner. Would I be able to survive or would I become just another forgotten victim like so many others?

II

> Not ignoring what is good, I am quick to perceive a horror, and could still be social with it - would they let me - since it is but well to be on friendly terms with all the inmates of the place one lodges in.
>
> Herman Melville

No matter how prepared you are, some things always take you by surprise. Sometimes this is good and sometimes bad, then there are the times when you don't know which it is. I had been taught from the academy on to dislike and distrust convicts, therefore, I was caught unawares when I met a new convict named Michael Allen. As a new convict he was a fish. To the guards that means orientation status and nothing coming until he moves to the main yard. But to the convicts it means two words, fresh meat.

These "newbies" are quickly tested, probed for weaknesses, sifted for anything of value. If these fish don't instantly stand up for themselves, it becomes day one of a waking nightmare that will last until they either parole or die; perhaps, even these will not let them truly escape.

I was the floor officer in the orientation block when Allen was brought in on a chain with five other convicts. Three of the cons were old hands at this, as they had been in and out of prison their whole lives.

"What's crackin', Stogie?", a burly black con addressed me familiarly. "Same shit, different day. I see you couldn't stay away."

I've only been working here for five years, but I've figured out the game. Everybody wants to be remembered, to be noticed, so I pretend to remember; even though they come and go at such a rate as to make it impossible. Only the lifers never leave. They are like an old piece of furniture, comfortable in its familiarity.

"I see you're still chomping on those damn engines," he threw across the dayroom. "You always were a bright one," I shut back.

Sometimes I can't help myself. He was trying to put on a show for the others, but I've never been able to stick to someone elses script. He muttered something and slunk into a sulky silence like the rest. As I glanced down the chain I caught the eyes of one locked on me. He was a tall white boy, who looked like he'd been raised on a farm, big from the ground up. As I shifted my glance back to his face, I saw a gleam in his eye and a smirk on his face. My first instinct was to go over and smack it off, but then he cut his eyes towards the black con and swung them slowly back to me and nodded. The smirk was gone and in its place was a grin with no good intent. I was confused, an awkward sense of pride welled in me, as if he had patted my shoulder and said good job. I was not sure how to react so I abruptly turned and left the other guards to put the cons in their cells. Much later, I would try unsuccessfully to forget this meeting.

It didn't take long before trouble started on the row, and not surprisingly, the black con was right in the middle of it. His name was T-bone, he was a crip, and he had gotten wind of Allen having cash money - which is against prison regulations, but is a way for fish to buy what they need immediately. We later heard the details leading up to the incident from one of our snitches. I sometimes think there are more snitches in prison than guards. They are on every yard, in every block, in every pod, and yes, they mainly do our job for us.

It happened on a Saturday afternoon. Another guard and I were standing in the dayroom while the gunner was releasing for yard. T-bone and another black con sauntered up to Allen and started gesticulating wildly while their voices grew increasingly louder, I knew this was Allen's test. I didn't rush to break it up, as I said before, I'm just a minimizer. I watched Allen closely and was somehow disappointed when he only stood utterly still with a blank look on his face.

T-bone reached out arrogantly to grasp Allen's arm, as he too had mistaken the look on Allen's face. Allen hit him in the throat with an open right hand and then clubbed him to the ground with two hammerlike left hooks to the head. At once he turned to face the other con who was in full retreat, hands raised before him as to ward off a horror. Allen sprang at him with a ferocity I'd never seen before, he hit him viciously with lefts and rights and when the victim started to crumple he held him up and began to smash knees into his face. The sound of breaking bone filled the dayroom.

It all took place so quickly that my partner and I stand stunned. Finally, the gunner pressed the alarm and started screaming "get down", "get down", while chambering a round. This brought us out of our stupor and we ran forward plying our batons and pepper spray simultaneously. We used them mainly on Allen as he was the only con left standing. T-bone had never risen, but lay grounded, gagging from his ruined throat. When we gained control of the situation I looked at Allen, he was lying belly down, cuffed up on the tier, when his eyes met mine, the gleam was still there and the grin was a bit wider. It was at that moment, I knew we had a different kind of convict. I nodded slightly and he nodded in return and looked to the floor, as alarm bells shattered the air and medics rushed to attend victims.

It's my job to house and feed convicts, also to protect them from each other; in theory at least, there are times when you feel the urge to jump in and fight side by side with someone, and then there are the times when you want to stand stock still and watch some piece of garbage get filled with holes and secretly cheer the assailant, but of course, you can do neither. So maybe you are a bit slow responding to an alarm or extra quick to work your baton with such efficacy as to point you an assailant. Really, it's only a matter of perception, isn't it?

Allen was sent to the hole without ever making it to the mainline, which is unusual, most cons take a little longer to get into trouble. When he finally reached the yard six months later, he received quite a reception, as rumor outran him. It didn't take long for him to attract a following and he was reluctant to play the role assigned him, he chased most of these away, but not all. Another convict called D-Man, the D being short for dumb, attached himself to Allen like a Siamese twin, and even though D-Man wasn't the brightest he and Allen clicked from day one.

All this attention did not go unnoticed. It placed him in direct conflict with a con named Snake, who did not like being outshone. Snake was a big brute, all muscles, tattoos, and a complete lack of conscience. He ran the yard for the Aryan Syndicate. The prisons most notorious gang. They assaulted, extorted, murdered, and basically did whatever the hell they wanted. Snake had had cons killed for lesser offenses, and he personally had two prison murders on his jacket, he was the wrong man to cross.

Respect is a curious concept. It barely registers with us on the outside, but in here, it's as if the entire world were made of the very letters which spell it out; take one letter away and the world crumbles. I once heard an old convict explain it to a youngster: He said respect had nothing to do with courtesy or manners, it wasn't a thing one should be given or giving freely, it is simply what you think of yourself and what you made others think.

Their definition is vastly different than most. They view respect as a physical thing which can be sensed, touched, grasped to yourself like a lifeline. It's your shoulders, your arms, your rage, your will to power. It's what you take and keep, what and how much you can force on another. Respect is offense, aggression, body counts, whoever displays the most receives the most.

This perverted idea of respect explains much, if not all, of their interactions with others, and why most cannot make it on the outside. There is a fundamental flaw in their thinking which prevents it.

Maybe, this is what we should be working on before releasing them on an unsuspecting society, or maybe, we know exactly what we're doing?

III

I've made my way through this world poorly. Looking back, it is difficult not to dream of revenge; but that is a childs fantasy, to which I am no longer entitled. Besides, here, I have my hands full with reality. I come from a small town and a smaller family, I'm not used to crowds; the closeness, the noise, the stench, the desperation. I feel a constant sense of anxiety, which demands my full attention to keep it from surfacing and consuming me.

Life here is fairly simple, because it's stripped down to the core. There are no distractions; all niceties and accessories have been discarded. You learn to meet your needs or you learn how swiftly the end can come. You need to make selfishness your companion; ah, not much change here, we should all be pros at that. The struggle for existence moves selfishness right up the ladder of values, till it's perched atop the lofty heights, disdainfully distancing itself from mans works.

You must learn Brutality and Hardness, it might surprise you how easily they come, their willingness an embarrassment. What is difficult? To live in a pit of belly-crawlers, while trying to retain a small piece of humanity. Life is simpler when there are rules, it eases the burden of decision and indecision, without them all is confusion and loss. We are too far from our Beginnings to lovingly labor with the Faustian soul; we have confined ourselves, stilted our growth, with all of our teaching we have untaught ourselves the basics; yet, deep down the knowledge still resides, it only takes circumstance to recall it.

I've been here only a handful of years, and already everything that came before is fading as swiftly as the remnants of a dream. Soon, I will know nothing but this world, and this life, that frightens me more than anything. The small piece of my former life which I retain, I have tucked away into the deep recesses of my mind, and only occasionally look at it from a distance, too wary to approach, for fear of its power. I have only this life now, and if I am to survive I must forget all.

IV

When youngsters come in they are quickly set upon, it's like watching birds of prey dive-bomb their victims, they never see it coming until the talons close around them. The older convicts scramble, trying to snatch up a protege, while others just look for the weak to do their bidding. It was in one of these instances that the strong undercurrent of dislike between Allen and Snake had its first eruption.

A young fish named Tommy appeared and Snake was first on the scene, trying to attach an anchor to his claimed property, but no sooner had he turned his back, Allen swooped the boy away and began his schooling. Here is another way Allen differed from most cons, he didn't school his youngsters into becoming better criminals or prison gangsters. Don't get me wrong, he didn't turn them into angels, but he did teach them priorities. They were highly efficient in violence, but never for violences sake. He taught them that their place was on the outside and their responsibility was to their families. That it didn't matter what the next man thought of you, but what your wife or child did.

In this environment it's difficult if not impossible to stand alone yet the other guards and I watch as Allen bucks this trend so easily that we wonder if maybe we are wrong. He is a violent man, at times this violence is breathtaking in its scope and rawness, but he has earned the handle 'Teacher' for more than this. He's constantly studying, and shares what he learns with those who are willing to hear.

"Snake isn't gonna like you pouncing on his fish." D-Man aired dryly. "His likes or dislikes don't concern me."

"I'm just saying, the kid would have found his way to you on his own."

"Maybe, but I wasn't willing to take that chance." I'd be damned if I was going to sit back and watch Snake ruin another good kid. I don't have much to offer, yet, I have a mountain of sins to atone for, maybe, if I can help this kid and the next, I will have gone some distance, I will have made a start.

"Speak of the Devil, heads up teach," D-Man's warning snapped me to attention. "So, I hear you've found yourself a little pussy," Snake spat out.

I grinned and said, "I don't know what you're talking about. Probably one of your morons feeding you some bullshit." Wolf and Bull, two of his knucklebusters, trailed him as usual. Wolf was a sneaky one, you had to keep an eye on him at all times, while Bull was as big as a house and so far beyond dumb that they had to create a new category of stupid for him.

I could feel D-Man tense at my side and I knew if anything went down, it would be two on three, and I liked those odds.

"I'm gonna give you a warning," Snake happily informed me. "You keep your nose out of my business, if you want to keep it on your goddamned face. This yard is mine. I got dibs on anything and everything. If there's some crap I don't want, well then, eat it up, but if you step on my toes again, you won't even see it coming."

I didn't answer, just stared and unclenched my fists, as I could see he was in the mood for talking not fighting. I let him blow off steam, these days I know when he's serious. When he sits back to watch while his goons come slinking around, that's the time to beware. Bull nodded heavily to me as they walked away.

D-Man said, "damn, I was sure we were going to the hole."

"You know Snake ain't gonna do shit himself," I replied. "But, keep your eyes open and be ready until we get home." I knew how Snake liked to make little visits to his victims right before all hell broke loose, and I wasn't convinced his warning was just a verbal one.

I could see Tommy walking towards us from across the yard. The realization scorched its way through me like a bolt of lightning, the warning had been given, now it was time for the example.

"They're gonna do Tommy, let's go." I spit it out so quickly, D-Man didn't even understand, but was immediately at my heel. Even as I said it, I knew it was too late. As I silently watched, two cons approached Tommy, one from the front the other from behind. Before he knew what was happening. The one behind grabbed him in a full Nelson and the other began stabbing him repeatedly in the stomach and chest. He was struggling and kicking but his protests quickly grew heavy and I could see his fight fading. He was looking in my direction as he slid gently to the ground.

The alarm was blaring and the gunner was yelling. "Get Down." Two warning shots from his mini 14 rifle slammed across the yard, echoing their violent intent. A third round found the con with the knife, it entered his back, and like a lover, blew out his heart when it was done. He collapsed in a pile, useless. All became quiet, not a word uttered, no snide comments made, as everyone had just caught a possible glimpse of their future and were too scared to tempt it.

The guards came and did their job, carting the bodies off like so much refuse. They stripped everyone out looking for wounds and weapons, then escorted us back to our cells to be locked down for a couple months, just enough time to plan for our next yard.

As D-Man and I sat in our cell, neither of us wanted to speak the obvious, that the decision had been taken from us. When we came out, the entire yard, guards included, knew what was going to happen; It was only a matter of how creative and violent we could be. There was no thought of getting away with it, as that is not the idea; you want everyone - enemies above all, to see you at work. You want them to know that it could be their turn next.

When Tommy was murdered, I had a feeling that it was the beginning of a slow end, for either Teacher or Snake, or both. I was also sure that there would be plenty of bodies strewn in their path. It was disconcerting to find myself rooting for one, but let me explain. There's good and bad even among convicts, it's only different by degrees, and while one is blatant, the other is subtle and must be searched out.

Many times I've seen cowardice sheathed in violence. I've seen four or five cons jump on one man and scream and howl like they were the craziest killers around. Yet, I know if they were forced to fight one-on-one, it would be an entirely different story. In here, the most common courage comes in the form of numbers, which isn't courage, but mob frenzy. Convicts redefine everything, this makes it easier to live with the want. I have only seen real courage a few times, and once was in here.

I or any other guard could have easily searched Teacher and D-Man's cell, found weapons and rolled them up to the hole. This would have avoided some problems, but sometimes delaying a confrontation is simply hiding from the cause; sooner or later, confrontation is inevitable. So, none of us searched their cell. We waited for fate to have its way, and hoped no guards would be hurt when the day came.

I have seen the cons who hang around with Teacher, and they are of a different make up than the rest. They are the ones who go back to the outside world and make it. They become good employees, good neighbors, good citizens. Most of them are not like this when they arrive, it's only after spending time with Teacher that they come to this realization, that they begin to think of others first, that they become men.

Under the influence of Teacher and Snake, I've seen good men become better and bad men become worse. I wonder if it's natural inclination or just what they're being taught? I've seen Snake turn petty crooks into cold blooded killers. I've seen young men buy into his hype, only to fold when the shit hit the fan. They would have a sudden awakening and walk up to the nearest guard and check-in or lock-up. These cons are now considered punks, they can no longer walk a mainline without getting assaulted. Countless young men have been ruined in this way. When you strip a man of his coating, you leave him naked to the world, and no matter what he does, there is no coming back, he's but a shell of his founding and already gone. When this happens, the other cons revel in it, as if it were a party. Yet, what they are really celebrating is, it was not them who were exposed, and they are safe for another day.

Believe me when I tell you that there is a battle being waged in here, whose outcome affects us all, and it has nothing to do with the physical. Young mens minds are being bought, sold, and traded like thrift store merchandise, and then, discarded just as quickly. These young men will not listen to cops or guards, parents or family, but they will listen to a convict like Teacher, and he's our last best hope to save even a handful.

The day finally came. Everyone was filled with a giddy sense of violent expectation, and I am ashamed to say that I was among them. It's easy to look forward to these days when you are but a spectator. I don't know how the participants feel, but I imagine a case of butterflies that would turn your bowels to water.

Before we unlocked for yard, I walked by Teacher's cell to get an idea of how he was making out. I'm not sure, but maybe I was thinking that he wouldn't came through, couldn't bear the burden any longer. Even the guards had high expectations of him, although, none higher than what he set for himself. I was strangely reassured when I saw him sitting on his bunk reading a book as usual, D-Man was seated at the desk eating a sandwich, also as usual. The calm before the storm always amazes me, everyone turns into the perfect gentleman, introspective, pensive. I used to think that they were just brutes, mindless to the danger they were about to face. But, over the years, I've come to realize that it's not a frank disregard to the danger, but instead, a kind or quiet homage to the courage it takes to face it.

Everything that day seemed oddly preordained from the day he stepped foot onto a prison yard; free will took quite a blow. As the convicts started to flood the yard, it all seemed like slow motion, slow swimming gaits held up progress as they sluggishly moved to their area of the yard. Teacher and D-Man emerged from the building as if vomited, they came pouring and tumbling and covering all in their path with the scent of violence. They rode their way straight to the tables where the white convicts gather. They did not stop for the usual handshakes and pats on the back; this forfeiture unmasked intent and scattered all.

Teacher turned directly into Bull and plunged his knife deep. You could hear the hiss of escaping air as the knife unsheathed from his lung one of two things happen when you get a knife sunk into you, fight or flight. Bull chose the former, and since he already had his hand filled with have is own weapon, he immediately began stabbing Teacher. The two stood toe to toe carving deep fissures and mining holes into each other like determined workmen.

Simultaneously, D-Man began a savage attack upon Wolf. He opened his throat from ear to ear with a box cutter, and continued to slice him as if he were a coroner performing an autopsy. Wolf was game and tried to fight back with one hand while clutching his broken throat with the other. You could see him weakening rapidly, his strength ebbing as his blood found its way through the cracks of his fingers, plump dark droplets chasing his life away. D-Man did not realize that he had already given the death blow, but held him still in a viselike grip and tried to carve his eye out of his skull.

Bull was a big man, but did not work with the power of belief. Oh, he punched plenty of holes into Teacher, just not with the intent of ending him. Teacher, on the other hand, was swinging like the axman, trying to bite deep into the heartwood. Guttural grunts echoed from Bull with every thrust of Teacher's knife, the pain and confusion were taking the fight from him. The sound of the Blockgun boomed repeatedly, but the blocks bounced off the combatants ineffectually, dropping harmlessly to the ground, their energy spent.

Wolf's knees gave way. No longer seeing the need to hold up a ruin, they gave over to fate. He no longer fought back or defended himself, but lay still with a faraway stare of one who has hit upon a revelation; D-Man continued his deadly work.

Bull was giving ground and sank slowly to a knee when the mini 14 sounded out, its piercing cry ripping through the scene. Teacher turned and searched out Snake, who had watched the fight from a safe distance, but he was too tired and too wounded to finish it. So he pulled D-Man off of Wolf's still form, retreated a few feet and got into the prone position.

Reality crashed back with a roar that left my ears ringing and my skin tinging. I stood flat-footed and breathless, as if it had been me fighting. Guards were spilling out of every building, handcuffs flashing as they were snapped onto wrists. One guard even rolled the body of Wolf over and cuffed him. I wondered, if maybe he was afraid of Ghosts. Everyone was on the verge of hysterics, fighting to restrain the fear from flowing forth.

I helped to strap Teacher onto a gurney and rushed him to the prison infirmary, where his bloody clothes were cut away from his punctured body. He was a mass of broken tissue. The flesh stood up around the wounds to make it look like a mountain range, full of serrated peaks and blood filled valleys. He refused the anesthetic, just laid stoically while his wounds were cleared and sutured. Is this his self imposed punishment for having failed Tommy, or for failing himself?

In the following days people - guards and cons alike, spoke of nothing else, as if they were all high on the same drug and they couldn't get enough. Was this some primal urge which we could not escape, or was it just the ripples of fear still sounding from the depths?

Teacher and Bull recuperated in the infirmary for a couple months Bull had permanently lost the use of one lung and was placed on dialysis due to kidney failure. When Teacher was fully healed, he was moved to the hole and put into a cell with D-Man, who was fighting a murder charge; what were they gonna do, give him another life sentence? Wolf was buried in a paupers grave as no one could be found to claim his remains. The hands on the clock kept their constant vigil and the world went on as if nothing had happened.

V

Once again I'm sitting in the hole and it will be a long stay this time as everyone and their mother is pissed. I look at the bright side, this is my vacation, time away from the madness that is the yard. Here you go everywhere cuffed and escorted, which means people aren't roaming the tier all day. You can actually relax and take your shoes off, this does wonders for you mentally as well as physically, your mind and body have the chance to heal and forget, and that's exactly what I needed.

Don't believe it when you hear that hole time is the hard time. The mainlines are the warzones, the hole and SHU is where you recoup all your spent energies. They are where you have time to study, to learn the basics of strategy and subtlety, to learn not to volunteer - either yourself or information. Minding your own is a skill most fail to learn, often to their detriment. Hole time is mandatory every few years, without it you'll either go soft and lock up or let down your guard and became a victim. It grounds you, bringing your priorities back to the fore. It seems odd to speak of the hole in positive terms, but everything has its good and bad, and this place is no different.

"How long did you get?"

I still had my cuffs on when D-Man asked the question. I waited until the skrew uncuffed me and left before I answered.

"I got less time than you, brother. Thirty six months for attempted murder, but I'll only do a little over twenty seven, then I'm a free man."

D-Man had picked up five years hole time for Wolf's murder, and surprise, surprise, the D.A. rejected the case against him. They only pick up on short timers, gotta keep the prisons full, right?

Neither of us wanted to voice the obvious, that I was going to be cut loose long before him, and since we weren't really sure of the fallout from our escapade, we wanted to go back to the yard together in order to watch each others back. We knew full well that if Snake had his way, we'd be "put in the hat." Marked for murder by the Aryan Syndicate.

"You know we could have avoided this mess, right?" D-Man asked.

"No, we couldn't," I replied. We had had this conversation a dozen times and we both knew it inside out, D-Man is only playing his role. He would voice the question and then listen as I bounced all the possibilities off of him. In this fashion, we would find our way to the nearest truth, or at least, truth for us. It's hard to find someone like him, as most like the sound of their own voice too much.

We are nonconformists, and sinfully take pride in that alone. This nonconformity encompasses both sides of the wall. We do not care for the hypocritical laws outside, which are subjective in their application, nor the quasi laws within these walls, which are an ugly reflection of one mans ego. We have our own morals and principals which we will not compromise, this inevitably leads to conflict; but somewhere, sometime a man has to do more than just talk a good game, he must take a stand regardless of the consequences. This puts all he believes to the test, and shows if he is either constant or just a weather-vane.

D-Man and I chose to break away from the prison norm. We still follow some rules if they coincide with our own, such as; we will not walk the same line with garbage; rapists, child predators, snitches - but we do not victimize our own for a few bucks, or for self importance. We've decided on the course of taking up the education of the younger cons, trying to teach them that prison is not the place for them. We do this by showing them everything they're missing on the outside, it's fairly easy. Families; wife, children, parents, and above all women! You don't realize how much you miss the sound of a womans voice, or simply her scent, until the occasional male guard comes by your cell at mail call. You are instantly struck by a sense of déjà vu and the memories crowd their way in like excited children, all willy nilly and undisciplined, but also with an unbridled joy. Everyone tries to stop her and strike up a conversation in hopes of prolonging the momentary freedom, to ease the lonliness for female companionship. When I speak to a female guard I'm reminded of my mother, my aunts, old girlfriends, it's a respite from this reality and a remembrance of one past.

It's not difficult to convince them when you use the truth. The method does not matter; connive, shame, bludgeon, frighten, the outcome is all. Between D-Man and myself, we have gotten through to quite a few. Before they parole, they always ask, what can I do for you out there? We only have one reply: Don't ever let me see you again, and happily, in most cases this has been the result. Occasionally, I receive a card during the holidays, and that's good.

"How long do you think we'll be sitting in this craphole before heading off to the SHU?" D-Man broke in.

"That skrew said it's about a six or seven month wait right now, so we have about two months to go."

"We're gonna miss the whole damn football season," he complained for the umpteenth time.

I knew how D-Man would rant if given any encouragement, so I held my tongue and hoped for the best, even though I was feeling just as anxious as he was. Administrative Segregation - ad seg, or as it's better known, "the Hole", is only temporary housing. After your case is heard and your sentence handed down you're moved to the Security Housing Unit - SHU, here is where you serve your time.

Since the Hole is temporary your property; books, paperwork, envelopes, and the rest is held until you arrive at the SHU. Once there, you're given your television and the rest of your allowable property. The rest you are forced to mail home at your own expense, if you're poor and have no money it's destroyed. We all know how degenerative television is, but let me tell you, when you spend twenty two and a half hours a day locked in a cell it provides an outlet of escape which helps you cope.

"Teacher, D-Man, are you guys busy?," our neighbor yelled through the vent. I was quick on the trigger when I said "it's Your Turn" to D-Man, as neither of us liked him, it was a choice having to speak to him, so we both tried various methods of getting out of it. "Crap!" D-Man spat out and shot me a disgusted look, to which I feigned innocence and smiled as wide as possible.

"No, we ain't busy. What's happening?" D-Man spoke into the vent. "I got a kite for you guys. You want to fish over and get it," he asked.

"Gawddammit!" D-Man swore under his breath, in his newly acquired southern accent. I have no idea where this came from, he's from California. One thing we both hate to do is fish, throwing some twined up string down the filthy tier and pulling in some stinking hairballs the size of tumbleweeds, and a kite filled with drama, was not our idea of fun.

"I'll be over in a minute," D-Man growled.

The whole time he was fishing, he was muttering and cursing and testing out his new accent, he put on quite an entertaining show. When he finally got it reeled in he put the line away and washed his hands vigorously, then turned and threw the kite at me. I knew it was coming, it's part of our routine. I unfolded the kite and read it aloud;

Respects to you both. Hey, these pigs are asking me to take a cellie, should I? I don't know the guy and I don't wanna do the cops no favors. Oh yeah, can you shoot me a few shots of mud? I'm out again. Alright get at me. I gotta bounce.

With/respects Ghost "I gotta bounce? What the hell does that mean?" D-Man asked confusedly.

"Shit, I don't know. Some new age slang these morons are picking up somewhere. Probably the same place he picked up his sagging britches" I answered, just guessing. Then added, "You notice how he asks for something in every damn kite he sends us?"

"Hell yeah, he's a damn panhandler, and he knows what's up with the cellie situation.

He only asked to cover for the real reason, begging."

"You're probably right, but I think he's also looking for a way out. We gotta try to set this kid straight," I replied. The rules for the white convicts regarding cellies are pretty simple; it's mandatory. The reasoning behind this is, too many try to hide out; also, not many have the mental fortitude to remain single without going a little batty, paranoia is a constantly attacking gremlin, and once it sinks its claws in, it's over, when someone has a cellie. They're much more likely to behave accordingly, because there is somebody who can put hands on them at anytime. Rule enforcement is simpler when there's a physical threat behind it.

D-Man was already bagging up the coffee, which left me to do the talking. "Hey Ghost," I called.

"Yeah," he answered immediately.

"Damn, what were you doing, standing at the vent listening?" "No, No. I was just cleaning my sink."

"Yeah right," I said. "Anyway, check it out. You know the way we do it with cellies, so I'm not gonna explain. I don't want to tell you what to do, I'm just gonna give you some advice and you gotta trust that I'm not steering you wrong. First of all, these skrews wouldn't be trying to move this guy in with you if he was a piece of shit. They protect those guys because they're afraid of being sued. Secondly, they probably got this wood sleeping in a fucking wet cell and if you deny him, you're gonna make his stay alot longer. You know how miserable those wet cells are, it's where everyone cuts their hair and toenails, it's beyond foul. Whoever he is, if he comes over here and finds out you were stalling, he might not be too happy." I finished up subtlety.

"I'm not trying to deny cellies. I just want to cell with someone I know; Ghost whined out petulantly.

Everyday we had to listen as this kid spit out his lame ass war stories, which were nothing more than slap and tickle wrestling matches, but he would build on them every time with the patient practice of one accustomed to lying. At that moment he sounded like a child, and anger surged, as I knew he was playing a role with me. Whenever he was trying to get out of doing something, he reverted to this scared little kid act, but I knew in this instance he was not acting, so I pushed the anger down and tried to help him before he made a mistake that he couldn't come back from.

"Look Ghost, we all want to live with one of our homeboys or friends, but all the whites are doubled-up right now, you know that. You also know if you refuse him what's gonna be said and what's gonna happen. You'll be off roll call and it will only be a matter of time before what went down here catches up with you," I explained patiently.

"Hey, I ain't scared of taking a cellie, I'll live -"

I cut him off as I didn't want to hear his bullshit. "I know, I'm just giving you advice like I'd give any other wood."

Alright," he said reluctantly. "When the cop comes back I'll tell him to go ahead and bring him over."

"That's the ticket. Shoot your line, D-Man has some mud for you." I ended the conversation.

That night Buzz moved in with Ghost. He was an older con I knew from the yard. He was very much set in his ways and didn't tolerate anyone with opposing ideas or habits. On the big yard he wasn't allowed to live with youngsters because of this and his violent streak. He was from an outlaw biker gang and looked like Sasquatch's older, bigger brother. He was doing a life sentence for bludgeoning to death two members from a rival gang. Needless to say, I had an uneasy feeling about him moving in with Ghost, and it wasn't only from his reputation, but from the fact that everything I touched these days seemed to go to crap. I was overburdened with guilt as it was, I didn't need to add someone or something else to my list.

I let about ten minutes pass, enough time for them to get acquainted and then called out.

"Hey Buzz?"

"Hey, what's going on Teacher," he answered. "How are you and D-Man doing?"

"We're getting by, just waiting for the chain to the SHU. Right now it's hurry up and wait, but we'll be glad to get out of this pigsty." I replied, "what brings a nice friendly guy like you back here?"

He laughed before answering, "You're not gonna believe this. Some freaking faggot tried to hit on me!" The incredulity in his voice was almost comical. I would have laughed out loud but the situation called for a little tact, only the guy it happened to could laugh, anyone else and it would be taken as disrespect.

"I guess I don't need to ask what happened next?"

"Shit, I only hit that thing one time, but its jaw broke in four places, he said disgustedly. "I didn't even want to touch that motherfucker, but what can you do, you know?"

I glanced at D-Man who was grinning from ear to ear. I smiled too and we quietly shared a laugh. He felt that whatever happened to a person, they had it coming, because they had somehow brought it on themselves. I don't know if this belief was karma, or simply its plain cousin, what comes around goes around as D-Man would never explain it fully, but what I do know is that he was getting a kick out of Buzz's situation.

"Sorry about your luck, Buzz, there wasn't anything else you could do though." I said placatingly. I wanted to get some info about the yard, so I continued, "what's the word going around about D-Man and me?"

I could pretty much guess, and his hesitation added to my certainty. He finally came out with, "Snake has said that you two are through and everyone is going along with it to stay out of trouble themselves. But I'll tell ya, alot of woods ain't cool with it. They all figure it was a personal deal and it's over, but you know what time it is, no one is gonna stick their neck out for the next man. I'll tell you straight up, you two are solid in my book." The outlaw bikers had never gotten along with the Aryan Syndicate, so his empathy was questionable.

"We appreciate that Buzz, and the heads up as well." I said. "Now it's my turn to share. You have a pretty good kid for a cellie, he's just green is all, but he has alot of potential. If you two don't get along, D-Man or I will swap cells, one of us will more in with you and the other with Ghost. I'd hate to see anything happen to him, he's too young to be judged like us."

"Alright, thanks. I'm sure we'll be fine," he countered. "I gotta get settled in, so I'll talk to you guys later."

"Okay. You two have a good day."

The skrews have been messing with us lately. They're mad because we won't enlighten them about our incident, and when you get the skrews mad you're up shit creek. Curious things start happening that no one can explain. Our property came up missing, our canteen ducats were misplaced - two months running, we've been moved three times for no more reason other than to make us uncomfortable. But when you live in an 8 x 10 concrete box, strip naked squat and cough in front of a yard full of men - with the occasional female guard thrown in for good measure - you have a very high threshold for the uncomfortable.

We should have been in the SHU by now, but here we still sit. Everyone else has left, only to be replaced by new faces, this place never stays empty long. There was a riot on the mainline between whites and blacks, it involved about fifty cons, so the place is jam-packed once again. Most of these will serve four to six months then get kicked out to a different yard, but the guys who have priors, well that's a whole different story. They'll wind up doing years in the SHU for the same crime; maybe justice isn't about fairness after all.

Our new neighbors are two woods, Scotty and Mark, who were involved in the riot. Well, actually one of them was, the other laid down, which is the ultimate crime. Scotty was a skinhead and gung ho about anything racial. He would preach to you for hours about conspiracies and Jewish plots, if you let him. Some of it sounded plausible, but don't they all? And in such a shrunken world as this it's hard to care beyond your own survival, even if they are true.

Needless to say, Scotty was not the one to lay down. Mark was in his early twenties and came from a well off family, which is not usual in here. Most convicts come from poor surroundings and careless upbringings, so, of course, his outlook on life was completely foreign to most. As he had never had to do without, he had an easygoing attitude about money concerns, which spilled over into other areas of his life. He didn't take anything serious, all was an adventure to be shrugged off and discarded when it lost its appeal.

Here, even the most insignificant thing is taken with unwarranted seriousness. As most have nothing, everything is attached with an overexaggerated sense of value. Mark could not understand this way of thinking and now he was in a situation he couldn't shrug his way out of. Scotty asked our advice about 'dealing with' Mark, I like to give people a second chance, especially the youngsters, so that's what I told him.

"You know you two have to go a few rounds, just don't let it go too far, and when it's over make sure he knows why it happened, and that it's over and forgotten." I finished with, "If you want, I'll talk to him when it's done."

"That'll work. I'm gonna wait until after the late count," he said. Then asked, "can you keep watch for us and give a knock if someone comes?"

"That's not a problem, but you two shouldn't be at it for too long, anyway I was a little worried that he might get carried away and hurt Mark more than he should. It wasn't about the ass whipping, it was the lesson that mattered, he needed to be taught to face his fears and meet his obligations, and that the principal and task were one and the same. There are no free rides in this life and the sooner a person learns that the better.

They went at it that night and we were happy to hear that Mark stood his ground. Oh, he took a pretty good beating, but what's important is he didn't back down and he stood and fought back. That's life: You can never conquer it, but you can earn your right to it.

Since Mark didn't get involved in the riot, he was gonna be kicked back to the yard, and in most cases when a riot occurs, it goes on for a year or more. Each side wants to get their runbacks, so the initial riot leads to two or three more. Then there are the times it goes on indefinately, everytime the doors rack cons just rush each other on sight with no end to be seen. Even though the names and faces change, the governing factor still exists and is in full control; fear. No one wants to be a victim, so they take the easy solution, perpetuate the cycle. The cause of the riot is long forgotten or was never known, so most have no idea what they're fighting about and no idea how to stop it. The guards play their role too. They nurture the hatred between the convicts, and with the gentleness of a loving mother they encourage one side while secretly warning the other.

Shortly before Mark was to go back to the yard I called him to the vent to try to explain a few contradictory things. As he only had two years until his parole date, we had been encouraging him to stay clean and make his date, also not to come back, but then with the next breath we told him he had no choice but to get involved in the next riot, his confusion was obvious.

"Mark, come to the phone." I called into the vent. "What's going on, Teacher?" he asked.

"Just thinking about you leaving and want to get a few things straight. Also, if you have any questions, now is the time to ask." I replied.

"Okay."

I went on, "I want to make sure you fully understand our last conversation about the riot. The easiest way for me to explain is this, all societies have laws which govern behavior, on the outside and in here and if you don't obey these laws you get into trouble. The difference is punishment. If you break the law outside, you are sent in here; in here you break the law, you are stabbed and ostracised. I know it's odd to expect men who can't obey the law outside to come in here and toe the line, but that's how it is. We can't live without rules, without structure; all sheep need a shepherd. No matter how we protest, we need laws to govern our lives. Also, you cannot follow the rules or one society while living in another, because circumstance is different. Yet, there is a similiarity between these two societies that will always hold true; bystanders, the innocent, those who passively watch life from a safe distance, these are the ones who get victimized. It's an ugly and unfair truth, but it is a truth nonetheless. In the second and third waves of a riot, who are the ones victimized?"

He answered quickly, "the ones who wait."

"That's right." The ones who wait to see if anything is going to happen. The one who stand on the fringes thinking it's safe and hoping all trouble will pass them by. The ones who pick up a Bible in hopes of defense. But you know as well as I do, these are the ones who are picked off, the ones who by their voluntary separation from the Herd, make easy prey and are struck down by an opportunistic aggressor. Everyone likes to think they're the individual, but the unvarnished truth, especially here, is that protection lay only with the Herd. I took a breath, stalling for time. I realized that I was speaking to myself more than to him and my actions of late gave the lie to my words. I had never been able to take my own advice, this will probably cost me one day, but today I am only concerned with his future.

I continued, "take all I'm saying is keep your nose clean and concentrate on making it home. You have people who need you, and not just for what you can do for them, but simply because they love you. When you go back to the yard, if nothing is going on then just mind yourself, but if a riot jumps again you have to do your part. You'll lose ninety days good time, but at least you'll make it home, if you sit out again chances are you won't. Do you understand?"

"Yeah, I understand," he answered noncommittally.

He doesn't realize that I'm only concerned for his well being and only want to help, he's still too young to be able to judge the value of advice, there is nothing more I can do. I clearly understand Claus' frustration, voiced in his 'I stand here.'

"Alright then, it was good to meet you and you watch yourself okay. And I hope I never see you again." I finished. I know it sounds rude but it's the best goodbye you can give to a con who is short to the pad. It means, don't ever come back to this shithole. The next day he left to the yard and two years later, when I got cut loose he had already paroled. I never heard from him or about him again and that makes me smile.

VI

The days passed, unconcerned with human cares they carelessly rose and fell in an unmoving tide. Before I knew it, my time in the SHU was quickly coming to an end. I had but a few days left and was feeling anxious, I didn't want to leave D-Man alone. I didn't fear for him, as that was unnecessary, I was worried that he would always choose the physical action first and I didn't want him in any more trouble. I decided to speak with him before I left.

During our time in the SHU we had discussed much, yet surprisingly little to do with our situation. I guess this was due, in part, to the fact that we both already knew our options, and of those, one outcome was most likely. Therefore, we spoke of everything but.

I don't know if our time passed slowly or quickly, I've seemed to have forgotten their differences, all I know is that time passed. The prison offers college courses by mail, so we both enrolled. We are taking intro courses to Philosophy and Theology, strange, I know, but I have always been curious about the common threads which run through most Mythology. My mistake was equating Mythology to Theology. Others in our block are also taking courses, and while I applaud the effort, the results are far from encouraging the old adage: a little knowledge is dangerous, has never found soil so fertile. What they learn is twisted and molded like clay, to fit into their preconceived notions, the end result being a slightly more literate criminal. This is not always the case. I've met some cons who went into their studies like a blank slate and came out better men for their efforts, but this is rare.

Interspersed between our studies were our workouts. These are mandatory as you need to be able to protect yourself, plus, it's a good way to get rid of frustration and anxiety. We would often get carried away and go to the point of exhaustion, where we could barely lift ourselves off of the floor. Immediately after one of these workouts, D-Man said, "You're gone Friday, we got one good workout left, then I gotta go back to the bullshit routine I knew exactly what he was talking about, we worked out together and pushed each other hard, also, we used each others body weight to lift. I would stand in his hands and he would bench press me, now he would have to go back to push-ups and he was not happy about it.

"Yeah, I'll have to drive your ass into the dirt tomorrow," I said laughing, because I'd never been able to do it yet. When it came to working out, D-Man was a beast.

"Good luck old man, but we both know you'll be limping out of this cell come Friday," he shot back.

"Now that we're speaking of Friday, I have something else that I think we should discuss."

"Shoot."

"We both know where we sit and what's likely to happen when I hit the yard. But I want to talk about you and your next move." I started.

"I think we both already know the answer to that," he stated.

"I think you're jumping the gun a little. If circumstances change, then our plan should change too, I don't want you going off half-cocked and whacking the first guy you can get your hands on. We're both doing live in this shithole, the mainline is our streets, our version of paroling, so if we happen to hit a yard where we can get a little action at a phone and some yard time with actual sunshine, I think we should take advantage of it. Also -"

"You know damn well their not going to let that happen," he interrupted. I knew he was speaking of the Aryan Syndicate. I also knew that we had already agreed on an offensive strategy at all times, but I've been having my doubts about the wisdom of that.

"You're right. But they don't have people on every yard, just sympathizer and wannabes, and they don't want none of us, you know that. But that is not my concern, I'm worried that our actions don't reflect our beliefs. If we want these youngsters to listen to us, then we have to live what we preach." I stopped him before he could interrupt again and went on. "I know this will put us in a precarious position and I don't care for that aspect of it either, but I can't let that be the determining factor in how I behave. Look brother, I've never tried to tell you what to do and I'm sure as hell not about to start, but if our actions don't match our speech, we're gonna lose credibility, and no one will listen to a damn thing from us. We chose this road long ago and I haven't traveled this far only to turn aside now."

"Huh," was his only response, but he grunted it out in a questioning tone and I knew he was thinking about it, that's all I could ask.

When Teacher was brought back to the yard, it was through a rigid silence that he made his way to the block. The yard was full of cons and most nodded, but none approached or spoke, even though they liked and respected him, they were not willing to share his trouble. Snake and a few of his friends were moved to another yard, the captain was hoping this would avoid more problems, but the cons kept them distance still.

It is surprising that I can still be surprised, for I've seen it all. There are only a few types of convicts and all are out from the same few molds. There is the programmer: This is the one who comes to prison, follows all the rules and paroles, he doesn't take part in prison life and is looked down on by the other cons, and in many cases, these are the one who are victimized. The wannabe: These are the ones seduced by prison. They think the gangsterism is cool. They get caught up in the life and even pitch dirt a couple times. Then they realize they're in over their heads and lock-up. The gangster: Those are the convicts who were seemingly born for this life, they kill; steal; assult; plot and connive, with an impunity that goes beyond frightening. They have no greater ambition in life than to be the top dog in prison.

Every now and then the odd one will roll through who doesn't fit into any of these molds, and no one knows how to take him, guards and cons alike. Generally, the guards will just shove him into one of the preexisting categories; we don't see the individual, only a continuation of the mass. But in our defense, we are overworked and undermanned.

For the first few weeks that Teacher was back the tension was high, every yard, every dayroom, we expected something to happen, nothing did. As scared as the cons are of the Aryan Syndicate, they live by the Maxim: out or sight out of mind, and all the members are slammed down in the hole as soon as they're discovered. Teacher was a physical presence that no one wanted to take on, so the yard settled into a quiet acceptance, which Teacher surprisingly went along with.

Teacher was given a job in the kitchen and a new cellie, a youngster everyone called Splinter, this was because he was so small and skinny, that he wasn't big enough to be a wood, only a branch off the tree. His real name was Matthew Lee McKinley and he was the only one willing to move in with Teacher. Alot of guards fought this decision, especially the women. As Splinter had just turned eighteen, this would be his first cellie and most did not want him around Teacher, because his fault or not, violence seemed to be attracted to him.

Splinter came to the prison when he was seventeen, he looked thirteen, so, many of the female guards mothered him. I don't know if it was conscious or just a deep seated maternal instinct, but woe to those who tried to mess with him, they quickly found themselves on the losing end. Splinter would act like he hated it when others were around, but secretly he basked in their attention and they loved that they had someone to mother hen. The only reason the move was approved is because we are always struggling to find more room, overcrowding is a huge problem and double-celling cons frees up that room.

That afternoon we brought Teacher to Captain Schmidt's office to speak about him moving in with Splinter, there were a few guards milling around waiting to have a word with him as well, and if I had to guess, I would bet they were going to threaten the hell out of him.

As we stepped into the captains office, he was reading Teacher's enormous C-file and shaking his head, but as he wore a slight grin, I assumed he was enjoying himself. Every convict has a Central File, it documents his every move throughout the prison system, achievements and failures, behavior, enemies. This helps us to better know a con, also to keep known enemies seperated.

"You know the Aryan Syndicate has a contract on you?" Captain Schmidt said without warning. Teacher remained still and gave no response as expected.

"My Gang Investigators have been hearing your name all over the prison grapevine, people debriefing are mentioning your name, people who are just plan scared to have you on the yard are dropping kites left and right. It's my job to warn you, so considered yourself warned," he continued. "Got it?"

"Yes sir." Teacher answered.

"Okay, now on to the cellie issue. I know there isn't gonna be any problems, so I'm not even gonna warn you, but I will give you some advice, don't get this kid into any trouble. There are alot of folks who will hold you personally accountable, understand?"

"Yes sir."

"Before you get out of here, there are some people next door who would like to have a word with you, and if I was you, I'd listen. Alright, take him to the conference room, Walker." The captain dismissed us.

We walked down the hall and I could feel Teacher tense as we entered not knowing what to expect. Inside not surprisingly were three women, all guards. Mrs. Brian was the eldest and quite obviously in charge, as the other two were taking cues from her and following her lead.

I instantly knew what was happening and had to suppress a grin. Teacher sat straddling a chair, hands cuffed behind him, he looked straight ahead and didn't say a word. Mrs. Brian came to stand in front of him and looked him over with a feigned distaste, which did not have the desired effect as we all knew she was sympathetic towards him.

"I have no idea why the captain agreed to let splinter live with you," she finally blurted out. Everyone, guards included, called McKinley by his nickname.

"He is only a child and I swear to you, if anything happens to him around you, because of you, or by you, you will regret it for the rest of your life. This prison is a small place, and there is nowhere you can go to get away from us. Yes, I said us. I am not the only one who feels this way, and if you think life is difficult now, by God, let one little thing happen to that child and you'll find out the definition of difficult. He has eighteen months until he paroles, and we are going to make sure he does, any way we have to, do you understand?"

"Yes ma'am, fully," Teacher answered neutrally.

"That's good. But I want a promise from you, that you are going to make sure he doesn't get into any trouble or got hurt."

"The only thing I can promise you is that I'll do my best to watch out for him, but I can't be with him all the time and I can't make his decisions for him -"

"You don't have to," she interrupted. "If something happens, you just let one of us know," indicating the other women with a stabbing gesture of her hand, "and we'll make his decisions for him."

I could see he was fighting to keep a smile off his face, I was struggling to do the same.

"You know I can't do that," he carefully responded. "I have to live here, and I don't think frequent visitations to the guards would be good for my health, but if it's something small and not prison related, I'll let you know. You have my word I'll keep an eye on him, I'm sorry, that's all I can do."

Mrs. Brian stood still and seemed to be weighing her options, probably wondering if she could extract anymore from him. I was surprised she had gotten as much as she did. She made her mind up about something, because her next words were, "we are holding you personally responsible for his safety," and then in a quieter voice, "you know I trust you."

It wasn't said as a question, but a fact, I was stunned by the underlying honesty and her implication. She knew that he could protect Splinter better than a whole prison of guards and she openly showed this to him.

He sat quiet for what seemed an eternity, he and Mrs. Brian holding each others gaze. Abruptly, his face softened and he let out a pent up breath, "Thank you," was all he said.

As I was escorting him back to the block, he was smiling. I thought, perhaps it was over the womens display, and stayed silent, as it was somewhat comical. Yet, as we continued, it started bothering me that he could disregard their obvious concern so easily. "You know, they only spoke to you because they care about Splinter. There's no reason to simply shrug off their words with a laugh."

He looked at me genuinely amused, "You misunderstand me Stogie, I value their words and intent highly. It has just been a long time since I've seen anyone give a damn, and I'm smiling because it makes me remember better times and better people."

We finished our walk in silence, and I delivered him back to his cell. Alone I made my way back across the yard, I couldn't help but think, than maybe he was a better man than I had given him credit for.

Well, I'm back on the yard and things are not what I expected, which is a pleasant surprise. I have officially been made a Babysitter, but I can't complain, as I would have taken the job on myself; It just seems strange to have the approval, tacit or otherwise, of most of the guards. This was both good and bad. I could appreciate the female guards stopping by with extra lunches or trays to make sure Splinter was eating right, because I benefitted from that too, but the fact that so many eyes were on us made it impossible to do anything in secrecy as well as highly uncomfortable.

Splinter wanted me to sling some ink on him pretty bad, he had what we call ink-fever, a burning desire to get inked by anybody, no matter how good they are, or bad, it's difficult to find good tattoo artists in here, as most don't have the equipment or time in order to become proficient. He was wound up with enthusiasm when he found out that I was one of the better artists and he could not leave me alone. Day and night he was on me about getting 'shirted', I had absolutely no intention of giving him even the smallest tattoo, I knew he would be showing it off for the entire yard, Mrs. Brian and coterie included. I didn't want to face three angry surrogate mothers, I'm no genus, but even I know that's a no-win situation. He finally broke me down I told him I'd do his tattoos on one condition; he had to get Mrs. Brian's approval. I congratulated myself on a fine solution, he would be pestering Mrs. Brian from now on. She wanted a child, now she had one.

So it was a surprise when only two days later Splinter came home and told me he had gotten 'permission' for a few tattoos. He wanted a heart with roses behind it and mom written across it, the second was his last name across his upper back. I knew right then that this kid was much shrewder than I had thought. I told him I'd have to confirm with Mrs. Brian, to make sure he wasn't yanking my chain, and if she said yes, then I'd draw up his patterns in the next few days. Over those following days he almost drove me crazy, every five minutes it was, are you ready yet?; why aren't you ready?; I'm ready to go, are you? My God, if I wasn't bold already, I would have pulled my hair out by the handfuls. I have no idea how parent do it, but they have all my sympathy and respect.

I checked with Mrs. Brian and she okayed it, but stressed he could have two only, and no racist or gangster stuff. There was nothing to do except get to work, but one thing I had decided on early, I was going to make it uncomfortable, inflict a little more pain than was necessary in the hope of dissuading him from wanting any more. Deep down, I knew this wasn't gonna work and I'd probably be visited sometime in the future by his 'mother', who would tell me that he could have a few more, and then a few more. what the hell had I gotten myself into?

I had just come home from work and Splinter was sitting on my bunk watching soap operas, thanks Mrs. Brian. He barely glanced up couldn't peel his eyes off the t.v. He would watch them and then go out into the <u>rotundra</u> office and sit around with the coterie clucking like a hen. Anyone else, I would have put a stop to it, other cons do more than gossip if you hang out with guards, but he was learning necessary things from these women and I didn't want him picking up prison habits. I knew I could protect him until he paroled, but what they taught him would help him where I couldn't.

"You ready to get started, or do you wanna keep watching your soaps?" I asked nonchalantly.

He jumped up so quick, he banged his head into the top bunk. I smiled as he rubbed his head and cursed.

"I been ready since the day I came to prison. Hell yeah, lets do it," he said. "I didn't know you had the patterns ready."

"I finished them up yesterday."

"What, you mean we could've tattooed last night?" he blurted out incredulously. "No, we couldn't've," I said.

"Why?"

"Because, I hadn't cleared it with your mom, yet." I answered with a feigned disgust, to which he only grinned.

To show you how persuasive he is, he went from being allowed two tattoos, to a full shirt, as long as it was half sleeves! Basically, if a T-shirt would cover it, he could have it. So, for the next four months I worked on his ink. I did his arms from the elbows up, his chest and back, he was in heaven the entire time, no matter how much it hurt. I did find the sessions to my advantage as well, he had to sit still for the tattooing, so I took these opportunities to school him.

At first he tried to watch t.v. while I inked, but I quickly changed that, I made lecturing and tattooing go hand in hand, if he wanted one he had to accept the other. He wasn't too happy about this but his desire for ink was too strong for him to say no. So all the while I was inking him, I spoke about family, responsibility, becoming a man, taking care of your elders, and so on. Most of the conversations that I imagine fathers have with their sons. He had no choice but to listen, and over those months I could see a change in him that made me proud. I was even commended by Mrs. Brian for the good influence I'd been on him. Praise is addictive and I wanted more.

One day while we were speaking of the need for him to be law abiding, he interrupted with, "hey Teacher, if what you say is true, why do you do the things I've heard about?" When I just looked at him blankly, he added, "You know, stab people, beat people, I know you're done alot of crazy things in here, but you're telling me to do the opposite."

I couldn't think of what to say, should I lie, should I play the innocent role - it's not my fault, society failed me -, or should I tell the truth? I could only do one thing.

"Okay look, I know it may sound like a cop-out, but my life outside these walls is over, I'm gonna live and die here. Since I'm a permanent member of this society, I live by its rules, not all, but most. If I had a chance to go back to the streets, believe me, I would do absolutely everything by the book. I've seen and done this and I'm over it, I want to go back to the real world, but that will never happen, so I can't think about it, you understand? If I thought about it all the time it would drive me crazy. The reason I spend so much time lecturing you, is because I don't want you to wind up in the same position as me. I want you to go out there and experience life, get married, have children, watch them waddle around all clumsily and grasp your finger in their little hands. Look around you, this isn't life in here, only a slower form of death. Look at the guys you know, half of them have a life sentence, the rest have 30, 40, 50, years. What do you think happens to someone after they've done that much time in prison? Even if you have family who'll accept you, there's no going back. Time is a thief little brother, and if you don't watch out he'll rob you blind."

I could have went on and on, but I felt I might be losing him as well as myself. I was going down a road which was too dangerous, I knew I needed to back up and stick to safer routes.

I've been on the yard for a year now and I'm amazed that I've lasted this long without anything negative happening. It's nice to go to work and come home tired but oddly satisfied; to go to the yard and socialize and get some actual sunshine; to sit in the dayroom and play cards; none of this is possible in the hole or SHU, it gives you a sense of freedom. I know it's strange to speak of freedom in prison, but there you have it, everyone must find their own.

I think I can pinpoint the day where I made my mistake, although I never looked at it as such, but it's the day I gave my enemies all that they had been waiting for. For years everything had been personal, so the majority of cons didn't take or and either side, but now I had broken the cardinal role, I had taken up for a guard, only to the point where I spoke on his behalf, but that was more than enough.

Splinter was a night porter, at two in the afternoon, he came out to sweep and map the tiers and scrub the showers. We had dayroom time after dinner, then the porters swept once again before being locked up for the night. Splinter came home wired up every night because he knew we would be tattooing, but this night was different. When he came in

I could tell something was wrong, he was quiet, subdued, which was contrary to his character.

"What's got you all hemmed up?" I asked.

He was slow in responding, but finally came out with, "I heard some crazy stuff that I wasn't meant to. I don't want to go around repeating it, but I think someone should know. I don't know what to do, teach."

He was looking to me for guidance.

"Look, little brother, you know you can tell me anything without compromising yourself, we share confidences. More importantly though, whatever it was you heard, ask yourself if it goes against your beliefs, if not then forget you ever heard it, but if it does, you can't stand idly by or your beliefs become hollow." I gently explained.

"I don't want to get into trouble Teacher."

A scared child was looking at me, my anger was sudden and deep, not with him, but whoever it was that had been careless enough to be overheard. I have no children, nothing that will reach beyond myself into the future. Yet, I have the urge to protect the young, defenseless; the urge to stamp out any and every threat. All this welled up in me as I looked at Splinter that night, standing there small and frightened, yet wanting to do the right thing, to show himself worthy of his newfound morals.

"Sit down and tell me what you heard, I'll take care of it for both of us."

Stogie had done a few cell searches that night in a different section and hit Cyco and Cowboys cell. Everybody, skrews included, knew that those two made moonshine and sold it, that was their hustle. They had to, as neither had anyone on the streets to look out for them. Stogie and the other skrews had always looked the other way because they never caused any trouble, but this time something was different, he took all their wine and cooking paraphernalia and they were freaking pissed. Stogie only did it because a certain sargeant - who was an uptight asshole, was working, so his hand was forced.

Most cons know that this comes with the territory, sometimes you take a hit and you have to suck it up and start over. But Cyco and

Cowboy had different ideas. Splinter was sweeping in front of their cell, underneath the stairs, and heard them plotting Stogies murder.

Suddenly I understood his reluctance, this was a situation where sticking your nose in his liable to get it chopped off. The relationship between guards and cons is contentious in the best of times and down right nasty most of the time. If a guard is beaten or stabbed, the whole yard will suffer the consequences. Cells will be ransacked, televisions broken, family photos strewn on the ground to be trampled under foot, in many cases, property will be thrown away never to be seen again. There has always been an Us versus Them mentality in here, a holdover of the dislike for cops on the street.

Most guards are just regular folk, here for their eight hours and paycheck and then home to their families. Alot are decent, easy going people, just trying to get by like everyone else. This is not a popular view in here, but for as long as I've been down, I've never seen Stogie mistreat or disrespect anyone who didn't have it coming, so I felt I had a responsibility to step in and cool down tempers, if possible, or go to the hole, if necessary.

Cowboy worked with me in the kitchen, but I decided to approach them when they were together, as things tend to get misunderstood when they are second or third hand. Plus, I didn't want him going back and running his mouth, that would give them a chance to plot against me, then I'd have to watch both at all times and that is just a pain in the ass. Besides, it's best to deal with something as quick and efficient as possible, because the waiting is always the hardest part, it eats away at your nerve.

I decided to speak with them on the yard the following day. That night I got my knife out and readied. Splinter was anxious all night, full of questions wanting to know what I was going to do, he also wanted to help. He only had five months until he paroled. There was no way in hell I'd let him go with me. In fact, I told him he had to stay home from yard the next day. He had the anger of youth, instant and unthinking.

"I'm not a child. I can make my own decisions," he blurted out angrily. "You owe me," I told him.

"What. What the hell are you talking about."

I stared at him for a minute with a look that backed him up. I saw fear in his eyes and knew I was the reason, I didn't like that.

"I took you in, I protected you, I tattooed you, I taught you what you need to live a decent life outside these walls, and if you don't feel that you owe me your allegiance, then you damn sure better know that you owe me a favor." I stated forcefully. His initial enthusiasm was dampened somewhat, as if I'd thrown a wet blanket over him. "That favor, I'm calling in. I don't want you on the yard tomorrow, okay?"

"Teacher, I just want to help, exactly because of those reasons."

"I know, but don't you understand. That would make us both hypocrites. All the preparing we've done to get you home would be wasted if we turn around and let you get involved in some worthless prison crap. If you want to show me what you've learned, you'll stay home. But you're right, you're a man and I won't tell you what to do, I only hope you make the right decision." I finished reasonably, hoping he would see logic.

Generally, after we shut off the light and T.V. for the night, we would lay there and bullshit for awhile until one or the other fell asleep. That night we were both to wrapped up in our own thoughts, sleep was long in coming and the silence made it longer.

In the morning, he told me that he was staying home, not because I asked, but because it was the right thing to do. So on a different day, he lightened my load and put a smile on my face.

"You two want to spin a few laps with me?"

"Sure Teacher," Cowboy replied suspiciously. He and Cyco shared a look that put me on my toes.

As we headed for the track they jockeyed for position, making sure I wasn't behind them. Sometimes having a reputation is a disadvantage. I walked in front of them trusting they wouldn't act out blindly, we made it to the track then walked on side by side.

I figured direct would be best, "I heard what Stogie did to your cell."

"Yeah, everybody has. That son of a bitch took everything." Cyco spat out. "We don't give a damn about the wine, but he took all of our equipment, stingers, buckets, pipes. You know how hard it is to replace that stuff? We don't got no damn money."

"Pipes?"

"Yeah. We got our hands on a few pieces of PVC pipe and rigged them to our still and had a drip system. The shit practically cooked itself."

He was working himself up even as we were speaking. I knew I had to blunt his anger somehow or this little stroll was gonna turn ugly.

"You know the woodpile will pitch in and restock you guys in a day or two, you can be up and running within the week."

"We know that," Cowboy said, "but we got other ideas. There is a disrespect issue we gotta deal with," he finished coldly. I knew he was only posturing, because that's the game in here. You always say the worst and hope someone is there with a bit of sense to talk you down. I was encouraged by this, they seemed to be reading from the expected script, so I knew my next move.

"Look fellas, I'd hate to see something happen where it only gets worse for you guys. I'm sure you know what the consequences would be if something happens to that skrew, so I'm not gonna mention them. But I'd like you to think about this, our version of respect is not theirs. Someone can only disrespect us who practices the same form as us, otherwise it's unintentional. What it comes down to is this, Stogie didn't disrespect you guys, he's just a skrew doing his job and if you go after him, alot of us are gonna get swept up as collateral damage. This would start a war that's alot bigger than you two, and in the end all of us will be in the SHU for the rest of our lives."

I could see my words were getting through as both looked alot less certain than just a few moments ago. So I decided to keep the advantage and continue.

"I gotta tell you guys, if I was gonna crack one of these skrews, it wouldn't be Stogie. He's actually one of the decent ones, he looks the other way and lets as go about our business. As long as you don't throw something in his face, he's pretty cool for a skrew."

We walked in silence for awhile, as it stretched I knew it was working on their nerves. I also hoped these 'talks' wouldn't go on for days, as they often do. I have little patience for this kind of thing, feel like a damned therapist.

Cowboy finally broke the quiet. "I agree with everything you said, but that pig put us on the spot and you know damn well if we don't deal with it we're done on this yard."

"I don't know anything of the kind. I'm a wood on this yard and you know how I feel. I suggest you talk to a few of the fellas out here right now, you might be surprised by their reactions," I said. "Alright, I'm gonna take off. I'll stop by tonight at dayroom and we can talk some more, if need be. Whatever you two decide, I know you'll give us a heads-up so we don't get caught holding."

"That's a given, Wood. We'll see you tonight. Hey, thanks for the time, huh?"

"No problem."

That night we were put on lockdown while the Goon squad ran roughshod through the block, hitting houses at seeming random, but everyone knew this was for show, as all the cells searched were those of whites. Warning calls were ringing throughout the block, "Gooners walking, Gooners walking." For these searches, they always bring the handheld metal detectors, so you can't 'hoop' your knife or you'll set it off. Then you'll be put on 'Potty watch' until you crap it out for them, then it's straight to the hole. When you hear the warnings sound, you hide your knife and dump any contraband with a quickness.

The Gooners went straight to Cyco and Cowboys cell, which was not very surprising. The way those two made such a production out of their anger, every snitch on the yard knew exactly what they were contemplating, and from that point on it was only a race to see who could give up the information first and get their gold star.

They brought them both out cuffed and from the way they were mad dogging everyone, I knew that they had been caught with something. From what the rumor mill turned out, we later found out that they were gonna be put in the hole regardless. 'Confidential information' said they were gonna move on a cop, so there was no way the brass was gonna keep them on the yard. I felt bad for them because these are the hardest cases to defend yourself against. It's not like the outside courts, where you get to face your accuser. Here, snitches mostly make stuff up and there's no way to fight them as the prison protects them. Hell, the guards are the ones who feed them most of the crap they spit out. I just hoped that they caught a break and beat it somehow, I wouldn't mind seeing them back on the yard.

The night we rolled up Cowboy and Cyco was a revelation. I came on duty at two in the afternoon and was sent directly to Captain Schmidts office. When I arrived he looked angry, and I instantly started sifting back over the last few days trying to remember what I had done wrong. He looked up and nodded to the chair and continued reading.

"Tell me what's been going on in your block lately," he said.

I was thrown off by the question, as not a damn thing had occurred, everything was running along smoothly, to the point of being boring. When you've worked here as long as I have the days run together, and one becomes indistinguishable from the next. This union produces an ugly ash gray palette, which promises and delivers anonymity.

Without a word, he shoved a loose stack of folded paper across the desk, where it stood teetering, as if in anticipation of being read. I could tell at a glance that they were "kites" from convicts. They were always ripped and folded the same way, and I could see the obligatory microprint writing that was almost impossible to read. I put on my reading glasses and reached for the first one with a sense of trepidation, was someone snitching on me? It would be unpleasant to have to explain yourself because of an anonymous accusations now I knew how the convicts felt.

All the kites were basically the same. I had disrespected two convicts cell, and now they had been making knives over the last few days, and from conversations they had had with other cons their intent was to "deal with me."

I was more than a little shocked and very aware of the captain watching me. I imagine he was trying to gauge my reaction in order to make a decision, so I tried to laugh off the first few kites, but the more I read the larger the pit in my stomach grew and my laughs slowly died away. How close had I come? I wondered.

The captains voice intruded, "Mike, you didn't have any idea things had gone this far?"

"No, not at all," I answered slowly. "I was just in the dayroom with them last night and I didn't notice anything strange - it was only a cell search."

"Speaking of strange, see what you make out of these", he said, handing me two more kites.

I spread them out and read them catching his meaning immediately. They had essentially the same info as the others, but these added a twist. Apparently Teacher had gotten wind of the situation and had talked them out of it. There was no reason given, only his intervention.

"Has anyone tried to speak to teach - I mean, Allen, about this?" I knew the answer even as it was being voiced.

"I sent two escorting officers to pick him up, but he refused to come out of his cell and I can't force him. I seriously doubt he would speak to any of us, anyway."

"So how are we going to play this? I asked somewhat hesitantly.

"We, ain't doing anything. You will not be involved," he said forcefully. "Those two are going to the hole, that's for damn sure, and that block is being turned upside down even as we speak. Maybe we can throw a few more of those morons in the hole as well."

"What about these last two kites saying they were talked out of it?"

"I don't give a damn if that's true or not, we'll let someone else deal with that. I want them off my yard. Nobody even thinks about threatening one of my officers, that shit don't fly on my watch." He was almost yelling.

I don't know if this was his idea of reassuring me, but all it was doing was making me more nervous. I wanted to get out of there and head to my block, where I hoped to find everything normal. As I rose to leave, the captain told me 'The Squad' would be running my block for the next few days and that I'd be working in a tower. This is where they put guards to protect them from cons. But there was a bonus; I'd be allowed to claim all the overtime I wanted! Money, todays great cureall.

That night, sitting alone in the gun tower, I wondered why Teacher would put himself in a bad position with the other convicts for a guard. Was there some ulterior motive, one that had nothing to do with me? Perhaps, he didn't want his program disrupted and decided it wasn't gonna be personally. Yet the more I thought about it, the easier it was to reject these ideas. I had watched him over the last ten years and as he aged, the one thing that had not changed was the way in which he conducted himself. He was always honest, even when he couldn't tell you what you wanted to know, he wouldn't lie, he simply wouldn't answer. He never practiced subterfuge. This brought me to the only logical conclusion; he helped me for the sole purpose of helping me.

VII

The prison is split into two yards, each holding a little more than 1000 convicts. The only contact these yards have with each other is through the PIA. This is the Prison Industry Authority, it's where convicts go behind a wall to work. There are boat and shoe factories; an optical plant - which makes glasses; mechanics shop; bakery; main kitchen; all of these serve the needs of the prison and help make it less dependent on outside resources.

Since cons from both yards work here, it's a hot spot for information. The cons pass kites and verbal messages back and forth with an efficiency and regularity that puts the postal service to shame. They check on new guys who hit the yard, making sure they didn't lock-up or were victimized on the other yard or at another prison.

Our policy is simply to move a victim to the other yard, and hold our breath while waiting for the inevitable. When they're assulted there, we transfer them to another prison and wish them luck; it's like sending a lamb to the slaughter. If it seems redundant and ineffective that's because it is.

Cowboy and Cyco spent four months in the hole and then were released to the other yard, they couldn't be found guilty as there was not enough evidence, so they were freed. The yard they went to is where Snake had set up shop and take over, in order to get on his good side the two did more than hint that Teacher had stopped them from killing a cop, they went as far as saying that he "might" be working for us. In here statements don't need to be qualified, as rumor is taken as fact, especially if it concerns your enemy. This was exactly what Snake had been waiting for.

Instantly, the traffic in kites between yards was revved up. Snake was promising, cajoling, threatening, and buying anyone and everyone he could, in order to have Teacher hit. But as I said earlier, cons are a pretty scary lot and when it comes right down to it, the only neck they look out for is their own.

Teacher was brought to the captains office again and warned of the threats. He sat unconcernedly listening, made no comment, then quietly left. I knew he wasn't stupid, so it was difficult to fathom his lack of worry over possibly being murdered. He reacted as if we had told him it was chow time, or you have to breathe to live, or some other mundane statement; what seemed so wrong to us was perfectly natural to him, just another fact of life. It's a helluva life these cons live, if it may be called that.

I felt compelled to help him in turn, but I had no idea how to go about it or even where to start. The only thing I knew was I'd have to do it soon, because with all these threats coming in, he wasn't going to stick around long, he'd be on the offensive shortly. I knew the only thing keeping him here was Splinter, he wouldn't take off and leave the kid unprotected, but Splinter had only two months left, so I would have to work quick.

I didn't want to make the situation worse, so I decided to approach him while he was at work, where there were fewer eyes to see and fewer tongues to wag. As I was walking to the kitchen, I was still trying to think of what to say, when a voice brought me up short, "How ya doing, Stogie?"

I looked up to find Teacher standing outside the door to the kitchen, leaning against the wall, looking as relaxed as could be.

"Pretty good. How about yourself?" I replied.

"I'm good too, just taking a break. It's nice to be outside."

"I can imagine, it beats being locked in a cell, huh?" "Sure does."

This is generally the extent of conversations between guards and cons as no one wants to be the guy who crosses that invisible line.

We both stood in a comfortable silence and gazed out on an empty yard, the yard that looked so menacing when it was strewn with convicts, looked surprisingly innocent now, the aura they left was as transitory as they themselves. Over the tops of the buildings you could see the low rolling foothills in the distance, and the few trees which top them, lining the horizon, standing still as silent sentinels. It's a beautiful view from a prison yard, and as I glanced at Teacher, I could understand his wanting to take it in, it was a respite from the ugly world in which he lived. I didn't want to disturb him, but I had to tell him

"Thanks," I said.

He kept looking into the distance and I didn't think he was going to respond, until he finally came out with, "For what"?

"For taking a couple of idiots out of a bad mistake, and for saving my family and me alot of heartache and worry." I stopped, suddenly very aware that not only was I grateful to a criminal, but I thought of him as an equal, and perhaps, even a friend. I didn't know if I should go on or if I had already come too far to stop.

A stray thought wound its way to the fore and became insistent. I had heard it rumored that a society is judged by how it treats its inmates, maybe I am being judged right now.

"If things had gone differently, I might not be here. I don't know who would take care of my family - it's a big deal to me. I know you can't confirm anything and I don't want you to, but I owe you, and if I can help you in any way, all you have to do is ask."

He didn't respond, and I felt a tug of disappointment. I don't know what I was expecting, but it doesn't matter, as I said what I needed to. I turned to leave, when his voice stopped me.

"Hey Stogie - I'm glad everything worked out."

Every since the plot to kill me had been uncovered, the sergeant and captain have been giving me first dibs on all overtime, which is good since I'm up to my neck in bills, and for some reason, the more I try to work my way out the deeper I become buried. So I've been pulling double shifts three days a week. The extra shifts have been in PIA, from eight in the morning to two in the afternoon, then my regular shift goes from two till ten. Hell, I'm spending almost as much time in prison as the prisoners; that can't be good.

Working in PIA is unsettling, there are very few guards and no gun coverage as it's behind the wall. There's what we call free staff, these are civilian instructors. They're behind to teach the cons how to work in the individual areas, they are not guards.

If anything happens, fights, stabbings, riots, they run from the incident while pushing their alarms; we run towards it. This is not a slur against them, it's simply a fact, what they are told to do. With no chance of being shot, the cons rarely stop an assult of their own accord, they have to be beaten off with batons or pepper sprayed the hell out of. For this reason, most cons who are chosen to work back here are proven programmers.

So you can imagine my surprise when I found Snake working there. With his assultive history, there should be no way he is allowed back here. Obviously, he has a friend or influence somewhere, that is a shame because it reflects poorly on us guards.

When I first saw him, he was across the room hidden in partial shadow, openly staring at me. When our eyes met, a slow grin spread searchingly across his rugged face, rising and falling as if having to struggle over the terrain. I've never seen a smile so ugly in aspect or intent. I stood still staring back, I didn't want to show any weakness, as nothing summons the shark's swifter. There was still some residual fear from the knowledge of what "they" wanted to do to me. This fear expressed itself in the worst case of butterflies imaginable.

Snake started towards me, homing in as if I were a human beacon, his grin ever widening and an ugly sparkle in his eye. I knew he could sense my fear and was feeding off of it, but I couldn't move. He stopped a few feet away and slowly came out with.

"I see you're still plugging along, old man."

We were the same age, but where he was a wall of muscle, I am pretty much made up of beer. It's a difference which neve strikes you until you are faced with its physicality, then, you know you've made a fatal mistake.

"Why wouldn't I be?", I asked, hoping he would be smug enough to implicate himself, he only laughed.

"People fall from all kinds of diseases, Stogie, you know that. You never know what's lurking around the corner, biding its time, waiting to pull you down. You just can't be careful enough these days, can you?"

So much for subtlety, he just laid his threats out for all to see. Yet, I'm thankful for his arrogance as it awakened my anger.

"Is that a threat from you and your friends?"

He wore a satisfied look. I wish I hadn't said anything.

"I don't know where or who you could have gotten that idea from."

The emphasis he put on the word 'who' led me exactly where he wanted.

"I always thought you were cool, Stogie. You do your job. I do mine, and we never mess with each other, has something changed?"

He was good, that quick he'd turned the situation around and was the one asking questions.

"You know exactly what I'm talking about, your two friends are on the same yard as you now. One big happy dysfunctional family, right?"

He smiled like I had given him just what he wanted.

"And your friend is still on the yard with you, isn't he?", he said confidently.

I had made a mistake in opening the door and now all I could do was deny and protest, which I would not do to a stinking piece of garbage like him. In the future, I would have to avoid these conversations.

Tonight a storm hit the prison, the howling winds tore and buttered at the walls, seeking out every crevice and weakness in seeming disgust at the perverted use they'd been put to. The yard door banged back and forth in its track, the continuing pounding keeping rhythm with my heartbeat and encouraging it in its efforts. The power has gone out too, now dark cells match dark thoughts, one spurring the other to ever darkening depths. Sometimes it is hard to catch your breath, the sheer amount of thoughts, of what ifs, of fears, simply overwhelm and leave one grasping for escape.

My cellie paroled three days ago, so I am alone. This makes the night revel in its strength, as it forces but a single foe; where there is human contact the battle is shared.

But things are looking up, D-man will be out of the SHU in a week and he will be coming to this yard as he has enemies on the other. I use this knowledge to strengthen my resolve and push all seductive thoughts out of my mind, as it is too easy to become lost in them.

I can hear whispered snatches of conversation on the tier, restrained voices struggling to hold themselves back. In these instances, life reverts to its most primitive, the thread stretching back to our origin; man alone in a dark cave.

Borne on its winds, the storm seems to carry a warning, its sense so strong as to be palpable. I'm not superstitious, but I feel something coming and I know it will leave negation in its wake.

As the days disappeared, time worked its magic, my fear slowly sank below the surface of remembrance. Yet, much of the time I feel adrift, as helpless as kelp on the oceans face, moving to and fro at the whim of another. I struggle to reach the shallows, as the depths are too deep. My legs dangle, feet clutching as if they had the ability to grasp, seeking out firm ground to plant themselves upon.

This job is like any other. You get bogged down into a routine that drains your enthusiasm for the work, then you settle into complacency, but here complacency can get you killed. Over the following months my guard has slowly lowered as nothing has happened, and it's impossible to keep it up indefinately. So I've settled into this limbo existence and sleepwalk through my days.

They're not much to speak of, the daily grind of waking, working, and going to sleep. Three days a week I was spending sixteen hours at the prison, when I'm home my children are asleep and I know nothing of their waking lives, which I was extracted from long ago. Standing in their midst I have become an absentee father.

My wife and I rarely speak anymore, unless it's with raised voices, but even this has faded as we have nothing left to say. We used to speak simply to hear each other. I would ask questions just to hear her whispery voice, I could listen to her speak all night. She has seen me at my best and worst and loved me throughout, yet now, my indifference has sapped the strength from her feelings.

Life is interrupted at intervals with accidents; sorrows, misfortunes, that are generally brief in duration, then life resumes its normal pace, but in here life itself is the interrupter. Here, life is lived from one violent episode to the next, everything in between is nothing but down time and filler. During the lockdowns the cons are forced to find another activity to pass the time, but everyone knows these moments of respite are fleeting and artificial. All are waiting for the doors to rack, for the next burst of life.

Somehow my life has adapted itself to these tracks and is relentlessly steaming ahead, I can't jump off or stop it, I can only hang on for the ride. It is like a soldier returning from war, he has lived so long with the constant threat of danger, that everything else has an artificial quality to it. His senses have been honed to the point were everything was sharper, livelier, tastier; you subtract the danger and all becomes dull, food is bland, family's a chore, life is hollow.

This has become my life and I don't know how to fix it, how to retrieve the past. The only thing I know now to do is work, so I keep working. I occasionally bump into Teacher when I am on the yard, we nod and exchange how ya doings, then go our own ways. We never speak of the debt, nor has he called in the favor. A few months back D-man was kicked out of the SHU, he and Teacher are living together again. I am glad Teacher has a true friend, I am sure it makes life easier.

We had an incident in PIA today, a convict had his hand smashed in a 22-ton press. This machine is used to make license plates you place a rectangular piece of metal into a mold, you then step on a pedal which brings the press down, while safety straps pull the cons hands out of danger. The safety straps on this particular machine had been cut. This time when the press descended a scream rang throughout the area followed by an eerie silence. I rushed over to the press and saw a con standing hunched over with his back to me, he was cradling his hand. At the sound of my voice he turned and held out his appendage, his hand was smashed as flat as a sheet of paper. The bones had been flattened and ripped out the meaty sides of his fingers and thumb. He just stood there staring at the dangling thing attached to the end of his arm, trying to figure out what it was. It was so thin it seemed to ruffle in the breeze like a flag. Looking at it I knew this would be his standard for life. The shock of his face was complete, he didn't moan, cry out, only stood there unable to comprehend his ruined self.

"Shit happens, right Stogie?" an amused voice said behind me. I turned to find Snake eyeing me coldly. Whenever anything horrible took place, he seemed to be in his element, and would swell up and smile like a proud father. It is true that misery loves company, I see it every day, yet, even the miserable hang their heads in despair at times; not Snake, he revels in it. When things are at their worst he thrives, when bodies are on the floor a smile plays over his face.

"Get your ass back to work!" I yelled, turning to help the injured con. He was rushed to an outside hospital as his need was beyond the prison staff. I knew it was useless as there was no fixing what had been undone.

Later, as I sat thinking about the 'accident', Snakes voice was worming its way through my head. I knew with a certainty that he was involved, he had either done it himself or had it done, he had plenty of flunkies for that kind of work. As I wrote up my report of the accident, I decided to add a postscript about Snakes possible involvement, hoping that whoever investigated would take a strong look at him. More than likely, nothing would come of it, but if there was even the smallest chance that I could get that animal sent to the hole, I would take it.

D-man's back and all is well, I didn't realize how much I missed the guy till he showed up with a smile on his face looking as crazy as usual. If they thought that four and a half years in the hole was going to change or tame him. They were sadly mistaken. His ways are set as firm as those visages routed out of Rushmore.

After Splinter paroled I started up a lucrative tattooing business. Since I was single-celled for awhile I would have people sneak into my cell for the night, I'd hook them up and they'd be gone come breakfast. As there wasn't many artists on the yard, I was making good money, so when D-man showed up, I had a bunk for him and a cell full of food.

The first few days we drank so much coffee and ate so many spreads, that we were in a continuous race for the toilet.

Spreads are just a bunch of crap thrown together in a plastic garbage bag and cooked with boiling water; top ramen noodles, dehydrated beans, cut up sausages and peppers, and finally, crunched up chips. It is not as good or bad as it sounds, but when you're used to eating the swill served here you can choke down anything and we did.

D-man was actually notorious for the amount of food he could put away and the speed with which he did it, I swear he didn't chew, but just shoveled it in and swallowed. Guys used to bet on it as if it were a sporting event, of course, without his knowing, but even when he found out he didn't care, as long as his plate was full.

Things on the yard have been pretty mild, some fights and a few stabbings each month, all stemming from debt. Gambling debts, drug debts, whatever one can imagine somebodys got their hand into. It's all ran of the mill for prison, I'm just happy the yard is running smooth. It means we can program; yard, phones, packages, canteen, it's nice for a change. When shit hits the fan it's all taken away. D-man came at a good time, he'll get a little taste of freedom, for awhile at least. We all know the good times never last.

Our first priority was getting him a job with a pay number, so we'd have some extra canteen money rolling in, and not just any job but one with a good pay number. Alot of jobs in here pay less than ten dollars a month, the way D eats that won't cut it. He wanted a kitchen job, but even the skrews knew about his eating habits, and they weren't going to hire him just to get cleaned out, so that was out of the question. Foodwise, he'd have to make due with whatever I brought home.

When he heard Snake was working behind the wall, he immediately wanted to go there. He tried to convince me that if we could find a skrew to hire him, he'd be able to kill Snake with no one being the wiser. Of course, that was out of the question, as I wouldn't be there to help there was no way I was going to let him go. Besides, we both knew damn well that if Snake came up dead, everyone in the entire prison and probably the surrounding town would know exactly who had done it.

That's the main problem with prison, no one knows how to keep secrets any longer. "Look, we gotta deal with him, sooner or later. It's only a matter of time before one of his flunkies lands over here, and if we don't know him he's got the jump on us. I don't mind getting a little R & R out here, but not at the expense of some lame cutting my throat. I'd feel alot better if we were on the offensive and had a plan of attack." D-Man said.

"I agree with you about having a plan, but one of us going back there by himself is a bad idea, he has at least 3 homeboys with him, that we know about, so it would be four-on-one." I had to slap him before he interrupted, "I know what you're gonna say, you like those odds, well I don't. I want to get him as bad as you do, but I want us to be around when it's over, this isn't a damn suicide mission."

"How the hell are we staying on the offensive, just sitting here on our asses?" "Boy, you're all fired up to go right back to the hole, aren't you?"

"Hell no, I'd just feel better knowing we had something in the works."

I knew exactly how he felt. I'd spent the last few years out here thinking of ways to get my hands wrapped around Snakes throat. Knowing he was just on the next yard, so close I could almost see him, but he might as well have been halfway around the world for all the access I had to him. It was frustrating to know that he was doing the same crap over there that he'd been doing here. I wondered how many youngsters he'd ruined so far? D-man was right, he needed to be dealt with.

"I hear ya, brother, the only thing we can do is stay ready. If any of his people show up, we'll knock 'em down before they know what hit them, and we can try to find a skrew who'll put us in PIA - together. It might take awhile, but there's one thing we can count on, people always forget, so we're bound to get our chance, someday."

As long as I've been working here, I've never been approached by a con and asked to do something for him or bring something to him. There are a handful of guards who dabble in this kind of activity. Most are innocent enough, bringing battles of ink, smut magazines. Maybe some fast food, all things a prisoner can't get on his own.

I don't know what drives these guards, perhaps empathy or since most are young, that need to be liked and to be popular still influences their actions. Whatever it is, it sets a chain of events into motion of which they're not aware. Once you do something for that first con, word spreads like wildfire, jumping from con to con, spanning the empty area between yards and taking up once again as it touches down on the other side. Saying yes that first time is the mistake, like vultures to a carcass they hone on to the weakness and when you next look up there will be a long line of petitioners awaiting your voluntary services. Word eventually comes full circle right back to the guards, and since most are not eager to inform on their friends, it sluggishly works its way up the totem pole. When the sergeant or captain gets wind of it, they stamp it out, for two reasons: First, it could lead to something bigger where they'd have to fire one of their own; secondly, the idea of helping a convict, in any way whatsoever, is utterly repugnant to them. Once you've been in the system long enough to make captain, your feelings toward convicts have been shored up by years of struggle and hatred.

Cons know who and who not to ask, thus, my surprise, when I was approached one day during lunch hour in PIA. Two cons I knew, associates of Snakes, asked if they could have a word with me. I was instantly on guard, one hand on my baton the other on my alarm button.

"What do you fella's need?" I asked, my voice hitting a high note on the last word. I winced, might as well just tell them that my sac climbed up into my stomach.

They stood smiling, knowing exactly what had happened. In that moment I hated them beyond words.

"Whoa, Stogie, no need for all that," he said, indicating my hands. "We just want a friendly word, maybe we can do each other a favor, tit for tat, ya know?"

"I seriously doubt that you or your friends have anything I need. You have something to say, just spit it out."

"Alright, if that's how you want it, no small talk. We have ten thousand dollars with your name on it - and don't act like you don't need it, we know all about your, how should I say it... financial problems - all we want is a small favor." He finished, holding his index finger and thumb almost touching, to indicate just how small it was.

"You gotta be kidding me. You're actually trying to bribe me! What is it you think I'm gonna do, help one of you escape?"

"Before you go off half-cocked and get all self righteous on us, maybe you should listen, I'm sure -"

"Hell no!" I interrupted. "You came to the wrong cop."

They both started laughing in my face, an open, mocking laugh. Something was wrong, they weren't even the slightest bit nervous.

"You're not a cop, Stogie, you're a prison guard, a glorified babysitter. You shower us, feed us, clothe us, and finally you put us to sleep like the good babysitter you are. But that's beside the point, all we want is for you to give a certain guy a job back here. See, no drugs, no escape plots, just a simple favor and the money's yours. Think on it for awhile, there's no rush."

A speaking hunch sot through me, "who is this certain guy?" I asked, knowing the answer full well, but wanting to hear it said aloud.

"Let's just come to an agreement first, we can work out the details later. How does that sound?"

During the conversation, only one of them spoke. The other was slowly edging around my side. Recognition dawned in a flash, if I said no, they were going to do what the others had left undone, kill me. Like floodwaters breeching a rivers bank, the old fear came rushing back with no regard for anything in its path.

I stood frozen, no thought, body unresponsive. I couldn't move, couldn't speak, and I knew if they attacked me I would stand like a rabbit in the headlights and they would do their work and I would be gone. It was frightening how easily my mind accepted this outcome, maybe I was done struggling.

A voice cut through the scene like a razor, "what the hell is going on here?"

Relief surged through me like a drug, leaving me light-headed and weak, I had to lock my legs to keep them from buckling.

It was Sergeant Atkins. Big brass, ex-military, and like all military once a soldier always a soldier. Everyone called him Atty, he still wore a crewcut and gave orders like he was drilling recruits. He was annoying as hell, but I'd never been so happy to hear that voice, as I was now.

One of the cons spoke up, "hey, Atty, were just shooting the breeze before we have to get back to work."

Atty glanced at his watch, "You assholes were supposed to be to work five minutes ago, instead you're over here dicking around on my time, I won't have it! I'll bounce you two out of here so goddamned fast you won't know what hit you till you're crying on your cellies knee. Now get!"

They sauntered off, unfazed by Attys tirade. He spoke to everyone like that, most found it amusing, he even had his imitators.

He stood in front of me, scrutinizing me so closely I thought the truth was scrawled across my face, plain for all to see.

"What was all that about, Stogie?"

"It was nothing, surge, just talking about last nights game. Must've lost track of time, it's my fault." I answered shakily.

Atty just stared at me. I knew he didn't believe a word I said, and I have no idea why I lied, maybe it was the shame I felt at my own impotency.

"Yeah, right. Don't you go getting all buddy-buddy with these losers, you hear?" "Sure, I got ya, Atty. But don't worry about me forgetting which side I'm on, that'll never happen." I said with a surety I did not feel.

VIII

Once again the holidays near and bring with them memories better forgotten. Where most feel joy, I feel only dread. I sit in my cell and listen to the carols endlessly repeating on the radio, and it's like someone knows. I watch the happy parade of commercials, sitcoms, and movies all pitching the same line and I know that only a fraction of life is portrayed but I understand, no one wants the truth, especially during these times.

I've spent many years away from my family and friends and I guess deservedly so, so the holidays no longer mean what they once did. Now they are but a reminder of loss, of what once was, just another obstacle to be overcome. This is my busiest time of the year, but not for the reasons you might think. I stay busy from sunup to sundown, in order to have less time and energy to think, the less thinking the better.

The prison is crowded and rowdy at all times, even the holidays. Most are too ignorant to realize what they're missing and the rest are too self absorbed to care, but you can always spot the individual who knows - who understands that something is being taken from him, just as he took from someone else - by the way he sinks into himself, not wanting to come up for air. These cons recognize and could commiserate with one another, but that would be letting themselves off the hook, and that wouldn't do.

I'm lucky I have D-man with me as he instinctively knows how to make things easier, and his big solution to the holiday doldrums is to get so shitfaced we won't even know what day it is. I am skeptical, but I trust him as his solutions have proven correct in the past. I'm just happy he didn't suggest the one we used a few years ago, a fistfight.

I was in a funk and trying to shake the state, but for some reason I couldn't. As a good cellie should make time easier, he suggested a whole list of possibilities to which I shook my head and muttered. Finally he got fed up and said, "we ought to just go a few rounds, that'll snap your ass out of it!"

It doesn't matter how close you are to someone, when those words are uttered, it's a challenge pure and simple. And if you don't step up then you've lost something, something intangible and manmade, but something nonetheless. I instantly came off the bunk, wired from head to toe, "You might want to think twice about this, brother." I said. He only backed up and turned the light off, then went into a crouched stance. His hands coming slowly to the sides of his face, they seemed to frame the grin playing around the corners of his mouth. Without another word I waded in and as we fully embraced it, forgetfulness came.

His solution worked great. The only problem was we beat the living crap out of each other, to the point where we were laid up for a week, and in here it doesn't pay to be out of commission. After we were done we shook hands and laughed our asses off for the rest of the night. It was then I realized, everything has a price and as long as you're willing to pay, you might find a measure of relief. I was in a great mood for the rest of the season.

Our cell stinks and the fruit flies and gnats are driving me crazy. I spend half the day stalking around the cell swatting them and the other half trying to fan the smell out by waving a towel, it doesn't work. D-man baby sits his huge bag of pruno, constantly heating it up so it cooks faster, and that makes the smell even worse. The hotter it becomes the more it bubbles. He sits as if in a trance and watches the bubbles rise to the surface where they loudly pop. He hovers like an anxious parent; man I'm having second thoughts about this.

The pruno has been cooking for six days, so only a day or two left before our little shindig. We already have it worked out to get a bag of ice from the kitchen to take the edge off the taste and make it half-assed drinkable, but my hopes are not high, as D-man's the uncanny ability to make all his pruno taste like dirty socks, and takes great pride in the fact.

He's camped out in front of the open bag again, so I ask, "Hows it looking. Think it will be ready tomorrow?"

"Oh hell yeah. All the pulp fell, so it's good to go. Should be nice and sour."

He looked at me slyly and I knew what was coming. Before he could get a word out, I said, "no".

He tried to look innocent and hurt at the same time, "no what?"

"You know what."

"I have no idea what you're talking about."

I imitated his voice, and said, "We have so much, we might as well have us a little taste test right now. We can probably have a few cups each."

"I'm shocked you would say such a thing, put such words in my mouth," he replied in a feigned accent and indignant tone. The one he used when he knew he was caught red-handed and guilty as hell.

"You say the same thing everytime we drink!"

He started laughing, "Yeah, okay. But since you brought it up this time I'll go along with you." He started opening the bag, "let's strain this and have us a wee nightcap, what do you say?"

There was no use arguing, as he saw both sides of the argument as his opinion just expressed differently. So I got up to help as he knew I'd do all along. We strained the pruno through a pillowcase into a plastic bag and threw away the 'kicker', then cleaned up the mess. We filled our cups and pounded down two each, the rest of the night is a blur of smack talk and laughing our asses off. The man knew how to make some mean wine.

We woke the next day with slight headaches, but the cure was at hand. We washed up, ate a little breakfast, then we were off to the races again.

As we started in things were dicey right from the start. With the first cup it felt like someone was stomping my guts with steeltoed combat boots. This hair of the dog thing was a little more difficult than I had thought. D-man made a bitter beer face and hopped around on one leg while chicken winging his arms, yelling, "yee haw!" That is a sight to see. I forgot my stomach instantly and got busy pouring us another cup. The first cup went down like liquid fire and the heat was quickly spreading, I had the feeling things were gonna get wild today.

By noon we were three cups in and had three each remaining. I was so drunk already, I was humming along to the hated Christmas music. We could hear cons up and down the tier, just as drunk as we were, singing the carols, it sounded horrible, like being forced to watch American Idol. But it was the funniest damn thing we'd ever heard, all these hardcore convicts choiring out Silent Night. I laughed so hard my stomach and face muscles started cramping.

D-man said they sounded like a bunch of scraggly alleycats and went to the cell door and yelled, "there ain't no pussy in here, so why don't you fuckers shut the hell up!"

"You're just mad cause you never had no pussy!" someone yelled back.

I almost fell off the bunk I was laughing so hard. A deep red crept its way up his throat to his face, and in no time, he was doing his best imitation of a rosy red apple.

He glared at me and turned back to the door and screamed out, "You're a pussy!"

By this time I was gasping for air, rolling around on the floor pointing a finger at him, he looked throughly disgusted, which made it that much funnier. Finally he started grinning and said, "screw you too, virgin boy!" That set off a new round of laughs.

We had both been arrested so young that the older cons used to tease us about being virgins. They would hook us up with women to write, telling us we could at least get our cherries popped through the mail, talk about safe sex. So now whenever we're drunk we always clown about it.

I got off the floor and weaved my way to the desk, "time for another cup, D. Get over here, it's your turn to pour."

"It's always my turn to pour," he complained. "Hey, we all do what we're good at."

"That must be why you talk so much," he muttered. "Bingo. Now make sure you don't spill any."

"Ah, shut the hell up!"

After a few more cups we settled into a comfortable stupor, a steady stream of smack which washed away all worries and troubles. Flowed back and forth. I was roasting his stature and verbal skills, or lack of, and he was on me about my age and being bald. Same old material, it's just alot funnier when you're drunk. Then he went to his old stand by.

"You remember when I beat the crap outta ya a few years ago?" He threw out casually. "Man, that was a good time."

"Your memory is as short as you are. If I remember correctly, and I do. You were laid out cord sleeping like a fat ass baby."

He walked over and peered down at my face, then started laughing. "Damn, you actually believe that, don't you? You're so full of shit you're gonna drown as in it. Wouldn't that be a pretty sight, a handsome man like me turned into a crap covered cutlet! You better stop tempting fate with all that lying or she's gonna take it out on both of us. I don't like the idea of all my fans not getting to see my handsome face because you got us swimming in a sea of shit."

I just nodded and laughed, too entertained to interrupt. I tried not to think about his 'fans', as he had no one. When he was sentence to life in prison his girl and his family cut him loose, then all his friends fell by the wayside. I guess, out of sight out of mind works on both sides of the wall. I knew why we were so tight, I'm all he has in either world.

We drunk till eight thirty that night, both of us puking a few times. We just rinsed our mouths out and kept going. The next day I was just happy to find that all the puke made it into the toilet and not on the floor, I've had a few hangovers made worse by having to mop up puke; man, that'll almost make you stop drinking all together.

The holidays are a great time for making money. Most of the guards try to swap shirts, hoping to get time off to be with their families. The young guys who are still bachelors and the older guards whose kids are grown and gone are the ones who end up working through the holidays. We get paid time and a half, so no one is complaining.

    I can't remember when I started working the holidays, I still have a young family, so I should be at home, but for some reason I keep volunteering for overtime. My family used to miss me, my wife used to complain, but no longer. I've done a fine job of seperating myself and the only real connections I feel anymore are within the prison walls.

    The holidays are a strange time in here, it's almost as if a play were being acted out and everyone participates knowing their roles. If just one guard or con breaks character, no one yells out while we are given the chance to backtrack and start over. Instead reality crashes down with the blow of a hammer and what were only surface cracks become gaping crevasses, and no one here is equipped to deal with that.

    Knowing all this I still prefer to be here rather than home. I think - no, I know, something is wrong with me.

    Many times during the holidays we run on a skeleton crew, just enough guards to hand out the food trays and push the buttons for entry and exit, so the prison is always on lockdown, no movement equals less work. This makes it much more difficult for convicts to make their way through unscathed. As I walk from cell to cell unpadlocking the tray slots in order to slide a dinner tray through, most of the cons are standing ready, almost at attention, fidgeting and rocking from foot to foot. They immediately start up a pointless conversation, spouting off about anything and everything, just needing to speak and be spoken to. I don't know if emotions have a smell, but they most certainly have a feel. As I engage in conversation, I can feel waves of anxiety and desperation leeching out of their pores like slow rising groundwater; inexorable. Their strength has me reeling and I can feel them blooming and spreading deep within myself, it's like a contagion. The look in their eyes tells you they are barely holding it together, the restraint close to its breaking point. It's a dangerous time, if they lose concentration for the slightest moment they will drift off to someplace they don't want to be and the journey back is impossible for some. You might wonder, if things are so bad here, why do I still work here and even put in for overtime? I'm afraid to search out the answer, as it might be uglier than I'm prepared to face. What I do know is that I seem to be fortified by their pain.

The prison population is in constant flux. Like a living breathing - entity. A ripple started at one end works its way through the entire thing. When a body is subtracted here, one is added there, making good the loss, perpetuating the cycle. New faces continually flood the yard, so from day to day you're forced to deal with the unknown con, the unknown element. They had been con lockdown for ten days, so when we let them out to the yard they were practically sprinting from the buildings, making their way to the doors and fresh air beyond.

I was standing on the periphery of the yard with two other guards, keeping watch. Other groups of guards were stationed around the yard at intervals, this spacing ensured a quick response time to any incident. As the cons were released the noise level rose, they were all speaking and back slapping at once. The new guys who had been placed on the yard during the lockdown were now being interrogated; who were they?; where were they from?; why were they in prison?; the same unending drama unfolding only with new participants. I saw Teacher and D-man approach several white cons and strike up conversations, they were all short and the two quickly moved on, all seemed well. Then I saw a con I recognized from the hole, he had been on the other yard before being rolled up for drugs, he was a friend of Snakes.

I had a bad feeling that today would not turn out well for someone. I walked over to the sergeant and aired my concerns, he disappeared into the captains office saying he would check on it. As I stood waiting my discomfort grew, but I had a welcome realization, I was not worried about myself but for Teacher.

When the sergeant reappeared he didn't look too happy. If he had gotten his ass chewed out, I knew it was about to be handed down and braced for it, instead, what came out was even more shocking.

"That son of a bitch shouldn't be on this yard, but the snitch who put him in the hole is still on the other yard, working!" He said the last word while stabbing the air with angry quote marks. "So this guy can't go back and we can't keep him in the hole, his SHU term is up.

Apparently, we don't have enough information about his connection to the Aryan Syndicate to transfer him out of here, even with your situation."

He gave me a hard look as if he were contemplating something, then said, "this goes no further than us, got it?" I nodded my confirmation and he went on. "The higher ups are hoping these scum deal with each other and save us the headache. We are suppose to sit back and watch and not interfere. The old "two birds with one stone" crap."

We were going to let this con move on Teacher just to avoid a headache, I couldn't believe it. I should have thought before I spoke, but fear gave wing to my words and they flew of their own accord.

"Are you fucking kidding me! Were supposed to let Teacher stand out there, in the dark about what might take place, no warning, heads-up or anything? He's a good guy and doesn't deserve this." I stopped and took several breaths. I was so angry I was shaking. As the next words left my mouth, I knew I was going too far.

"I'm gonna warn him." I started to turn away, but the sergeant grabbed my arm and spun me around, he looked throughly disgusted.

"You'll do no such thing! What the hell is the matter with you, he's a goddamned convict! You better remember that before you cross a line, Mike."

"Before I cross a line? We're crossing one now by just standing here, we're supposed to be the good guys."

As he let go my arm, I did not think of my family or my career if you can call being a prison guard a career - but only of a debt could I stand here and watch as the man who had saved me was attacked and perhaps murdered, when I had openly acknowledged my debt to him? Did my word have no meaning or worth? No, I couldn't do this. In trying to protect him I would also be protecting myself.

I quickly scanned the yard looking for Teacher, I would tell him now. My eyes located him exactly where I knew he'd be, he and D-Man were at the white cons workout station doing pull-ups. I let myself through the upper gate, which seperated the yard from the main complex. This area included the canteen, education, program office, library, and cons were only allowed through this gate if they worked here or had a ducat.

As I started across the yard I saw the new guy walking in a group of four cons, they were headed directly toward teacher and D-Man. I don't know why or how, but I knew what was about to take place. I couldn't push the alarm or yell out, as nothing had yet occurred. As the group came up behind Teacher, the new guy seperated himself and went into action. His right arm came up over Teacher's right shoulder, the sun glinted off a metal object sending rays of blinding light piercing through the sky.

I had stopped walking, not consciously, but something primitive had taken over. My body betrayed my intent. The help I so wanted to give stayed locked inside, too weak to battle my fear.

Helplessly I watched the offending right arm inch its way around Teachers neck like a lovers embrace and saw back with a premature violence born of youth. Red drops crept to the surface following the razors track, as if their job were to mark its progress. Even from this distance I could see his face laid open from the tip of his chin to the back of his neck, a single red line seperating top from bottom ran along his jawline and disappeared behind his right ear, which was now missing its lobe. The cut was so straight as to have been done with the help of a ruler.

Teacher acted instinctively, his body leaned onto his left leg and turned into the cut, in one smooth motion he uncoiled and sprang forward, his left fist connecting solidly with his assailants chin. The sound was like the crack of a high powered rifle reverberating through the prison yard.

The new guy collapsed in a splay of arms and legs that were jerking and locking in all directions. Teacher hunched over him like a mountain, overshadowing and dwarfing him. He backpedaled while looking for other enemies. D-man made a beeline for the convulsing body and I knew what he had in mind. His left hand dipped into his front pocket where he kept his weapon, I had sudden flashes of the last con he had knifed and felt like retching.

Teacher intercepted D-man by grabbing his shoulders and pushing backwards, D-man was struggling to get loose and in his frustration tears brightened his eyes; he wanted, needed, to hurt someone very bad.

I heard Teachers voice carry soothingly across the yard, "no, he's not worth it," over and over, all the while backing him further away.

The alarm was blaring and guards were running, converging on the incident. Everything seemed hazy and slow, all sounds were in the distant background. My eyes were locked on Teacher, he and D-man were squatted down about fifteen feet from the now quiet body, and were pushing something into the ground. Teacher had pulled his shirt off and was calmly holding it against his face.

As the rest of the yard was laid out and flex-cuffed, two guards escorted Teacher across the yard to the medical center, a nurse was keeping stride holding a compress to his face.

I went to stand next to D-man, knowing there was one way in which I could help. As our eyes met, I shifted my gaze to the newly turned soil then back again, the question obvious, he acknowledged it with a barely perceptible nod, and I knew I was being trusted. I shuffled slightly to the right and stood upon the small grave, my weight compacting the soil, hiding the intrusion, burying my debt.

D-man didn't look at me again, I got the feeling that he was waiting for me to turn him in and he didn't want to press his luck. I knew a line had just been crossed, that line the sergeant warned me of, but whatever the consequences, I didn't want to think of them.

Teacher let the RN clean his newest wound, but refused sutures or any further aid, as that would have created more evidence against his assailant and that is akin to snitching. He was fortunate his attacker had bad aim, a few inches lower and his jugular and carotid would have been severed, as it was he would be wearing a nasty scar for life; yet, on him it was one among many and would quickly become lost in the crowd. On any other con it would have been a sign of disgrace, as facial scars are inflicted on purpose and on a certain type of convict, a sort of mark of cam warning all newcomers, but Teacher wore it as one would a medal pinned to the chest, proud and on full display, inviting reactions and questions alike.

IX

"Mike, how is the writing coming along? Have you been doing it every day, like I asked? Do you feel that it's helped straighten your thoughts out?"

Man, she really knew how to ask questions. I wish I knew how to give her the answers she wanted or even the ones she needed, but I'm still looking for them myself, so I'm of little or no help to her. But I have to give her something, that is after all the purpose of these meetings.

"The writing is more difficult than I expected, but I'm making headway. I'm not going to tell her what type of headway, as she will read into it whatever she wants; people have an uncanny way of hearing what they want and of supplying their own meaning to your words. I don't want her reading it till I'm done, I don't think I could stand the looks nor the revolt she would feel toward me. It will be easier done all at once, like ripping off a band-aid, only in this case the wound beneath is far from healed.

"Go on," she encouraged.

She doesn't like single sentence answers, ironic since that is her mode of conversing. The more I speak the more I trip up and let things out I'd rather not. She knows this and pushes me onward.

"Things are slowly becoming clearer. Although, the more I write the more questions seem to appear. I know that's contradictory, but it's true."

I could see I said the right thing as she grew excited.

"Share some of these questions with me and we can work on them together." Maybe I didn't say the right thing after all, now I would have to discuss this."

"Okay... I've began to wonder just how important the truth really is. When it goes beyond the individual to whom it belongs, doesn't it become subjective to the point of change?"

"Subjective in what sense, Mike?"

"Do you think circumstance alters truth? We know murder is wrong, but how does a mother whose child has been molested feel about it? Do you remember the woman who shot her childs assailant in the courtroom? She was not convicted of murder. Don't you think truth had become something entirely different to her?"

Dr. Adams held her hand up to slow me down. After months of having one-sided conversation with me, I've finally given her something and there was no way she was going to be rushed.

"Let's take these one at a time, okay? First, I believe circumstance may alter the individuals view of the truth, but not truth itself, that remains constant. The important thing is why you think it alters. This could be a mechanism you're using to excuse actions you're not proud of."

And here we go. She is so damn happy it's almost disgusting. When I ask the most innocent of questions or show the slightest emotion she seem to feel from it and grow larger before my eyes. Not for the first time, I wonder if our roles shouldn't perhaps be reversal. But like it or not, I had started this conversation so I would have to see it through.

"Isn't truth defined by man?, and anything manmade is subject to bias from our very nature. So truth is defined with the imprint of the individual, making it slightly different due to circumstance." I stopped to gather my thoughts, I was doing a smash-up job of explaining myself. I needed to try a new tact, "look Doc, this is difficult to explain - lets say we have five people who are presented with the same situation or problem, isn't it likely, even proable, that all five will react differently, even giving different justifications for their actions?"

"Yes, I would agree with that." She answered, somewhat reluctantly, as if sensing a trap.

"Then the truth of the situation varies according to the circumstances of the five individuals, in essence, making five truths. I understand this is an abstract notion, but the fact is people are judged everyday by a rigid, single defined version of truth. You and I may agree on the fundamental meaning, while having completely different versions of the truth, right?"

"Of course, we can come to truth by different paths, but when we finally arrive it will always be to the same place. Truth is simply fact, Mike, and fact cannot be altered due to ones view of it. I believe what you're speaking of is the journey, the steps or process one takes before arriving. This journey is as you've said, subjective, but when it is over we all find ourselves in the same spot, the objective truth. Does this make sense, does it help you clear things up?"

I could see she views truth as a scientist does, in a sterilized lab free from any outside influence. Truth in all its pristine glory, seperated from the realities of life. Isn't it strange that she subtracts the very thing that gives it meaning?

"Mike?"

"... Yes, of course, you're right. I understand now, thank you."

She doesn't see that her argument has made my point much clearer than I could, there is no reason to continue as it will only reenforce her bias.

"You're very welcome," she said happily.

As our session continued, I had already checked out to be with my own thoughts. I still said yes occasionally and nodded often, but I no longer heard what she said. After our conversation, I could only think about what she was writing in her short, slashing motions, filling her notebook with the worst, I imagine. That perhaps I am detached from reality, living in a world of my own creation, or I am some kind of psychopath just out to work the system. As strange as it sounds I wish these were true, then I would have an excuse for my actions.

The holidays are finally over and I am thankful, as my anxiety has slowly bled back to a normal state, at least, what's normal for me. My days are full of nothing and my nights more of the same, don't pity me though, a state of numbness is highly desired in here, as it deadens everything.

D-man has been upset with me since the day of the incident, I think he believes I've gone soft, and he's not alone in that thought. Other cons who used to drop their eyes to the ground when I walked by now stare boldly, an unvoiced challenge inviting me. The first time in my life I had backed off and tried to let the authorities handle it, the first time I've tried to consciously steer my life in a different direction, it's backfired on me. Where I thought to solve some of my problems I've only created more, and the easiest solution would be to return to my old ways act first question later. But that feels like one more surrender in a long line of them. Is that what life is, endless surrenderings, one after another until you have nothing left?

"What are you thinking about?"

D-man finally broke the silence, which is a good thing, it means he's no longer mad. "Just about how things change," I answered.

"Yeah, tell me about it." I knew he meant me, and his tone left no doubt as to his thoughts about it. We would have to get this cleared up before it began to fester.

"If you have something to say, spit it out!"

He looked at me knowingly, "there's no reason for me to say what you already know I'm thinking."

"You of all people know what I've been trying to do. Well I tried, and it didn't work, but I'm telling you right now I won't let anything like that happen again. What I did was harder for me than turning around and ripping that fuckers head off, but I'm through with well-intentioned words and empty promises. I have to try to live according to what I believe or at least what I think I believe. The only thing that has surprised me through this entire event is your attitude and your doubts. I never expected that." I had to stop before I went to far.

"Well, Goddamnit! You know I never doubted you, I'm just pissed you held me back.

Hell, I'm just pissed at the world, you know that."

"Yeah, I know." And I did. Change is alot harder than I thought for some reason, I thought I could just change my mind and everything else would simply full into place, that was naive, the world doesn't work like that.

"If you didn't like that I have more bad news for you." That got his attention, his head snapped forward and his eyes narrowed. "I'm not going to fall back into my old ways simply because I don't like this first outcome. I'm still going to give this new road a try, I can't quit at the first bump in -"

"So I'm just supposed to stand there while some jerkoff tries to slice your freaking throat, or mine? You can go ahead with your new way of thinking, I'm gonna stick with what's been keeping me alive."

"Lets get something straight, brother. I never asked you to go along with this and if you don't feel comfortable, maybe we should remedy that."

"What the hell does that mean?"

I was hesitant to give an answer that would push him away, but the reality was he could not believe in one set of rules while trying to live by another, and by keeping him with me, that is exactly what I'd be asking him to do.

"If you're not around me, then you won't be forced to deal with situations in a manner you don't think appropriate. I believe it would make things easier for both of us." He stared at me for awhile before answering, as if having a difficult time unscrambling what I had just said. Finally he barked out a laugh devoid of any laughter, and said, "You gotta be fucking kidding me. I was good enough to start this process with; but not to finish it, is that it? You have a fine way of treating friends."

I tried to interrupt, to explain that that was not how it was, but he steamrolled right over me.

"I didn't sit on the edge of the pool dangling my feet, testing the water I fucking dove in head first right by your side, and now you're making decisions for me like I'm some damn pup who doesn't know any better. I didn't know you thought so little of me."

He was right. I thought I had thought it through and came up with a perfect solution. When in reality I had only outsmarted myself convincing myself that the only way to protect my friend was to put distance between us.

"I'm gonna tell you something you're probably not gonna like. Ever since you've tried to become this new person, your attitude and behavior have grown sketchy, where before you would act on instinct and get things right, now with reflection you get them wrong, you overthink everything. You walk around like a man wearing a suit two sizes too small, constantly fidgeting, adjusting, always uncomfortable and making those around you equally as uncomfortable. Let me tell you, that suit ain't gonna magically grow and you ain't gonna shrink, so you see the problem? You're wearing something that doesn't fit you. I'm not suggesting that you give it up completely, I just think maybe you should have it altered so it fits properly. And one more thing, I ain't going anywhere so you can stall that shit!"

When someone is ripping you a new one and you have no response, there is probably a clue in there somewhere, an answer waiting for your attention.

The cell door opened unexpectedly and I was instantly on guard. I got up and went to the front of the cell cautiously, as you never know what's awaiting you on the tier. It could be the 'Goon squad' coming to raid your cell or something innocent like a phone call, but if one of your enemies is on the tier, hiding under the stairs, then even the innocent has the potential for danger.

I saw D-man walking down the tier and when he looked up and saw me, he immediately looked to the ground. He wasn't supposed to get off work for a few more hours, so I knew something was wrong. As he approached, I stood aside and let him enter the cell, and stayed there until the door was fully closed, then turned to D, "what's going on, why are you home early?"

"My boss had to take off, so he cut us all loose."

He was distracted, he didn't look at me when he spoke, so I knew there was something more. I would wait and let him come out with it in his own good time.

"Since you're home early, what say we get some tattooing done? I have a few more patterns roughed out and the big one is done. We can get that bad boy outlined and halfway shaded tonight."

I had drawn a dragon that would start at his wrist and wound its way up around his arm, climbing till it eventually reached his shoulder, while its head rested on the side of his neck. It was a cover-up, as he had a couple of old unfinished tattoos he wanted gone.

"Yeah, we can do that," he said with little enthusiasm. Now I definately knew something was wrong.

As we got everything ready and settled in for some serious inking he remained silent, which was fine with me. When I was first learning to tattoo, it took so much concentration that I couldn't have spoken if I wanted, but as I became better it grew easier and required less of me. I found I could let my mind wander, I could even have full blown conversations without missing a beat. I discovered that it could be meditative, even theraputic. Whenever I felt anxious or hemmed in I could grab for the tattoo gun and simply check out.

About a half hour into our session D-man finally spoke, and as much as I wanted to hear his voice, I wished I could have shut my ears to him.

"Ghost is dead."

I felt as if he had punched me in the chest, I couldn't breathe. A foreign feeling surged through me. Was this my fault?

"Who did it?" I asked, already knowing.

"Word coming out of the hole is they found him hanging during night count. His cellie was asleep, or so he says."

"Was he still with Buzz?" "Yeah."

I knew there was something he wasn't telling me. Normally, he would be cursing him into oblivion, making threats of gruesome retaliation. Yet now, he was uncharacteristically quiet.

"What else?"

"Okay, but I don't want you to read too much into it, you know, start moping around acting like everything is your fault."

I stopped the gun and looked at him, "Will you just spit it out already you're acting like you have some damn national secret!"

He took a breath and said, "even though he was found hanging, they're investigating it as a murder because he was beat up pretty bad. They think Buzz beat him unconscious, then hung him up to make it look like suicide. Buzz always was a stupid bastard."

I slowly set the gun down and stood. I needed to move, to clear my head, so I began pacing back and forth in my matchbox sized cell. It only made the feeling worse as the cell constricted more than my movement. The truth hammered through me, as relentless as a driven nail, I'm the one who talked him into taking a cellie; I'm the one who eased his fears; I'm the one who set the wheels in motion, which ended up in the murder of a kid. God, I need to get out of this cell, everything is closing in on me. I need to look at the sky and feel my smallness.

"I know what you're thinking and you gotta let it go, brother. Whatever happens in another mans cell is not your responsibility." D's voice was softer than I had ever heard it before, as if he could assuage my guilt with its texture.

"But we both know that nothing would have happened without my intervention." "Dammit! What you did was right. If he would've denied a cellie, he'd have been done."

"Yet he didn't…and he is done anyway. Don't you see the problem there? We make rules, that if followed are supposed to help us, but the rule he obeyed killed him instead. Doesn't that make the rule illegitimate?"

"You're opening a huge can of worms here, Teach. Maybe we need to slow down and look at the consequences before we leap into the fire, huh?"

"Bullshit! I'm already in the hut with the Aryan Syndicate. Hell, for that matter, so are you, and to tell you the truth I couldn't care less but this is an entirely different deal."

He gave me a flat look, "why have you become so anxious…so jumpy lately?"

His question struck true. He amazes me everytime with his intuitiveness, but this time more than any other I knew the answer.

I've been in here almost 20 years and I'm tired of playing at life, just plain tired. I find myself constantly daydreaming; my focus, which was once so sharp is gone. I dream about being on the outside with my family, living a good life, being a good man. And I've begun to think that maybe these dreams could be real someday, if only I change. Perhaps they are a glimpse into a possible future if I choose a different path. Daydreaming is a nice escape, but in here, it leaves you haunted by possibility.

"If anyone knows the answer to that, it's you. You've been down as long as I have, don't you feel it?"

He didn't respond immediately, but I could tell from the look in his eyes that he understood perfectly.

"Why don't you tell me what 'it' is?"

I laughed, because he had done it again, right to the crux.

"I wish I could tell you, brother, I really do, but I'm not sure myself. It could be a single thing like aging, mortality, responsibility, or a culmination of things showing me I've wasted my life. Whatever 'it' is, I can't shake it."

"Does it have to do with the violence in here?"

I'd actually thought of that many times and came to the conclusion that violence is simply another part of mans nature, and without it we would be incomplete. I believe we can only know and define something through its opposite. We know truth through lies, war through peace, good through bad; if you subtract one you subtract both. Therefore violence is integral to our lives, the only question is how it's used.

"No, it's not that. I think it's the chance that I could have been something better, and the possibility exist, however slight, that I still can."

X

We sit in our cells and wait for the 4:30 count, shortly thereafter dinner is served. But what happens in between is what everyone is really waiting on, mail call. It's peculiar how such a simple thing can make or break your day. Everyone pretends like it's no big deal, when their name is called they feign surprise while nonchalantly gathering their treasure in protective arms and hoarding it.

I know cons who have been down 30 years and have never received a single letter, junkmail telling them they may have already won a million dollars. Yes; a letter from someone who loves them, no. I don't know how they deal, maybe it was like that before they ever came to prison. If you watch closely, you can see how it affects them. They are cut off from the emotions which the rest of us share, it's as if they've been excluded from a private club which the rest of us take for granted. To have someone who cares whether you're alive or dead is a powerful thing. It's no wonder that they have little to give, as they've never received anything.

"Allen, last two?" "Eighty eight."

"Here you go. Hold on, I have a couple more for you." The skrew slid two letters and a book catalog through the side of the door. As usual, there was nothing for D-man. When you have a cellie who receives nothing it puts a damper on your own joy. I've tried to set him up with pen-pals in the past, but they never lasted beyond a few letters.

I think he has lost the ability to communicate, or worse, he has given up on the idea. Regardless, I'll keep trying.

"Hey, I got a letter from that kid I told you about, Splinter." "You mean your son?" he said rolling his eyes.

He had heard how I was overprotective of him, and even though he had never met him, he took every opportunity to goad me about him.

"Damn right!" I answered happily.

"I thought you told him not to write? Shit, he's already disobeying you."

He wasn't gonna let this go, he was having too good a time and I play right along, as I enjoy it too.

"What can I say, you know kids these days, they do whatever they want." "Hell no I don't, and I don't want to."

I threw the catalog to D so he could flip through it while I read my letters.

I could feel pride swell within me as I read Splinter's words. Man, he was really doing it! The kid was making good.

"So what did he have to say?"

I had to clear my throat before I answered, damn allergies got me choked up.

"He's doing great. Has a job working for his uncles construction company. Has a few girls he's seeing, and get this, he thinks his parole officer likes him!"

We both started laughing. But I knew it was likely, as all the women here liked him, although not in the manner that he would've liked.

"You better tell him he's fishing in the wrong pond. He's liable to swallow a hook and be the one dangling."

"You're probably right, but a good woman is exactly what he needs. She'll sure as hell keep him on the straight and narrow."

"Look at you. You're all puffed up like a damned peacock!" He was right.

I thought back to one of our previous conversations about helping youngsters in here, I had had a difficult time explaining the whys and what fors, but realization hit me like the break of day; slow, all encompassing, and filled with the awe of possibility.

I held the letter in my hand and shook it at him, "This is it! This is the answer to the question. This is the possibility that has been nagging me. I had assumed all along that this change was to help me, but what if it's meant to help others instead? What if this helping others is my eventual salvation? -"

"Knock it off! You're starting to freak me out. You're sounding like Dr. Phil, and believe me, that ain't a good thing!"

No matter what he said, we both knew that I had hit upon a truth, at least a truth for me.

Every year we shuffle job positions throughout the prison, there are a few reasons for this. First, it ensures no overfamiliarity between guards and cons, this is mainly a problem for female guards. Over the years I have seen quite a few guards fall into relationships with cons. Of course, they are instantly fired, but many of the relationships don't end there. I have actually seen cons parole and marry these women they got fired, but the opposite is usually true though, these women are used and when caught they are tossed aside by guard and con alike.

I've also seen male guards form attachments, fostered in some misguided sense of empathy. They start bringing things to the con which are not allowed, little things at first, like something from their lunch or a dirty magazine, but this giving always progresses, and without realizing it items grow in size and illegality. They soon move on to bottles of tattoo ink and finally to the sharing of other cons c-files, and when these cons are assulted for being child molesters or rapists, the guard has just become a criminal.

Second, in a job where routine is law boredom comes quickly and with it comes a relaxing or lowering of your guard, that's not an option here. Dead in the midst of the unchanging moment violence erupts to change everything, and if you are not aware, it could affect you or a fellow guard.

We bid for the jobs we want and in the end whoever has the most senority gets the position, and as I'm the old guy around here, I generally get what I want. This year I've put in for a position in PIA. I need a break from the yard for awhile, I've seen enough stabbings and riots to last me a lifetime. Plus, as I've been feeling a strange sense of kinship lately, an absence is in order.

Snake and his flunkies are still there, but aside from one unnerving conversation they've kept their distance and I've kept mine.

The free staff here do all the work. So I just show up, strip down the cons when they arrive and depart and the rest of the day sit with my feet propped atop my desk thinking how nice it is to get paid for relaxing. I guess you could call this step one of my retirement process, but I'll tell you what, if steps two and three are anything like this I just might stick around a bit longer.

I have asked a friend to keep me informed of any overtime possibilities in the kitchen on the yard, the kitchen where Teacher works. I don't really know my own reasoning and it's probably pointless to go, but I have an urge to be around him, to speak to him; it's the same urge which drove me off the yard.

A few weeks later I received the call for a full shift. I was disconnected to find myself happy for the first time in months. I was anxious, my palms were clammy. What the hell was wrong with me? I was acting like a kid going on his first date, maybe this wasn't the best of ideas.

I showed up twenty minutes early to relieve the staff on duty, it's a courtesy we all try to give. It takes so long to get out of the damn prison we try to give each other a head start. When I arrived the cons hadn't shown up yet, but would be in soon. So I went into the blank cube of an office and put my feet up. Man, I really had to stop working so hard.

Teacher was the head man, so he'd be the first one in. He had to get the ovens turned on, the stand-up warmers going, pots and pans out, basically all the prep work for the rest of the cons. I heard the gunner crack the front door to let him in, and as he walked by the office he did a quick double take, then poked his smiling face through the door.

"Well, well, well, look what the cat dragged in. What brings you slumming?"

His smile and good mood were infectious, and I knew instantly I was right to come. "It would take alot more than a cat to drag this old body around. Hell, I can barely do it myself these days."

"Come on, Stogie, you're full of it. You ain't but a handful of years older than me, and for all that relaxing you do you sure ain't used yourself up."

We both had a good laugh as my 'hard work' was legendary.

"Yeah, you got a point there." I paused before asking the question, not knowing if it was going too far. "So, how're things going around this dump since I left?"

He gave me a look that seemed to search for some meaning behind my words and must've come to the conclusion that my intent was innocent, because he visibly relaxed and said, "Same as they always have, Stogie. Same shit different day, some day different shit. There's no rhyme or reason, no start or finish here, only the never ending ride." He cleared his throat as if realizing he'd said too much, "I'd better get to work," he said as he walked off.

I sat quiet listening to the other cons drift in, accompanied by their ever present noise. I replayed what Teacher had said, that is how I would've answered if asked, but knew instantly that was false; I'm not brave enough to let others know my real thoughts.

The first few hours is where all the work takes place. After everything is cooked and trayed up it is delivered to the buildings where it is passed out cell to cell by the guards. This is downtime for the cons in the kitchen. They have about an hour to relax before the trays are collected and returned to the kitchen for washing and packing away till the next day, when the process repeats itself.

During this lull, I went into the chow hall which is no longer used, to try to catch Teacher alone. The chow hall is a long rectangle of a hundred feet or so, with two rows of octagon, stainless steel tables with four bolted-on-seats, each running down the middle. Its function being lost, it is now used for storage and for breaks. In the center of this rectangle on the outer wall is a door which opens to the yard. I walked over and keyed the door letting the hot, stale air out, as well as the cons. They all went out and sat on the loading dock, I sat out there, too, and bullshited a little, but mainly I just listened.

They spoke of sports, television, and of course, women; the number one topic here. After ten minutes or so, they started drifting back into the kitchen, singly or in pairs, so trained they could barely handle a taste of freedom. Only Teacher and I remained. I knew he would stay out as long as I allowed and I found I didn't want to go back inside either.

"I heard you were thinking about an early retirement, Stogie, is that true?"

The question caught me off guard as only a few knew of it, but then, there are no kept secrets in here. Curiously, I felt no urge to lie or avoid.

"Yeah, you heard right. Although I'm surprised it's common news."
"Nothing common about it, Stogie. And you ain't surprised."

It disturbed me how he kept using my name. It seemed his constant reminder to both of us of the distance that needed to be kept, the formality, but I wanted to speak where no names were necessary.

"So what're the reasons for wanting to hang it up?"

That is the question I've been asking myself for the last few years, and I don't care to share the answers.

"Same old story, I guess. You wake up one day, a day just like any other, and you're suddenly weary of this life. You can't see yourself doing it for one more day. I think I've seen enough of the dark side of life, I need to get away before I lose the ability to enjoy the other side. I'd also like to forget... this." I waved my hand about the yard, taking in everything, from buildings to concrete walls, barbed wire death fences to –. I stopped, this revelatory answer shocking me. This was the answer I'd been looking for and it simply poured out while speaking to a convict.

"I know exactly what you mean," Teacher said, filling the odd silence I had created. I looked at him. I had forgotten for a minute that he was there.

He went on, "You have the option to get out, to start fresh somewhere else. That's priceless and shouldn't be wasted."

I didn't know how to respond, so I simply said "Yes."

"One bad decision will snatch away that right as if it never existed. The right to choose, to come and go, to run from a weary life."

He fell silent and I knew he was speaking of himself.

Everyone knew what he was in prison for, us guards included. The courts had released a sex offender who preyed on children. He was relocated to a neighboring county as the outcry in his own was too large. The accepting county happened to be where Teacher lived, in one of its smaller towns, and the commonality among small towns the world over, is, there are no secrets. So when this new guy showed up, it was with a curiousity born of nosiness that his entire past was dug up and splashed across the town. Beside the fact that he was a child molester, everything else was only fanciful accessories, added and expanded with each retelling. The one other relevant fact of the story is that Teacher, only fifteen years old, kidnapped and killed the man. As far as I know, he had never committed any other crime, outside of prison that is; nor had he ever shown any remorse. The latter is what will keep him in prison until the day he dies. The parole board likes to hear those magic words, "I'm sorry," whether they're sincere or not. What they don't understand is that sometimes some people aren't sorry, and sometimes they shouldn't be.

The guards feel empathy for him, as most have children, and many of us have fantasized about doing what he did. As I looked over to where he was sitting, I could see that scar trailing its way along his lower jaw. It had happened months ago, yet, it stood out in stark relief, the skin as tender and pink as a newborns. He had other scars, too, ripping through his eyebrows, splitting them in half. His hands were busted up as well. Ragged tears, poorly mended, circled their way around and over mountain sized knuckles, a few of which were caved in from constant work. And I knew of the stab wounds and razor slices which crisscrossed and pocked his body. God, life had been cruel to this man.

A voice surprised me, "Hello Mike." I looked up to see Mrs. Brian standing directly in front of me.

"Hey Dorothy, how're you doing?"

"I'm doing very well, thank you." She stared at Teacher until he finally broke down and glanced at her.

She seemed pleased with his squirming. She nodded and said, "Mr. Allen." "Mrs. Brian," he imitated her monotone greeting.

She continued looking at him, "Well, do you have something for me?" "Excuse me?" Judging by the look on his face he was clearly perplexed.

"Am I going to have to spell it out?... very well. You have a message for me from someone who recently left, I believe." She stood tapping her foot in punctuation, perturbed at having to deal with a child.

Knowing dawned on Teacher's face. His eyebrows huddled together and his eyes narrowed, "You've been reading my mail." It was not an accusation so much as a simply stated fact.

"Of course, I have."

"Then you already know the message." "Yes. But I'd like to hear it from you."

I listened to this strange interplay, throughly bewildered, but curious as hell. What in the world could these two have in common? And then I knew, and felt myself grinning. She always knew when to lighten up a mood, God bless her.

He muttered something unintelligible, then began in a voice so low I could barely hear him.

"Splinter sends his... warmest regards," then spoke a little lower, "and says he misses you like h...heck." Not to worry as he's doing fine. He would like to call you, if it's okay."

Mrs Brian was beaming as she looked back and forth between the two of us.

"Thank you, Mr. Allen. Tell Matthew I miss him, too, and I'm happy he's doing well. If he keeps it up, we'll think about the phone call." She paused for effect. "Now, if you gentlemen will excuse me, I have work to do." With that she set off across the yard, looking for all the world like the cat who ate the canary.

I glanced at Teacher and he looked as ragged as an old dishtowel put through the wringer and hung out wrinkled.

He mumbled, "What the hell have I gotten myself into?"

I knew I shouldn't, but there was no stopping it. I burst out laughing. Before long Teacher was laughing, too, and we looked like a couple of idiots out there hee-hawing away.

XI

Everything is slightly out of focus, blurred just enough to make recognition difficult, yet, out of the haze faces appear, oddly familiar, and drift away as quickly as they came. I must be seated, because everyone towers over me looking down in seeming judgment. There's someone sitting in front of me, off to the left and facing me. He is speaking quietly, all the while his right arm slowly raises and points in my direction. I cannot make out his face, but his voice and manner are such that should know him.

There are crowds of people all around me, packed in so tight they seem to be sharing one breath; I can hear its rhythmic in and out. Their voices rising and falling as waves, every broken crest washing me in angry accusations, then retreating to gather its strength. Had I done something wrong?

A woman is walking toward me, she is dressed in a dark, three piece suit that makes her look severe. She is attractive nonetheless. Her hair is heaped atop her head like a pile of dead leaves with a few wisps escaping to hang limply around her face. Contempt leaves her eyes in a rush and pins me to my seat with its intensity. She says not a word, but somehow I understand her fully. As she slowly backs away her right hand comes to cover her mouth, like a woman about to cry, but as her cheeks balloon I knew she had no tears for me, she was simply trying to keep something down, to hold back the nausea. What had I done?

She melts back into the undulating mass only to be replaced by Mrs. Brian and her coterie. This is the first face I've known and I take comfort in it. As they stand before me their clothes begin to shift. One moment they are wearing their guards uniforms and the next they are draped in dark mourning garb. Then, finally, they are covered in judges robes, whose color bleeds blood red to black, then back again.

My comfort is gone. Those who had been my friends are something different now. I can feel heat radiating from them and I know it is the product of hate, its thickness almost chokes me. Mrs. Brian leans forward onto the table, her arms supporting her weight as her face inches ever closer. Her anger is suffocating. Her voice come out in a hiss, nothing like her normal one, "You are the worst of the worst, and no punishment they give you will ever be –."

I came awake in a jolt, sweat bursting out of every pore. What the hell was that all about? I looked to the other side of the bed, but it was empty and had been for some time now. My wife had taken to sleeping in her own bed, in her own room. So the comfort I was seeking was not to be found.

I hurriedly tried to gather the loose threads of the dream, hoping to make some sense of it, but it was gone, only a vague sense of uneasiness was in its place. Even though it was 4:19 in the morning, I had to move. Going back to sleep or sitting still was out of the question.

I showered, dressed, and left the house on foot. I didn't know where I was going, but it mattered little. The chill morning air woke me quickly as I headed toward town. All was quiet and dark, not even the usual sounds of early morning rang out. Houses I passed were seemingly empty, devoid of life. Windows black as eyeless sockets stared at me with a silent knowing. The unease of the dream was becoming manifold. Maybe if I ran I could outpace it. I wasn't dressed for jogging, wearing blue jeans, a flannel and boots, but as I started my legs stretched out with an unknown hunger, eating up the ground.

I ran for miles. Even as my lungs tired my legs churned faster and faster until I was in full flight, barely skimming over the pavement. I could feel moisture in my boots, wet and sticky, and knew my feet were taking a beating. I didn't care, I kept pushing. Something was bubbling up inside me and a scream tried to rip its way out of my throat, but I had no wind to lend it so it soared silently upwards as useless as a prayer. Tears squeezed out of the corners of my eyes to be torn away by a hungry wind.

I collapsed on an empty bench in front of an empty market and drew in ragged breaths. I was running from something, but I had no idea what. I had the sudden urge to get on a bus and never look back. Perhaps, I could outdistance whatever it was that was hunting me. Stay out of its sights by staying on the move. I knew no one would miss me. It would be a favor to all, but I've never been altruistic, so I turned and headed home.

Over the following weeks, as I sleepwalked through my days the dream never fully left me. At home or work it would strike suddenly and with force. I'd never had a dream that became part of me before, growing in strength with the passage of time. As I couldn't shake it, I kept trying to find meaning in it.

While sitting behind my desk daydreaming, yet again, I heard the alarm for the main yard ring out. I sat still, knowing some act of violence was taking place and happy that I was behind the wall so I didn't have to witness it. Within thirty seconds the call came over the loudspeaker for secondary responders, this meant a mandatory response from every guard. In most cases only the guard working the yard where the alarm occurs need respond. The secondary responder call means more help is needed and is generally sounded for riots or staff assults. No guard likes to hear this call.

As I sprinted through the PIA work areas, I barely noticed the cons assuming a squated position and clearing a path. I burst through the gate opening to the prison yard and searched out the location of the incident. It was easy to find as all guards were flowing in the same direction, as if the ground were tilted toward the spot.

As I ran toward the building I could see it was no riot as all the cons were proned out, and when you step onto a yard during a riot it is sheer hell; as confusing as a Jackson Pollack painting, it leaves you grasping for meaning.

As I neared, I saw between 12 to 15 guards brutally applying their batons. Once started, the weapons seemed to have a mind of their own, rising and falling in a practiced choreography, and landing with thick thuds. I couldn't make out who the cons were, but it looked to be a couple of Mexicans and a white. I couldn't understand the frenzy of the guards till I spotted a small group huddled on the ground about fifteen feet from the action. It was a guard being tended to by medical staff, surrounded by a ring of guards holding their batons at the ready. You could tell by their white knuckles and clenched jaws that these too wanted to partake in the violence which was so tantalizingly close.

I approached the downed guard as I had no interest in joining the melee. It was a woman, one of the new cadets fresh from the academy. She was very young. There was blood matted in her blond hair, it ran down the left side of her face and pooled in the hollow at her throat. The nurses had her jumpsuit ripped open down to her navel, and were working on a stab wound in her lower stomach. As I looked back to her face her eyes met mine, and we shared a moment of pure fear which was unspeakable. I looked away as I had nothing to offer her.

A few sergeants had taken the scene over and were screaming at the guards to step their assault. A few had to be physically restrained. The three cons were a bloody mess. The smell of shit was strong in the air, they had been beat till their bowels let go, and more. I didn't recognize the white con, I doubted anyone could in his state, I could only tell he was big and bald. He lay unconscious, battered into a welcomed oblivion. There were open gashes all over his head that were weeping blood and a clear liquid. His hand was partially covering his face. I knew he had been trying to protect himself with it, as it was swollen to a grotesque size and a few of the fingers were bent into unnatural positions, imitating broken matchsticks.

More nurses arrived and rushed to the injured guard, none seemed concerned with the convicts and I couldn't blame them.

The prison was placed on 'state of emergency' lockdown, that meant absolutely no movement. If you're dying in your cell, sorry about your luck, because you were going to meet your maker from that same cell.

It took a few hours to get all the cons secured and escorted to their cells, then the investigation began.

The Investigative Services Unit or ISU started taking photos and collecting evidence. They wanted to interview their snitches, but that had to wait. They found two weapons, a knife and a razor blade melted into a plastic cup handle. The three assailants were ID'ed and everyone was stunned into a betraying silence. The first two were Mexican gangmembers, part of a group called MS-13. They dealt in anything and everything; murder, drugs, prostitution, human trafficking, so this was no leap for them. But the last one turned out to be Michael Allen, Teacher.

None but the first responders could be interviewed, as all other parties involved had been rushed to the local outside hospital. I had a bad feeling about the incident. Some guards had gone too far, Civil Rights groups and Internal Affairs were going to be climbing all over this, and that meant some peoples futures were in serious doubt.

Captain Schmidt was raging through the scene like a man afire, he wanted every guard in the center of the yard immediately. As the call went out, guards came at a dead run and skidded to a stop. No one wanted to be the last one to show. At these moments, you can see the familial like atmosphere shared by all guards, the care and concern shown when one of their own is hurt.

After everyone arrived silence took over. All that was heard was the clicking of dry throats, nervously swallowing, and the panting for breath. The captain started in.

"Okay. Everyone who was directly involved in the incident, step to your left." As bodies started milling sluggishly around, the word "now" rang out like a shot. Instantly everyone was all business. About twenty guards seperated from the group and stood shifting their weight nervously back and forth.

"Before your written statements, you're going to come to my office one by one and give an oral report to ISU and myself. The rest of you will turn in your statements before shift change or no one leaves, and I mean no one. We're on 'state of emergency', so you all know the program; bag lunches and no movement, period." He took a deep breath and went on in a softer tone. "Officer Lowe is fine. She suffered a cut to her scalp, which is where all the blood came from, and a stab wound to the abdomen." I could hear angry mutterings all around me. I knew they wanted nothing more than to go from cell to cell visiting vengeance upon the cons. I had done that many times in my years. "... She will be up and moving around in a few days, and back to work when she feels up to it. Visitation info will be posted in work change tomorrow, as of now, there is none. Warden Garcia will be here in a few hours, so I want everything smooth when he arrives." He looked to his right, "You follow me, the rest of you back to work."

At work the following day, rumor was rife. Everyone was speaking while no one listened. Snitches were being brought in and wrung out by their handlers. Officer Lowe gave a complete rundown and a clearer picture started to reveal itself, a very different picture. With this revelation came a sinking feeling that a mistake had been made, and perhaps, a crime committed.

One of the gangmembers was in a medically induced coma, his injuries being so severe as to threaten his life; the other was not far behind. Teacher had a broken hand and arm, it had taken 252 stitches to close all the wounds on his head and face. Three days later, he was transported to the prison infirmary, I was there, waiting. He was unrecognizable. His head was inflated like a balloon, his eyes swollen shut. He couldn't breathe through his smashed nose, so his mouth hung slightly open. He had a razor cut from the top of his right shoulder to his left waistline. The fact that he had received that wound while defending Officer Lowe and the others as a sign of our gratitude was a slap in the face.

During an attempted interview, he muttered a single sentence, "I have nothing to say," then refused to speak further. I tried to speak to him, even Mrs. Brian came and hovered over him, he ignored everyone.

The events of the incident were pieced together over the next few weeks. Officer Lowe had been conducting cell searches while the cons were on the yard, it was easier to deal with an empty cell. She came to a cell which housed the leader of MS-13, a con called Malo, which means bad, and he lived up to the name. Inside she found drugs and a knife.

The porters on the tier immediately passed this information on to the yard, where it quickly made its way to the gang leader. He knew he was headed to the hole for a handful of years so the decision he made was to stop her from passing the evidence along to the captain. He posted two of his subordinates at the front of the building with instructions to attack her as soon as she exited.

Luckily, Teacher happened to be standing outside the door to the kitchen, on one of his breaks. As the assult started on Officer Lowe he instantly jumped in. Contrary to what everyone had assumed, he fought on her side, dragging her attackers off, only to have them direct their attack on him. When the first responders arrived, they took everyone down, assuming that all the cons had been involved in the assult. Nobody could blame them, who in their right mind would think a convict was helping a guard?

We guards strongly dislike Internal Affairs. We believe they have forgotten which side they're on. Their sole occupation is trying to get their own fired on trumped up charges of excessive force and other crap like it. But in this instance, the charges were very real. Teacher had been brutally beaten for helping one of us, it didn't get much worse than that.

Once again, Teacher came to the aid of the guards, however unintentional; he refused to cooperate with I.A's investigation. No videotaped interview, no statement, no naming names, not a single word, nothing. I.A. tried to bribe him, offering him an immediate transfer to a lower level prison, an Heroic Act commendation, which would knock a year or more off his sentence, they even offered to share all the evidence they had gathered so he could use it for a lawsuit, which would have netted him easily thousands of dollars, he refused everything with a flat stare and silence. He had all the power, he was in the perfect position to take revenge on any guard he chose, yet he didn't use it.

I've really done it this time. Every con in the entire prison system was gonna want a piece of me, because I'm now the guy who sided with the guards. I'm having a hard time believing all this really happened, but my wounds don't lie and they give strength to truth. I'm in a bad position now. The worst imaginable for a convict. But fate is as unforgiving as it is undeniable. When I decided to change my ways, they were not moved in the slightest. I might live my life differently but the thread has already been spun and the end already clipped, I was but taking a different path to meet it and at the rate I'm going, that end will be soon.

My head is finally starting to clear as the drugs wear off. The pain throbs in rhythm with my heartbeat and surges through my body. My eyes feel like pincushions and my vision is swimming. I hate to admit it, but I hope they keep me here for a while, I'm a sitting duck in this condition.

People are bustling in and out of my room at all hours, most I simply ignore, while others, like Mrs. Brian, I listen to without responding. Just her presence is a comfort and she seems to realize it, it's almost like having my mother here, almost. She doesn't care that I don't speak, she moves around the room carrying on a one-sided conversation, happy enough for both of us. I know the guards regret what happened, but I don't know who to trust so I lump them all into the same big ball; better safe than sorry.

But soon I'm going to have to break my silence. I'm worried about D-Man and his reaction. Whatever it is, I know it will be bad news for someone, more than likely a guard. With as sorry as everyone feels, there's a good chance they will let me speak to him, especially if I drop a lug that it will ward off anymore trouble.

I've been stopping by Teacher's room everyday. I sit with him for 10 to 15 minutes, neither of us speaking. There's always someone there. Constant movement swirls around him making his stillness that much more pronounced.

It's been two weeks since the incident, the investigation and lockdown are ongoing. Officer Lowe was released from the hospital last week after receiving a full spectrum of antibiotics, the cons like to smear their knives in feces, which causes severe infections. She has been hosting a continuous stream of visitors and well-wishers. The two gangmembers are still in the hospital, but will be transferred to another high security prison soon. They can no longer be housed here for fear of retaliation from guards. Shit, they already got their issue; one has permanent brain damage and the other is so scared he's singing his stinking little heart out. Half the yard has been rolled up due to his snitching. The problem with that is investigators are trying to clean up loose cases by having him lie, most of the cons will end up beating their cases.

I stood to leave and as always, I said, "See ya tomorrow, Teacher." When I reached the door I heard my name whispered. I turned to find him staring at me, but wasn't sure I'd heard him correctly.

"You said if I ever needed a favor, to ask," he said.

His voice was hollow to the point of being cavernous, it seemed to sound up from some infinite depth. Stupid I know, but I was proud he spoke to me first.

"Whatever you want." I responded.

"I need to speak to my cellie, to let him know the truth and that I'm okay, before unlock happens. I'm sure you know why."

Yes, I knew. D-Man would come out looking for blood, half the guards at the prison were planning on staying home that day.

"I'll speak with the captain and come back to let you know. I can't make any promises, but I can stress the need to defuse the situation."

He nodded. As I turned to leave, he said, "and Stogie, whether you swing it or not, you and I are square."

When I came back later that afternoon, it was with good news, the captain had agreed to let him speak to D-Man. Officer Lowe and her husband were standing in the hallway outside Teacher's room. She wasn't in uniform, just slacks and a blouse. She looked healthy but nervous, her husband was standing behind her rubbing her arm with one hand while patting her shoulder with the other. She was facing the door to the room, but looked as if it were an insurmountable mountain.

"Well, look who's back to bother us," I announced as I approached not wanting to intrude on a private moment.

"Hi, Mike. It's good to see you." She said, somewhat tentatively.

"I should be the one saying that." I gave her arm a gentle squeeze and she smiled sadly. "How are you doing?"

"I'm fine. It just feels... different being back."

"Speaking of which, if you don't mind my asking, why are you here? I heard you were to be gone a month."

"I am." She turned slightly toward her husband, "Dan and I wanted to come and talk to Allen, to thank him for... you know."

"That's a great idea. I have some good news I was just about to deliver, so maybe I can go in first and prime him for you. He hasn't been too thrilled with us lately."

"Okay. That sounds fine."

"One more thing. He looks pretty bad, but most of it is superficial and he's recovering fine. Just keep that in mind, okay?"

I went into the room and told him that D-Man would be brought over later that night and that he had visitors.

"Thanks Stogie, but I don't want any visitors."

I told him who it was and that she needed this more than him. He stayed quiet for a few minutes and I thought he would say no, but then he nodded, "Yeah, okay, let her in, but you stay, too."

I went to the door and motioned them in, holding it open while they entered. I heard a sharp intake of breath, followed by a frightened whimper I turned to see Heather covering her face with one hand while hugging herself with the other. I had warned her, Teacher was a gruesome sight. He had sustained a fractured skull and the left side of his head was still swollen. He had staples closing a wound that ran from his hairline down his forehead and split his brow in half. There were others spread over his head and face, but that one was the center of attention. He had also lost five teeth. Curiously, out of all his numerous wounds, that seemed the only one which angered him. His bruising had reached the stage where it began to look like marble, intricate designs swirling and chasing each other across the surface of the skin, but a closer look showed their depth.

Heather walked slowly forward as if pulled, fighting every step. She stopped at the bedside and placed her hand on the cast which encased his broken arm. She didn't speak, nor meet his eyes, she stood simply and stared at his arm. Time moved slowly as her hand moved back and forth on the cast, the motion seeming to calm them both and communicating some unspoken message.

Teacher reached over and touched her hand lightly, "it's okay, I'm fine. It's not like I was a model to begin with, right? Then I'd be angry!" He was doing it the right way, easing the tension, making it easier for her. "And I'm happy you're okay, too."

She grabbed his hand in both of hers and squeezed as she raised her eyes to his face.

She smiled tearfully, turned and left the room without a word.

Her husband came over and shook Teacher's hand, "I don't know how to thank you." "You just did."

Later that evening I helped escort D-Man to the infirmary. He refused to come out of his cell till I told him what it was about and who wanted him, still he was suspicious. As we walked across the empty yard, I could feel his tension mounting, it didn't help that the only people in sight were angry guards.

Since the incident with Officer Lowe alot of bad shit had gone down. Cons were extracted from their cells and beaten right on the tier, a warning plain and clear. Block guns boomed from the buildings day and night, so much pepper spray was used, it simply stopped dissipating, the prison sat in a perpetual fog of it. All walked around with eyes watering and noses sniffling, there was nothing to be done. Neither side would give in.

We finally came to the infirmary and entered. There were more guards and many nurses, all milling around aimlessly. As we made our way to Teacher's room, eyes met and quickly slipped from D-Man, his reputation was every bit as known and feared as Teacher's. It's strange what guilt can do, make the good seem bad, the guard seem criminal. But in the end only the conscientious feel its tug, and that is what seperates us.

I keyed Teacher's door and let D-Man in, "I'll uncuff you through the trayport," I told him. He said nothing as he bent over and shoved his hands through the small opening. After I released him, I watched as he walked over and shook hands with his friend. No word passed between them, yet, they both turned and pinned me with a look, simultaneously. I nodded and walked away.

"Damn, brother, you look like Frankensteins' ugly cousin." "I took a beatdown, what's your excuse?"

"I don't need one, there's no excusing this much fine, anyway."

We were laughing and joking as usual. It was our way of dealing, it made things easier.

"So what's the deal with the skrews bringing me over here?"

"Right to the point, huh? They feel guilty, so they're giving me a little leeway. I know the lockdown is still on, but what's the word on the yard?"

He was quiet for awhile, and I could see he was trying to think of an innocent way to tell me I was up shit creek.

"I've been fishing and kiting for the last two weeks and I'm freakin' sick of it. The woodpile ain't too happy with you, but you already know that. We're all still in the dark on the details, so why don't you tell me what happened."

Good question, parts of it were hazy and some were just plain blank, but as he was going to sink or swim with me, he deserved an answer.

"First, let me ask you a question. What would you do if you seen two pieces of garbage beating a woman? Would you stand there and watch, turn away, or would you intervene?"

"Here's a better question. Why are you always asking me questions to which you already know the answers?"

I smiled. It was a good to see that my actions and my absence hadn't changed a thing between us, we fell right into our normal mode of conversing.

"You know damn well that I would've ruined those punks." He was right, I did know.

"Okay, point taken. I don't remember much after the clubs started their tap-dance on my head, but everything up till then is clear. I was on a break, standing outside watching the yard. I noticed a few of Malo's homeboys standing by the front door whispering with the porter, they took off and I didn't think any more of it. About five minutes later they came back, all nervous and twitchy. I knew something was in the off, but just figured they were going to hit one of their own. Then the door racked and that new female guard stepped out, I got a bad feeling quicklike. You know how the new ones are always gang ho, they're always the ones getting attacked too. Those two idiots became all business, so I pushed off the wall and headed in that direction. I didn't plan it or think about it, I just reacted. Sure enough, the little dark one. I don't know his name –"

"Diablo."

"Figures. He came out of his pocket with his hand filled and rushed her." I stopped for a moment remembering the scene. "That is the first time I've been scared in 20 years, and I didn't like it. My decision was already made, so I went with it."

"I yanked them off of her and we had a three man smackdown going for a minute, but they were so little it wasn't much fun, or challenging. I put one down quick and was dealing with the other when the first guards showed up, late as usual. It was all downhill from there. I don't blame the guards, they saw one of their own down and cons fighting. Shit, I would have done the same thing. It's easier to put everyone down and ask questions later, right?"

He didn't answer and I didn't go on. We gathered our thoughts separately, trying to think of the right things to say.

"It's not that easy and you know it." Now we would get to the meat of it.

"First, we don't let one of our own get cracked without retaliating. Second, you helped a cop. The woodpile doesn't know what the hell to do; stab a cop for what was done to you, or stab you for being a traitor! And of course the Mexicans are hot for you. They've been politicing all hush hush with a few of our shadier characters, I'm not sure where that's headed, but I wouldn't worry about that, we'll just kill them off, do everyone a favor."

I took in what he said. "I figured that would be the way of it. Moving on the guards is not an option, so what's our play?"

"Oh, just like that, it's my decision? Hell, you're supposed to be the brains in this outfit, I'm just here for my looks," he answered in all earnestness.

"Man, if that's true, we're in some serious trouble."

The laughter died slowly and was replaced with a comfortable silence, one born of familiarity. Sometimes that's enough.

"You should've seen her, D. She went down so easy, just crumpled to the ground and curled into a tight ball, like she could shut out all the bad by not acknowledging it... Goddamn, I wanted to kill those bastards! I still do."

"I wish I could've been there with you, but no worries, I'm there on the next go-round."

"I know."

This ride never ends. Whether I'm good or bad, trying to help people or hurt them, it all seems to end in the same place with the same consequences. I'm starting to think there is little if any difference between the two, and what there is is only cosmetic.

"I want you to go back and explain my side to the woodpile, and let them know I'll be back as soon as I'm healed up. If the Mexicans are pushing the line hard, I'll deal with them personally." I quickly held up my hand. "I know, we will deal with them. Also, I don't have a grudge against the skrews, so they shouldn't either. I know alot will be happy to hear that, the last thing they want is a war with the guards. You still have my property, right?" He nodded. "Don't let the skrews roll it up, you know they might try some underhanded shit."

"Don't trip on our cell, I got that under control, but I'd like to see them try, might be fun," he grinned wickedly. "You heal up, because we got us a rough road ahead."

He went quiet for a moment and gave me a shrewd look that was a warning of something to come.

"You're not going to take up this Hero business permanently, are you? I'm not sure your mug could handle any more thanks." He wore a smile more fit for a guilty child.

I felt myself smile in return, and knew that no matter what happened next, I had done the right thing.

XII

I'm in the hole again, walking my circles in this small box of a yard. They won't let me have a cellie, so I am alone this time. I can hear the guards practicing at their shooting range, the shots ring out like laughter. There must be something funny in all this, but for the life of me I don't know what.

This is the first time I've been in the hole where I was actually innocent. Guilt and innocence, I always thought there was a vast gap between the two, but I find the cell doesn't discriminate. My circles feel exactly the same, my loss, too.

I'm told I'm only being kept here till they can figure out what to do with me. They don't want to send me back to the yard because they're convinced I'll be murdered, and I can't argue that point, but they're growing increasingly frustrated as I won't cooperate with them. I know it's only a matter of time before they remember I'm a convict not a hero and wash their hands of me. I will make it back to the yard.

The guards who beat me came by to apologize. The funny thing was they had an attorney with them and looked to him everytime they spoke, as if asking permission. The suit asked me to sign a waiver of liability. What they were really worried about was a lawsuit; so much for sorry. I signed it and told them no hard feelings, I didn't want their money, I don't take revenge in that womanly fashion; besides, I just didn't care.

They even sent a shrink to speak with me. I guess they thought I was in shock or denial, or just losing my mind. They couldn't understand passing up all the free money involved in a lawsuit and I sure as hell wasn't going to explain. The conversation went as expected, he asked routine questions and I told him what he wanted to hear, then he left, never to be heard from again; nice job, Doc. Now you know why the only place you can land a job is in prison.

He asked if I had ever thought of suicide, recently or in the past. What could I say, everyone has a bad day and thinks how simple it would be to ease the pain? Or how alot of folks would be better off with my exit? Or thinking these thoughts and overcoming them is where true strength lies? No, he doesn't want to hear any of that, so I simply said no and he walked away with another job well done.

They gave me a commendation for an Heroic Act, telling me it would look good at my parole hearings and would go a long way to changing peoples minds about me. But the Board denied me 15 years at my first hearing, that was after 20 years served. One more denial like that and I'll be leaving here in an Heroic Box, so much for change.

A piece of paper and the opinion of strangers is not going to change me, I've already done that job myself without a carrot dangled in front of me. I didn't have to get involved in the incident, I could have turned my back and sat on my ass like the rest of the cons, they think a good deed is only so through acknowledgement, but sometimes, that only devalues it.

Time seems to have come to a standstill. The days and nights pass, I wake and sleep, go to work and come home, still nothing changes. I wonder if it's only me or if this is the way of things, is this how everyone feels? I want to be a shepherd, not a sheep. But as I look around I see no one is keeping an eye on anyone, anymore.

I don't like the knowing. I don't like the mundane, the Rut, but it's all I have and I'm afraid to lose what little it is. What is worse than the Rut, is Death? Death could be glorious or hideous, but ultimately it is unknowable; so at least the Rut has that going for it.

I sit at my desk and watch the cons work and watch them haze, in either pursuit their lethargy is as contagious as pity, and just as disgusting. They're like walking, talking, sleeping pills; and instead of being separate, I feel one of them and feel nothing.

The clock on the wall has lost all meaning. I could sit here for 8, 16, 24 hours, and it would feel the same! I could sit here infinitely and not miss a beat, because there is no beat to be missed. Something has gone wrong or at least I hope so, I hope this is not normal. I have to believe there is something better.

I watch Snake off in a corner, surrounded by his friends, if that's what they can be called. They are always busy whispering and hustling, the lethargy has passed them by. I know he's selling drugs, the whole prison knows, but no one does a thing about it, everyone is too comfortable with the status quo to even bother; the infection runs deep.

He and his friends take turns secreting their stash in their rectums, so nobody knows who has what on any given day. The one thing I do know is shortly after they arrive they start handing out little folded up rectangles of magazine pages, and I know damn well what's inside. This has been going on so long that they are just the newest faces in the same old sorry play. There is one new twist though, Snake has decided to conduct his business right in front of me. I don't know if he's challenging me or simply letting me know who really runs the show here. Either way, there is no respect in his eyes when he looks at me.

"What's going on, Stogie?"

I looked up to see Snake standing in front of me without a care in the world. "Nothing. What do you need?"

"I don't need a thing, Stogie, but you look like you could use a friend, or at least someone to lend you an ear."

"You serious? When I start looking for friends like you, then I'll know I'm in trouble."

"Yeah, maybe you're right. And seeing how you treat your friends, it's probably wiser to be your enemy, at least none of them are taking a beating for helping you guys."

He stood there laughing and I knew he was talking about Teacher, and I knew I shouldn't rise to the bait, but the fact that he was right galled me.

"I don't think you'd like to find yourself in that position, either. You know, you could be rolled up any day, for anything that I just happen to find, or make up. You're only here because I don't give a crap about you and neither does anyone else."

"Ah, come on, Stogie, we both know that's not true. I have alot of friends that would do anything for me, no questions asked. And I'll tell you something else, it's always better to make a man a friend rater than an enemy, you never know what pitfalls you may avoid or what benefits you may reap." As he finished, he turned and walked away.

I thought about what he'd said, and for once, the guy actually made sense. If there was one thing I could use in my life it was some friends. The ones I claimed now were that in name only, pale imitations of the real thing, but I have no idea how to find real ones and what Snake offered is a long way from ideal, an offer coupled with a threat.

The strange thing about Snake and Teacher is that even though they live in the same environment, inhabit the same space, they seem to come from opposite sides of the spectrum. Yet the more I think about it, the more similarities I see rather than differences.

They seem to be like diverging branches of a tree; to the eye they are separate and traveling in different directions, yet the mind knows that they have sprung from the same root. So can they truly be fundamentally different?

Teacher speaks and acts with an intention of helping others, yet every journey takes him down the path toward violence. Because his intent is innocent, does that make him somehow less culpable, any less the monster in the end?

Snake's intent is clearly written on his face for all to see. He likes to think he's the clever deceiver, but he lacks the brains and subtlety for that job; most would think this a character trait, this lack of ability to be a politician, but not on Snake. He is a user and manipulator, yet he's honest in both.

Which one is really practicing deception? I'm starting to think that the one who first convinces himself, the one who believes his own lies, who gives rise to hope, is the real artist. Regardless of their differences, they share a common trait that is enviable; they command respect in their spheres of influence, by friends and enemies alike. That is something every man should know. The only ones who have it are those who demand it and have the strength to enforce that demand. Once, respect didn't have to be enforced, it was a gift gladly given, but like many things these days respect has become an antiquated notion.

Maybe this is what I've been lacking in my life, why everything seems so hollow. We are after all social creatures and what could be more natural than wanting the regard of those around you?

Anticipation is a hell of a thing, whether you're expecting something good, bad, or unknown, it can tear you up with the waiting. Two days ago I was told I'm going back to the yard sometime this week, since then, all the possible scenarios that could occur have been playing on a non-stop loop, filling my head with crazy scenes, crowding out all other thought. It's impossible to keep my mind on any task that does not involve my returning. The few words I have with staff or my neighbor are forgotten with the same breath they're uttered. I have but two thoughts: what are the consequences for what I've done, and how will the cost be extracted?

I wish they wouldn't have told me till the day I'm to go. Someone must've known that their perceived kindness was instead a cruelty. The waiting is taking its toll. No matter the outcome, I'd rather get it over with.

My every thought ends the same. I hope I'm able to keep D'Man out of the mix. Everytime he's been thrown in the hole it's been on my account, I can no longer accept that guilt; my own overburdens me.

I hear the section door loudly slide open and a minute later two skrews are posted at my cell door.

"Time for you to check out, Allen. Are you all packed up?"

My time had come and none too soon, all that thinking was driving me up the wall. "I'm ready. Do I get a cellie?"

"Yeah. The captain shuffled a few people around and came up with an opening for you. You're sure you're ready?"

"As I'm ever gonna be."

They cuffed me and escorted me down the hallway, a few of the skrews nodded as I passed, some even called out Farewells, their intent in line with the original meaning, they knew as well as I what was waiting for me. The two skrews escorting me were young, neither knew my name or situation and that was fine with me, as there was no need for unnecessary conversation.

No matter how many times you leave the hole or SNU, when you're making that long walk back to the yard it always feels like the first time, the first time you climbed off the bus and saw the prison in all its undisguised nakedness. War stories you've heard take turns battering your stomach, sending it into convulsions. After all these years and all the truth I know, I feel it, too, and am glad for it. I can only imagine when that feeling stops and one becomes numb to the world. Whatever happens, at least I'm not dead yet.

As we step through the main gate the yard's empty. What a pitiful sight it is, just a vast expanse of cages and enclosures standing with gaping maws ready and eager to swallow their prey. What mind could have thought this up? It had to be one with no idea what freedom really means, or the taking of it.

It's early afternoon, the yard should be full of cons. I turned to one of my escorts, "Is the yard on lockdown?"

"Yeah. For about 4 or 5 months now. From what I hear, they should be coming up for air in the next month or so."

I haven't missed a thing. They've been on lockdown since I left, the skrews must have been pretty pissed, glad I missed all that. As we walked along the perimeter wall we came abreast of the program office and Captain Schmidt just happened to be standing there. It was obvious he'd been waiting for me. The two young skrews stiffened at his presence.

As we neared he ran a critical eye over me from head to toe then back again, his eyes drawn to the damage. He winced slightly and I knew in that moment he was sorry for what had been done.

"Uncuff him," he ordered.

My escorts looked a little unsure, but jumped to obey. As the cuffs came off, that extinguished sense of freedom rekindled with a fierce spark. I rubbed my wrists as prisoners are prone to do, not because they hurt, but to rid them of that sense of confinement.

"I wasn't sure if they were going to let you back on my yard. Truthfully, I was hoping you would have been transferred out of here, to a decent place, maybe."

"They tried that, but I wouldn't agree. Felt too much like running."

I didn't have to tell him that running was not an option. I have to live here for the rest of my life. This is my home and no one should be forced to run from home.

"I hope you're not coming out looking for trouble."

I had to laugh at that. Finding trouble had never been a problem for me, and now it would be a whole lot easier.

"No sir, just back for your fine hospitality."

Now it was his turn to laugh. "Right, because that's what we're known for." "How is Lowe doing?" I asked.

He hesitated, trying to decide whether to answer to a convict. His guilt must've decided for him.

"She no longer works here, but from what I'm told she is doing well. I'm sure being away from here is… helpful."

"It's probably for the best then."

Silence enfolded us, but it was comfortable. Only the two escorting me seemed put off by it.

"Well, I hope everything works out. If you need anything let me know." The captain said, breaking the silence.

"Thank you sir, but I'm sure I can handle things."

"Yeah, that's what I'm afraid of." He nodded to the guards, "Why don't you boys get him along to his building now. So long, Teacher."

The two young skrews exchanged a startled look and immediately took a keen interest in me. The captain was enjoying it, he had eated me, obviously. I had some kind of celebrity status among the guards, but my only concern was my status among the other cons.

"Which way are we headed?" I prompted. "To seven building," one stammered out.

That's the same place I was housed when I was last here. A sneaking and rather pleasant suspicion came over me. I didn't want to get my hopes up too much, as that's a study in futility. But no one can forgo hope, it's much too powerful, and in this imperfect world of ours, it is much needed.

"Who am I moving in with?"

"Uh, Taylor, I think," one said, while the second nodded his agreement.

I smiled. The captain had done me a favor, after all. He didn't bother waiting for me to ask as he knew that would never happen.

The two guards were eyeing me like a car wreck. Morbid curiosity mixed with an underlying horror, which was not strong enough to make them turn away. At least they had the good grace to show a sense of embarrassment when I caught them. The effect was they continually dropped their eyes.

Into the building we went. The same section, the same cell loomed before me, and even though in appearance it was a clone to every other cell, to me it was home. Differences lie in the little things and can be deceptive. A smiling face stood guard at the door beaconing away the unwanted, while welcoming the wary wayfarer. My anxiety disappeared in a flash as I realized that as much as things had changed, the important ones remained. As the door slid open I was greeted with the words, "Welcome home, brother."

The days and weeks that followed passed with an unrepentant rapidly. Those times we want most to last are always the quickest gone, and the ones we would forget, if we but could, linger and cling like a sickness. We fell back into our old routine as if nothing had happened, and for awhile I forgot what lay ahead.

In the mornings, D would roll out of bed and hit the floor for his obligatory set - of what he called - wake-your-ass-up-push-ups. I went along as it actually worked, it got the blood flowing, but I still relied on my morning shot of mud. We'd take turns cleaning the cell, then sit around and wait for breakfast to make an appearance, after which we'd get ready for the workout. For a while I was convinced that the only reason D'Man was glad to have me back is so he could use me as pigiron.

One morning about two weeks later our neighbors got into a cellfight. They were both Crips from L.A. we didn't speak to them, nor they us. None of their people were on the tier, so they were stuck down in the corner surrounded by enemies. That's not that unusual and it's only a big deal when a long ass lockdown rolls around, because then you're trapped in a 10 × 8 box with another man 24-7 for months on end. You can go into it the best of friends and come out the other end hating each other. All the little things you used to like about him are now the reasons you want to rip his freakin' head off. You have to learn to let the little stuff go and become good at 'tunnel vision'; the less you see, the less annoyed you'll become.

It was obvious our neighbors hadn't learned this, for they reached their breaking point. They were going at it pretty good then we heard a television explode, so we knew it was serious. A T.V. is one of the few possessions were allowed, so breaking one is serious business. Our first thoughts were hopefully we'll get some new neighbors, some woods. Yeah, I know, one man's misfortune and all that, right? Everybody is always jockeying in here, so it's only natural.

The skrews came hauling ass through the section door, and with as fat as most of them are, that's alot of ass to be hauling. Heads swiveling back and forth trying to locate the incident by sound alone. Sometimes it takes them an eternity. Funny stuff, not for the guy getting his ass kicked, but just in general.

They finally came to the right cell and started yelling and pushing alarm buttons. When this had no effect they did what they always do, pepper sprayed the hell out of them, which meant spraying the whole section. As D'Man and I had been through this countless times, we were prepared. You have to soak your towel in water, wring it out and fold it into a square, then hold it over your mouth and nose while breathing slow and steady. It filters all the O.C. out of the air. The one thing you don't want to do is panic, because the faster you breathe the quicker it will put you down.

The two were screaming that they couldn't breathe, but the skrews won't open cell doors till combatants are proned out on the cell floor. The skrews were screaming, "Get down, Get down." It finally sank in because they told the Gunner to rack the door. As soon as it opened you could have ear a stampede of boots, heavy breathing and muffled grunts a batons finding soft flesh echoed throughout the section. Even skrews needed to blow off steam, right? This was the perfect time.

A few minutes later they dragged the two out of the cell and got them to their feet where they wobbled like newborns on the plains; defenseless. They half-walked, half dragged them through the dayroom and out the section door, accompanied by hooting and hollering. This noise came from the cons whom everyone calls 'inmates'. It's a derogatory term which the skrews apply to us, cons use it on those who still fight with their mouths. They haven't pitched dirt, haven't earned their bones, but still feel the right to express their worthless opinions. They're easily differentiated from the 'regs' or 'regulars'; where they are loud and visible, the regs are quiet and unseen; they know it's best to save energy for when it's your turn.

I lowered my wet towel and said, "Well, I guess the show's over for now." "I wish they'd turn the purge system on to get rid of this stink!"

From his mouth to someone's ears, as soon as it was out the fans kicked on and the outer door was opened. This draws the pepper spray outside. The whole section was coughing and blowing their noses, the 'inmates' didn't know the wet towel trick and I wasn't about to share it with them.

When I first came back, the days were filled with enough drama to make soap operas look tame. D'Man told me where the woodpile stood in regards to what I had done, and I was surprised by their reaction. Apparently, D had played up the fact that it was a woman who'd been attacked; there's a special brand of justice for wife beaters here, and it ain't pretty, so that was a point for me. Then he played the 'Race card', and yes, it can be used by white people, too. He pointed out that she was a white woman attacked by two Mexicans, so it was basically my duty to defend her. The only ones who bought that were the white supremacists, who were instantly on my side, vowing to back me up come hell or highwater.

The only problem we could foresee was the Mexicans, as it was their people I had jumped on, but here again D'Man had a ready solution. As they ran the drug trade on the yard, they knew any lockdown, especially if it were racial, would bite deep into their business and empty their pockets. So D offered them a two-fold deal: I would go into a cell with whoever they picked and handle it one-on-one, or we would all mind our own and get the program running so we could make some money. Being the 'Entrepreneurs' they were, they chose the latter, with a few conditions.

D'Man was no genius, but he could read people as easily as breathing. He would have them saying whatever he wanted all the while believing it was their own idea. Where I expected to find just the opposite, he had every white on the yard applauding my actions. The guy was amazing, in different circumstances he could've been somebody. Not to say that he was nobody now, but his political skills are such that he could've ridden them to the top. I guess he's the proof that it's a fine line between a criminal and a politician; context is everything.

It's easy to separate content from context grammatically. To misquote someone for our own advantage or for their detriment has become a staple in our political world. But what happens if we define content differently? If content were to represent life, then context would be the circumstance and event which revolved around it. Mistakes made would be easily seen and easily corrected. One is not punished indefinitely for making a grammatical mistake, but taught how to fix it, and as life is held to a loftier position, should not the same standards apply? When did we become a people who prize the cheap and cheapen the prized?

XIII

Every race has a con who represents it on the yard, who is their leader, their shotcaller. For the Mexicans, this was Scar. He had complete control over his people. He decided who stayed and who left, the latter usually surrounded by nurses and strapped to a gurney.

It takes a certain kind of person to fill this role, which is the same for every race and gang in here, and Scar fit it to a tee. Aggressive, violent, greedy, ambitious, and above all, no conscience. These types are anachronisms not only in time and place, but to civilization itself. They are the basic Alpha Male, but where even the Alpha Male will draw a line at certain actions, these, in here, are not constrained by their setting.

I was on the yard ten years ago when he earned his nickname by taking the yard from his predecessor, it wasn't a peaceful succession. It was like watching a junta unseat a third world strong man, with machetes. He came away with a rictus grin and one eyebrow cocked up, as if being pulled by a fishhook; at least his outside now matched his inside.

A few days before the yard came up I received a kite from him. He wanted to talk, just the two of us, to see if we could work out this problem. I sent word back agreeing.

"I don't trust that slimy little bastard!"

"Dammit D, how many times do we have to go over this? I don't trust him, you don't trust him, hell, his own people don't trust him. But even if he has some scurry ass shit up his sleeve, we have to try, and if it all goes south he's gonna get the worst of that deal."

"That's exactly what I'm talking about. You got it all planned out to crack him, don't you? D'Man said accusingly.

"You know damn well that ain't the case. I'd like to stay on the yard for awhile, I'm sick of the hole. Do you actually think I'd plan to take off and leave you here in the crosshairs? You know me better than that, brother, or at least you used to."

He had the good grace to look sheepish, but he wouldn't let it go.

"Look, all I'm saying is I think it would be better if I were at the meeting. You know, just in case something goes wrong."

He was acting like I was some old man who couldn't take care of myself. Every since the incident with the skrews he'd been hovering over me, like I was broken or something. I started getting angry just thinking about it.

"It doesn't matter what you think, this is how we're doing it! You need to get it out of your mind that I've gone soft or grown too old for this game. Let me be the first to warn you, nothing has changed in that regard. If someone feels the burning need to test me, well, I welcome it. And if you're afraid I'm gonna take off to the hole and leave you again, there's a simple remedy for that. You just get on the first motherfucker you don't like and fielddress him. We'll meet up in the back and laugh about it, how's that sound for a plan?"

I thought by his reaction that I had gone a bit too far, then I saw that old grin of his pulling at the corners of his mouth.

"I was wondering how long it'd take you to get back."

Yeah, I knew he had. Alot of people had, myself included. "I was never gone, just trying something... different."

"Whatever it is or was, I'm glad to see the spark back."

It's funny how he and I saw this completely different. He thought of it as a regeneration, where I was once derailed I'm now back on track; but I saw it as an ember, easily capable of burning out of control, one that I thought extinguished. But I guess, you can never run for enough or fast enough to escape yourself, and no matter what change comes that ember always retains the possibility to reignite.

The day finally arrived for yard release, the lockdown was over. Now the question was; could we program or were we headed straight to the hole? D'Man and I had gone over every possibility so many times as to make the day boring, now that it was at hand. I found myself strangely calm. I guess talking something to death is a real possibility.

D still didn't like the plan, but at least he was no longer worried. He even seemed to relish the prospect of a little action, but then he always did. He's obviously been on the mainline too long. He's like an old steam boiler, you have to release the pressure regularly in order to avoid an explosion. I myself had no intention of going to the hole if I didn't have to.

In a few months I'll have been down for 21 years and suddenly I've been feeling claustrophobic, no matter how hard I try I ain't seem to find the cause. For all these many years, the confined spaces and the closeting away of humanity's refuse has never touched me. As I sat in my little cell crowded of everything but thought, I wave layer upon layer around my protective cocoon and nothing ever got in. You must even learn to shield yourself from yourself, as that is truly the most dangerous enemy. I've received phone call after phone call informing me of Death. Grandparents, aunts, uncles, younger brother, and finally father, a seeming endless parade of loss; but just as a knife taken to a piece of wood, the whittling cannot go on forever, eventually the material will disappear. But even these I never allowed in. Perhaps it's not the dead but the living who strike such a chord, who by means of mortality burrow their way in, whatever the cause, I find this change has been forced upon me and all I can do is follow.

Everything has reversed itself, in these quiet moments alone is where I feel most anxious, and in times of impending confrontation I am most calm. There must be something to be learned here.

As the cons come streaming forth from the building, they sound like a fast moving river, gurgling and bubbling, full of excitement. Everyone gazes upward, the sun is a white hot orb burning down on us. After six months of darkness it's like a new discovery or the face of a loved one; even though it may hurt, you dare not look away for fear it may disappear.

I saw Scar across the yard and nodded, we would meet up in awhile and see what happened. I was more concerned with my own at the moment and somewhat surprised at my reception, many cons shook my hand and welcomed me back. A handful stayed away, guilt by association was a defenseless crime in here and subject to the same punishment as the original offense, so I couldn't blame them.

Everywhere I went D'Man was my shadow. He was so close I could hear his breathing, could feel the heat coming off of him. Others felt it too, and kept their distance. Those brave enough to approach did so with empty hands in plain sight and peaceful intentions clearly outlined on their faces. There was no way D'Man was gonna be left behind again, that much was clear.

As the yard time slowly slipped away, I began to get the feeling that no one wanted to do anything. Nobody wanted to be the one who stack his neck out for something that was none of his business, and then got it wrung. Plus, the six month lockdown had tamed more than a few.

"I guess I should get this over with," I said to D'Man. "Don't worry, you don't have to be far away, just for enough to make it look right, okay? Keep your eye on the Mexican tables, if shit goes wrong, that's where his backup is coming from."

"You think I don't know that? I got that under control. If anyone tries to close that distance they'll never make it. You just concentrate on Scar."

"That's the plan. See ya on the other side, brother."

I quickly scanned the yard and found Scar and his homeboys staring at me, and every damn guard on the yard as well. Hell, heads were hanging out of every window and poking from every doorway, all wanted a front row seat. If someone was going to be killed, they sure weren't gonna miss it.

Scar indicated it was time to talk and I began to walk toward him. As he came forward he looked as unconcerned as those around his table. We knew each other well, strengths and weaknesses; the advantage lay with the one who could put more check's in the first column, and I knew that was me. He was a drug addict and that need is what controlled his actions, so going to the hole where he'd have to do without was not an option. I didn't discuss this with D'Man, he would've said I was putting too much stock in a faint idea, and he might've been right.

We stopped about three feet from each other, the perfect striking distance, we didn't bother shaking hands as we were far beyond the point of pretense.

"Either way this goes down, we can make it quick and easy, and keep our people out of it." I said into the silence.

I could see he didn't like playing second fiddle. He was used to people jumping at his every word, so I decided beforehand to press him. I wanted him to know there would be no concessions. We would either let everything go or we would settle it here and now.

"Two of my people are gone and you had a hand in it, now I'm just supposed to act like it never happened? You know I'd be out of a job pretty goddamned quick if I did that." He finished with a grin.

"So what do you want?"

I could tell by the greed that lit his eyes, this was only a negotiation, anything physical had passed. I sagged a bit with relief and was disconcerted to feel that way. I hope it didn't show on my face.

"I need a few things to make my people happy, to make them forget any insults. First, I need to have a working relationship with your peoples' head, and as he doesn't like me you need to make this happen. I'm tired of being in the blind when you guys do crazy shit! Second, I want you to walk over to my tables and apologize for Malo and Diablo." The last came out with a knowing sneer and I guessed it was a make or break proposition. So maybe this was his trap and I'd been wrong after all. Not much of a trap though, but then he'd never been one for subtlety, especially when brute force was such an abundant commodity and so easily utilized. All my instincts were shouting to just do him on the spot, they weren't much for subtlety either. I could sense that he, just as much as I, didn't want this to go south. So I had to assume that it was only a test. Without this show his people probably wouldn't keep him around, so he was in just as tight of a spot as I was.

"You want me to help you save face, is that it?" I asked.

"Call it whatever you want, but you know, whatever happens to one of us happens to both of us. So it's in our mutual interest to look out for each other, right?"

I could feel eyes all over me, questioning why I was standing still speaking, instead of stabbing. A crawling sensation worked its way up my spine and I knew itchy trigger fingers were yearning for release, in that moment, I knew violent tendencies were not the exclusive property of criminals.

"This has nothing to do with Malo and Diablo, does it?"

"Fuck no! Those two are done, but that's an issue for my people. What we got going here is only between you and me and consolidating power."

"Okay, I agree. But I need one thing from you as well." "What's that?"

"After we're done with your people, you come to my tables and tell my people how it stands with those two and how it stands with us. You don't have to give a reason, their status is good enough. It will ease a lot of tension and defuse a potential explosion." He couldn't say no without looking weak, so I had him.

He gave one of his ugly smiles and said, "nice."

I turned to give D'Man a sign, then walked toward the Mexican tables. I still wasn't 100 percent sure of Scar and was ready just in case things turned ugly, but he proved true to his kind, only interested in covering his own ass. I apologized and there were a few mutterings and a chorus of 'orales' around the tables.

It was the first time I had apologized to anyone for anything. It wasn't as difficult as I believed it would be, and I didn't feel lessened by it either. Even though I wasn't really sorry for a damn thing I'd done, the fact that my actions affected others not even involved in the incident, was a revelation to me.

We next strolled over to the white tables and went through our little act, both performing our assigned roles. As he left, we shook hands, and as we let go the tension parted, too.

Sweat broke out all over and what little breeze there was seemed to rush toward the invitation. When they met a cooling calmness covered me and I felt better than I had in a long time.

The sun still rode high in the sky, but the burning heat was replaced by a warming comfort.

The yard came up for program yesterday, and I sat at my desk barely breathing as my ears strained for the slightest sound. I was waiting for the alarm and the certain news it'd bring. For some odd reason I thought it might sound different, mournful maybe. But as the minutes, then hours, passed in an undisturbed rhythm, I felt a vague sense of disappointment, as if I'd been cheated. Things seem to have gone his way again.

I looked around at the various work stations and could see the same expectation and disappointment written on the faces there. For the first time I found myself rooting against those I had once favored, and it was not a comfortable feeling, as it put me on the 'other side'. I can't pinpoint when this change took place, I only know that it has a mind and will of its own and is inexorable. I now spend my days wondering if I'm becoming someone else or if this had always been me, just well hidden. What surprises me most is the lack of a fight, I thought I would have put up more of a struggle; perhaps my fighting days are over.

I've watched Teacher for almost twenty years. I've witnessed his daily struggle to be something he is not, and now I realize I was fighting that same battle, here and at home. I always thought my family got along better without me, so I kept my distance. But the truth is, I'm the one who does better without them, and when I realized that everything became easier. Some people never figure this out and go through life butting them head against the wall. Acceptance is a wonderous thing, it frees you from other's expectations.

"Hey Stogie, what gives? You've been sitting here like a statue all day."

I didn't have to look up to know who it was, the arrogance in his voice identified him as surely as a fingerprint or DNA would've. As usual, his timing was perfect. Whenever my questions became most persistent, bang! There he was. It was almost as if he could read my mind, maybe I was just that easy.

"Just working hard."

"Right... I hear the other yard is up and running. Everything being all peace, love, and understanding over there. Didn't see that coming."

"They're programming just like your yard, what's the difference?"

"I'm glad you asked. The difference is we don't have an insider working for your team on our yard."

He would never let hatred for Teacher go, it was a piece of him just as sure as his arms or legs were. But now I could see it from a different perspective. Teacher had broken the code that cons live by, and Snake being the top dog, the enforcer of that code, would be stained by his presence until could wipe it clean. So in a real sense he was justified in his hatred.

"Not that you know of."

He gave me a questioning look, "True." He leaned forward onto my desk with his palms flat. I could see the corner of a fifty dollar bill poking out from between his scarred fingers. "You know I've been trying to get my tattoos finished, but I'm all out of ink. I only need one bottle to finish up and I'm hoping to knock it out this weekend."

I waited for him to continue, to say the words, but he only stared down at me. I looked from his hand to his face and back again, suddenly I knew my answer. It came so easily, it must've been there the whole time.

I reached toward his hand and he moved back, just a little, making me reach further, then he left the bill behind, as if it weren't good enough for him. I quickly palmed it, "I'll be keeping the change."

His only response was a smile.

Over the next few weeks I formed a strange relationship with Snake. It's difficult to explain, but I found myself drawn to him, even liking him, I was doing him small favors almost daily. I brought him tattoo ink, cigarettes, CD's, even fast food. He always paid for everything, making sure there was plenty left over for me.

Even though what I was doing was illegal, I justified it to myself with the reasoning that it was nothing harmful, it wasn't drugs or weapons. I simply ignored the fact that that's where all his money came from, and it was illegal. To begin with, cons weren't allowed to possess money outside or their trust accounts. Plus, the guy ran every dirty rocket on the yard. Once you turn a blind eye to something it becomes easier and easier, till there is no longer a need to, because nothing bothers you anymore.

The day came when Snake asked for a real favor. This was a different thing, there was no money involved, no debt to be repaid, he was asking as one friend to another. I didn't realize it immediately, but the more I thought about it the more I understood that we were indeed friends.

"You think you can get a partner of mine a job back here?"

"I don't do the hiring, but I might be able to put a good word in. What's his name?"

"Jude Burden. He came out of the hole about a month ago, we're just trying to find him a job with a pay number so he can look out for himself. He's a good guy and I guarantee there'll be no problems with him, if that's what you're thinking."

The name was familiar, but I couldn't place it. Trying to recall him was like the dying echoes of a rung bell, the harder you listen the fainter the sound. I had the sense that I should know him and I should be careful, but it was only a dim echo of a warning and I ignored it.

"I'll see what I can do. Any particular spot?"

"No. Anywhere back here will be fine. Thanks, Stogie."

XIV

The prison offers a variety of self-help courses, most of which are mandatory for lifers to enroll in if they want a chance to parole. These courses sound helpful on paper, but it only takes one attendance for reality to set in. The instructors hired to run the classes are only vaguely familiar with the content, therefore they bluff their way through with generalizations and guilt. In the end, they hand out certificates without teaching a thing.

I've never taken a course, never saw the need. I've always assumed I'd die in here, never even coming close to the idea of paroling. This is after all California, where prisons are a business and business is good. I'm only surprised the state hasn't started running tourists through, letting them gawk and snap photos; but never feed the animals! California's newest - and oldest - amusement park; Penitentiaryland. I'm sure it would make loads of money.

But my thinking has changed recently, I have a new neighbor. He's an old Italian guy, almost fifty, goes by Johnny, although he spells it crazy with a G and a couple of I's. He was transferred in from out-of-state, after catching some big time gang murder. Everyone back home wants him in a box for it. Of course, the cops are trying to get him to turn, he'll have none of it. So here he sits, far away from family and friends for his own safety; at least that's the excuse they're using. I don't ask about his case and he doesn't volunteer anything, but everything else under the sky is open game and we speak freely.

He's been living this lifestyle since he was fifteen years old, so even though it's all he knows, he's grown weary of it and his conversation reflects this. Like most people, convicts prefer to speak of anything but their own reality, and Johnny was no different. The guy really had his shit together. He's been a good distraction for me, it's been a long time since I've had someone like him to talk to, too long.

One morning I was walking by his cell and stopped to say hello. I found him sitting quietly in the dark, t.v. and radio off. He was perched on the edge of his bunk gurgoylelike, elbows planted on his knees, staring at the floor. The bold spot on his head, where fate was marking time strand by strand, was clearly visible. He suddenly looked very old. I stood quietly for a full minute, waiting for him to move, to notice me, my concern mounting with every tick. He never budged, simply sat stonelike.

"Hey Johnny, what's happening?" I heard my voice rise and crack as I tried to sound normal.

He looked up with deep set eyes, which seemed to have-sank overnight. They were completely empty, like no one was home. A quiet voice whispered its way out of his slack mouth, "nothing's happening... nothing ever happens, that's the problem. I can't watch t.v., can't read, can't get lost in my puzzles... all I have is this," he swept his hand around the cell to indicate his meaning.

I knew what he was talking about. You can only fool yourself so long with outside distractions, but the day inexorably comes when these pale and grow transparent, then all you're left with is a stark reality. People work hard to keep these moments of lucidity from rising and overwhelming them with their naked truth, but no amount of work can keep them at bay forever, and when you've really screwed your life up these moments are beyond brutal.

He needed help to take his mind off of it.

"Are you up for some cards? I'll see if I can get your door racked and we can play in the dayroom. That sound cool?"

I could see the gratitude carve itself into deep lines around his eyes. "Yeah, sure. I'll bring the coffee."

His eagerness was almost painful to see, I turned aside so there'd be no witness, and hoped when it was my turn I'd be shown the same courtesy.

I'd been coming back from work, so I grabbed a quick shower and then settled down to hot coffee and two-handed pinochle. He talked, I listened. He went quickly, jumping from topic to topic without rhyme or reason, only needing the fog of words to forget, they seemed to come of their own accord, erupting like a geyser and landing indiscriminately. I encouraged him in his efforts, as I knew firsthand that when the mask slips it needs to be righted, before it's too late.

We played for a couple hours, or at least pretended to while he talked himself out. The gunner told us time was up, we had to take it home because the yard was coming in. We walked back to our cells slowly, neither wanting to be locked in. He turned and stuck his hand out, as I shook it he started to say something and then stopped, I knew from the sudden pressure of his grip what he meant to say. As I let go, I said, "Happy Thanksgiving, brother."

"You too," he said, disappearing into his dark, empty cell.

I turned to see the first guys coming through the door. D'Man was in the lead, wearing his trademark grin and bouncing on the balls of his feet as he walked. Right on time. Johnny's mood was contagious, and I sure as hell didn't want to catch it.

"What did you bring me to eat?" he spat out.

No preface, no small talk, just straight to the important stuff. As I watched him wipe his shoes on the floor towel, then wash his hands, the familiarity of the movements let me slip willingly back into the mindlessness of habit. My shields were quickly back in place. "A bag of turkey, some stuffing, and six pieces of pumpkin pie. Somebody's coming up short on their tray tonight."

"That should just about cover my lunch."

"That slimy particle board furkey is all yours, but we're halving the rest." "What the hell is furkey?"

"Fake Turkey. I just made that up, how ya like it?"

He gave a sad little shake of his head, "it's a sorry sight to see how delusional you're getting in your old age. You better leave the wordsmithing to the pros and stick to what you're good at."

I knew he was setting me up, but I didn't mind being the straight man, "and what would that be?" I asked.

"Bringing me food and tattooing!"

"Yeah, well, Happy Thanksgiving to you, too, asshole!"

I filled him in on Johnny's being down and asked him to look out for him. D'Man had a knack for talking people back from the edge without their knowing; the guy has some crazy skill I'm not sure even he's aware of.

We skipped lunch because the woodpile was throwing a spread in the dayroom after dinner. We pounded a few cups of water and loaded up on the coffee, that would see us through until it was time to eat. D knocked on the wall and told Johnny the water was hot, the universal phrase for 'Fix a shot of mud.'

D'Man went to the door and struck up a conversation with Johnny. There was a thin concrete wall dividing our cell, the doors so close they were almost touching, and the fact that the entire door, from top to bottom, had thousands of holes just big enough to poke the tip of your pinkie through, making it look like a piece of steel Swiss cheese, made it easy to talk to your neighbor.

I listened to them go back and forth for a few minutes, with the coffee they'd drank, they would be rambling till dinner showed up. I grabbed a pen and some paper and sat down to write my mom a letter. Since we couldn't be together for holidays, this was our way of pretending. We would set aside time on that day and it was like spending it with each other. I don't know if it was supposed to make the separation easier or just let the other know you were thinking of them, but it somehow helped. The old maxim: time heals all wounds, has never proven true here, but when time is the wound, what can you expect. As the years rolled relentlessly by, filled with mistaken memories and what ifs, the letter writing grew increasingly difficult. But I pushed through with tradition and filled a few pages with falsehoods, telling the truth was out of the question.

Many years ago when I first came to prison I tried to let my family go, thinking I'd be doing them a favor, somehow sparing them. I told them to forget about me and go on with their lives. I thought I was being noble or honorable, or some other word invented to make you feel good about yourself. I figured a quick death would be easier than watching me rot away till I was little more than a walking corpse; or watch me serve twenty years only to be murdered by another con or shot by a skrew. I was wrong. If she could've, my mom would've ripped my ears off through the mail! I'd never seen her so angry before and I've not made that mistake since.

She used to say, God sent you only what you could handle, so he must think very highly of us. How does one argue with that kind of reasoning? I think I agree with that Wily Scotsman who said, "If there is a God, he is one of limited intelligence."

I finished my letter, then filled out a request to attend an NA class. Yeah, I surprised myself with that one, but Johnny's voice was persistent.

There's nothing longer or as seemingly neve-rending as a four day weekend in prison. Time in here naturally flows slower, the last thing it needs is an aid. Most times half the guards call in sick, so the prison is slammed for lack of staff. 96 hours of sitting around on your ass may sound like a small vacation to some, but believe me, here it's nothing more than a punishment. Everytime a door slides open or the jingling of keys is heard, heads snap around looking for the source. A voice would come floating down the tier and everyone yearned for contact with it. The only thing to do was rein yourself in as tight as possible and pray for Monday.

During this time D'Man and I took turns talking with Johnny, as we knew all this cell time was harder on him. We took our usual coffee breaks, the three of us getting wired and chopping it up. Everything seemed fine, I thought he had shaken off his funk and was back. But on the morning of the third day D'Man gave a knock and called out, "water's hot, Johnny." He got no reply. He knocked again and still nothing.

Johnny woke up earlier than any of us. He was up doing cardio at 4:30 every morning.

I told D to knock louder and he practically pounded a hole through the concrete. Still no response.

"Something's wrong," he said.

"Maybe he just slept in." As soon as the words left my mouth I knew they were false. "Bullshit! That old bastard never sleeps. I'm telling you, something is wrong."

He went back to beating on the wall and calling Johnny's name out, there was a fear in his voice I'd never heard before, he was close to panic I looked at the clock on the t.v. screen, it read ten till six, the skrews wouldn't be in with breakfast for another forty minutes. I didn't know what to do. If I called out for the skrews and nothing was wrong. I would look like a freakin' jackass. But as I watched D'Man's futility, I knew he was right. A sudden surge of urgency took hold of me, I went quickly to the cell door and pushed D'Man aside. I began to yell,

"Control, A section, man down!"... "Control, A section!"... "Control, A Section, man down!" No one answered.

Panic flooded me and I started kicking the door, each kick rang out like a shot and sent on echo racing around the deserted dayroom. An angry face appeared at the tower window, its voice booming out, "What the hell is going on?"

I wanted to kill him instantly. Sorry lazy S.O.B... "Man down in cell 102, Get somebody in here!"

I watched him squat down reluctantly and speak to the floor staff through an opening. About a minute later, the section door slid open and two skrews came plodding in, as disinterested in their work as beasts of burden. When they reached the front of Johnny's cell, one of them croaked out, "Oh shit!", and my stomach fell.

It's hard to recall exactly when the descent started and impossible to guess where it will end. The only known, is it won't be any place good.

When I showed up for work Monday morning, the new guy I'd helped to get hired was there, standing next to Snake waiting to be let in. I did know him, it was Buzz, the con who had killed his cellie and gotten away with it. It had seemed a small favor when asked, but I should've known better, there's no such thing as a small favor here. I opened my mouth before I thought; isn't that how the downfall always got its start, biting off more than you can chew?

Buzz and Snake were acting like long lost friends. They worked in the same section, ate lunch together, palled around all day laughing behind big fists. I'd never seen Snake work on someone this hard before, if Buzz had had a baby Snake would've been kissing it. It dawned on me what he was doing. He was recruiting Buzz to be a member of the Aryan Syndicate and I had helped. There was nothing I could say or do about it without divulging my own guilt, and as a new path was already lain before me, it was simpler to follow than to fight; so I did nothing.

An hour before quitting time I was walking around surveying the work areas, making sure they were cleaned up and put back to rights before everyone left. When I rounded a corner I almost ran into a knot of bodies. Snake, Buzz, and two others were huddled up whispering. As I interrupted, they turned as one and seemed ready to pounce. Snake stepped forward and extended his hand, "What's up, Stogie?"

I had never shaken hands with a convict before, it just wasn't done. But seemingly of its own accord my hand rose and slipped into his, effortlessly. I contemplated my traitorous hand, but my behavior no longer shocked me, I was growing accustomed to these strange new happenings. As we shook I could see the others sharing a knowing look, as if they were all in on the same secret.

"Not much. Just doing my final walk-through before taking my old ass home." Deprecation came easy around him.

"Shit Stogie, you ain't old. Besides, you know what they say about old violins." "Yeah, I know. But this violin is missing a few strings."

"Hell, ain't we all?" he said with a laugh. Everyone followed suit and soon we were all cutting it up pretty good. "I got something that'll make you feel ten years younger, guaranteed."

He motioned to one of his buddies who turned toward a desk in the corner, I noticed four cups surrounding what looked like a homemade pitcher. It was some kind of clear Tupperware that had been melted into an unnatural shape and it was filled with what looked to be water, but as I watched the con fill the cups I knew it was something much stronger.

"How did you get that back here?" I asked lamely.

Snake smiled and glanced around as if making sure we were alone, he really loved this act.

"We don't bring it, we make it here," he almost purred out. "With the kitchen, bakery, and paint shop all right here, who's gonna smell a little ol' bag of moonshine cooking?"

"If you guys get caught you'll be fired."

"Now, why would we get caught, nobody but us"... here he included me. "Knows about it and we sure as hell ain't saying anything."

He fisted two cups and thrust one toward me. Once again my hand acted of its own volition. I found myself holding a cup of homemade prison hooch, surrounded by killers, while Snake made a toast to friendship and loyalty. I took a healthy slug and teared up as it burned its way to my middle and through reality. I finished off the contents in hurried gulps, much to everyone's surprise. They didn't know that I 'self-medicated' daily and their moonshine was nothing more than a wake-me-up.

I felt like I was watching myself from a distance, my words and actions controlled by someone else, someone who had very different plans for me.

Snake's voice cut in, "we shared with you, maybe next time you'll share with us, huh?"

So they did know.

"We'll see what happens." I answered noncommittally.

"Good enough," he said while handing me another cup. "Go ahead and get you another pull before we split."

The rest of the day I thought about what I'd done, and how it felt normal to be drinking with them. I didn't know what it meant or what it might lead to, but for the first time in ages I felt comfortable in my own skin, it was no longer constricting. As I made my nightly run to the liquor store. I grabbed two fifths instead of one and felt no different for it.

I sat on the toilet at the front of the cell and stared out the door. D'Man was standing by my side, neither of us spoke. The skrews were gathered into small groups all along the tier and into the dayroom, they were talking and laughing, I guess it's what passed for morgue humor.

Nobody feels at ease around a dead body. I understood the need to defuse the tension, but the disrespect was gawking.

They finally got his body cut down and four skrews managed to manhandle him up onto a rolling gurney that was parked between our two cells. As they laid him down his head lolled towards me, there was a braided piece of sheet still noosed around his neck, it was dug into the skin so deeply I could only see parts of it. The end. Where the guard had sawn through was frayed and began to unravel; a slow imitation of his life. His dead eyes looked directly into me. They had bulged so much the eyelids and sockets couldn't contain them. His visage had turned a white I had only read about, with the exception of his lips, which were a dark bruised purple. Now I comprehended the horror of the 'whiteness of the whale'. It is the cornerstone of every foundation, the beginning of every palette; yet, it was nothing. As I looked at him, I wondered why death had to be made so repulsive? Is it so we fear it more than natural? Is that even possible?

A handful of medical staff milled around as they had nothing else to do, the situation had progressed far beyond their limited skills. The prison shrink was going from group to group speaking quietly, lying a reassuring hand on the occasional shoulder for comfort. Next he walked from cell to cell asking if everyone was okay.

A few years back the court mandated that mental health care be brought up to current standards within the prison system, as there are more than a few crazies in here. Drug abuse and physical abuse take their toll in the body's soft spot. Since the ruling a shrink walks the tiers every two weeks, zooming by without a word. I guess he believes those needing help will holler up when the time comes, he doesn't realize that for those who really need it it's already too late.

When he made his way to our door, D and I were in the same positions we had held all morning, to move seemed sacrilegious. Johnny's body had been taken away, so he stood directly in front of our door and asked in his practiced rate, "are you gentlemen okay?"

This is his contribution to the prison, correct grammar. As if calling a pile of dung a rose would make it so; that believes perception can be changed by mere words.

"Do you really care?" I asked.

He looked incredulous, or at least attempted to. "Of course I care. That's why I'm here."

I let the silence stretch between us, it helped to calm me. "What was his name?"

"Excuse me?"

"I said, what was his name?"

He looked at the folder in his hands nervously, then glanced around for backup. "Uh; I'm not sure... maybe you could help me with that."

"That's what I thought. If you care so much, where were you when he needed help?" I had meant the question like a blow and hoped it would have a like effect, but he wasn't taken aback at all. I guess the first thing he learned was there's no guilt in the failure of your job. He had obviously taken that lesson to heart.

"Do you know something you'd like to share?"

"No thank you." I stood and turned the light off, then moved into the darkness.

Shocked at his dismissal, it took him a moment to recover. He said into the dark, "If you need to talk you can send for me." With that he moved on to continue dispensing his medical magic.

On Monday morning I was called out to attend an NA meeting. The weekend was over and forgotten in haste, there wasn't even a mention of Johnny, it was as if he'd never been. The whites wouldn't speak of him as he was one of theirs and his perceived weakness was an embarrassment. The other races scrupulously avoided the whites, they didn't want to precipitate an incident and go right back on lockdown. This was another of those unwritten rules which everyone followed.

"Why in the hell are you going to a drug meeting?" He was instantly suspicious. "Hopefully to learn something."

"All drug addicts are scum. There, now you're up to speed, so you can just go to the yard and workout with me." I didn't answer, so he went on. "This is bullshit, you don't even do drugs! You have something planned, don't you?"

"How many times do I have to tell you, I'm not going anywhere without you. Stop acting like a jealous girlfriend. I'm going over there to learn something, and you don't have to be a drug addict to go to an NA meeting."

I could tell he wasn't fully convinced by my answer at all. It took alot of patience to be D'Man's friend, but knowing his past, I was willing to make the effort. When he was a child his family had left, one at a time till no one remained and he was alone. So his lack of trust, even among friends, was understandable.

I threw him a bone, "if you want to go with me, let's go. But don't get bored and walk out and don't do anything stupid, like jump on some lame. I'd hate to end up in the hole for beating up the entire NA class!"

He looked me over through narrowed eyes trying to discern the truth, but the invitation had its desired effect. Finally he shook his head and said, "as fun as that sounds, I think I'll pass."

"Okay then, I'll see you here after yard. Whoever gets back first has to get lunch going, deal? And don't be slow dragging just so you don't have to cook."

He tried to look shocked at the accusation, "how dare you!" he couldn't even finish before he started laughing, "Yeah, okay."

We left the cell together but parted as we hit the yard, I headed to the education department and D went to the white's tables. I greeted those I knew along the way and kept an eye on those I didn't. Some nodded in turn, while others merely blinked, too practiced in caution to let association be known. I played along.

When I entered the room where the meeting was being held, I wasn't surprised by those already there. Most of them were guys hiding out, trying to stay off the yard in hopes of not being assaulted. They never went to dayroom or socialized beyond the circle. They came to yard once a month to collect their canteen. Then quickly disappeared back into their cells, breath held in expectation of safety.

A few looked up at me with recognition and nervously nugged their neighbors. As more eyes found me I could see fear light them from within. Maybe this wasn't such a good idea. Luckily, the free staff running the meeting had no idea who I was, she smiled and welcomed me. She handed me a clipboard asking me to sign in, then grab a chair in the circle. As I sat, those already there slowly edged away from me gathering on the opposite side of the small room. This didn't go unnoticed.

More inmates filed into the room, till eventually the circle was filled in. At 9:30 the meeting began, the woman conducting the meeting came and sat beside me, as the chairs on either side were empty.

"My name is Miss Mitleid, but you can call me Mary. I'll be your instructor in this course. I'm glad so many of you showed up, hopefully we can help each other." She glanced down at a clipboard in her lap and scanned a few pages. "What I'd like us to do first is go around the circle, everyone introduce themselves and give a quick synopsis of how drugs and drug abuse have affected your lives. Does that sound okay?"

There was a general assent and the first guy stood and started babbling about how nothing was his fault, it was the drugs that did all those horrible things, life just wasn't fair. I tuned him out and looked around the room. A skrew was standing at the door staring at me through the glass panes, as our eyes met and held a knowing grin spread across his face; he thought he had it all figured out. I turned and caught Miss Mitleid watching us both, she quickly looked away.

I ignored the skrew and kept my attention on Mary. She was very young and somewhat pretty in a tomboy kind of way. She was as tall as an average man, but painfully thin. She wore her hair pulled back into a ponytail high on her head like a young girl, it gave her an almost childish look. There were ink stains on her hands attesting to her vigilance, and an eagerness in her eyes showing her desire to help. Yet, I don't think she had the slightest idea of just who the men who sat around her were, what they were made of, and their true reasons for being here.

I fought the urge to leave as the sniveling droned on and on, but something held me in place, maybe the memory of Johnny. My turn to speak finally came without my realizing it.

"Mr. Allen, we're waiting on you," even her voice was young. She reached out and placed her hand on my forearm; it was cool and dry and sent a warm tingle racing up my arm. I stood abruptly.

"My name is Teach... Michael. I don't have a drug problem. I've never used them." I sat down.

Mary looked confused.

"Michael, you don't have to hide anything here, you're among friends. Feel free to speak openly."

"Okay."

She sat waiting for me to go on, but I remained quiet. She voiced the question that everyone in the room was thinking.

"If you don't have a drug problem, then why have you come to this meeting?"

I thought about it for a minute and wasn't sure myself. I gave her an answer I thought plausible, which was the only answer I had.

I turned in my chair to face her, "You teach people how to function without the aid of drugs, to discard their faulty thought process and learn to solve problems through logical thinking, right?" I didn't wait for an answer, but forged on. "I thought there might be something worth learning, that I could apply to other areas in life. I don't really know what I'm looking for, but I don't want to chance that what I'm seeking is hidden somewhere or in something that I simply passed up."

I didn't like having to explain myself in front of these 'inmates', but even as I had been giving her my answer I knew that it was fundamentally true and that I wanted to stay. I watched her eyes following the scars on my face, trying to relive the journey that had given them birth. I didn't need or want anyone's pity. I stood to leave, "maybe this isn't the place I thought it was, thanks for your time."

She popped up before I could turn, spilling her clipboard to the ground. She touched my arm again, this time gripping it tightly, the warm sensation spread. "Please, Michael, sit down. I didn't mean to suggest you had to leave. You're more than welcome to sit through the meetings, perhaps you'll get lucky and find what you're looking for, okay?"

"Okay."

XV

"So, what did you learn today?"

Here we go again. I had just come back from another meeting and he was gonna have his fun. I grunted in response, hoping he'd leave off. I should've known better, once D'Man gets his teeth into something there's no shaking him loose.

"Come on, you've been over there three times now and I know it ain't for the company."

That was an understatement if there ever was one. After the first meeting they figured I hadn't come to kill any of them, so they went back to what I assume was their normal routine, and let me tell you, it was an ugly thing to behold. They blamed their moms and dads, brothers and sisters, friends, dealers, anyone and everyone for their drug use, excluding themselves of course. Some would tear up and wouldn't be able to speak. Mary would sit holding their hands, softly talking them through, telling them it wasn't their fault, it was the disease's fault; it was quite a show.

I knew there was nothing for me to learn here, at least nothing useful. I had almost decided not to come back, then I really noticed Mary. No matter how petty or transparent, she would listen willingly and try to help with whatever problem was presented to her. I no longer listened to the inmate's lies, as they would say anything to hold on to the safety and security of this room. In the beginning I wanted to let loose with some beserker rage and see if I could take them all, but I quickly overcame that urge and settled in to study Miss Mitleid.

I couldn't understand what drove her. In the face of obvious lies, she still felt the need to give succor. Was it because she was a woman and more inclined to be sympathetic? That seemed too simple of an answer, a lazy man's answer. She was much too smart not to be aware of the lies. Perhaps, she was feigning ignorance in order to keep them talking, hoping they would reveal more as they went on. I didn't know, but there was something compelling about her. Everyone wants to change or change someone they know for the better, whether they know it or not; yet, this compulsion is usually driven by selfish reasons, but in her the opposite seemed true.

Once again D-Man's voice broke in, "Maybe you and that cute little teacher got something going, huh?"

I had to laugh at that one, as I knew I looked a poor imitation of her monster. Besides, I had long ago forfeited the right to anything of the kind.

"Yeah that's it, she has a monster fetish."

"Now we're getting somewhere. Keep going, I want to hear it all." He was warming up now.

"You know damn well there's nothing to tell. I've learned more than I care to about those inmates though, a sorrier pile of crap I've never seen. Hell, we know who needs that class, it's the guys out here slinging all the dope, but those morons need a Cowards Anonymous class! they were gangsters and killers on the outside, but now that they're locked up with the real thing they've had a sudden change of heart."

"If it's so miserable, why are you still going?" "For her."

He grinned salaciously.

"It's not what your dirty mind is thinking. There's something to be learned from her, but I'm not yet sure what it is. Plus, I feel sorry for her, sitting in that room surrounded by garbage."

D knew when I was serious and would either let it go or change the subject to something light. The latter is just what he did.

"We got a new wood down the tier, moved in with old man Joe. I'll give you my last candy bar, if you can guess his name, but if you don't get it, then you owe me, bet?"

"Alright, bet. But on two conditions, I get three guesses and one hint." "Okay, you're on. What's the hint?"

"Is it his real name or a nickname?"

"Damn, you're a cheater! But that's okay, cause you'll never got it anyway. It's his real name."

"Let me think about it for a while."

"You got fifteen minutes, then that candy bar is mine."

He's probably gonna be eating one of my candy bars, because D never bets unless he's confident of winning. That's a result of doing without his entire life.

I thought of ol' Joe. He's an 85 year old convict, doing life for double murder. He committed his crime when he was 75, you don't see that much in here, it's mainly a place where you start out young and grow old quick; the physical outpacing the mental. Joe has Alzheimers. Some days he wakes up unaware of what he's done and where he's housed. He wants to know why he can't walk out into his garden whenever he'd like. On these days he fusses and yells alot, then settles back to whimper like a child. The cons and skrews alike look out for him. Whoever this new cellie was, I felt for him as he was gonna have his hands full.

Joe's case read like a bad tragedy. Two repo-men came to his house to take his truck back to the lot because he had missed his last three payments and hadn't responded to the mailed warnings. When he looked out his front window and saw two strangers climbing into his truck, he made a natural assumption, they were stealing it. So he grabbed one of his many guns, a 357 magnum, marched down the front steps right up to the truck and opened fire. The two men were waving frantically, trying to explain that they were only doing their job, but it was too late, no one can outtalk a gun.

When the police searched his house they found fourteen envelopes sitting atop his television, addressed, with stamps affixed. Most contained letters to his family, the oldest going back six months. Among them were three envelopes containing his monthly payment to the car lot. He hadn't forgotten to pay, only to mail them. He was given 50 to life, which is a death sentence at any age. Justice strikes again.

"Alright, time's up. Let's hear it." D-Man said from across the cell.

"You know, even if I win you're gonna eat one of my candy bars. So why don't you just tell me the answer while we dig in?"

"Hell no! You're not gonna take the fun out of this for me, nice try though. Now let's go."

I hadn't given the name any thought, I'd been too busy thinking of Joe. "Okay. How about Cleotis?"

"Strike one." "Jaydn?"

"Jaydn! What the hell is that? It's not even a name. That's strike two, one shot left, better make it good."

"I heard it on t.v., some made up Hollywood crap. Alright, how about Demarquan?" We both burst out laughing.

"I wish that was his name, then we could take turns beating the crap out of him without feeling guilty." D-Man finally said. "You're not gonna believe his real name, it's Freakin' Shelley! He said his parents were expecting a girl and already had the name picked out, so when a boy popped out his dad refused to change it, he liked it too much, that's some tough luck, huh?"

"Yeah, that's pretty rough. I bet he can fight his ass off though."

D was still laughing. "Oh man, it gets better. He's only eighteen, 5'3, and a hundred pounds soaking wet. He looks like an ugly little girl!"

That set us off for another five minutes.

After regaining some composure, I grabbed a couple of candy bars for us. "Man, talk about getting the short end of the stick."

"Oh, he got it alright, got pummeled by it! But I talked to him on the yard about Joe's situation and the kid seemed pretty cool. So I don't think there's anything to worry about there."

I find that I fit right in. I should be disturbed by that revelation, instead I'm relieved. I have found those that I got along with and even enjoy being around, but more importantly, they feel the same of me. It seems a homecoming of sorts.

My daily alcohol intake has gone up considerably since I've begun taking my lunches with Snake and Buzz. I bring a fifth in my thermos and we lounge around pounding shots as if we hadn't a care in the world, and right now we don't. I tried to get them to sip it, but that rubbed them the wrong way. Buzz said that was for gentlemen, with a heavy emphasis on gentle.

Snake helped pay the tab. He had given me a few hundred and promised more as soon as he worked out a few kinks, he wouldn't say what those were and I didn't ask. But I didn't mind pitching in, as I was drinking my share and probably more.

During these lunches the conversation varied little, their interests and vocabularies were as narrow and confined as their world, but as my own was nothing to brag about, I found I wasn't pushed aside as usual. They would see new types or whiskies in magazines and ask me to bring them in, we were drinking something different practically everyday. Even the guy at the liquor store commented on it, he had taken to calling me Mr. International.

As lunchtime rolled around, I was making my way to our regular spot, Snake, Buzz, and Jimmy V were already there, doing their best to look suspicious as hell; it must've been in their genes. I pulled up short as I heard his name, it had been quite awhile since I thought about Teacher. I leaned against the wall all ears.

Jimmy V was another friend of Snakes, I didn't care for him, the V was short for violence and he had more than earned the handle. He was doing LWOP, life without the possibility of parole for killing two state witnesses in a drug case, with his bare hands.

"We know neither of you can get over there, but I'm clean, I'm not associated with anybody. I say we get me a job over there and I'll take care of your problem."

I recognized Jimmy's voice, it was always tinged with an eagerness to please.

"That's not how things work around here. You don't do the saying, I do." Snake always made sure to remind everyone that he was the top dog in this cage. "Listen up, we're only gonna get one shot at him, and when that time comes the job has to be done right. I don't just want him stabbed or sliced up, I want him fuckin' buried, understand?"

"You don't think I can get the job done?" Jimmy V asked.

"That doesn't matter. The only thing that matters is he gets dead! If that means putting three, four, or even five guys on him, then that's what I'm gonna do."

I could see him getting worked up just speaking and didn't think introducing alcohol at this point would help the situation. I decided to leave when he started speaking again, and no matter what I ordered my feet wouldn't move.

"If you want the truth, here it is, I know for a fact that you couldn't handle him. You've never seen the guy, never been there when he's in motion, never seen him work. The guy is a flat out beast. He never panics and he never plays. I've seen him attack and be attacked, there's no difference; he is always the aggressor. He doesn't just try to defend himself, he puts the person down as quickly and brutally as possible; like a mercy killing for a wounded animal. Me and Buzz were there when he treated Bull like a side of beef at a butchers market. He stood toe to toe with a guy almost twice his size and used him like a pincushion, and look at Bull now, he's fucking worthless. Better had he died than to have lost his nerve!" Snake went quiet for a moment letting all this sink in, then continued, "so maybe you could or maybe you couldn't deal with him, I'm not concerned either way, but I won't take the chance that he walks away again, you got it?"

Buzz must've noticed me eavesdropping, because he got Snake's attention and nodded his head in my direction. Snake immediately spoke up, "come on in, Stogie, we ain't saying nothing that you can't hear."

I couldn't walk away now pretending I was never there, so I took a deep breath and stepped in. I held up the thermos in front of me almost like a shield, "I brought lunch."

I didn't know if I should feel flattered or frightened that he didn't try to hide their conversation from me. As we sat there drinking our lunch, it amazed me how easily and deeply I had sunk into this company. I felt

I should have some regrets or a tinge of conscience, but where warning bells should have been sounding there was nothing but contentment.

"Hey Stogie, I need to talk with you before the day's over," Snake said. "How about now?"

"No, in private."

"Alright. After lunch come over to my desk, everyone will be back to work." "Right."

As we finished off our lunch, Jimmy V was telling war stories, every time he came to a part where he was stabbing someone Buzz would explode with laughter, braying like a donkey. I found myself laughing along just as loud. Jimmy relished the attention and became much more animated, talking faster and louder, standing so he could reenact the grisly scenes. In the middle of one story I glanced over at Snake and caught him staring at me, instead of looking away he smiled a wide, slow smile, which failed to penetrate my liquor haze. I briefly wondered what it was he wanted to talk about, but quickly gave over, whatever it was would probably be good for all of us.

That night in the dayroom I met Shelley. D-Man hadn't been exaggerating when he'd described him. The poor kid was everything D had said and more. When I first laid eyes on him I almost burst out laughing, as his ears and head looked to be doing battle for dominance. I'd have to say at that moment it was a tie. He must've known he had this effect on people, because he wore a permanent don't-mess-with-me-scowl, but on someone of his stature it only added to the comedic effect.

D-Man had made a good impression, because Shelley nearly attached himself to him. He shadowed his every step, bouncing around at his feet like a pup looking for attention. The tables had turned, now D would feel the weight or responsibility firsthand. I was gonna make sure he knew Shelley's schooling was all him. The fact that he was housed around us would make things a lot easier.

"So how are you and the old man getting along?" I asked him.

"We're good. He bosses me around, but that's cool, reminds me of my grandad. Plus, he takes like five naps a day, so I have the cell to myself, mostly."

"Yeah, Joe's good for that. You know D-Man is gonna put you on a study program soon, are you ready for that?"

"Not really. I never was much good in school and I doubt I've gotten any better, but I told him I'd try."

I liked this kid, he was real. Too many try to be something they're not when those prison gates shut behind them. That way lies heartache.

"You and me both. But you'll find out we don't study like in school, we learn what we need to survive in here, and more importantly, what we need to make it on the outside. Don't sweat it, D-Man knows what he's doing, and he'll help you through."

"He told me pretty much the same thing."

"Do you and Joe have everything you need, food, coffee, cosmetics?"

"Yeah. Everyone looked out pretty good, especially D-Man. He brought us a whole bag of stuff."

I smiled inwardly. The kid had already found D-Man's soft spot and D was hiding it from me so I wouldn't ride him. We'll see about that.

"Alright. But whenever you two run low just get at us."

Later that night, back in our cell, D and I talked about Shelley. He didn't need any encouragement in taking Shelley under his wing, in fact, he had basically laid claim to him already, warning off a few old gangsters. That was news to me. I would have to keep my eyes open and hands ready; it's funny, the further you try to get away from something the more it becomes a part of you. We were going to preach to this kid about following the rules and becoming a better man, all the while protecting him and ourselves with that very violence we were warning against. I wonder if there are exceptions to being branded a hypocrite; if there are ways of avoiding consequences when ones' intentions are true; or is this just hope giving self-delusions?

"Are you ready to pull an all-nighter and get some work done?" I held up the tattoo gun as I asked.

"We don't have any patterns hooked up, do we?" "I have one."

I placed the gun on the table and reached for my art folder, inside was three pieces of white paper taped together, making one huge sheet. On it lay my last month's worth of work. I unfolded it and handed it to him.

"Holy crap! When did you draw this?"

"I've been working on it off and on for the past month. Whenever you were gone." "It's freakin' awesome! But I don't have anyplace to put it. The only bare skin I have left is my lower back and this is way too big."

I stayed quiet and let him work it out. It finally dawned on him, he snapped his head toward me. "This is for you, isn't it? After all these years. You're finally gonna let me ink on you. So what changed your mind?"

I'd asked myself that very question. I've been here for 21 years and have never felt the need for a tattoo, but it struck me like a bolt one day. I could pay homage to my greatest desire, the one thing I'd never have; freedom.

"I like the symbolism."

He was excited, "You better get some coffee started, this is gonna take a long, long time. Man, you've already got it dittoed up and ready to roll. You've been planning this, haven't you? Nevermind, it doesn't matter. As soon as they clear count and roll the bar we're getting to work."

And that's exactly what we did. It took six and a half hours with a few coffee breaks thrown in, but we finished and had the equipment cleaned and put away by four in the morning.

"No use going to bed now, I have to be at work in forty five minutes." I said. I couldn't lie down anyway, my back felt like a blanket of fire.

"Sleep's overrated. Turn around so I can admire my handiwork."

I did as instructed, I was too tired to argue. From the moment he'd finished he'd been going on and on how he was the new Michelangelo, I couldn't dispute it, he'd done an incredible job. I had to stand with my back facing the mirror above the sink, holding a homemade handheld mirror over my shoulder so I could get the full effect. It was more beautiful than I had imagined.

From the tips of both shoulders, spreading across the wide plain of my upper back, stretched an eagle in full flight. His head rested on the nape of my neck, beak unhinged in the act of screaming defiance. His talons punched from the center of my back, grasping for that elusive thing which we all seek. His feathers looked as if they were ruffling in the breeze, stretched to their fullest, giving maximum effort and wanting nothing less.

I couldn't peel my eyes from it, neither could D. It was exactly what I'd wanted and D-man had delivered.

"Thank you, brother."

"No sweat. I got a lot more inking to do before we're even. I'm just glad to be able."

We weren't going to be doing anymore, I had what I wanted and was done, but I wouldn't tell him that now, he was too happy.

As I listened to Snake pitch his idea, which came as no surprise, my mind drifted, touching on images and happenings from my past. I tried to connect the dots, hoping to pave a road that led me to my current place. I guess, I wanted to see the why of it or maybe I was only looking for excuses. For mitigating evidence. Everyone was always searching for the easy way out, and I discovered I was no exception. I needed someone or something to blame. Yet, secretly I knew, if I were given the chance to do it over again, the outcome would be the same. So maybe instead of blame, I owed thanks.

Helluva place for contemplation, a fold-up desk in a prison work area, drunk off my ass. I can't imagine this is where I do my best thinking.

Snake was rattling away, expending a lot of effort to convince me to go along with his plan. It was wasted effort, as he already knew my answer, or should have. You don't ask somebody to do that, unless you know the answer in advance.

"You can save your breath, I'll do it."

He looked like he'd just won the lottery. For a second, I thought he was going to jump over the desk and hug me, instead he took a few deep breaths and plunged ahead.

"Stogie, we're gonna make so much money and so freakin' easy, it's almost a joke. The risk to you is nonexistent. If anyone gets popped, it will be my guys on the yard selling it and none of them knows where it comes from, so we're all safe up here at the top. We can keep it at once a month or double it up, it depends on how much money you want to make, and I've never met a man who wants to make less. I can move as much as you're willing to bring in."

"Let's stick to the plan and keep it at once a month for a while, if all goes well we can always up it. Give me the contact info so I can get it done tonight."

Snake wrote a name and phone number on a dog-eared piece of paper and slid it across to me. It sat in the middle of my desk, bent edges pointing toward me like accusing fingers. I crushed it deep into a fist, squelching any protest that might have been made.

I napped through the rest of the workday, then gathered my stuff to leave. On the long walk to my car I had to pass through a few security checkpoints along with many of my fellow guards. I nodded and waved to those I knew, shared small talk and the usual jokes. Strange, I was still playing my role perfectly and everyone believed me to be the same, I even felt the same. Somehow, I thought the change would be discernable to the point of obviousness, but it was my secret, and mine alone.

This was an unexpected bonus. I could come and go between different worlds, ghosting through as if I belonged, yet not having to follow the rules of either. It was all so easy.

I stopped at a pay phone to place the call, as I didn't want to do it from home, no reason to take unnecessary chances. I pulled the paper out of my pocket and smoothed it on the pane of glass enclosing the phone. As I dialed I read the name scrawled on the bottom, Animal. That sounded promising. I hung up after ten rings, waited a minute, then tried again. On the sixth ring a voice came growling out of the earpiece.

"This better be fucking good!"

I hesitated for a moment, wondering if I should just hang up and walk away, then decided it was too late for that.

"This is Stogie. Snake gave me your name."

"Well, Goddamn me. I thought he was blowing hot air, but here you are. So, what's the deal?"

How things change. This prison gangmember was asking me for instructions, awaiting orders. I cautiously wondered if that made me a member, too. I had to push down a surge of excitement at that thought, but promised myself to explore it later, and maybe even speak to Snake about it.

"One pound, broke down and packaged into one and two gram increments. That's easier for me to carry and easier for Snake to sell. Also, bring the addresses for a couple of drop-boxes. He's going to do most of the sales in cash, but some will have to be mailouts. They have to be clean and untraceable to us."

"Already covered. Where and when?" "Do you know this area?"

"Yeah. I'm only ninety miles away, I can be there in under two hours."

That was a little disconcerting. I hadn't expected things to move so quickly or easily. I'm used to cons talking big and producing little; in an effort to escape their impotency, most live in a fantasy world built of self-deceiving lies. It was one thing to deal with cons in a prison setting, where there was some measure of security, but to come face to face on the outside with no backup, no alarms, no weapons, was an entirely different thing.

There was an old fear nestled deep, which woke filled with anticipation. The attraction one feels toward fear is primal; there's no reasoning with it, no logic to unblind it, it's drawn to its source like the pull of a tide. You don't deny it, but simply follow and hope to survive.

"There's a laundromat on the corner of fourth and the Boulevard. It sits behind a gas station, out of the way of prying eyes. I'll be there tomorrow night at 7:30. How will I recognize you?"

He laughed. "Don't worry about that, Stogie. I know you. See you then." He hung up. On my drive home I could still hear his laughter. I consoled myself with the belief that it wasn't mocking, not really; but I've become fairly adept at lying, so I'm having trouble buying it.

XVI

Everywhere I went D-man would show up with someone and tell me to take my shirt off. It had been a month and instead of tiring, his strutting and preening had only grown. It didn't help that with every showing he was showered with praise. Cons telling him how great he was, begging to get even a small piece of his work. They were willing to pay top dollar and he was more than willing to take it. His next few months were booked up solid. It had taken quite awhile, but I was glad to see he finally got a hustle going, no more being dependant on someone else.

I grew fed up and refused to show it anymore, but he was waiting for that with a time tested solution, which I'm embarrassed to admit worked, he resorted to flattery. One day while doing bar work on the yard, he told me my eagle looked like it was in flight when I did pullups. I was secretly pleased with the picture that presented and found myself on the bars more frequently. Like I said before, he's a lot smarter than he lets on. So before I knew what happened he had me stripping my shirt off again, I was his walking, talking, business card.

I was on my way to another NA meeting, even though I was running out of questions and finding no answers. If there were none to be found here, I'd have to move on and search elsewhere. What makes this so difficult is I'm not sure what I'm looking for, and in that ignorance I might overlook it even if it presents itself.

As I entered the room all the same blank faces were there staring back with no curiousity, no questions, no imaginings. They might as well have been part of the room. If I wasn't careful I might start feeling sorry for these losers.

Mary sat in her usual spot, busy with her notes, always busy. Was she really that driven or was she covering for something? She wore no ring and seemed too young and career driven to have children. Perhaps all this compassion she showed was the flexing of her maternal muscle, kind of like the practice before the real thing, maybe this real thing was what she is hiding from.

She looked up and smiled, "hello, Michael." "Hello, Miss Mitleid."

"Mary, just Mary. As usual you're the last one to arrive, so lets get started, shall we?"

I didn't know if she was peeved or just stating a fact. I took my usual spot and said nothing.

"Today we're going to do something different. I want all of you to imagine how your lives would be if you had never been introduced to drugs. For the next fifteen minutes I want you to think of your families, your jobs, your futures. Use all the information we've gone over these last few months and try to build an alternate reality; one in which you never came to jail, never hit your wife or child, never lost sight of what was important. Plant it firmly in your mind just as if it were true. Does everyone understand?" She looked around at the nodding heads and wordless mouths. "Okay, let's give it a try."

She glanced at me, "Michael, do you need a different exercise?" "No, thank you."

At her questioning look, I said, "I'll just use a substitute."

She nodded her agreement and went back to her notes. She seemed almost afraid to be away from them, even while speaking, her hands constantly fingered them, as if to be reassured by their presence.

I played along with her experiment, but instead of drugs, the thing I subtracted from my life was violence. I went back to before I came to prison, to before I had killed, and realized that even then I'd been surrounded by violence. Although, I had never participated in it until that fated day.

I killed a child molestor, or at least, a man I assumed was one. Even now, I felt morally justified in my actions and was giving myself a convincing speech about it and all the violence that followed, as if one were related to the other and could be excused for that reason. Every stabbing or beating I'd perpetrated was trying to ride those same coattails, but this exercise was to imagine your life without that handicap, not make excuses for it.

I tried again, this time excluding violence altogether. I could see myself giving support to family in times of need; having a wife who loved me and children whom my mother could spoil, and who could in turn divert her thoughts away from her losses; family events filled with happiness and the usual good-natured bickering, no awkward silence as someone questions the presence of an empty chair; being an integral part in the lives of others, a part that were it missing would be missed.

I stopped suddenly and looked around, there was an alarm pounding in my head, warning me to stop. I've spent 21 years ruthlessly suppressing hope, and this one innocent game had brought its greedy head rearing up demanding more. I could already feel it feeding. I couldn't do this. I rose and made my way to the door, blind to what was around me. I heard Mary's voice chasing me out the door and down the hall, I ignored it. I needed to be outdoors among convicts, I needed to forget.

I hit the yard at a run and breathed deeply. The air was thick with fear, hate, and desperation; I was shamed to realize these were what I needed, these were the things which had kept me sane all these years, that kept me forgetful. To tell yourself there is no hope of ever leaving this place alive is a harsh truth, but worse by far is to let even the tiniest trickle of hope in, and stand by helplessly as it consumes you. I had gone to Mary for help and instead had been ambushed and ripped open.

I was sitting alone in a laundromat waiting for a drug dealer; when things change they really change. There were only two others present, an old woman who was muttering to herself as she counted her small stack of coins over and over and a middle aged man who was an obvious bachelor as even the clothes he wore were dirty; a married man would never get away with that. He kept cutting his eyes toward me, wanting to strike up a conversation to relieve the boredom, but laundromats are no place to make friends, it's where you ignore others hoping they'll return the favor.

I'd been sitting in the same spot for 45 minutes, and just when I started growing nervous a face materialized at the window and beckoned me with its eyes. Well, here goes nothing, I thought. I walked into the parking lot and saw him in the far corner, climbing into a nondescript truck.

As I neared, he indicated I should get into the passenger's side, which I did. I looked him over, thinking I would recognize him as one of the ex-cons from the prison, but I'd never seen him before, although he did fit the profile. He was big and muscular, tattoos covered all his exposed skin excluding his face, which was home to a large, bushy blond goatee. His hair was long and oily, pulled into a ponytail which fell to the middle of his back.

He gave me a knowing smile, which said he knew exactly what I was thinking, then he opened his mouth and lent it proof.

"No, you don't know me." His words floated out or putrid breath, maybe that's where he got his nickname, I thought. "No worries though, I know you. I've been keeping an eye on you for a while now, and I'm satisfied we can do business safely."

It struck me suddenly, this man, this stranger, knew everything about me, where I lived, worked, my family, he could've easily killed me any time he wanted and still could, but they needed me, they had plans for me. I wondered how long this had been going on, this surveillance, but decided not to ask. Obviously, I was more important alive than dead and that is always a reassuring thought, as well as very satisfying.

He lowered the armrest in the middle of the seat and a large Ziploc baggie came tumbling out to rest against my thigh. I stared at it, not knowing what came next.

"That's yours, take it. It's all there, packaged like you wanted. The addresses, too.

Give me a call when and where to pick up the money and to drop off the next load."

I nodded and grabbed the bag, placing it inside my coat. I was surprised at how small it was.

He started the truck and stared at me. I took the cue and quickly exited. He backed up then stopped to put the truck in drive, but before he did he leaned across the seat and rolled down the passenger window, "by the way, Stogie, that's a good looking family you have. Make sure you take care of them, ya hear?"

As I watched him drive away I wanted to laugh, he didn't know me as well as he thought or he would have known that I'd lost them long ago, so his threat was empty. I've never been the loving husband or doting father and recently that has never been more true. My family sensed that lack of familial connection and pulled away to live their own lives, and I willingly watched them go. It's uncomfortable to live in the same house with complete strangers, you never get past that awkward stage where you tiptoe around on your best behavior, excuse me and thank you the most frequent words in your vocabulary. Finally, the threat had no punch because I had no idea of deviating from our plans; I was exactly where I wanted to be, doing exactly what I wanted to do.

When I brought the drugs to Snake the following day I carried them in my lunch container, packed like a sandwich. I didn't need to be so cautious, I was simply having fun with the cloak and dagger bit. For a guard, walking in and out of the prison with whatever you wanted is a simple affair, no one ever suspects their own, that's too much like questioning yourself. It's not till it's too late people say, "he was always a good neighbor... but oddly quiet"; blind faith, a badmans most useful ally.

As Snake eyed his cache, his hands trembled ever so slightly, he'd never had a hold of this quantity in prison. I had opened a whole new world of possibility to him and I could feel the power which that gave me, I wouldn't have to ask about my position, I would dictate it. He had given me something, too, and when I inspected it closely I saw five one hundred dollar bills rolled so tightly that they were skinnier than a straw. He always caught me off guard with the ease and amount of money he had.

He must've seen the look on my face, because he said, "that's yours. And every shipment you bring in you'll get the same. You can make thousands if you want, we all can."

"Thanks," I said lamely.

"No need for that, Stogie. You're one of us now."

I reached out and shook his hand. Buzz and Jimmy V were quick to follow suit, soon we were shaking hands all around laughing about our good fortune.

Snake was not averse to sampling his own product, almost before I knew what he was doing he had opened one of the small baggies and dumped its contents onto a piece of paper. There was a pile of white powder which seemed to catch the light and send its reflections menacingly through the room, in some strange attempt at warning; a message as clear as the bright colors on poisonous animals. I glanced at the faces around me and saw the want and need clearly defined, it was practically etched into their faces. Here was the weakness that hadn't yet presented itself. Every weakness is exploited, the question will be, am I to gain or lose from this? Only time would tell.

I saw her coming from a mile away and knew there was no escape. As much as I liked her I wasn't in the mood for her lecturing. So much for my break, I started back into the kitchen when her voice brought me up short. Damn, the whole yard must've heard her!

"Mr. Allen!"

She knew how to stop a man dead in his tracks. I turned, and like a condemned man resigned to his fate, watched her approach. With Mrs. Brian it was always wiser to submit than to fight, at least that way you could retain some of your dignity, otherwise she'd strip you bare and send you slinking away like a bad pup.

"Hello, Mrs Brian. How are you?" "I'm fine, thank you for asking." So far so good.

"The real question is how are you?" She let that sink in a moment, then went on. "It came to my attention that you stopped attending Mary's class. In fact, the last time you did attend you left abruptly and rudely. Would you like to tell me why?"

Hell no. I wouldn't. Especially with half the yard staring at us and most of them snickering away.

"No ma'am, it's personal... but I'm sorry about having been rude and will apologize when I get the chance."

"Well, your chance just presented itself. Mary has a class later today, shall I tell her to expect you?"

Man, this conversation had gotten out of control, quick! Out of my control at least.

Maybe I could change the subject.

"How is splinter's new job going?"

Since he had stopped writing, Mrs. Brian has been good enough to keep me updated on his progress, information she holds like a bargaining chip. She's a wily one.

"It would seem we both want answers," she replied sweetly.

Two could play this game. I smiled innocently and said, "ladies first."

She crinkled her nose up and made a humph sound, but I knew she was having fun.

"Matthew's doing fine. He doesn't like the work much, but is sticking with it. He's taking a computer class at the local college and is very excited about it, he says all his videogame skills are finally paying off. And, of course, he sends his best to you." She added that last bit reluctantly, but I understood.

"Thank you." She always softened up whenever she spoke of splinter and I was grateful she kept me in the know.

"I will try Mary's class again, but sometimes it's difficult for a lifer to imagine a life beyond these walls, which is what she asks of us. It's a dangerous game. You've read my life, you know I'm never leaving this place. You've been there on more than one occasion when I've received news of deaths in my family. It's for these reasons that I spend every waking hour - and sleeping hour if I could - keeping that life locked securely away. We've both been here long enough to see people go crazy, losing whatever tenuous grasp they had. Even though I sometimes think it would be easier, I don't want to be one of them. If I constantly think of what could have been, of the life on the other side of these walls, that's what will happen."

Quiet stretched between us. She looked a little overwhelmed at what had been said and I was sorry I'd gone so far, but her opinion mattered, so I wanted her to understand.

"I didn't realize," she said softly. "I will speak to Mary -." "No, that's okay. I'll speak to her at class today."

Again silence.

"That's fine, then. Do you have any messages for Matthew? I'll be phoning him tonight."

"Just tell him to keep up the good work, he's making us all proud."

She started to leave, then turned and said, "You're a good man, Michael." That was the only time she ever used my first name.

After work I wanted to make a beeline to my cell and birdbath so I could head to Mary's class without the funk of the kitchen attached to me, but as I entered the section I saw three skrews and a nurse sitting around a dayroom table talking with old man Joe. I walked over to his cell and found Shelley looking frightened.

"What's going on with Joe?"

"Hey Teacher, he's on a bad one today. He's been calling me by his sons name all morning and when I tried to correct him he started crying. He forgot where he was and who I am. He wanted out of the cell, so I called the tower and asked if he could talk to the nurse. They've been out there for about twenty minutes and Joe doesn't look too happy."

The kid was worried. He'd come a long way from when he had first arrived, he'd gone from not giving a crap to being as protective as a family member, it was good to see that change.

"You did the right thing", I told him. "I'm gonna see if I can help out."

I walked apprehensively to the table, not sure what I was going to see and not wanting to see the worst.

"Hey Joe, how's things?"

"Teacher?" He looked up at me through bleary eyes, confusion warring with recognition.

I rested my hand on his shoulder and wondered at how spare it was, all the muscle seemed to have fled, leaving behind an abandoned framework.

"Yeah, it's me. How are you doing?"

"They won't let me see my son, Teacher. I need to make sure he's taking care of his mother, she's not young anymore." A note of panic slipped into his voice, "tell them to let me see him!"

God, this was bad. His wife has been dead for twenty years and he hasn't spoken to his son since, only his two daughters stayed by his side. Nothing good was gonna come of this. As horrible as it sounds I wish his senility would take him fully. So to spare him the painfully fleeting moments of lucidity, which are growing shorter and shorter.

"We'll see what we can do, Joe," I said. Then addressed the nurse. "You know his situation, right?"

"Of course, I've read his file."

She didn't like being questioned by a convict. The skrews on the other hand knew I looked out for Joe, so they gave me some leeway.

"Then you know that she's been gone for twenty years." "Who's been gone? What are you talking about?"

Woman or not, I really wanted to smack the shit out of her. It was difficult keeping my anger in check. The skrews were becoming annoyed with her, too. You would expect someone in the health-care profession to show a little sympathy or at least insight.

I looked down at Joe and mouthed the words "his wife". This had the intended effect. She started speaking softly to him, telling him she would help call his family and get everything straightened out. She left about ten minutes later, with old Joe at her side holding her arm and one of the skrews trailing behind; he seemed to unconsciously be riding drag, wiping away any vestige of Joe's existence.

As I watched him leave, he seemed to diminish with every step. He looked small and fragile, almost like an infant. He was hardly here at all. I knew with a certainty that I would never see him again, and for the smallest of moments, I wondered if perhaps he was the lucky one. His journey almost done, his rest so near. But it was only a second, harsh reality elbowed lesser concerns aside. I would have to worry that question another time.

I left the building without a shower and still in my work clothes, made my way across the yard in a daze, thinking, would Joe's present be my future? As much as I try to forget this place, I can't imagine forgetting everything. The blessing of forgetting the painful, the bad, seemed nullified by the cruelty of forgetting the joyful, and the good; balance has never seemed so unequal. It's a trade off made vulgar with its tit for tat logic.

I entered the class late, interrupting an exercise already in progress. I didn't look at anyone, just went to an empty chair and sat. After a moments silence the voices rose as the conversation resumed. One of the 'patients' was going on about how when he got out he was gonna start his own business custom detailing cars. He would be free of drugs, able to concentrate on career and family. He seemed to have it all worked out and Mary was enthusiastic in her encouragement, but he and I knew better. Half the guys in here, including him, had drug debts on the yard. Some even looked loaded as they sat slumped in their chairs. It wasn't my place to point them out, to expose their lies. Besides, I don't think it would've had any effect, Mary had her own motives for doing this work and I knew she wouldn't be deterred by the motives of others.

"Okay, let's move on. I'd like to go around the circle and have everyone tell us what's the one thing you hope to gain from this class? Can we start with you, Michael?"

"I would prefer to go last. I'm not quite sure how to phrase my answer. Is that okay?"

"Of course, we'll just start in the other direction."

"Mary?" She turned her head and raised her eyebrows in a questioning manner. "I'm sorry for walking out."

Surprise shown bright on her face and she was not alone. Cons in the group were exchanging odd uncomfortable glances. She quickly regained her composure and smiled, "thank you. Alright let's begin."

I was thankful she didn't make a big deal of it, but accepted it in the same manner in which it was given.

The exercise started and the first guy said "sobriety", the rest followed with predictable answers, mainly what they thought Mary wanted to hear. A few openly plagirized quotes from the source material for the course. Mary didn't say anything, I believe she was just happy they were actually reading it. When my turn came, it was much quicker than I anticipated, I still hadn't formed an answer. I decided on a different tact.

"May I ask you a question?"

"Of course." She was always so quick to accomodate. "Why are you here?"

She looked stumped.

"Excuse me? I'm not sure what you mean."

"Why do you come here." I motioned around the stark concrete box we were all huddled into. "You're young, educated, and if I had to guess, I'd say you had a much better job prior to this one. Yet, here you are in a room full of drug addicted losers. People who've had two, three, four chances at life and failed. Something brings you here, the same thing that drives you to do this work, and I'd like to know what it is."

The room fell quiet and I could see her mulling it over. The silence was so complete I could hear the breathing of those nearest me, I felt the urge to end their suffering, I've been having alot of urges like that lately.

"To be honest, I've never really thought about what brings me here, initially, it just felt like the right thing to do. I knew long before I came that I would be doing this sort of work, helping those who lack the resources or know-how to help themselves. You're right about my previous job, I worked as a nurse and grief counselor at a private clinic. I still do the counseling, but gave up nursing in order to run NA meetings, which I do at two prisons and various places on the outside."

It was strange to hear her refer to life beyond these walls as the 'outside', but that's what happens to those in here, even the temporary ones are affected.

"It's very rewarding work," she added.

Her work seemed to revolve around the downtrodden and dying, those who have and will cause death, those who are not long for it, but haven't realized the futility of fighting. I wonder if she knows this, and if so, does being around so much death confirm her life, without which, she may be dull and dispirited?

"Rewarding how?"

"It gives me a sense of purpose. When I help others, I feel it helps me, too. I know that by doing this work I'm able to make a difference in more lives than just my own, and every life I touch may go on to touch others... it's akin to a pebble dropped into a pond, the ripples can spread as far as the weight of the pebble can take them; the greater the weight the more far-reaching. The weight of my belief is very heavy and I hope to make a big splash!" she laughed in deprecation, but the truth was in her eyes.

"Your job as a nurse must've had more immediate impact. There you were actually saving lives, while here you're only hoping to have some future impact; you've given up a sure thing for a maybe, a possibility. Why did you decide to take that gamble?"

"Well, nursing did give me access to the instant gratification of saving a life, but here, the delayed satisfaction of possibly saving 20, 30, or even more lives is for me well worth the trade-off. In nursing I could help one or two people at a time, while here I'm given the chance to help whole groups. If I was offered a forum where I could help hundreds or thousands at a time, I would move on to that."

"I didn't know nurturing was so ambitious."

She was growing uncomfortable with the closeness of my questions and I couldn't blame her, I hardly knew what I was gonna ask next, but I wanted more so I hurried on. "You said helping others gave you a purpose. I think what I'm trying to ask is, does life need a purpose in order to be worth living?"

"I really don't know the answer to that. I guess it's possible it doesn't, but I know for myself, a purposed life is much more rewarding. It makes everything richer, sharper; family, friends, careers, pleasure, all become more valuable."

"And you know this from experience?"

"Yes, I believe everyone does. You may not know your purpose, yet, but when it makes itself known and you look back on your former life. It'll be with an almost sadness for time lost. The contrast is so stark it's almost like switching from black and white to color, you'll wonder why it took so long to awaken and be forever grateful it did."

She looked around, embarrassment coloring her cheeks a light pink. I knew she hadn't meant to go so far, to share private thoughts. I jumped in to dissolve the awkwardness, "thanks for your help, Mary."

"You're welcome. Now, I believe it's your turn. What is it you hope to gain by being here?"

"I think I've already gotten it. I appreciate you letting me sit in on your classes, but I won't be coming anymore."

That night as I lay in bed, D-man and I spoke of old man Joe. He said the skrews had come and rolled-up Joe's property, he was being rehoused in the infirmary and wouldn't be back. I felt guilty as there was no compassion or empathy eating at me, but the turn over rate here is so high, that if you go down that path you'd be lost forever. You can only spare the slightest moment, if you hope to spare yourself. I wondered what Mary would think of that?

D-man's breathing grew slower and deeper, he'd fallen asleep, the rhythmic sound was comforting in its companionship. I replayed my conversation with Mary and tried to fit it together with what I already knew, it was quite a puzzle. I realized Mary would have a ball trying to solve it, or rather me. She had used the word rewarding twice, I wonder if she'd still be doing this work without the 'pay-off', or would she move on to something else."

Ego gives lie to altruism, but then, nothing is ever as pure as its ideal. Mary's work does help people, but more importantly, it helps her.

First Johnny. Then Joe. They fell prey to something more deceitful than the physical; the weakness of self, of one's own mind. That's the battle here, to retain some individualism, while at the same time not straying too far from the herd; maybe that's the battle everywhere? But prison is the basest form of "intellectual castration". There's no healthy ego, self, will, all thoughts are one and the one is singular, live! We are but sheep herded from pen to pen, bleating our discomfort but never our outrage. We are fed, bathed, and clipped!

XVII

I'd lived with D-man so long that it was strange to be talking him into moving out, but Shelley needed a cellmate and it was only natural that it be him. I wasn't sure who I'd live with as I had no friends outside of D, at least none that I trusted like him. I would just wait and see who the skrews threw in. D-man didn't like it one bit.

"I don't see why I have to move out to help Shelley. I can do it just fine from here!" This was going to be more difficult than I'd thought.

"We've already talked about this. If you move in with Shelley and I get another youngster, we can look out for two instead of one." He didn't seemed convinced. "Look what happened to Ghost. If one of us would've been in that cell he would be here today, he would've made it home to his family. If we're serious about helping these youngsters, we can't go half-stepping, we have to jump in with both feet and get it done right."

We both knew it was only a matter of time before one of Snake's associates showed up and tried to move on me, for that reason. D didn't like to be far from me, he wouldn't be left out again. He was on a whole protective kick, but when confronted he would deny the hell out of it. Nothing was gonna change his mind, so I gave up and accepted the inevitable.

"Look, I'm all good with helping the youngsters, you know that, but we have to stay alive to do it, right? I just don't think we should help others more than we help ourselves. I know that sounds greedy, but it's The Law of Nature, The Law of Survival. You're the one who told me that anything taken to an extreme, even something good, becomes a vice. So what if the helper forgets himself, then what?"

"Good point," I grudgingly agreed. "I'm gonna have to stop sharing so much with you, you're starting to use it against me. I'm not saying that we let our guard down, I just think we need to put more effort into this newest endeavor; I think we can do both." I raised my hand to forestall his next interruption. "Hold on. If it meant one of us moving to another block or yard, I could see your point, but we'll still be on the same yard, block, and tier. Hell, we'll only be a few cells apart."

He was searching for an argument, anything to put a dent in my logic, but he knew it was sound, so he took to muttering and cursing, which was the usual indication that I had won. I decided to toss him a bone.

"Besides, he wants some ink and you need someone who is more willing to flaunt your work, I'm resigning. You have me marching around half-naked, like I'm working a catwalk!"

"Woe is me! You can keep pretending you didn't like it, but we both know better. You were strutting around like a natural."

We started laughing. That was always the sign the argument was over and we'd come to an agreement, no matter how grudgingly.

"Don't be jealous, brother, you're either born with it or you're not."

Yeah, this would go on for a long time, but the amount of time you play has to surpass the amount you argue or something ain't right.

Later that day D-man packed his stuff and moved in with Shelley, who was as excited as a puppy upon its owners return. He was bouncing around between the two of us, more of a hindrance than a help, but moving is pretty easy in here. You just lie an open sheet on the concrete bed and stack all your stuff in the middle, bring the four corners together and tie, you sling it over your back and tramp down the tier like a hobo along the tracks.

D-man had alot of stuff. He ended up with three hobo bundles, plus his television and radio. We took our time walking the stuff down the tier and making the return trip. I suspect we were dragging it out on purpose, trying to delay and ignore the finality of it, but eventually we found nothing else to move and stood empty handed in front of his new cell with his new cellie. Shelley didn't feel, nor could he have understood, our reticence about letting this moment go.

"Alright Shelley, this old thing is your problem now. Good luck!"

"Old thing! Shit, do you need some help finding your way back to your cell, grandpa? I know how you get confused these days, and I'd hate for you to wind up in the wrong cell."

"No you wouldn't. You'd love it."

We always downplay or make fun of the things that scare us most. In D-mans case, growing old and feeble while surrounded by enemies was it, so he was constantly clowning about old this, old that. He'd seen a program on PBS about the aging prison population, it showed 60 and 70 year old cons incapacitated, having to be bathed by lower level cons. He talked about it for weeks, obsessing on it, and finally said he had a favor to ask of me.

"If I get that bad or just grow too damn old, you have to end it for me. Don't leave me like that, dependent on this scum in here. Give your word."

He was seldom serious, but this time was different. His eyes bored into me and he was on the verge of pleading. His fists clenched and released repeatedly, as if hoping to convey the urgency of their message. I knew I could never do it, but I told him yes, hoping it would give him a small measure of comfort, or at the very least, move us onto a different topic.

Old man Joes situation had plucked that same fear laden chord or else we wouldn't be joking like this, especially in front of Shelley, who treated Joe like his grandpa.

Shelley stood quiet, a frown smeared across his face like an unwashed youth. He didn't like the joking, but was smart enough not to voice it.

I turned to leave, "I'll see you two at dayroom, bring your wallets, it's poker night."

I hadn't lived alone for quite awhile. Being single-celled was okay every now and then, for a little break, but it wasn't something I wanted to get used to. As much as I like the quiet, it's easier to appreciate in small increments, when it's continuous, it loses some of its luster. I know cons who refuse to have a cellie, and the longer it goes on the more they retreat, preferring isolation. I used to think of this as a form of devolving, but now I see anyone smart enough to separate from the herd must be on to something.

I caught myself making comments to the television, aloud, forgetting that D-man wasn't there to chime in about whatever stupid thing we had just seen. At first, it's funny. You giggle as you look around your empty cell, realizing no one's there and feeling slightly embarrassed, but after a week you start to feel a little uncomfortable with your 'slips' and wonder if they might lead to larger ones. You have to chase these thoughts away before they take root.

It had been two weeks since D-man moved and surprisingly I was still single, the skrews are generally good at filling cells almost immediately. There are so many bodies crammed in here, it would be hard not to be good. But the day eventually came when I was to get a cellie, and I found myself regretting it.

Two skrews came to my cell, one of which I knew, he was my floor staff, a regular, but the other wore the jumpsuit of a 'gooner'. Gooners made up I.G.I., the institutional gang investigators, the most hated group of skrews in the prison. I had no idea why he'd be at my door, he's usually busy chasing his tail in circles looking for imaginary monsters, and when he doesn't find them, he simply creates them; a God in his own right.

"Hey Allen, do you want to come out for a cellie interview?" "I don't need an interview, just bring him in."

"I wish I could, but we're not allowed to do that anymore. We have to make sure people are compatible before sticking them in the same cell. It's the new policy."

He seemed to sense my hesitancy. "Look, I.G.I. is only here for the same reason as me, because we have to. There's no funny business going on, you have my word."

"Okay, let's go."

My cell door opened and the three of us walked through the dayroom toward the section door. I heard D-man call out, "where ya going, brother?"

I looked back over my shoulder, "to get a cellie, I'm told. They have 'em lined up against the wall and I get to take my pick."

"In that case, pick a rich one. I'm tired of your broke ass!"

A few laughs followed me out the door. We entered the rotundra, a small space with an office for the skrews and one for the counselor. You have to walk through this area to enter or exit the building, a lot of shit goes down here. There are two cages standing against the wall, a bit larger, but roughly the same shape as coffins. They're used for cons released from the hole, new arrivals, or people involved in incidents. They lock you in till they figure out what to do with you. Inside, there's just enough room to spin a tight circle, but not enough to squat down, so you're forced to stand the entire time. I was locked in one for fourteen hours once, not a pleasant memory, but they were kind enough to feed me through a tray slot attached to the cage door. In comes a paper plate with no utensil, you just rip off a corner and use it as a makeshift spoon, all the while standing.

My potential new cellie stood enclosed in one now. He looked like a scared pimple-faced teenager.

"Hey Cole, why don't you let him out." I pointed to the cage.

He undid the masterlock, then stepped back. The kid came out looking jumpy, he kept looking back into the cage like he thought it might come after him, and faced with me he didn't get any less nervous. I'm a lot slower to anger these days, but when I see a scared kid my hackles rise and a slow simmer begins.

I walked up to him and forced a smile, "name's Teacher, good to meet you." I stuck my hand out.

He took my hand and gave it a vigorous shake, as if I was a long, lost friend. "Folks call me Billi Mac. That's Billi with two eyes." He pointed at his eyes when he said this. "It kinda rhymes with chili mac, 'cepting mac don't rhyme with mac, do it? I never noticed that before, have to work on that. Anywho, it's nice to meet you, too."

He was pumping my hand the entire time he spoke, and I was having such a hard time making sense of his rambling, that I didn't realize we were just two guys standing there holding hands. I jerked my hand free and unconsciously dry washed it. He didn't seem to mind a bit, but kept right on talking.

"So, it's Billi Mac, then?" "Yup. Sure 'nuff."

"Where you from?"

"The center of the universe, of course. I live on a farm on the outskirts of Bakersfield, miles and miles of beautiful dirt as far as the eye can see." He raised his arms to indicate his body, "look at me, I'm all stringy muscle, it comes from those skinny chickens we raise."

Man, this kid was wired different.

I looked over my shoulder, "Hey Cole, where's the off button on this one?"

He and the gooner were all smiles, "Why, what-ever are you talking about?" he asked innocently.

"What did I ever do to you?" I mumbled as I turned back around.

"... Sure ya know. The most famous country singers come from Bakersfield, too. Merle Haggard, Dwight Yoakam, I could go on and on, but I don't want to sound like I'm bragging, my mama says that's unbecoming. I know you've heard of -"

"Hey," I interrupted, "why don't we grab your stuff and move you in."

All he had was a bedroll, containing two sheets, two blankets, and a pillowcase, and a brown lunch bag with a fish-kit inside. The fish kit had a spoon, cup, pen filler, and a bar of state soap that will peel your skin right off.

"Sounds good to me, I'm tired of standing in that cage. I need to find a comfortable seat and make friends with it."

"Alright Cole, I'll take him. Do we have to sign anything?" "Yeah. You need to sign this "marriage chrono"."

An ugly name for what is essentially a release form. If one of us kills the other, they don't want to be held responsible for it. We signed.

"You can go back to your cell, Allen, we need to speak with Smith for a minute."

A sneaking hunch ran up my spine and I looked from Cole to the gooner. Oh well, there wasn't much I could do besides warn the kid, so as I walked away, I leaned toward him and said, "don't believe the crap these two are shoveling." He nodded his response. Maybe he wasn't a dim bulb after all.

On my way back, I stopped at D-mans cell and ran him down. We knew I.G.I were trying their lame ass scare tactics, which almost never worked; unfortunately, some fell prey and were then placed on other yards in the employ of the skrews, which generally led to them getting dead. So much for a helping hand.

I sat in my cell, waiting to see how this would unfold, hoping the kid wouldn't buckle. I knew I was in for it this time, the kid would never shut up; at least he had a funny accent. I'd heard of Bakersfield, had met plenty of people from there, but none had ever talked like that one. Maybe he lived in some remote, backwoods area of the city that was lost in a time warp. There had to be some excuse.

The thought was cut off as my cell door popped open. I was instantly up. Billi Mac came sauntering down the tier like he owned it, smiling like he'd just come home from a long trip. My God, he was even bow-legged. I wondered if he'd been riding those skinny chickens? This couldn't get much worse, hopefully.

I always knew things would go further, they seldom stop at a safe spot enjoying what they've earned. No, they always push the envelope, wanting more, not knowing when to leave well enough alone.

When Snake said he wanted to talk, I knew we were headed somewhere new. Generally, whenever he had a new idea, he was filled with a contagious energy, which infected those around him, but this was different, there was a hardness about him that made me instantly wary.

"What's on your mind?" I asked cautiously.

"Business. Mine is being fucked with and I don't like it."

This was news to me. "What are you talking about? Do we have some kind of problem?" This was the day I'd been waiting for, the day the house of cards came tumbling down. Strangely enough, I didn't care at all.

"Yeah, we got a problem. My guys are getting pinched on the yard and I'm losing money and product by the crapload. I don't care about the bodies, I got plenty lined up to take their place, but I won't tolerate these fucking snitches dipping their filthy hands into my pockets and taking what's mine!"

His fists were sinking into the desktop, forearms corded with an angry muscle that was twitching and throbbing, begging to be freed. He was mad. I'd never seen this side of him. I was suddenly very aware of our isolation and grateful that we were on the same side; although, I've seen how he treated supposed friends in the past, and that gave me pause. He stared at me unblinkingly, pinning me to my seat. I could see his question plainly, was I the one snitching?

"Tell me what's happening and how we can fix it."

I must've said the right thing, for he leaned back in his chair and smiled, something he rarely did, and of which I was glad as it revealed too much; a lie is much easier to live with, without those small flashes of intruding truth.

"That's what I was hoping you'd say."

"You know where I stand by now, or at least you should, so there's no use for questions."

He started laughing softly, "have you ever heard the saying: the one you trust the most is the one you watch the closest?" He went on, not waiting for an answer. "Who would've ever thought that a skrew would become a member of the Aryan syndicate and work for me? The funny thing is, you're the only one I trust, the rest of these morons don't know the meaning of the word. I see white, black, brown, and any mixture even a mad scientist would have trouble dreaming up, tattooed with the Chinese characters for 'Trust no man', then they step foot onto a prison yard and get taken in by the first con to show an interest. But you, you're different, you live a life outside of these walls where trust is a given, and still it took you twenty years to trust me, so you understand."

He stopped and took a few deep breaths, as if preparing to plunge into icy water. Instantly, I understood the meaning of his words. I was to be entrusted with something beyond what we had done so far, and I was to be the only one. A surge of excitement shot through me, I was nearing the top of the ladder, new doors would be opened, new secrets revealed.

"I need the names and housing numbers of the rats giving my guys up, giving 'our' guys up."

We both remained quiet. I could see him anticipating my response. He had laid it on the line, becoming a "Knight of Faith" and taking that necessary leap. Now I knew where I truly stood, my own sense of value rising; who knew where it would stop?

"Okay. But it's gonna take some time, and if you whack all of them at once, it's going to open some eyes and raise unnecessary suspicions."

He let out the breath he'd been holding, "hell yeah! You're as solid as they come, Stogie. I'm not worried about the time-frame, just get the info when you can and we'll put them on a watch list for now. We'll work on a few "accidents" and take them out one at a time, nice and slow."

I'd crossed the line long ago, but this, this felt altogether new. I had been vaguely disappointed that this change hadn't brought exactly what I'd hoped for. Don't get me wrong, there was a certain excitement at flouting the law, and doing it under the very noses of my bosses and coworkers only added to its allure, but still, it didn't seem enough. Now things were different. I felt a strange power in me, completely foreign, something of which I had no prior knowledge. Yet, it called to me, gently at first, but as its awareness grew so did the strength of its voice, till it was ringing throughout my body. I couldn't fight it, did not want to, there was no contending with it, regardless. I gave over and felt a strength I had never known, a strength which was now mine; the power over the lives of others.

It now resided with me, who lived and who died. A single word born from a bad day would put someone in the ground. There would be no oversight, no orders to follow, the decision would be mine and mine alone. If others knew of this, how gently they would tread, how differently would they treat me! But part of its power is its secrecy; you can't let them know until it's too late to make a recovery. I've heard it said, that 'ultimate power ultimately corrupts', but that's just the fanciful phrasing of the meek, hoping to be given something, praying to inherit what is only for the taking. This world was built by strength, and through strength it is maintained and progressed.

That evening during dayroom, I introduced Billi Mac to D-man and the rest of the woodpile. He got along well and soon had everyone smiling and laughing, that's a good talent to have. I sat and listened, amused, as he and D-man went back and forth over his name.

"No, I'm asking you what's Billi Mac short for?"

"It ain't short for nothing. I always thought it was long myself." "So it's your real name then?"

"Oh no! Don't let my mama hear you say that, she'd whip ya till you was hollering for mercy. She don't hold with folks changing what she done."

"Stop!" D-man blurted out. Frustrated beyond his limits, he was close to snapping. I stepped in and said, "Billi Mac, just tell him your real name."

"Oh, is that all he wants? I could've done that long ago, if he had just asked."

He turned to D-Man, stood straight and proud, and said, "My proper name is Daniel Elijah Smith. My Mama said I was such a good baby that I deserved two names from the Bible, and you know what? I think she was right."

Man, this kid was almost as priceless as the look of disbelief on D-Man's face. "What the...! How in the hell do you get Billi Mac from that?"

"It don't come from that. My best friend back home goes by Billi Mac, too. He's gonna be a famous wrestler someday, that ol' boy could put a cow on the ground in three seconds flat. So I took it for him."

"A cow? All cows do is stand there eating."

"You got that right. That's what makes 'em so hard to get down, they're practiced in standing."

"Should I even ask what his real name is?" D-Man was staring right at me when he asked this, and I was having a hard time keeping a straight face.

"Joseph Stalin McGillicuddy. His folks named him after a famous scientist in the old country, hoping the smarts would rub off."

D-Man's gaze travelled between us, then settled on me. "Holy freakin' crap! You got your hands full, brother. Best of luck with that."

D sat down next to me and Billi Mac went to play poker with Shelley. I noticed D watching Shelley closely, he looked like a protective father hovering around his kid. It was good to see. We might be able to pull this off after all.

D-Man's voice brought me back, "You hear the latest going around about Stogie?"

He was filling me in on the weekly gossip. He always had one ear to the ground, picking up even the slightest echoes, which left me free to concentrate on other things. We'd been hearing some disturbing things about Stogie lately, but I found it hard to put faith in any of it.

"Nah, what gives?"

"It seems he's in Snake's hip pocket these days."

"I don't believe that. Stogie isn't a hero, but he's always been a stand up guy. I don't see him getting tangled up with the likes of Snake. If I remember correctly, he's always hated the guy."

"More like feared him, but you might want to hear the rest before you start sticking up for him. A few woods from this yard are working back there, they're seeing this stuff daily, with their own eyes, and they have no reason to lie. Stogie spends his lunch hour drinking with Snake, Buzz, Jimmy V, and a few others. He supplies the alcohol. What's worse, he's been muling crank. The entire other yard is tweaked out of their minds, half of them are in debt so deep they have no chance of paying; there's either gonna be a mass exodus of lock-ups or Snake's gonna start a bloodbath. There's other stuff, too. You know wherever drugs are involved sick shit happens…" His word trailed off into a forced forgetfulness. I knew he was leaving something unsaid.

"You might as well finish, I'm gonna hear it anyway."

"Word going round is those in debt are being forced into prostitution, and most are youngsters. He's keeping them high, so none have run off and told yet."

I didn't know what to think. I've been down for 21 years and have only seen one queer, he was run off the yard so fast all I saw were the soles of his shoes. I thought of splinter, Billi Mac, Tommy, and all the other youngsters I'd known, I couldn't imagine any of them in that situation. But then, if it hadn't been for the intervention of me and D, they would've been alone and quickly targeted, if not for prostitution, then for something else. I felt the old anger returning, like a dam bursting, its waters, which once gave solace, were now spilling with a rampaging fury, attacking all they once helped. I had spent the last few years fortifying myself against this, all for naught. Easier to change water into wine; the politician into an honest man; war into peace, than to evade what nature and the fates have in store for you. You may attempt change, closeting your true self away, but it's only an elaborate game of hide-and-seek; where all the hiding places are known, the seeking is but a ruse. A feeling of helplessness threatened to sweep me away. I had to get control of myself, to use my anger constructively. This has been a long time coming, he and I have been enemies for over twenty years and something had always kept us apart, kept us from that final conflict we were destined for. I would fight it no longer, instead I would give over and resolutely follow the path that lay before me. I would joy in speeding the day of our meeting forward. My every thought and action would now be geared toward that day. I would need help with the planning, generally, I would turn to D-man at times like this, but if at all possible, I want to keep him out of this one, as I knew deep down this could be the end and if so, I'd make it one to remember.

XVIII

I wasn't quite sure how to go about collecting the names Snake wanted, without being too obvious or raising too many suspicions. I knew most of the guys who worked with the snitches, they were in the Gang Unit and were pretty free with their tongues, if the latter were sufficiently wetted. Perhaps all I had to do was hang out with them for a while, spring for a few drinks and let their natural tendencies take over.

It's peculiar how we adopt similar attitudes as the convicts we're supposedly better than. The guys in the Gang Unit hate snitches almost as much as the convicts do. They demean them with the very same insults; they speak of their loss of manhood; their no longer being able to look at themselves in the mirror; and they laugh about it, as if it were something of great hilarity that we should all partake in and enjoy. They never stop to think that their jobs are made possible almost exclusively through the existence of these snitches.

But this weakness is my advantage. This bragging, this wagging of the tongue for entertainment purposes, will give me what I need without my having to work too hard. I only need to put myself in close proximity, so my ears could freely hear what was already being noticed.

I was an alcoholic and everyone knew it, so hanging out at the bar would raise no eyebrows. Over a period of weeks, I started making daily appearances at the guards local watering hole. It was a seedy little dump, called, appropriately enough, the Stool Pigeon. Everyone loved the irony. It was a dark place where guards came to wash away all they had seen that day and days before in the liquid of their choice, and when they'd drunk enough, they would vomit up things they were supposed to keep quiet.

But no one ever said a word against it, as everyone knew they were amongst friends.

This was almost too easy. Where I thought to find stiff resistance was nothing but pliant flesh, easily molded. Civility had done the prep work, these milled around like the domesticated stock they were. I thought I would feel the intruder, out of place and as easily spotted as a wolf amongst sheep. But that was not the case, no one gave a second thought, or perhaps, not even a first. As I'm a veteran of 25 years, not many held higher seniority than me, even though I hadn't risen in the ranks - at least the ranks which they knew of - due to a supposed lack of education, I was still afforded some courtesies.

I walked by a table occupied by three guards from the Gang Unit. They sat away from the other guards, wanting to retain their special status, their feeling of uniqueness which their job brought. They practically marched under a standard. But the feeling was mutual, the regular guards disdained them their airs.

"Afternoon, boys."

"Hey Stogie, pull up a seat, the first one's on me. So what's the good news?" The short, stocky one named Fred asked.

This has been our routine for the last week, we take turns buying rounds and then I direct them to the soil I need turned.

"Life's short, boys, life's short. You want the bad news?"

"Lay it on us, Stog. Just make it quick, my beer's getting warm." Steve, the consummate drinker said.

"My wife is trying to prolong mine. She wants to put me on some macrobiotic diet, where I eat a bunch of vegetables and nuts. It's some Buddhist crap. I don't think she's ever noticed the Buddha's fat ass belly, that wily ol' bastard was sneaking beef and beer on the side."

There were laughs all around.

"Tell you what, Stogie. I'll spring for a platter of hot wings, I hate the thought of you stuck out to pasture, grazing away on shrubs. That's a waste of a good beer belly." Axel interjected, good-naturedly.

More laughs rolled round the table. It was as if they knew what I'd come for and were eagerly playing their parts.

"I'll take you up on that kind offer," I lifted my beer on a toast, "and here's to growing as fat as the Buddha, God bless him!"

These three did everything together, drank, ate, drove iron; they have the same crew cut and obligatory tribal band tattoo around their bicep. They were relatively young and single, with too much money and free time, and for all their bravado and show of not caring, they were quick to accept an outsider and quicker still to spill their secrets.

The beer and wings were flowing freely and disappearing as fast as they were tabled. I began supplementing every other round with shots of Jack, that really sped along nicely. We reached the fertile grounds I needed tilled laughing and joking and no one the wiser.

It began innocently enough. Just a casual remark about a known snitch who worked in PIA, but that's all it took. Soon, they were being cursed roundly around the table, 'they' being the snitches. Complaints flowed as easily as the liquor and had the same ability of lowering inhibitions; a complaint is never lonely long, others rush to it naturally and crowd around wanting as much to be heard.

"Shit, I got a guy over on B yard who thinks every piece of information he gives me should knock a month off his sentence!" Said Steve.

Axel laughed as he chimed in, "does he know you don't have that kind of authority?" "Hell no! And I ain't gonna tell him. The guy's gold, he knows everything going down on the yard, which means I know everything. Get this, he comes in one day and tells me he's been keeping tally, and by his reckoning he should be paroling any day!" Here he burst into laughter.

"What are you gonna tell him when his parole date never comes around?" I asked.

"I ain't gonna tell him anything. I'll just throw his ass in the hole or threaten him with it." He looked around the bar, then leaned into the table and lowered his voice, "if he doesn't like it, I'll leak his name onto the yard, then sit back and watch my headache disappear. He sat back and gave a slow, knowing grin, which the others shared. Well, we weren't that different after all.

"Don't tell me you're talking about that old queer sunshine! That penis-leech doesn't know a damn thing, he just makes shit up to get in good." I laughed condescendingly, knowing it would egg him on. "I can't believe you fell for that. Maybe I ought to help you do your job, I'd hate for you to get fired!" The punctuation struck home and produced the desired effect.

He gripped the tables edge, white knuckled and red faced. His words came fast and hot, carving the air between us like a knife's edge.

"Don't try to tell me how to do my job, Stogie! You think I don't know a convict from a con artist? Truth from lie? Some nobody punk who's trying to play me from the real thing? I have my finger on the pulse of this prison, nothing happens that I don't know about."

He grew still, struggling to get hold of himself, but I needed him to continue, I was growing tired of being in the company of morons. Provokingly, I smiled wider and said, "sure you do."

He picked up the thread and continued, much more smoothly, more self-assured.

"Let me ask you a question, do you remember Bull, a high ranking member of the Aryan Syndicate? The one who had a knife fight with your pet convict, Teacher?" My look of surprise made him bold. "Yeah, I thought you would. When he was recuperating, who do you think was sitting by his bed everyday? Who do you think conivved and cajoled, encouraged and persuaded, till finally convincing him that it was in his best interest to work for me? While you were sitting with one for the simple sake that you were worried, I was doing my job, I was creating an asset for the prison. Who do you think coached him for the role he's now playing; the weak, enfeebled victim of an attack? It's a role which keeps him from having to get physically involved, it has its own built-in excuse. With it, we keep him on the yard and in our service indefinately. So before you go throwing accusations around, you might want to know what you're talking about!"

I held up my hands placatingly, in mock surrender, "look Steve, I didn't mean anything. We're just sitting around sharing some beers and having a good time, whatever was said was only meant in a joking manner, not a personal attack. If you think I went too far I apologize."

"You don't have to apologize, Stogie." Axel quickly interjected. "We all know you were only joking. Why don't we just relax and you boys let me get the next round, I'm sure no one will complain."

That broke the tension. All the while Steve spoke, Fred and Axel had stared directly at him, willing him to shut his mouth. I could tell they were angry, but didn't know if it was because his lack of courtesy or his divulging of information. I would soon find out.

Steve reluctantly reached a hand across the table, saying, "Sorry 'but that, Stogie. I get a mite touchy about my job."

I took his extended hand and gave it a shake. "No need for all that, we're on the same side. And believe me, I know all about the stresses of the job."

And just like that I was back in his good graces, and with a few leading questions prompting him along, our conversation picked up right where it had stalled. Openly showing my admiration for his skill, he was soon lying the workings of his entire operation on the dirty table for my inspection, and with every ooh and ah pride danced in his eyes and spurred him to give still more.

I've been distracted for some years now, trying to live with one foot in this world and the other outside, even though I know it to be impossible, I have even preached against it, still I unconsciously try. I'd forgotten the first rule of life: You're either all in or all out; there is no hedging your bet, that only leads to a shadow existence which precludes you from making any impression whatsoever from acting upon that impactful deed that will be remembered. It's time for me to forget what I've learned, to furl my sails and let the wind go on without me; I've always known that its power was meant for another. It was time to ball up into myself and live fully in this world not of my choosing. As I sever all ties, I do not allow myself to feel the loss, that privilege too, is gone.

I started a new regimen of physical training. I've always been in good shape as D-Man is constantly pushing me, but I now went at it as one possessed. With no other worries or concerns, I had but a single driving force motivating me, one solitary need which eclipsed all others; to kill Snake.

The first weeks training left me stretched out on the rock, almost immobile. But the human body has a way of adapting, of quickly coming to terms with anything done to it; torture, deprivation, malnutrition, it will face and overcome all. If only the mind were as strong.

I was exercising twice daily, one cardio and one strength session. I did the cardio on the yard, running and hitting the heavy bag, and saved the latter for the cell, where I lifted water bags and D-Man. I knew what my enemies were doing and I was determined to be at my best when we met, to control what I was able and leave the rest to the Bearers of the Thread.

D-Man grew more curious by the day as he watched me go through my paces. His perception being as keen as ever, he wanted to know what I was training for, and when were 'we' going? I wasn't ready to have that argument. Yet, and an argument it would be. So I played it off as a New Years' resolution, hoping that would buy me the time I needed.

I'd just finished my jog and was walking laps to cool off, when I noticed Mrs. Brian and Mary on a course to intercept me whatever they had in mind, I couldn't take an interest in, as my world has grown narrow and permits but a single activity. I leaned against the chain-link fence feeling the diamond shapes press into my flesh, leaving their imprint, no matter how transitory. I looked to the ground, feigning interest, simply hoping they would pass by. I knew better than to run, there wasn't enough speed or real estate in this world to escape that voice.

Just as I feared, they stopped directly in front of me. "Mr. Allen, you can look up now, we're not going away."

I looked up sheepishly. I'd tried a child's ploy and had been called on it, it doesn't get much worse than that."

"Mrs. Brian, Mary. Yeah, I knew you weren't, but a man can hope."
"Well, I see you're as rude as ever."

"You just have a knack of bringing it out, ma'am. Usually, I'm very polite."

She sniffed loudly, making her thoughts on the matter perfectly clear. I glanced at Mary and saw her smiling at our interplay, maybe she was glad someone could get Mrs. Brian riled up and a little ruffled. I knew Mrs. Brian liked it. I felt for her husband, she probably tore him a new one every morning in lieu of a cup of coffee.

"What can I do for you ladies?"

"That's better. Now Mary has a question for you." Here, she physically pushed Mary toward me.

Mary seemed flustered. Her hand kept up a constant journey from her side to her head, snatching stray strands of hair and tucking them behind her ear, only to have them escape, calling for more attention. I couldn't imagine why she was nervous, but she needed the prompting of her companion, "go on Mary, ask him."

"Um... I was wondering, if you might change your mind and come back to class?" She must've seen the answer clearly on my face, as she rushed forward to make her case. "I'm not asking only for... myself, but for the benefit of the others in the class." Was she blushing? "When you bring up odd questions, which have seemingly nothing to do with our program, it makes everyone think beyond the written material. After you left, we openly discussed our last conversation, it brought much deeper answers. The guys were actually trying instead of just quoting the handbook back to me. I've tried to continue this trend, but my questions don't have the same effect as yours. I'm too in touch with the orthodoxy of teaching. I find it impossible to stray off course. I could really use your help."

She kept looking me up and down, and I could feel her need, it was almost tangible. She had used the word, myself, she had given a little in hopes of receiving yet more. This had nothing to do with me besides what I could give, how I could help her feed her need. But I had my own need these days, and it was all consuming. I had nothing to spare. Still, knowing this, I felt a sense of guilt for not being able to give her what she wanted; I guess empathy and selfishness are not exclusive after all.

"I'm sorry, Mary, but I can't come back." "Oh," she said, instantly deflated.

But Mrs. Brian would have none of it and came to her rescue. "Of course, you can come back. Don't be foolish!"

"No, Mrs. Brian. I can't."

She looked at me as if I were a disobedient child. In the blink of an eye, she was stripped of all her power, revealed for the little old lady she was. It was a hard thing to witness, as I was its cause.

She squared her shoulders and summoned a vestige of her old strength, "You are not the man I thought you were."

The omission of my name told me where I stood, to her I was as good as forgotten. "Oh Dorothy, it's not that serious." Mary intervened.

Mrs. Brian continued to stare at me. "Of course, you're right. It's not serious. In fact, it is nothing at all."

Without another word, she grabbed Mary's arm and turned to march away.

I leaned heavily into the chain-link and watched the two women walk away, neither looked back. I know what I had done was cruel, but the time for severing ties was at hand, and the quicker the better. The path I was on had no place for symbols from another world, they only distracted from purpose.

"I'm sorry, Mrs. Brian". I said low, as I hunched up and shook myself out. With a quickening pace I headed back onto the track, I needed a few more miles to shake this mood, but I knew it wouldn't be gotten rid of so easily.

Snake was so primed, he looked ready to blow, and I hadn't even told him what I'd found out. He knew I had some information, though, I'd made sure of it. First thing in the morning, I had strolled by his work area and given him a knowing wink while mouthing the word 'lunch'. I knew the curiosity would eat him up, he was not a patient man. He spent the entire morning trying to corner me, but I kept slipping away, happily watching his frustration grow. I had the power now and was enjoying the use of it.

Finally, lunch hour rolled around and I headed to our usual spot. As I neared, I saw the collection of usual suspects; Buzz, Jimmy V., and of course, Snake. They were eagerly awaiting what I had to bring and what I had to tell. Suddenly, it hit me full force, stopping me in my trucks; not only was I a member of the Aryan Syndicate, but by anyone's reckoning, I was its most productive member. They were constantly waiting on something from me. I was the only one who could provide most of the things they needed, without me, they wouldn't have squat. So, as I stood before them, I addressed them accordingly, "Afternoon, brothers."

There were nods and hellos all around, none seemed to notice my phrasing, or if they had it was readily accepted. Then I looked at Snake, who was studying me through half-lidded eyes, weighing the significance of my words. I felt as if I were perched on a scale which was tottering drunkenly, I had only to hope it would balance in my favor.

After an endless few moments, Snake stood and put his hand out, "afternoon, brother."

I had been weighed and measured and found not wanting. I experienced a clarion moment of victory, unlike anything before or since. I rode a wave which carried me from myself, away from this earthly boundness, and I knew instantly, it was a feeling I would chase to the end.

We settled down to our usual liquid lunch. As we drank, I retold the entire conversation from the bar. Everyone listened raptly, laughing and back-slapping, congratulating me on my ingenuity. When I came to the part where Bulls name was to be revealed, I drew it out a bit, for effect.

A stunned silence enveloped the group. Buzz wouldn't make eye contact with anyone, while Jimmy V. studiously studied the ground; he must've found something very interesting between the tips of his boots. Snake's face was red and growing redder by the second. He methodically balled his fists and released. I was confused, this was not the reception I had imagined. In my head, a celebration had followed my pronouncement, not a mourners mass.

Only later did I learn the significance of one of your own turning. The weight of all you once believed shattering with the fragility of glass. The quiet questions demanding answers; who vouched for him?; who worked closest with him?; was it just a case of bad judge of character or did this infection run deeper? Trust is out the window when everyone is suspect. In times like this, everyone keeps quiet and watches their back. This thing could easily snowball and a lot of innocent guys would wind up on the scrap heap.

I had to break the silence, it had gone from awkward to dangerous.

"You already told me the answer to this, but I need to make sure. He doesn't know anything about me or what we have going, right?" I asked Snake.

He gave me a disgusted look, "already concerned about your own ass, huh?"

"If that were true, I wouldn't be here right now and you know it. What I'm concerned about is us and our business. It only makes sense for us to cover our bases, if he knows even the smallest thing it could run us. But remember, you can't go right back and kill him, that would send up red flags all over the place. There would be an investigation and business would be over, period."

Snake gave a malicious grin. "I like the way you think. Don't worry about Bull, I'll handle that." He swung his gaze to Buzz and Jimmy, "you two old biddies didn't go gossiping around him or with him, did you?"

They fell all over themselves denying anything of the sort. One moment they were killers, the next nervous school children pointing a finger at a classmate hoping to slough off any blame. It would've been comical, if it wasn't deadly serious.

"Alright, enough! I know the four of us are solid. We have too much going for us to let someone fuck it off. Okay, Stogie, during your conversation with the gooners, did any other names come up in connection with Bull?"

"No, just his. And I don't think I'll be able to get anymore information from them, things got pretty heated and I don't think I'll be welcomed back to their table."

"Yeah, it's probably best to leave that avenue alone. The last thing we need is for you getting into barroom brawls." Everyone let out a nervous laugh, the tension was ebbing away in the face of our new challenge. "Do you have any ideas on how to collect the info we need?"

I nodded, that I did. "A few. If worse comes to worse I can pull a couple of overtime shifts during first watch, it's a ghost town then, so I could go over to the program office or I.G.I.'s little rooms and read through the confidential files."

"Perfect. There'll be no need to question any skrews or convicts, it'll be safer that way."

"With access to the c-files, we'll know everybody's secrets. We can use that info to extort some of these lames!" Jimmy V. said enthusiastically.

"That's true," Snake said, "but right now we have our hands full. If you come across any other info, Stogie, we'll put it in the bank for later."

Buzz rarely spoke more than a few words, so when he did it was a surprise. "While you're going through files, pull Teachers and see if he gave up cowboy and cyco."

Whenever Teachers name came up, which was frequently, it put Snake in a foul mood. He became defensive and aggressive at the same time. A lot of cons saw nothing wrong with Teacher, in fact, most respected him highly, but Snake would dispel them of that notion very quickly; and more times than not they'd be picking their teeth up off the ground.

He spoke in a tight, barely controlled voice. "It doesn't matter if he snitched on those two or not, he picked his side and it wasn't ours; that's all that matters! If anybody doesn't understand that or has a problem with it, well, we can work that out right now."

I watched his hand inch toward his waistband as he spoke, and knew he was going for his knife. I looked at Buzz, he sat calmly, neither responding verbally or with any sudden moves. Looking at him, I knew he was more than a match for Snake. As big as Snake was, Buzz was half again as big, and I had seen him work, he had a calm surety that was frightening. but he was smart enough not to provoke Snake on this.

"I never said he was right. I'd just like to know how much stock to put in the word of those two." Buzz replied smoothly.

Snake stared at him for a few heartbeats. "Sure, you're right. If we find out they've been lying, we can give them a lesson in our brand of honesty, the only brand that counts. Go ahead and check it out, Stogie."

It should've been strange, this sitting around with three convicts discussing the beating of two cons, while my word had already sealed the fate of a third, but it felt perfectly natural. It was difficult to see the true danger that lie in the words, they seemed so abstract. I knew a murder would take place in the near future and I had set it into motion, had made it not only possible, but necessary; yet, the reality escaped me.

Lately, I've been having a hard time with that, this floating between two existences, firmly planted in neither. I was starting to think there was something wrong with me, some deficiency, some lack of a vital component making me somehow different. Yet, if this were true, wouldn't I be exempt from the laws which govern the majority? And if so, I couldn't be held accountable for any "sins" I incurred while trudging my way through this life; that is a comforting thought.

XIX

I was sitting at my desk reading, the radio droning away in the background. When the skrew in the gun tower came over the intercom and announced, "everybody take it home, the programs' slammed!" The only people on the tier were the porters and a few guys using the phones, the rest were either at work or on the yard. I didn't hear an alarm, so we were probably going on lockdown for a power failure or a level one walkaway. That's what they call an escape down at the country clubs.

Nobody escapes from the level fours. Surrounding twenty foot high concrete walls, perimeter gun towers manned by bored skrews itching to try out their new rifles, and a "Death Fence" fed with enough electricity to zap your ass into the next world in the blink of an eye, keeps the bad men tucked safely away.

The cell door opened and Billi Mac came dragging in, which is the only way to describe his walk. The kid was so lazy he'd crawl if it were socially acceptable. I held up my hand and pointed to his muddy boots, he had a habit of tracking his work all over the cell. He sat on the toilet with a sigh and unlaced them, leaning them against the wall next to the door, then walked to the bunk and collapsed.

"I don't know how much more I can take of digging never ending holes to nowhere," he said, which was what he said nearly everyday.

He'd been given a job on the yard crew, but when your yard was just a square chunk of dirt, there's not much to do. The skrew who runs the crews has the cons dig holes and then fill them in; it's meant to keep the cons busy and tired, which it does if Billi Mac were any indication.

"We'll find you a better job soon, it's just difficult to find someone willing to hire your lazy ass."

"Well, that ain't hardly fair. I only appear lazy because I'm not particularly suited for this job. Now, if I were matched up with the proper job, I'd excel."

"And what exactly is the proper job?" I asked, not at all sure I wanted to hear the answer.

"I'm glad you asked. I've been giving that some thought -". "You sure you can afford it?"

He ignored my jibe. "And I've come to the conclusion that my proper job would be as an anatomy model for artists." He said with a straight face.

He was all ears and feet held together by a few toothpicks. "You don't say. And how'd you figure that out?"

"It was easy, really. To be a model, you have to be skilled in sitting still for long periods of time, and I don't know anybody who does that better than me."

I looked over at him and caught him smiling from ear to ear.

"You got a point there," I said drolly. "What's the word going around about the lockdown?"

He shot off the bed so quick he smacked his head into the top bunk. He hopped around rubbing his head, then must've came to the conclusion that no damage was done, because he said, "I completely forgot. Shelley's boss told him a guard was killed in another prison, so it's a statewide lockdown. He wasn't sure how long it's gonna last..."

I had already stopped listening, my mind racing ahead as I knew what was coming. I quickly went to the cell door and yelled over the din of voices, "excuse me on the tier. Hey D-man?"

A few seconds went by, then his reply, "Yeah." "Hey, did Shelley fill you in?"

"Just now. I was about to give you a call. We might be in for a bumpy ride, better batten down the hatches."

"I hear that. Alright then, brother, see ya on the other side of this. Thank you on the tier."

Billi Mac looked a bit confused and somewhat put out that I had cut him off in mid-sentence, but he was young and a fast healer, he'd be over it as soon as he opened his mouth.

"What was that all about, Teach?"

I hurried around the cell stashing certain things we weren't supposed to have, like our stinger for making hot water; a few razor blades, which got wrapped up and stuck in my mouth between the gum and cheek; two knives, which had to be wrapped in a wet lunch bag and hooped, the wet bag would throw off the metal detector.

I spoke as I moved. "Okay, listen up good. The skrews are good and pissed right now. One of their own got knocked down and it doesn't matter that it didn't happen at this pen, they're gonna act as if it did. They're gonna come through decked out in riot gear, putting on a show of force, but as long as you stay cool and keep your mouth shut, they'll just toss our cell and quickly move on to the next guys."

"Them fat, lazy bastards don't want none!" he laughed out. "That's exactly the crap I'm talking about!" I yelled at him.

I could see I'd scared him, so I toned it down a bit and went on. "Look, this is just a fishing expedition, plain and simple. They'll say they're looking for weapons and other contraband, but what they really want is that one con who'll make a remark like you just did, and when they find him, well, sorry 'bout his luck. This whole thing will be about revenge and reestablishing the pecking order. They want it known, only one dog runs this pound and you don't fuck with it without getting your ass handed to you."

I stopped to let it sink in, then continued on a brighter note. "We don't have a problem with these skrews and I'd like to keep it that way, but if things go south, you know I got your back. Shit, I'll peel them fools up one at a time and make 'em work like they ain't never, but - and this is the important part - only as a last resort and only if we're forced, got it?"

"Yeah, I got it. No brawling with the pigs." he answered sulkily.

I hadn't let him become involved in anything so far, no fights, no stabbings, no riots, and he was growing restless. He had even taken to provoking other cons, but they knew they'd be fighting me as well, so none had risen to the bait, at least not yet. I decided to offer him a little consolation.

"You're gonna get your chance sooner or later, don't worry about that, just enjoy the peace and quiet while you can, because when all hell breaks loose they're few and far between. Once you're involved in that first incident, you set something into motion which you no longer have control of; like lighting the first firecracker on a row, it's only a matter of time before the rest go off. I'm not sure why, but once you advertise yourself in that fashion, you'll have takers lined up around the yard. I guess it all comes back to pecking order and just how much of this dogpound you want to run."

I hadn't meant to ramble on like that, but my concern for the kid lent my tongue words which weren't its own.

"I hear ya, Teacher, loud and clear. I ain't in no all fired rush to fight the skrews.

Heck, I can see what they done to you."

That was a touchy subject, which I didn't speak of, but maybe this was the time. "You've been wanting to know for a while now, haven't you? I know you asked around."

He put on an incredulous look, "Why I never -"

"You'd do well to remember, this is a small world we live in." He started to protest.

"Nevermind, it doesn't matter. You want to hear, I'm gonna tell you. I'm sure you heard the story of why it happened, but let me tell you how it felt to be at the eye of the storm. First, you're simply fighting, and just like any other fight you don't feel anything, you're just trying to hurt the other guy worse than he's hurting you. But then the skrews jump in, angry and scared for their own, and the rules change abruptly. When the batons start landing, they're only a minor inconvenience, an annoyance distracting you from your purpose, then that one blow lands which knocks the stiffness from your spine, the pins from your knees, and before you know it you're stumbling around like a puppet hung on loose strings, not able to see what's right in front of you. You hit the ground and ball up because you have no choice, the party's just getting started. A few more solid blows to the head and you're no longer able to control your muscles, and here's where things start getting bad; with your muscles tensed they help absorb the blows, but now, when the batons land, they find soft, yielding flesh, no longer hardened to protect the insides. Your organs take the beating, your bowels let go, and what's worse, you feel every second like it's an eternity… so when you hear cons casually talking about fighting the skrews, you know they never have, because there's nothing casual about it at all."

He was chastened to the point of utter silence, which was a rare thing for him. I hadn't meant to scold or frighten, only to convey the seriousness of the situation, and I hadn't been entirely truthful, I didn't tell him that I submitted without a fight on purpose, but then, that was my business. What's important is the point got across, because it would be both of our asses on the line if it didn't, and I wasn't looking for a repeat performance.

"When do you think they're gonna show up, Teach?" he asked a while later.

"It could be anytime, I've seen 'em come in the dead of night, banging and shouting and scaring the hell out of people. This may sound callous, but hopefully they've had their fill by the time they reach us. Don't think that every convict on the yard isn't thinking the same thing, because they are.

I took comfort in the knowledge that D-man was having the same conversation with Shelley, and I knew he'd take care of his end, so my worry lessened.

A few days passed and nothing happened, which only made the anticipation worse, the longer it dragged on, the more it played on everyone's nerves. We only saw the skrews at chow time and count, otherwise, it was as if they'd vanished. I knew they were busy busting balls in another block. With no convicts to work in the kitchen, the skrews are forced to do the cooking and pass out the trays, when the trays finally show up they're almost empty, and what there is, most are afraid to touch. These are lean days.

Whenever something like this happens the first few days are always the worst. That's when the anger is raw, and unsolved, but it's a wearisome duty to keep it stoked, so it eventually cools, bringing reason and regret. This is why you want to be last, by the time they reach you their actions which seemed so reasonable are now an embarrassment of which they're ashamed, so they perfunctorily rush through your block handling everyone with the utmost care, and quickly leaving.

They hit us on the third day at seven in the evening, a bad sign. It was perfect timing on their part as everyone was stretched out readying to watch their favorite t.v. shows, their guard lowered for the night, big mistake!

They come with a noise that's all their own, a noise intended to cause panic and fear. It strikes straight to its purpose as most run to their doors to see the show instead of taking care of business, generally resulting in their going to the hole. They come in a line, shoulder to shoulder, marching lock-step; left foot forward, right foot matches; left foot forward, right foot matches. With every left-footed step a resounding thud is heard upon its impact with the ground. Simultaneously, they bash their batons against their plexiglas shields, adding to the rhythmic beat. It is a simple thing really, but when done right it draws the eye, especially when you're on the receiving end of its attention. Watching their approach, I'm reminded of passages of Greek Phalanxes closing with their enemy. Historians say this tactic was effective because their foes were simple and knew no better. Not much has changed over the intervening 2000 years, so much for evolution.

Most times having a reputation is a constant problem, skrews assume your guilt, while cons want to test themselves against you, but every now and then it has its advantages. The skrews, all of them, knew of my intervention in the attack on Officer Lowe, so I was treated with a deference that was uncomfortable, but nevertheless useful.

Billi Mac and I were cuffed and escorted to the shower, where we were locked in while our cell was ransacked. I left out a few odds and ends for them to confiscate, you never want to have too clean of a cell, it only makes them suspicious and they search all the harder. I watched as D-man and Shelley were marched through the dayroom, into the rotundra, and placed in holding cages. Shelley was staring at the ground the entire time, D-man had done his job well.

They were searching by race, and they always did the whites first as there were so few of us. When they got to the blacks and Mexicans their numbers were such that there wasn't enough holding cells to accomodate them, they had to be placed on separate concrete yards; at least they got some fresh air.

They were relatively quick and had us back in our cells in under ten minutes. The damage wasn't too bad, the sheets and blankets were scattered on the floor along with the clothes from our lockers. There were bootprints all over the stuff, so we'd be doing a lot of washing, but that was about the best we could've expected, we'd gotten off easy.

It was a different story for the Mexicans. The con who had killed the skrew was a southsider; a member of a Sũreno Street gang, which could be said for almost every Mexican in here, so they were the ones taking the brunt of the anger. Some were being dragged through the dayroom, arms and legs flailing, screaming their protest, all to no effect. They were handled as easily and as mindlessly as mannequins. Their property rained down from the top tier, creating an impenetrable curtain which gave only the odd glimpse of what was lurking on the other side. The heavy stuff, radios, T.V.'s, hot pots, fell fast and shattered on impact, but the lighter things floated this way and that way as if caught by a young breeze enjoying the play.

The noise was tremendous. It was the combination of many different activities occuring simultaneously, but like an orchestra, each played a specific part culminating in the whole. Batons were smacking into the walls looking for loose concrete, which was the telltale sign of a hiding place; boots were scuffing the floor, making their ear-splitting, high pitched squeaks, only muffled by the trampling of something soft; the small explosions of appliances hitting the floor were akin to a drumbeat keeping rhythm for the performance; the buzzing, angry voices blending together to create a constant quivering tension; all added to the rising crescendo, till suddenly, without warning, as if by the slice of a different baton, the music stops abruptly and the silence hums with the expended energy and you wait. You wait to see if it's truly over or if this is but the intermission between acts.

About half the Mexicans never made it back, they ended up in the hole for various "alleged" offenses, most for weapons beefs which shouldn't have happened since everyone had a heads up. Ah, but this was an old game with old rules; if you didn't have a weapon before, now you do!

The cons get back into the swing of things pretty quick, the concern for their fellow cons short lived. First, they get on the tier and vent their anger, after the skrews leave, of course, then they joke about what the stupid pigs missed. Finally, they settle back into their lamblike existence as if nothing had happened, and in truth, nothing had.

Billi Mac had never been through one of these before, so he stayed rooted to the cell door as if he'd sprang from the spot, while I lingered at the back of the cell, which was lost in shadow; in times like these I had learned that being inconspicuous was a wise thing. I went to the door and gave D-man a call on the strength, I knew all was fine and he confirmed as much. Billi Mac and I put the cell back to rights and settled in to await whatever came next.

The 'state of emergency' lockdown gave me the perfect opportunity to do the snooping I needed. When serious incidents take place. There's plenty of overtime to go around. Husbands talk their wives into calling in sick, hoping they'll miss any backlash against the guards, creating a noticeable lack of female presence and a lot of extra shifts to fill.

It was almost as if an unseen hand were aiding me in my search, clearing the path ahead of any obstacles, leaving me free to wander as I pleased.

I pulled three double-shifts in a row hoping to speed my search along. I thought I'd be rundown by it, but the opposite proved true; I was invigorated not only by what I was doing, but also by my continued presence within the prison. It almost seemed the longer I stayed the fuller I grew, my walls thickened up and the hollow places began to fill, with what, I do not know, but I could sense somewhat faintly, as if it were still in an embryonic state, a purpose. I had spent my entire life up till this point simply flowing with the current, heedless of direction.

I've stutter-stepped through life, leaving my decisions up to others, but no more.

First watch, otherwise known as the graveyard shift, is from ten p.m. to six a.m. It's a strange time to be within the prison walls. The place is devoid of convicts as they're locked up for the night, and a prison minus its inhabitants is strange, indeed; it's like a vein without blood, one would be hard pressed to define its function. There's a minimal number of guards working, as many are not needed. They ghost quietly around the buildings making no more noise than falling leaves, only the dry whispering of fabric rubbing against itself can be heard, and that just faintly. Every few hours they walk by the cells with flashlight in hand, making sure no one has run off or is swinging from the light fixture; the night seems to call to the weak, to those contemplative of leaving. Then they congregate in one spot, banding together to fight off the boredom and loneliness of the night, this leaves the entire prison open to my scrutiny.

The first night I got absolutely nothing done. I wandered aimlessly like a child in an amusement park, not knowing which ride to test out first. I fell prey to the temptation of going into every office, through every desk, handling personal momentos that were left behind to cozy up the place. On one desktop was a teddy bear with its arms spread wide, the words "I wuv u this much" stitched on its front. Splashed across the wall directly behind its head were 'victim photos'; cons beaten, stabbed, necks sliced open with the skin hanging loose. It was a fine contrast.

But on the second night I resolved to get down to business, I headed straight for the program office where all the convicts files are kept. I was somewhat discouraged by the row after row of filing cabinets confronting me, but I quickly discovered that everything was alphabetized and easy to access. I pulled ten files of names which I knew, leaving the empty spots open so I'd know exactly where to return them. Snake had given me a list of what he termed 'suspicious characters', it was half the yard.

The convicts C-file is broken into two major parts, confidential and nonconfidential, and these are further divided into various subsections. The larger part is nonconfidential and contains mundane chronological facts of the convict's time in prison; education, job skills, behavior, deaths in family, etc; but the confidential is where the good stuff is hiding. This section is full of juicy tidbits, to be seen by the very few, but not tonight. I scanned through the files quickly, ignoring the first part altogether, there wasn't much to find. Out of the ten only one was a snitch, and his name had been added to the list by Buzz, obviously Snake's judge of character was questionable. Throughout the night I combed through almost forty files, identifying four informants; 1 in every 10, that would be quite a blow to the convict mystique.

One file called to me, almost urging me to take it up, yet I refused, knowing the delay would heighten the anticipation and eventual gratification.

Every few hours I'd walk the count and check in with the other guards, as I wasn't a regular on this shift, I wasn't invited to sit with them, nor did I expect to be. As I approached the table I saw the makings of a card game in session, although it was doing its best to disguise itself from prying eyes.

"So Stogie, how're you liking the graveyard shift?" the first one asked.

"It isn't nearly as bad as I thought. With all this peace and quiet I can catch up on my reading. And I'll tell you something else, it's sure nice not having to hear the cons whine and complain all day." When all else failed and you wanted to get in good with other guards, the solution was simple, talk smack about the convicts. Our common dislike is the glue that holds us together.

"Amen!" exclaimed another, an obscenely fat, older guard, whose stomach was outpacing the rest of his body by a good three feet. "I worked among that scum for twenty years before switching to first watch, best decision I ever made. Plus," he added with a conspiratorial wink, "Where else can you sit on your ass for seven out of every eight hours, get in three good hours of poker, and get paid like we do?" he finished up with a wheezing laugh that disintegrated into a fit of coughing, then took a nip from a flask that had been securely anchored in the folds of fat that lay piled on his lap.

I joined in the laughter and the others did as well, it was a strangely quiet laughter. Those who worked first watch had a disquieting quietness about them, their speech, walk, even simple gestures. It was almost as if they were afraid of waking the beast. We all knew we had a good thing going, what they didn't know was that I had it better. What had started as monthly drop offs from Animal had escalated into weekly dumps, I was pulling in twice as much as my legitimate pay, and all in cold, hard, tax-free cash. As I hadn't much to do with it, I was just letting it pile up. It had already turned into quite a sum, forcing me to move it a few times to keep it from being discovered. Then I found the perfect spot, my locker at the prison, right beside my desk. It had a personal lock, so no one besides myself could get into it. It was actually the safest spot in the world, provided with all the safety measures the prison had, and the irony was worth as much to me as the money itself. When I placed it there, it seemed like a homecoming; after all, isn't this where it was made?

Business had really boomed and had come a long way from its humble origins. It had branched off into numerous unforeseen ventures. We had begun small, like any good business does, a little drugs with some extortion thrown in for good measure; it's not wise to put all your eggs in one basket, right? Then, I had brought in three cellphones for easier communication, soon Snake was selling individual phone calls to trusted cons. As the prison phones recorded every word, this was a way for cons to do business with the outside world, free from the big ears of eavesdroppers, that flourished into a full fledged phone business. I was buying cheap phones off the Internet in bulk, paying around twenty bucks a pop. Snake could resell them for eight hundred a piece, not too bad of a profit margin. And as one thing invariably leads to another, we soon found ourselves in the jewelry game. I bought bags of cheap knock-offs; rings, watches, chains, even sunglasses, and sold them at a 3 to 4 hundred percent mark up. I was amazed at the amount of money these cons could come up with, the yard was flush with it. Some days you'd walk onto the yard and it looked like a jewelry store exploded and rained its crap down everywhere. It was all so obvious, I grew a bit nervous, but it was plain as I looked at the other guards; they chose to see nothing and that is exactly what they saw.

On the third night, in the quiet hours just before dawn, I gave in. I pulled the only file that I really cared about. It was much larger than any of the previous ones, so large in fact, it took three folders to contain its bulk. I hefted it from the cabinet with eager hands and was pleasantly surprised by its weight. This would be some serious reading. It should've come as no shock, the guy had been down over twenty years and had been involved in so many incidents, I've forgotten most.

There were two desks in the office, I approached the nearest and set my burden down. I knew I could make this last till morning, could stretch the moment to draw every bit of satisfaction it had to offer, but as I sat I knew this would not be the case. I consumed it as a starving man does food, with no regard for the warranted moderation, and with the same effect. I sat satiated, but sick, dumbfounded with anger that churned and swirled demanding release. I needed to direct it at someone before it fed on my insides. Out of the chaos, the birthplace of all things, an idea slowly began to form. Just an inkling at first, but as it rose it fleshed itself as new creations do. When I turned it about, viewing it from all possible sides, its beauty and simplicity were too much to deny.

It had been a week since the raid, and word was going around that we were coming up for program any day. These rumors, like most in here, were started by the skrews. Not much else had gone down in the preceding days, a few more Mexicans were rolled up to the hole, just further fallout. There were probably a few in the first batch who were giving up everything and everybody, in order to get themselves out of hot water. After any major incident, you had to stay on your toes for at least a week, because that's usually when the second pile of shit hit the fan.

I was sitting in the dark, enjoying the quiet and my morning cup of mud when the cell door popped open, startling me. I looked up to the top bunk, Billi Mac didn't even budge, just snored contentedly on. It was only two steps to the door, so I was there and beyond before the thought finished. The tower screw had his arm out beckoning me forward. Even though it was 4:30 in the morning, I wasn't too worried as no one else was present. As I neared, he squatted down and poked his head out, "hey Allen, they just called for kitchen workers."

"Does that mean we're back on regular program?" I asked, trying to garner a little more information. Information is power and the screws are the prime source.

"I'm not sure. They've only called for you guys so far." "Probably tired of dishing out that slop, can't say I blame them."

"You're probably right," he replied good-naturedly. "Do you need a few minutes to get ready?"

"Nah, just let me grab my stuff and I'll be off."

I went directly to D-man's cell as I knew he'd be awake, long years of living with me had adapted him to my strange hours. I stopped in front of his cell and was not surprised by the scene presented, D was in full motion, well into his workout; steam was rising off his shaved head and his breath was coming in short, biting gasps.

"Morning brother. I see nothing's changed, still huffing and puffing while the children sleep." Shelley was curled into a ball under his blanket, the only part of him visible was a big toe sticking out of a hole in his blanket.

"Morning. You know the world ain't meant for the lazy, that's in the Bible or so your cellie says. Let me guess, he's sound asleep?"

"Yeah," I said, as I looked up at Shelley, "these two must be related. They're running kitchen workers, but the gunner doesn't know if we're off lockdown. If they run yard and I'm not back, keep an eye on Billi for me, he's been a bit restless lately."

"Done."

As always, his answers were short and to the point. A lot could be said for that, but then that'd ruin it, right?

"Alright, I'll see you out there."

I grabbed my cup and spoon from the cell, woke Billi Mac, and went to work. When I arrived at the kitchen, in place of my usual boss, sat Stogie. I hadn't seen him in almost two years, although I'd heard plenty.

I walked over to where he was sitting, "hey Stogie, how're things?"

He looked up, feigning surprise. He knew I worked here and had seen me come in, he was playing at something.

"Things are fine, I can't complain. Well, I could, but nobody likes hearing a grown man cry, right? So how've you been, Teacher?"

"Getting by, you know how it is, not much changes around here."

"Right, not much difference between here and the outside, in that regard." He stood, but kept the desk between us. He was acting strange, guarded, and that put me on my toes. Maybe I was placing too much stock in the rumors going around.

"So, how's PIA treating you? Do you like it better back there?"

His eyes narrowed with a newfound cunningness; this is definitely not the same Stogie I had known.

"Work's work, you know. But I'll tell you one thing, it's quieter and it's a more controlled setting, which makes it easier to dictate program," he stated forcefully.

"I'm sure you're right," and I knew exactly who was calling the shots. "I've been thinking of making a switch myself, I'd like to get back there where the good pay numbers are, all this making $45 a month, ain't cutting it; besides the state takes half of that for restitution, I might as well stand in line for government cheese."

I looked around conspiratorially, "don't tell anyone, but I swipe it back in the amount of food I take out of here." I laughed, trying to lighten the mood and ease the tension. He joined in and for a brief moment, I saw the old Stogie, the decent man who treated everyone in the manner they deserved, convict or guard, but the moment was fleeting, and left as fast as it had appeared; yes, he is learning from Snake.

"I don't know if the brass will let you back there, you have a few enemies who work there. Are you sure you even want to, knowing there could be…trouble?"

"All that crap's in the past. I'm sure I'd have to do a bit of persuading, but you know, it would go a long way if someone were on my side."

I was hoping he would remember the favor he'd offered so many years ago without me bringing it up. It hung between us like an umbilical cord, a constant reminder of an existing debt; now was his chance to sever it.

"I could ask around and see how the idea is received, but I can't promise anything. If all it takes is a nudge, then I'll be that nudge."

"I appreciate it, Stogie, and remember it's a two way street, if I can help you with any…problems, all you need do is ask and it's as good as done." I stared at him, letting my full meaning sink in. "Well, I better get to work, that slop ain't gonna cook itself. Talk to you later, Stogie."

XX

"Why don't you make like that thermos is your ol' lady and pass it around!"

Loud laughs followed. Everyone was in high spirits, literally. After ten days of lockdown we were all back in PIA and the whiskey was being greedily sucked down. I'd brought in extra as Snake had called and ordered it. They were putting it back like water and the effect was showing. Jimmy V held out his hand as he made his demand.

"Shit," Buzz held up the thermos, "If this were my ol' lady I wouldn't have to pass her around, that whore'd be bouncing from lap to lap like you were a bunch of Santa Clauses with bags full of presents!" Again laughter rolled around the group. The liquor had us all in fine fiddle.

We had a new addition to the group which brought our number to five. He was the newest member of the ARYAN SYNDICATE. He was short and wiry, with a crop of unruly hair so red it hurt your eyes. He'd been at the prison for seven years before being noticed; despite the beacon that sat atop his head, he had an uncanny ability to disappear into his surroundings. The fact that he could sit or stand as still as any statue helped in that endeavor.

But today he rocked back and forth as he yukked it up, this was his first go round with the real stuff and it plainly told on him. His name was Marcus Doolittle and he lived up to the name as if it were a challenge presented at birth. He was by far the laziest human being I'd ever met; if his lunch was farther than arms length away he'd sit and stare, going hungry before standing up to go get it.

His one redeeming quality was also his only skill, he could make a knife out of anything, and not just any knife, but one guaranteed to take a man's wind.

"Hey Doolittle, pass that nectar thissaway if'n it ain't too much work."

Snake was slurring his words and talking loud, too loud. It was time to put the liquor away. I rose and took the thermos, screwing the lid back on, I dropped it into my lunch bag. "I hate to put a damper on the fun, but we have some business to discuss, unless you want to wait till tomorrow?" I deliberately asked Snake.

"Nah, let's get her done. First, give these goons their phones back, they've been whining the entire time, and we need an extra one for Doolittle, even though he ain't got anybody to call."

"That ain't true," Doolittle retorted, "I'll call Buzz's wife!"

That set off more laughter, even I joined in. Whenever there was a search or lockdown I'd collect the phones and other contraband and store it in my locker, handing it out after. Every phone that is except Snake's. He had a good hiding place, and once he had it in his hand there was no getting it back from him; it was a connection with the free world and to power, one which he wouldn't give up.

I pulled a slip of paper from my breast pocket and passed it to Snake. The names of the four snitches I'd uncovered were on it, and he was gonna be surprised; no more surprised than by the revelation of Bull though.

As he looked over the list he grew very still, menace seemed to emanate off of him in waves. He ripped the paper into tiny pieces, dropping the fragments on the ground, where he proceeded to grind them into dust under the heel of his boot; a presage of what he had in mind for those named.

In a low hissing voice he said, "it's time to deal with this garbage. In the next few days we're gonna knock down a handful. We got some youngsters looking to make their bones, but I want a vet to go with each to make sure the job gets done right. Buzz, Jimmy V, I'll give you the targets, you can pick whoever you want to go with you."

"I work best alone," Buzz cut in.

"I know, but that's not the point here. We got kids that need to put in work and it's our job to supply that work and show 'em how it's done. No moves on the yard, I want them in the buildings, in blind spots. I don't want you two going to the hole, I need you here. Stogie, so you're in the know, we're putting Doolittle in Bull's cell to steer him away from our business; but the best part is we're gonna feed him false information and let him and his buddies handle some of our dirty work, get rid of a few 'undesirables' for us. When he's done serving that purpose, he'll find out that our little knifesmith does more than just make 'em."

Snake went on and on in his staccato like speech about killing half the yard, he was in a red mood today. Maybe all this liquor wasn't the best idea. If things went down like he was saying, and I had no doubt they would, the prison was headed for another long lockdown.

Grim grins greeted every pronouncement, as if gallows humor were the one true humor.

"Maybe I should keep the phones till this business is over?"

"Good idea, Stogie. A couple morons got popped with them on the shakedown and the skrews are going crazy trying to figure it out. Just leave 'em in there with all your money," he said smiling.

I looked at him sharply.

"Ah brother, don't look so surprised. Never think anything goes on around here without me knowing. Don't worry, I don't have sticky fingers. Besides, I've got plenty of my own."

I should've known better than to place it anywhere he could get a whiff, too late to move it now, he'd know and that would only make him suspicious. In any event, he was just letting me know not to underestimate him.

Buzz's voice cut in, such a soft voice seemed out of place in a body as big as his. "Did you read any other files while you were at it?"

That was the question I'd been waiting for, and I knew Buzz would be the one who posed it. There was no need for names, everyone knew which file he spoke of.

"Yeah, I read through our friend's file, or I should say, files, he has three." I paused, the moment lengthening enjoyably. Hungry eyes, whose curiosity only I could assuage, were fastened desperately upon me. Some filled with an eager vindictiveness, hoping my words would fall in judgment like a headsman's ax; while others craved redemptive words which would blow the cloud of doubt away from a man they respected. There were definite sides here and one was about to have their legs cut out from under them. For no reason I could grasp, I felt a strong sense of satisfaction over what was about to occur.

"So what's the word on our 'friend'?" Snake asked, staring directly at Buzz. He handled the word like it was a pile of dog crap he'd just scraped from his boot and flung away in disgust.

I'd practiced how I would phrase my first sentence. I wanted it to have immediate impact, to silence some while validating others; yet, I wanted a sliver of doubt which would encourage questions. I wanted to be center stage, the prime witness in the deconstructing of a man.

"Our friend and I have had the same employer for the last twenty years." I said it nonchalantly, as though I were speaking of the weather or some other item of little import, while inside my guts were churning in a nervous victory celebration. I'd given up names of snitches, which would lead to their eventual murders, but I was unfazed as there seemed to be a curtain of impersonality drawn between myself and those actions. But this, this was up close, face to face, it was almost as if I were driving the knife in myself. I wasn't simply reporting a fact, I was creating history. I held a man's past, present, and future in the palm of my hand and could snuff it out with the closing. Don't speak to me of power, I now know what it is.

Buzz was the first to react. "What exactly does that mean?"

"Does it have to be spelled out for you? It means he's a fucking snitch! He's exactly what I knew he was! He's an actor, whose holier than thou attitude, which everyone admired, was just that, an act!"

I knew Snake would defend whatever I said about Teacher to the death, as his hatred for him was equal to my own and that's what I had banked on. Snake went on at length, denigrating anything with the slightest attachment to Teacher, and like the good politician, he extolled his own virtues with the same carious breath. I interrupted his soliloquy with another bombshell.

"He asked me to try and get him a job back here," I whispered.

An incredulous silence greeted this statement. Disbelief, respect, and more than a little fear shone forth from the faces arrayed before me. Slowly Snake's face gave birth to a rictus grin full of portent. Slowly but surely the rest of the faces transformed, as if brushed by his contagion, all except Buzz, who, while still sitting within the circle, seemed to be far removed in unshared thoughts.

I'd put off the conversation with D'man long enough. Now that I'd spoken to Stogie, things seem to have taken on a momentum of their own which left me struggling to keep up. I felt as if I were in a race and losing ground with every stride; maybe it was the powerlessness one feels with inevitability? Like being a bystander in your own body, you stand pedestrian-like, as someone or something else makes your decisions. Free will is not much to brag about when all your options come from a pre-approved list. yet even knowing with a dead certainty what is going to occur, does not stop one from striving against the outcome, so I ran on hoping that through physical exhaustion I will sacrifice something now for an advantage then, and that the restored balance will come at an opportune time. Then again, maybe I was just trying to exhaust myself so thinking would be impossible, that would be a blessing.

D-man's on the pullup bars and with every lap I attack I can see his head rotating, following my progress, no matter where I am on the track, his eyes are on me. Yeah, it was time for that talk, before he did something crazy just to beat me to it. I slowed down to a fast walk and got his attention with a nod of my head, then glanced at the drinking fountain. He didn't say a word to anyone around him, but instantly set off, instinctively knowing he was about to receive an answer.

I arrived first, but waited for him before I drank or splashed water on my face; a prison yard is no place to bury your head without someone having your back. He slowed as he approached trying to act nonchalant, but eagerness was in his eyes, his step, the whites of his knuckles; I should've done this sooner to save him some anxiety.

I washed up and drank my fill with him standing behind me. "You want some?"

"Hell no, I hate water!"

He always said drinking plain water was a waste when you could have coffee or pruno instead.

"Yeah, I know. Just being courteous. We need to talk, want to spin a few?"

He didn't answer, but fell into step at my side, where he'd been since the day we met.

We walked an entire lap without saying a word. Finally, D broke the silence.

"You might as well spit it out, I doubt thinking it over is gonna change your mind." I laughed. He was right, as always. "I was just enjoying the company."

"Bullshit!" "I hear that."

We walked on. I didn't know how or where to start. I'd tried rehearsing this conversation, but it never turned out well, and I doubted it would now. The only thing to do was jump in and hope for the best.

"I'm going to the back to deal with Snake. Stogie's gonna get me a job back there."

He shot me a disgusted look. "What, am I stupid? I don't need to hear what I already know."

I was more than a little surprised, and it must've shown, because he went on. "You underestimate people too much. I know you're smarter than the average guy, but if the average guy's a moron that ain't saying much, is it?"

"Hold on. Before you go accusing me, you know damn well I've never thought you were dumb, despite your nickname and what you want people to think."

"I know, I know, you value my intellect," he said sarcastically. "I ain't some bimbo you're trying to bed, so save it. All I need to hear is how I fit into the plan, what's my part?"

It's the rare person who doesn't like to have their sails filled from time to time, and D-man is one of them. You hear people speak of wanting the truth, but that's seldom the case when it concerns them;

they'd much rather have it hung with false adornments, it's easier to look upon when clothed such. D-Man liked his truth ugly, the prettier it came the more suspicious he grew, but I needed to explain in my own words, so he'd just have to listen.

"Did you know that tolerance is a symptom of an aging society just as it is with the individual?"

He kept his silence and the sounds of the yard slowly bled away, only the harmonious fall of our steps was present, and their rhythmic beat encouraged my thoughts. "These last handful of years I've spent studying in hopes of coming across some secret that would change everything. I went through religion, mythology, psychology, history, and your favorite, self-help; but in the end they were all filled with ordinary words, written by ordinary men, for ordinary problems. There was nothing secret waiting to be discovered, no cure-all to fix everything; I only saw in them what I see right here, just plain life. I didn't want to change because I thought I was a bad person, it was the seduction of becoming something better than you are, something different. I fell victim to what's ailed mankind throughout history: the raising of man's laws above natures.

I stopped for a minute to refocus my thoughts. I had never aired them before, and when you give voice to unfamiliar thoughts they tend to take advantage of their newfound freedom and run riot on you.

"No one just wakes up one morning and thinks 'all my beliefs are false', I'd better change. This desire to change comes through continuous attack and brow beating by society until the free-thinker falls in line. Thousands of years of history, and not one culture, not one civilization, not a single people, have been born through tolerance and equality; these are only later symptoms of decay. This is the time when civilizations rewrite their own beginnings, conveniently forgetting the fact that just like man, they too are born in blood. And at some point, with a feigned sense of superiority, the intellect takes over from the natural and slowly gives away everything their earlier selves fought and died for. They're no longer what nature intended, but an artificial construct."

"So you agree with Snake now, is that it?" D cut in.

"No, he's a piece of garbage. Although, he's right in one respect; everything in life is a competition and competitions are won by those most brutal, either physically or intellectually, from the battlefield to the boardroom. So yeah, in the application of brutality I agree with Snake, but it's the "where and when" we differ. I still feel myself to be a part of something, he doesn't."

And that was it, what I'd been looking for this whole time, what separated me from Snake. No matter the truth or lies of a society, how it's founded and how it's governed, I still wanted to be a part of mine, and that meant protecting it from those who would tear it down or feed upon it.

"Are you gonna answer my question or not?"

"Yes. Your part is to stay on this yard and push our agenda, and if anyone gets in your way you show 'em how brutal life can be."

And for once he didn't argue, but simply plodded along silently. His steps had grown slow and heavy, reflecting the new weight placed upon him. Maybe he would opt out and do his own thing, but he had been with me so long, that even if this were not his in the beginning, it was definitely his now.

"No feedback, brother?"

"You haven't left me much to say."

"That never stopped you before, no reason to let it now." I laughed alone in my humor.

"I don't have any opposition because I know the reasons, and my silence is agreement enough, isn't it? I never pegged you for one who needed stoking."

"There's that humor I was looking for. Quit being so stoic, we both know you're the sensitive type."

That's all it took. He grinned, and we broke into a heated bout of slap boxing, which was as close as a man could get to the mushy stuff without feeling like a complete sissy.

A skrew leaned out the window of the nearest block and yelled, "You two morons knock that shit off!"

D-Man immediately answered. "Fuck off, copper! Come on down here and get you an issue!" We took off down the track before he could respond, we were laughing and joking, all felt right.

That same day the first of the four snitches was killed. His body was discovered by a guard during count. It was discarded under the stairs, pushed into the dark recesses with a blanket covering it. When the blanket was removed a vulture's feast was shown. The corpse was naked and had been so riddled with wounds, it looked as if hungry beaks had torn chunks of flesh away from head to foot. He'd been stabbed over a hundred times.

I didn't see the body, but I saw the effect on the guards who had, and that was more than enough for me.

The yard was slammed and guards from all over the prison were summoned to help conduct a search. I entered the conference room in the program office and was confronted with crying women and shaken men. The young woman who found the body was sitting at the head of a long table, tear-streaked face and shaking hands painted her as an accident victim, and in truth, she was. Mrs. Brian was at her side, whispering into her ear while rocking her as one would an infant; maybe the familiar motion would recall better memories.

A few men sat off in a secluded corner, one was continuously rubbing a hand back and forth across his cropped hair, the motion creating a sound of worked sandpaper. The words "I can't believe it" were being spoken like a mantra, so quick they came they seemed to form one long, unending sentence.

What was still abstract to me, was very real to these people. But then, I didn't have to see the outcome of my handiwork, so I could view the proceedings with a detachment which enabled me to see just how far-reaching, how powerful, my actions really were. As I watched the scene play out in front of me, I remembered a time when my word meant nothing; people would shrug it off as a joke or swat at it absent-mindedly as if it were an annoying insect; but now, it was as strong and contagious as any disease, affecting and infecting an untold number.

Captain Schmidt entered in a flurry of activity, and as ever, he was the calm at the center. His every move was crisp and precise, no wasted motion. Around him fluttered a number of nervous guards, lieutenants, sergeants, and plain ol' guards, all speaking at once demanding to be heard above the rest. It really was a hilarious sight. The captain marched right past me without a nod or even a simple gesture, no flicker of recognition lit his eyes. In fact, he didn't so much as look at me, it was as though I didn't exit.

He sat at the table opposite the women and commanded silence.

"Okay, let's calm down people. First thing," he looked to the gang investigator, "do we have eyes on the scene?"

"No sir. He was our eyes."

"Do you think that's why he was targeted, someone found out?"

"That's the assumption we're working from, sir. Although, we're not discounting other... possibilities."

"Such as?"

"Well...," the guy was nervous as hell and didn't want to answer in front of witnesses, "he was a drug addict who liked to gamble, so there's a chance he got into... trouble over debt."

"Got into trouble! He got dead! You knew of his "hobbies" and let him continue? The captain was relentless in his questioning. He could've been a lawyer, but then he'd have to take a pay cut.

"It's not exactly like that, Sir, we encouraged him to stop." "Why wasn't he removed from the yard?"

"The information he provided was too valuable. He was placed perfectly to give us what we needed. He was an immense help exactly where he was."

"Really. Have you taken a good look at that yard, it's out of control! It's inundated with drugs; there are convicts walking around wearing thousands of dollars worth of jewelry; we have convicts sitting in their cells texting away on their Goddamned cell phones!" His voice grew louder with every indictment, his stubby finger stabbing the air in punctuation. "And now we have the body of a man supposedly helping you clean up the yard, a drug addict and a gambler. You boys are doing a real bang up job."

"Sir, it's a slow -"

"Go get your buddies and round up your snitches, I want to know who did this." "But that'll blow their covers."

"Find a way. I expect to hear from you before the end of the day, got it?"

It was a dismissal and everyone knew it. Eyes were averted as the guy rose in reluctant resignation and made his way to the door.

"As for the rest of you, Sgt. Atkins is in charge of the search. I want that block turned upside down and all the crap shaken loose. Nobody goes home till we're done. I want half that block in the hole come nightfall. Get to it!"

We assembled on the yard to hear Atty give his speech. As usual, he was long on military speak, which no one fully understood - every other line a bad cliche from a bad movie. So we did what we always do on raids: go in, make a lot of noise, tear up cells, all the while remembering our real goal is to get out by shift change. I went straight to Snake's cell, hoping to be the one to search it, so as to avoid trouble, but when I arrived he was being cuffed by two young guards.

"Hey boys, go ahead and place them in the holding cells and help with the other escorts. I'll start searching."

They gave me a questioning look, which was gone a split second later; after all, I'd been working here as long as these two had been alive.

"Okay. You're the boss."

Bull and Doolittle lived in the neighboring cell, and as Snake and his cellie were marched away, I.G.I was there to pick up Bull, real smooth. I could hear Bull's voice raised in mock indignation, "Where the hell are you guys taking me?" There was a stiff falsity to it which reminded me of soap opera actors. The gooners looked embarrassed and uncomfortable, they knew this wasn't their game; they were used to being the unseen hand that snatched you up when you least expected it, faceless and nameless.

"Uh... You're going to medical," one of them stammered out. I laughed at their discomfort, and said, "good one."

They shrugged helplessly, as careless with their gestures as they were with their words. As the cell door opened to let Bull out I heard Doolittle's voice, "Come on back now, ya hear?" An amused lilt ran through it, injecting each word with subtle meaning. When they exited, I turned to Doolittle, "This isn't the time to be having fun."

"Ah, you're looking at it all wrong, Stogie. If you have fun and play the clown all the time, then they won't know when you're serious and they'll never see ya coming."

As I stood looking at him I realized he was sharper and more dangerous than I had given him credit for, maybe a little too sharp. He would bear watching.

"Do you have anything you need me to hold?"

"No, we don't keep the hot stuff in the cells, and just so you're not caught off guard, when your boys search they're gonna find another surprise."

He was wearing his crooked little grin and taking immense pleasure in all this chaos; it was then I realized where the true danger lie.

"What surprise are -." Before I could get the words out an alarm sounded, and there was yelling in the next section.

Doolittle's grin had widened, "Two for the price of one, Stogie. Don't look so worried, Bull should be spilling his guts even as we speak, you know, fingering the bad guy and all that." He was beyond smug, and as I thought of what we were doing, I felt a certain satisfaction myself.

"Who's taking the fall?"

"None of us, and isn't that all that matters?" "Yeah. That's all that matters." I echoed.

And he was right. As long as others paid the price we were untouchable, and in this environment it would be easy to maintain the status quo, as all eyes are attached to the surface, not caring or wanting to delve too deep. I couldn't foresee any problems, we had every angle covered, even the snitches were doing our bidding. We would be in business, a very long time.

XXI

I sat in the dayroom listening to the hum of excited voices. They were accompanied by eager smiles and clichéd phrases. Everyone knew of the murders on the other yard and were thrilled, something that was much easier to be since the danger was a safe distance away, and the victims were, after all, only snitches.

I knew what was working on them: an attraction to fear. It's some fundamental thing, instinctual, it goes beyond the bounds of logic and speaks to the animal side. It's the same principle at play as the one which draws good women to bad men. There's an underlying excitement, a sense of sharing the danger of the experience without having the responsibility for the action. Some are sufficiently strong to reason away this attraction, but they're the exception, most are subject to it in its full glory, with no distinctions drawn between sexes, they are played and played upon equally. Their primitive selves - which they maintain are no longer there - are stoked and stimulated simply by its nearness. When we give into this attraction, even in the smallest degree, it's to prove to ourselves that we are not fully domesticated, that we still have a streak of wildness, of independence; but distance is the key, the further away the action the safer it is to indulge. Just so in this instance, the other yard was an eternity away so the party was in full swing. Some people believe that good things come in threes, but these same folks ignore the fact that bad also arrives in groups. I knew these murders were only the vanguard of a parade of terrible events, of which I would take part.

D-Man was at the poker table, where he regularly raked in about a hundred bucks a month. The guys he gambled with had seen the world series of Poker on ESPN, and thought that watching translated into know-how, so it was easy pickings for D. He must've felt me staring, because he looked over with a questioning frown. I smiled and touched my ear while looking around the dayroom. He knew exactly what I meant and gave a sardonic grin rolling his eyes, then went back to his cards.

There's a concrete ledge which runs around the dayroom, it's one step down from the first tier and is used for sitting, it's also where the phones are attached to the wall. During dayroom every race sat at their own tables in their own area, these areas were separated by an invisible boundary which was encircled and protected; even when all possessions are stripped away from man, he'll still find something to fight over.

I was sitting on the ledge behind the white's table, Shelley and Billi Mac were on either side of me. I was leaning back so they could yack away at each other. Billi invariably got the better of these discussions, as he could talk anyone into stupefaction by the simple fact that he would never shut up. But both clearly liked it. As they grinned away while trading barbs, and they were good enough friends that everything was fair game, even mothers. I hated to interrupt their fun, but I needed to tie up a few loose ends which I had discussed with D-Man. Now it fell to me to break the news.

"Hey, before you two piss away the whole dayroom with your in-depth analysis of each other, we need to have a little talk."

They went quiet and looked at me, still grinning, probably thinking that I had just praised their talents.

"What's up, Teacher?" Billi Mac asked. "I hope this doesn't take too long. There's still a lot I need to tell Shelley," he finished with a knowing wink.

"Oh man, you're not gonna go on and on about how smart I am again, are you?" Shelley said, knowing he was setting himself up but he was a sucker for a good punchline.

"Of course I am, I never met a walking, talking, cowpie before —"

"To be continued," I interrupted. "Now, if you can shut up for a minute." I could tell Shelley was trying to think of a comeback, and wondered if I'd been that slow when I was young; I didn't think so, but then, I couldn't remember ever feeling that young. "Look, I'm starting a new job in a few weeks, so I'll be moving."

"What!" both exclaimed in unison.

"I know, it ain't cool, but that's life. We're lucky we have a heads up so we can dictate some of the changes. You two can move in together and D-Man can put another youngster in his cell, or you can figure out what to do on your own. There's no need to rush, so take your time and make a good decision; you might want to talk to D-Man, too."

They remained quiet, so I stood to leave them to it, when Billi Mac suddenly spoke up, "Why do you have to move just because you're getting a new job?"

He asked the one question I hoped he wouldn't. "My new job is in PIA."

I didn't have to say anymore, they knew what it meant. When we got back to our cell Billi would probably hound me and I'd explain it better then, but now I wasn't in the mood.

I went to the poker table and stood watching while not seeing a thing, my mind had already gone off, too busy chasing its own distractions to pay attention. Was I doing the right thing or was I being selfish? Maybe, in this case, selfish was the right thing. In any event it was too late for second thoughts; the wheels were already in motion, the gears churning toward a certain future and any back-tracking would only leave one crushed in their wake.

The following day I attended Mary's class. I hadn't intended to and I was halfway across the yard before I realized where I was headed. I still felt guilty for not helping her when she needed it, and for making her ask in the first place; but sometimes you don't have enough to help yourself and others too. I was nervous approaching the door, maybe she wouldn't allow me to sit in on her class anymore, ask me to leave, or worse, order me. I hesitated, my hand hovering just above the doorknob, I didn't want to be what brought out her bad side, what made her less. I let my hand slip to my side, this had been a selfish idea, concerned for my benefit, not hers. I turned to leave, glancing back one more time, Mary was looking directly at me, smiling as always and motioning for me to come in with a fluid movement of her hand. I entered the room and went to my accustomed spot, which strangely enough was empty, it was as if it had been awaiting my arrival.

"Hello, Mr. Allen." She said with the cool detachment of a professional something had changed.

I followed her lead, "hello, Miss Mitleid. Is it okay if I sit?"

"Of course, please do. We were just getting started." She looked to one of the other cons. "Please continue, Mr. Martin."

A con across the room started speaking about how drugs had made his life empty without his ever realizing it. How he had given up tangible things which had meaning for an illusory life. Familiar faces no longer bore familiar looks and I knew with a certainty that Mary had gotten through. She'd changed the environment. These guys weren't just going through the motions anymore, but were actually trying to learn something. No longer was their favorite word 'I', they spoke of others first and theirselves second, and only in relation to the whole. None sat slouched in their chair, simply happy to pass time in the relative safety of the room, but were attentively engaged even when not speaking.

I didn't speak and Mary didn't ask. I think she wanted me to see how far the class had progressed, all her effort had finally paid off and her pride was obvious; maybe now she would leave.

As the class came to a close, cons rose and made their way to the door. I watched them file out unhurriedly, they seemed to want to stay, but for a different reason than before.

"So what do you think?"

I turned to find Mary standing beside me, watching passively as the figures retreated. She wore a satisfied expression, but the eagerness that once lit her eyes had fled with the challenge.

"It seems you've gotten what you wanted, a receptive audience. I'm glad things turned out well. It was a lot different than last time I was here."

"Yes. As you heard, we've strayed from the approved material. I took a cue from some of the questions you asked me. It's a bit unorthodox, but so is this place. When I engaged them in personal matters outside the curriculum, they were more receptive to the required material later, and for that I owe you, so thank you."

"That's not necessary, I was only here to help myself."

"Isn't that what we're all doing?" She bent to gather her things, loose sheets of paper overflowed her too small folder, which she busily stuffed into place. She seemed to be stalling and covering for it with an excess of motion. Finally she stood, her arms full of work and her face filled with resolve.

"When this course is over I'll be moving on to conduct classes at the local college." So that was it. Even though I had known her intention all along, a rift opened, increasing the distance between us. Judgment found its way to my tongue, where I swallowed it back for the bile it was. It was hypocritical of me to expect to be surprised; I'd known her for what she was from the very beginning and had accepted it, and now to want better while I myself sought redemption daily on my own terms was foolish.

"Well, this place will be worse for your leaving, but better for you having been here. I wish you good luck with your new job."

She looked relieved. "Thank you, Michael. I knew you'd feel that way, that you would understand. I only have three more classes here. Will I see you?"

I'd seen all I needed, to come back would only encourage the truth to come spilling out and harm to be done.

"No. I only came today to see how things were going, and, well... I don't really know why, but I'm glad I did. Goodbye Mary.'

"Goodbye Michael."

As I walked away it struck me, if someone such as Mary, a good law-abiding, socially conscious woman, could pursue her aims regardless of the consequence, then there must be an inherent right in it, in the pursuit. As long as the aim is worthy, the means are merely secondary considerations; the old "sacrifice the few for the good of the many" argument. Maybe I was a Socialist, or maybe I was simply trying to justify my own impending actions.

I had another visit from Animal last night. He was dropping off larger shipments and picking up larger amounts of cash. I squatted in front of my locker, using a boot to stuff my duffle bag inside, it was full to the point of bursting. Since Snake had announced his knowledge of its contents, the locker had taken on a life of its own, everyone and their brother felt free to use it. Besides my money, there were also five cell phones, two half gallon bottles of vodka, a towering stack of smut rags, and six of Doolittle's homemade knives, which even I had to admit were really something.

Each knife was about seven inches in length, the blade slowly tapering to a razorlike tip. Like a dog's snarl, the edges were peeled back to uncover the meat of the weapon, which was murderously sharp and would leave anything severed in its wake. As you followed the blade back the last inch was runcinated, hungry teeth pointing toward the handle instead of the tip; making it easier to drag prizes out with every withdrawal. There was no guard between blade and hilt as the clenched fist served that purpose well. The last three and a half inches were wrapped with a braided piece of ripped sheet, which had been soaked in warm saltwater, and the wrapping was done while it was still wet; as it dried it shrank around the metal so tightly that the only way to remove it was to cut it off. Months ago Snake had asked me to bring a small whetstone and a handheld circular file, which was thinner than a Bic pen; at the time I didn't know what they were for, I did now.

The yard wouldn't be off lockdown for another week. So all the workers came from the other yard, the one on which Teacher lived. The place seemed empty as there were only half the number as usual, but that was fine by me, I needed the rest, the last few months had proven stressful, but productive.

I'd been thinking of ways to have Teacher pulled back here without my name being attached; if doing business with these cons had taught me anything it was to look out for yourself because nobody else would! The solution was simple, I'd get someone else to hire him. Buzz would plant the seed with the free staff who did the hiring, and I would vouch for Teacher, but only if asked. It would keep my name off any paperwork.

During the search somewhere between ten to twelve cons were rolled up and sent to the hole, which was about average for any good raid. A couple of black cons were cell extracted after threatening the guards who had searched their cell. They thought it disrespectful to have their family photos thrown on the ground. It's funny how they only notice disrespect when it concerns them; the trail of victims that is sprawled out behind them unemotionally explained away as a result of economic disadvantage at the hands of the "man". These guys come to prison, read a book by Malcolm X and become overnight revolutionaries – made from the stoutest paper, of course – only to be wadded up and thrown into the nearest wastebasket when self preservation comes into the mix.

Snake used Bull to full effect. The information he had Doolittle pass on was already paying off in spades; his two main rivals to corner the yards drug trade were gone, sitting in the hole on suspicion of murder, now Snake had complete control and one hundred percent of the yard's profit. Bull had spilled out the story that was written for him, and like a good puppet had danced when his strings were pulled. A few of the whites who disagreed with Snake's running of the yard were woven into Bull's story; Snake's thinking was why waste time dealing with them when we could simply be rid of the problem and go on with business as usual. Too bad this strategy didn't work on snitches, you can't snitch on a snitch. Besides, that's the one compromise Snake was unwilling to make; snitches had to leave the yard in a body bag or strapped to a gurney leaking like a sieve, period!

The day of the search a third body had been found hanging in a utility closet, which was used to store extra mops and brooms for the porters, but unlike the others, this one had been artfully done. The timing pointed strongly to a third murder, and the captain didn't believe in coincidence, but no matter how thoroughly they scoured the little room, no evidence was found. Violence is an integral part of the prison environment and one grows numb to it over time, but three bodies in a single day sobered even the most grizzled of veterans.

I made a quick stop at Snake's cell, letting him know that any other plans should be put on hold for the time being or the yard would never come up, and the captain, out of sheer desperation, might start snatching up the 'shotcallers.' He smiled and said, "Yeah, they're really shook up, huh?" He was enjoying his power and everyone else's vulnerability, and after a moment's thought, I saw no reason why I shouldn't do the same, as I'd played more than just a small part. I had come too far to turn back now, so there was no reason to sit around worrying while I could be enjoying it instead; Besides, turning back was no longer a possibility, if it ever had been. I'm not naive enough to think I can control fate, but I'm just arrogant enough to give it a try.

Two weeks later and I'm sitting in the usual spot, but this time I have company. Snake is across from me looking like an old, rung out dish-towel, explaining why he needs some of my money. During the lockdown they hadn't been able to sell any of the drug, so they'd used it instead. Part of the proceeds from the sale went toward reupping, and although Snake made alot of money, he also spent a lot. We were into Animal for ten grand, and brother or no brother, he wasn't getting off any more product till he got paid.

As I listened reality struck like a bolt of lightning: Snake ran the prison, Animal ran the streets, they couldn't get at each other, but there was one person they could both lay hands on, me. So, even though Snake was giving me the courtesy of an explanation, we both knew I had no choice, I would be the one held responsible for the debt and Animal knew where I lived, worked, and drank.

"Finally figured it out, Stogie? Had me worried for a minute, thought you might've gone soft in the head like the rest of these morons."

"Yeah, I understand perfectly. You put me in a spot I can't get out of, instead of helping me you're using me."

"You got it all wrong, now listen up. You'll get your money back and more, that's not an issue, but if you think this is some warm, fuzzy, we-all-get-along-gang you joined, you have a rude awakening coming. This is social Darwinism in its clearest form. You were brought in because you have something to offer, when you no longer have that, you become an obstacle, dead weight, get it? You're on the bottom of this totem pole, so don't think for one second that someone higher up won't step on you, squashing you and your insignificance in a heartbeat to keep from being displaced. That's how we stay strong, we encourage competition, even foster it; it weeds out the weak and strengthens the strong. This is no democracy, brother, where mediocrity is the goal. This is a struggle on the fittest, we fight for each other, but we fight against each other just as ruthlessly. Don't forget it. All that being said, I brought you in and I've shared more with you than anyone before, so don't think I'm gonna leave you stranded."

Despite his reassuring addendum, his speech had opened my eyes to a new reality; if I ever thought of displacing him and becoming the top dog, I'd have to reckon with the cannibalism that was the gangs foundation; no sooner would I ascend, then I'd start feeling the nipping teeth of those below.

He stood to leave, "bring a full thermos to lunch, we have some serious work to do. We have a few more loose ends to tie up, and we need to find a new way of carrying our goods to the yard, because after this next move all hell's gonna break loose."

That was the understatement of the year. Hell had already broken loose, but he was so comfortable in it, he failed to register the change. The crazier things became, the happier he grew. He thrived in the chaos he created because it destroyed the order which kept him in check. I'd come to realize that this was the purpose in his every act. He destroyed, uncreated what existed with no idea or thought of replacing it with his own creation, but simply of wading unscathed through the whirling vortices in his wake. In one sense, it was an attractive way to live. For down its path lie strength and strength is what every man or woman secretly desires; and in truth, only a small part of mankind are creators, the rest no more than sheep pointed to their proper pasturage. Then there's the other small part, the destroyers. These two groups bookend the majority, and one is as necessary as the other in order to maintain balance. So perhaps, Snake was fulfilling a needed function, and by following, I would too?

At lunch everyone drank sparingly, too engrossed with the business at hand to fully enjoy the alcohol. Snake laid out the bare bones of our plan and everyone took turns fleshing it. My part, which consisted of two things, was derived from necessity, as I was the only one with keys. I was to keep the gates that separated the work areas to the east locked for as long as possible, while keeping the ones to the west open to provide an avenue of escape. Leaving the gates open during work hours was normal practice, so there'd be no questions there, but the locked ones would need to be explained.

The second thing was to take the knives out of the locker and place them in strategic locations throughout the work areas. This was to be done the day of the incident and was the easier of the two tasks.

The area where Teacher would be working, like most of the areas, was outside. A chainlink enclosure took the place of walls dividing the whole into individual work areas. It was easier to organize and keep track of supplies and cons this way, not to mention cheaper. Buzz worked in the same section as Snake and Jimmy V. While Doolittle worked two sections over to the west; Teacher would be in the middle, surrounded.

Even though there was alot of bickering and complaining, I got the cell move done the following afternoon. Shelley and I swapped cells and I was back with D-Man. I wanted to spend a little time with him before leaving, and after he'd be able to move in whomever he wanted. It was good to be back. D-Man was an old hand at this business and knew how to act, he wouldn't worry me to death over the little things and the what ifs, instead he'd make sure I thought about the upcoming event as little as possible.

"Living with that kid done turned you soft."

D-Man was the only person I knew who could start a conversation with an insult. "What the hell are you talking about?"

"I've been jogging in place for ten minutes, warming up for the workout and you're still sitting on your ass daydreaming. Maybe you feel like writing in your diary, tell it all your secrets. You know, unburden yourself?" He was smiling as he bounced back and forth, I knew what he wanted.

I rushed him and we went at it for about five minutes, after which we were dripping with sweat; that's the best warm-up for any routine. I'd missed his smartass remarks. The one disadvantage of living with youngsters is they're reluctant to think of themselves as equals, so it ends up being a one-sided relationship, which quickly grows stale.

"We'll see if all that extra exercise you've been doing lately has paid off. I have a good program in mind, let's see if you can make it through without having to hug the toilet."

Crap! I'd conveniently forgotten about his crazy workouts. Oh well, it's probably what I needed. I'd be so tired I wouldn't have the energy to worry about anything.

"We might as well get started, you sure ain't getting any younger."

"You got some nerve, grandpa. I might not be getting younger, but you sure as hell are getting older. Before you know it the only workout you'll be able to do is "sweating to the oldies"! And I ain't talking about music."

"Alright, alright, if we keep this up we're both gonna have huge jaw muscles and not much else."

Be careful what you ask for. Three hours later I sat on the floor, slumped against the wall in a pool of my own sweat, at least I hoped it was my own. We were so beat we didn't bother with speech but simply used hand gestures and grunts. I pointed to the sink, then to my glass, he understood. We took down about a half gallon of water which made me feel even more sluggish, every time I moved my stomach sloshed. The sweat had dried and left tracks of salt behind to mark its passing, so I stood and went to the sink where I toweled off and drank even more water. I know, a glutton for punishment.

"Whose turn to birdbath first?" I asked.

D-Man looked up, he was beat. "Go ahead, I'll get the sink. I don't think you could handle it right now."

We always took turns going first, because whoever was last had to scrub the sink and toilet, which was almost like a second workout.

"At least I'm standing."

"Not for long," he said, slowly climbing to his feet. I started laughing and he was quick to join. "Alright, you won this round."

I was stunned. As long as I had known him he'd never made a concession to anyone, myself included.

"I'll make ya a deal, you do the cleaning and I'll make lunch."

"Sounds good. But it better be hot and it better be a lot!"

My thoughts exactly.

That night neither of us felt like going to the dayroom, I was so tired I wanted to drop in my tracks and curl up on the floor, but appearance was mandatory for the whites, so we sat there watching the clock seemingly slow down with every tick and prayed for dayroom recall. If anything were to jump, I realized there was a good chance that I'd be able to sleep right through it.

When we got home we climbed into our bunks and stared blankly at the TV, too tired to pay attention. We were just waiting for the skrew to count and roll the bar so we could crash. What felt like an eternity passed before we finally heard the doors that separated the sections pop open, an indication that count had arrived and sleep was close at hand.

As the skrew made his way down the tier, the distinctive click of keys banging into his baton marked his step. He stopped at our cell and peered in with his flashlight, "Allen, last two?"

Reroute mail, welcome at any time.

I climbed off the bunk and went to the cell door, "eighty eight", I answered.

He slid an orange, index sized card through the side of the door, "looks like you have a new job."

I took the ducat and said thanks. As I read it a calm settled over me, one way or another all would be over soon. I turned to D-Man and held up the ducat, his eyes fastened onto it as if it were alien, then slowly shifted to mine. For an endless moment I knew his every thought, felt his frustration and pain. He was fighting to keep himself in check. He got up suddenly and turned the TV off, then climbed back into bed and rolled to face the wall. There was nothing to do or say, so I simply followed his lead.

XXII

Six days. It doesn't sound like a long time and in actuality it's not, but when there's something waiting for you at the end, something only partially known and in no way good, six days can seem an eternity.

It was the morning after I'd received the ducat. I'd been unassigned from my kitchen job, so I had the next six days free before starting my new job. D-Man and I were waiting for morning yard to open, we'd been uncharacteristically quiet, drinking our morning shot of mud and cleaning the cell in silence. I had a lot on my mind, and D, aside from leaving me with the privacy of my thoughts probably had his own to work through. I hadn't realized how complete the silence was until he spoke, startling me.

"All these years I've been hoping for you to shut up, and now when I want to hear ya talk, you grant my wish. Just my luck."

"What?" I said. The words barely registering. "Sorry, I was zoning out."

"If you're having second thoughts about this whole deal, it's not too late to alter the plan a bit more in our favor. We can postpone till we find someone to hire me too," he smiled wickedly, "Then we go back there together and have a little fun."

"That definitely would've been my first option and you know it, but things are already in motion and I'm afraid if I stop it now it'll remain that way. As for second thoughts, they're only natural, right? When I'm there, they'll disappear as if they never existed."

He looked me squarely in the face, and with his usual stoicism said, "That's the last time I offer."

He was schooling himself to accept the role which had been lain out for him, and for a man like him that was a more difficult battle than anything in the physical world. He'd come a long way in a short time, which is more impressive as the paths available here are not those conducive to betterment, but quite the opposite. He had succeeded where so many others had failed, and worse, had simply given in without trying.

"Remember when we first met?"

He looked at me and smiled, "hell yeah, I do. Worst day of my life!" We laughed, "I was about to say the same."

We'd known each other for nineteen years now, almost my entire time in prison. When I was young and raw I hated everything and everybody, him included, but he didn't seem to notice or just didn't care. I easily ran every newcomer off, but no matter what I said or did he was always at my side, either quiet and plodding or full of useful information that eventually found its way through my thick skull. Without him I would've been dead or locked away in the hole forever; death by atrophy. I'd still done more than my share of hole time, but instead of constantly prowling for that next incident or next target, I had also learned to enjoy my time on the mainline. This world doesn't have much, and what there is, is very unappealing. There are two roads, victim and victimizer, anything beyond must be found and held onto by the individual, this is where D-Man helped me most. He made me see it was possible that while living here physically, mentally I was free to travel wherever I wished, and even though this mental life pales in comparison with its cousin, it is nevertheless enough to keep you sane.

"Bullshit! That was the luckiest day of your life. You wouldn't've known what to do without me, admit it."

I wouldn't admit it, at least not aloud; yet we knew it for the truth it was, and that was enough. Many precious things are locked away, their value lying simply in the thought of them; such was the case here.

"You're so full of it you're stinking up the cell!"

A voice came over the intercom, "Yard release five minutes."

"About time, I don't know how much more of your rudeness I can take this morning." I looked at him and rolled my eyes without responding. We were clowning around as usual, but the mood was forced. They were the same words and same jokes, but they had a strain attached to them that pulled the mouth into a false grin.

Six days.

We had to keep up this pretense, acting as though nothing had changed when in fact everything had. It was as if the incident had already taken place and we were in the unique and unfortunate position of suffering the consequences beforehand.

As we headed out the door to the yard, I found myself praying for speed, for the days to change their eternal habits and come and go with the speed of a wish.

"We were making good progress, then in our last few sessions you seem to have closed up. Has something happened that you'd like to tell me about?"

She never wasted a moment, but surgeonlike she cut directly to the heart of the matter.

"No, nothing's happened, maybe that's the problem. When I write I'm lost in the past and no matter how troublesome the memories, they're not nearly as unsettling as this limbolike present. I can be up at three in the morning or three in the afternoon and it feels no different."

"That's a natural stage of being locked up. You're used to a different routine of waking at a certain time, going to work and coming home, growing tired and going to sleep. Now that all that is gone and your body is trying to adjust, it will take a little time, but you'll overcome it."

"Yes, that's probably it, thanks."

She sat beaming across the table. I wondered if psychologists were this easy to please. She didn't seem to suspect that I always kept things from her. The very things that she wanted to know the most about were mine and I wouldn't share them freely, but what I gave her seemed to be enough.

"You mentioned your writing, how is it progressing?"

"Slowly." I said, which was a lie. The words were pouring out so quick, and with such insistence that I was having a hard time keeping pace. Many nights I was awake till the small hours scribbling furiously, hardly paying attention to what was being scratched across the page; I wrote as a laborer, unconcerned with rules or proper etiquette, but simply engrossed in the unearthing. I would read it aloud the following day and would be stunned at what I heard. The plainness and openness was shocking; why didn't I or anyone else see it?

"That's okay. The fact that you're trying is what's important. It may be difficult now, but I promise you, it will be helpful in the long run."

"I hope so. I will continue, I don't believe I could stop even if I wanted."

"Good. I'm glad to hear it. So, are you still having trouble sleeping? I know they've prescribed you some mild antidepressants which should help, but if the problem is persisting I can have them give you something stronger."

"That would be helpful. So far nothing I do seems to work, I've even taken up exercise, but I still can't sleep. I remember watching the cons working out in their cells and I'd laugh at the cliché come to life, but now I understand, it's not about becoming muscle-bound, it's simply a means of escape, of shutting your mind off to reality, unfortunately it doesn't work all the time."

There was no use lying to her about this as my face clearly told the truth. In the few months I've been here I look as if I've aged five years. Where before I had fine lines, now there were deep crows feet; the bags under my eyes were swollen and discolored as if I'd been on the losing end of a fight; my hair was rapidly thinning, making good the escape which alluded me. I was beginning to resemble the usual inhabitants of this place; thin, bald, and pale, with a permanent set of black eyes. I'd always thought that the cons conformed to a specific look on purpose, like the wearing of a uniform or badge, they wanted to be known for who and what they were; but the truth is much simpler and inescapable, internal forces outside the control of the individual, whittle away at your exterior till it matches your interior; thus nature has set you into your proper place and marked you out as a warning to all others.

As I was speaking she was reading from a slim file folder which was open on the desk in front of her, and I thought she hadn't heard me, but she suddenly spoke.

"The night staff say they find you awake at all hours of the night and always doing the same thing, writing at your desk."

It was a strange observation to make since I'd just admitted that very thing. Maybe she was just testing the veracity of my words or maybe she wanted to keep me talking. The first thing I had learned in the past few months was patience, so if it were the former I had proved to be truthful and if it were the latter, well, she wouldn't win a waiting game with me. I matched her stare and remained quiet.

"Are you having any other problems besides the sleeping and the growing used to this place?"

They seem like simple questions, even routine, yet they always had a significance beyond their surface. The fact that I've become a passenger in my own life I'd say is a problem. The utter helplessness of only being able to watch as decisions are made and buttons are pushed without your best interest taken into consideration. The sitting alone in a cell, staring at the wall fantasizing, purposely shutting out the truth or creating a new one to suit your needs, it's easier and more pleasurable to chase fantastic thoughts than to deal with what's in front of you.

"No, those are all. Everything else is as well as can be expected."

"You realize I'm going to have to see some of your writings soon? I'm not here working for you but for the court, and I've given you more leeway than I should've, but I believe the promise you made me. Perhaps when I come back next week you'll bring some with you?"

"Yes, I can do that." "Good."

I sat listening as Snake verbally added more bodies to the pile. He spoke as if word were deed and he fully expected it to be so, as though it had already occurred and he was only waiting for history to catch up and record it. I wasn't as confident as he was, some parts of his plan were going to be almost impossible.

The day of the impending incident with Teacher - which was only three days hence - Doolittle was to "take care of" Bull in the cell before coming to work. I was stunned by how everyone listened calmly,

Doolittle included, without making the obvious remark; there was to be four to deal with Teacher, but Doolittle was supposed to handle Bull alone! I couldn't see the logic in the idea and had to say something.

"Do you think it's a good idea for Doolittle to go at Bull alone?" "Don't worry about Doolittle, that's his job." Snake said offhandedly.

"But Bull is literally twice his size, and if things go wrong he'll have no chance to get away, being trapped in the cell." I wasn't so much concerned with Doolittle's safety as I was with my own if things went awry.

Snake gave a low laugh which dissolved into an ugly smile.

"What're you, his mother? Believe it when I tell you he can more than take care of himself. As for getting away, that's never part of the plan. We do it in a cell on purpose. If you send a man to do a job knowing there is an avenue of escape, when the going gets tough instead of pushing through he'll take it, but you put him in a situation where escape is not an option and failure is possibly death, that's when you'll get his best and more, he'll do things he never knew he was capable of. There's nothing in this world like a man fighting for his life... You're probably one of those guys who buys the pay-per-view boxing and MMA matches, right? Imagine for a moment what those fights would be like with no ringman and no rules; where the only man to leave the ring would be the only one who could, the chance of death makes a man more than he is. I'm gonna shatter a misconception you might have: We don't fight because we like it or because it's fun, we fight to outlive the next man, period! So when Doolittle goes about his business in those tight confines, rest assured, he knows the consequence of failure."

I looked at the others. Buzz and Jimmy V. sat with their heads bowed as if paying homage to Snake's eulogizing of violence. Doolittle returned my look with a flat, expressionless stare. He wasn't smiling or frowning, he simply had the look of inevitability, of one who was soon to face the possibility of death and had already reconciled himself to that fact.

Until this moment everything we had done seemed easy and exciting. We were making money hand over fist and all our actions were relatively harmless - or at least mine were - as most of the stuff we dealt in had been part of the prison environment from its inception and would be long after we were gone. Even the murders had seemed scripted and staged, following a predictable plot line; I wonder if this distorted view is a result of a society grown addicted to and made complacent by entertainment?

The possibility that Doolittle could be murdered in his own cell and bring all our plans crashing down brought the realization that it could happen to any one of us, and I was not as eager as he to face my own mortality. As I stared at him a chasm of difference parted between us, so wide and deep that I didn't see any way it could be bridged, and in that instant I knew I wasn't like him, no matter how much I wanted or pretended to be. In the midst of some kind of crisis I had found my life unsatisfactory and had adopted the first option that came along, not because I found it attractive, but because it was different.

I knew now that this was not the life for me, but the realization has come too late as this is not the life one can just walk away from. I've made a mistake, one I'll have to live and die with.

Snake was finishing his instruction to Doolittle, "... wrap his body in blankets and roll it so it faces the wall. It won't be noticed until the noon count and by that time we'll be done with our business, we're all gonna end up in the hole, but if we keep our wits about us and our mouths shut they'll never be able to prove anything. So we'll be right back after a little vacation."

"That's fine by me, I need some R&R anyway. All this highfalutin living out here is taking its toll on me." Jimmy V. chimed in.

"I hear ya. I think I've just about pickled my liver with all these fine refreshments Stogie's been supplying."

Doolittle had never heard a conversation in which he wasn't compelled to put his two cents in and now was no different. "You two speak for yourselves, my liver has grown fond of sleeping on a waterbed of vodka. I don't know how he's gonna react when I cut him off, I really don't." He put on his best worried expression and wrung his hands as he spoke.

Everyone busted up laughing, and just like that all the tension was gone.

"We'll see if we can't find you some pruno to tide ya over, you damned alcoholic." Buzz said, speaking his first words of the day.

"I'll take that as a compliment, thank you. It proves that I'm good at what I do, I can't think of anything more pitiful than being a mediocre drinker, I think I'd have to kill myself." Doolittle was feeling fine. As he finished speaking he drained the thermos as if dotting an exclamation point. "You'll have to bring us something special for the next few days, Stogie. After all, they could be our last," he grinned maliciously.

The old risk-reward argument came to mind, and though we were not dealing with money what we were using was far more valuable; life itself, and in risking it we either forfeited it or earned the right to live it.

Without a job I had more time on my hands, which is exactly what I didn't need; the one thing everybody wants more of is the one thing in plentiful supply here. It may run counter to popular belief, but all here wish for less; less time to think, to work, to be locked in a cage, and many wish for less time to be alive so the state won't grow fat on their carcasses. Time isn't wanted or needed here. All of its attributes are but a reflection of the beholder, so you can imagine the face it presents behind these walls.

I'm as ready for the confrontation as I'll ever be, mentally and physically I've done everything possible to be at the top of my game. It's strange though, even as I find myself eager for its approach, I'm hoping that possibly it will be the last, and afterward all will be peaceful. I don't know if it's the symbiotic relationship between war and peace, the eternal connection they share in the mind of man that makes it impossible to think of one without the other, but as I prepare for what could be my final chapter all I can think about is the peace beyond, and I know that can't be good.

"You're gonna have to workout on your own today, my boss has us digging holes for some new pullup bars. The bars aren't even made yet, the jerk just likes ordering us around." D-Man said disgustedly.

I'm thinking of taking the next few days off anyway. I need to rest and heal up, all those twice a day workouts are catching up. I can't show up for the big dance and be too tired to get on the floor."

He didn't respond. He had taken the view that if he wasn't allowed to speak of it then neither was I, not even in a joking manner.

"I'm just gonna cruise around with the youngsters today, maybe play some handball or basketball." I said.

"You're too old for handball, you'd probably wind up breaking a hip. You better stick with sitting in the sun, maybe we can find a nice blanket to fold up and lay across your legs." He laughed at his own joke and I joined, because if you can't laugh at yourself you're screwed.

"Those are big words from a little man who won't even be on the court to back 'em up. You'd best stick to digging holes, that'd be safer for your ego. Now that I think about it, it's best it worked out this way, I'd hate to demolish you and then leave, you'd probably never recover."

He was giving me one of his crazy stares, eyes and mouth drawn into tight lines. He called it his Clint Eastwood stare.

"You got some nerve throwing out a fake challenge! Well, guess what? I accept. We're playing both games, loser's the maid and cook for the next week. How's that sound?"

"Sounds like a guy who has to go to work and knows it." "Screw work, I ain't going!"

"You know your boss will fire you for that."

He barked out a laugh," hell, that's a bonus. You're just talking me into it."

"Okay. One game of each, winner take all. No runbacks or best 2 out of 3. Sound good?"

"Sounds like someone is gonna be making me lunch."

Yard came and D-Man, true to form, went to work. Don't let it be said that all convicts are worthless layabouts. No matter how much he complained about his boss I knew he loved going to work, not only to get out of the cell but he liked the idea of being a working man and the responsibility that went with it. Although he did talk his boss into letting him off an hour early so we'd have plenty of time to get our games in. All I had to do was kill an hour with guys half my age, which isn't as fun or as easy as it sounds.

Billi Mac and Shelley were standing as still as a couple of fenceposts when I approached; the youngsters were forever lounging while the older cons were constantly on the move, motion leads to exhaustion which leads to forgetfulness, a useful state of mind. Once the youngster's minds caught up with their bodies they'd be on the move too, always searching for that state where nothing's real but the present.

"Hey fellas, what's the good news?" I reached out and shook hands with both.

Billi Mac jumped in first just as I knew he would, "Shelly hasn't farted in a whole five minutes. I think that's a record for him."

"Shut your piehole or I'll eat a bag of spicy refried beans tonight and I won't go to the door to cut loose!" Shelly retorted.

"Like that makes any difference. You've already ruin't my nose with that fire coming out your behind."

"Shit, you'll find out how much of a difference -"

As I stood listening to them go back and forth, I was reminded of D-Man and myself. The only guy you talk that much smack to is the one guy you trust to hear it. These two would be okay as long as they had D-Man to keep them out of any major incidents.

"You two want to spin some laps or do you want to keep whispering sweet nothings to each other?"

That got their attention.

We took off to begin our circles. Walking is a big deal in prison, it's all about that motion I mentioned, and the fact that you're not a sitting target also encourages it; a moving target is much harder to creep up on.

As we strolled they kept up a nervous conversation about one of their friends, another youngster named Danny Boy. For a kid he was already as big as half the cons here, and in a place where physical size equates to respect, he was a step ahead of the pack, and naturally Billi Mac and Shelley looked up to him.

"I hate to interrupt your lovefest, but I think you two are misplacing your admiration."

"We don't admire him!" said Billi Mac, confirming the opposite. "Then why do you call him your friend?"

They shared a confused look. I went on to forestall any needless questions. "You should always admire your friends. People become friends because they admire a quality in each other, which they believe they lack and perhaps can acquire through association. It's nothing to be embarrassed about, it's simply true. No matter what you say I know you two admire one another. D-Man and I do, too."

"What quality does D-Man have that you like?" asked Shelley. It was a simple question with a simple answer.

"Loyalty. When he's your friend it's for life. It's not a commodity that can be bought and sold, or traded as if it were common, but a gift freely given, and once you have it you'll never be without."

I was getting off track. "Look, Danny Boy is an alright wood, but he hasn't any qualities that either of you don't already possess. You two read, study, have an active relationship with your families, are trying and succeeding in bettering yourselves, he has nothing to offer you. You know what his program is; he works out, eats, and watches about ten hours of t.v. a day; he's growing physically while withering away mentally. You two are so far ahead of him it's almost embarrassing; he should be seeking your friendship, not the other way around. I'm not trying to tell you who to be friends with because you already know who your real friends are, I only want you to know that sometimes it's necessary to prune away the stray branches in order to maintain the health and integrity of the tree... a wise man was once asked after a series of unfortunate incidents, "What do we do now?," without a moment's hesitation he answered, "We cultivate our garden." A true friend is someone who helps you cultivate your garden, "always remember that."

Neither looked as if they understood a word I'd said. In fact, they looked more confused than ever, but time would work its wonders and some years down the road, if they happened to look back, understanding would bloom and they'd curse youth for its ignorance.

"Well, I see D-Man headed this way. I knew he'd talk his boss into early release. I have to teach a lesson on the handball court, so if you gents will excuse me -"

"Hey Teacher, can I ask you a question?" Shelley cut in. "Shoot."

"Why are you going to the back alone? We talked to D-Man about it and he said we could probably get two or three of us back there, that would sure even up the fight."

I felt gratitude and anger well up at the same time. The fact that they wanted to take on my fight as their own spoke highly of them and of D-Man's schooling, but in doing so they pushed aside their most important lesson: Keep your nose clean and make it back to the streets.

"First of all, it's not your fight and no one invited you!" That cowed them a bit as both retreated a half-step in unison. "Second, you two have better things to do than to become lifers in prison, don't you? You have family and friends counting on you to make it back home, and now you want to possibly throw that chance away at the first sign of a good fight? Maybe I'm wrong, but I thought you two were smarter than that."

"That's not it, Teacher, we just don't like the idea of you going it alone." Billi Mac said.

I could see concern on their faces which were still unschooled at hiding their true feelings, and knew for the first time that I had more than just D-Man and that my time with these two hadn't been wasted.

"I appreciate the hell out of the offer and it means a lot to know you feel that way, but if I took you up on it I'd be a hypocrite. I'm a lot of things, but, hypocrite isn't one of them. Let me tell ya a secret; I'm not exactly thrilled about going alone, I wish I could take the whole lot of you; but I also know that courage, like any other muscle will atrophy and die without continual use. So we have to face our fears and overcome them or hide in the shadows and be overwhelmed by them, I choose the first."

"Not the courage speech again!" D-Man's voice sounded behind me. I turned to see him smiling. "Are you ready for that whupping or would you rather stand here spouting from your podium? Wait, don't answer that, I already know."

I couldn't help but think that that was the perfect way to end an awkward conversation, leave everyone smiling.

"Ask and ye shall receive. Let's go little guy, I'm about to give you a beatdown of biblical proportions."

XXIII

I awoke at 4:30 this morning, at least that's when I finally got tired of staring at the ceiling and climbed out of bed. I don't think I slept more than an hour the entire night, my mind wouldn't let go of the possibilities of the coming day. I'll have the chance to do something that should've been done years ago; get rid of Snake for good, and I'd only get one shot. Everything needed to go perfectly in order for this to work and those little details are what had kept me up all night. After years of waiting patiently I simply couldn't allow anything to go wrong.

I was up moving around the cell in the dark, trying to be quiet but not doing a good job of it. Finally D-Man spoke out of the darkness, "You can stop trying to be quiet, it ain't working!" He threw his blanket off and climbed out of bed heading for the sink and toilet. "And turn the damn light on, I can't see a thing!"

He wasn't a morning person. That was one of the reasons we were such good cellies, we never got in each other's way. I got up early and handled my business so that when he woke we weren't competing for the facilities, I'd just get out of the way. This had worked well over the years and no matter how he protested now, I knew he'd slept about as well as I had.

"We're gonna have to get you a walker and some bifocals the way you're stumbling around here." I said.

"I wouldn't be stumbling around if you didn't have me up at some god awful time.

How early is it, anyway, about six?"

There was a clock on the wall just beneath the bars of the guard tower, but he couldn't see that far, even though he pretended he could.

"No, it's a little after 4:30."

"Four freakin' thirty! What the hell am I doing awake? Oh yeah, you!"

I could barely understand him as he was sloshing handfuls of water onto his face while he spoke, but there was no mistaking the tone, he was none too happy. I waited till he finished and was patting his face dry before I spoke again.

"Can it. You know you were just as awake as I was. I heard you rolling around all night because I was doing the same. What kept you awake?"

He shot me an incredulous look, "take a guess, genius!"

"Man, you are some kind of crabby this morning. Maybe we should tuck you back into your crib."

"Shut the hell up!... You're really gonna make me say it out loud, aren't you?"

I didn't answer. We both knew what he was talking about, and yes, I wanted him to say it. It wasn't sentimentality or a sudden softness that had me pushing him; it was his final hurdle. He was being left in charge and he needed to be able to do more than just handle acts of violence, he needed to say what was on his mind without being embarrassed by it.

He stood unsurely and cleared his throat a few times. It was strange to see this man who was so dominant in the physical world suddenly transformed into an awkward, bumbling kid.

"You're not my best friend, you're my only friend," he began haltingly, "and I have a bad feeling about this whole thing. I was angry when I came to prison and that has only increased by being surrounded by garbage, but the focus and direction of that anger has changed and that is your doing. It's a debt I can never repay. I have the feeling this may be the last time I see you. I'm not gonna ask you to reconsider because we've already had that conversation, but I think you should at least take a weapon, we have plenty of good ones."

"You know I can't take that chance. I have to go through work change and their metal detector picks up everything, then I'd be sitting in the hole for a weapons beef and many would think it was on purpose."

A lot of guys who were forced to put in work conveniently got caught with their knives thinking it would be an easier route, but when they showed up in the hole, they found themselves in trouble.

"Screw them! If I catch anyone running their mouths, I'll make sure they won't be able to talk for a good long time."

He was getting worked up.

"I know, but you know as well as I do, we don't let others dictate our program. There's no reason to create a possible situation by being careless. I'll get a weapon back there."

"Did you get someone to set that up for you?" he asked hopefully.

"No. You know I don't trust anyone but you; besides, I can't take the chance of someone ratting me out. I'll borrow a knife from one of my dance partners, there are sure to be a few with weak grips."

"Yeah well, don't get too cocky."

I laughed as I saw all the steam had gone out of his argument. "There's a fine line between cockiness and confidence and you know it. I know what my enemies have been doing to prepare for this moment and I know what I've been doing, and I must admit, I like my chances."

D-Man stood and walked to the sink for a glass of water. As he passed me he said softly, "that makes one of us."

I was the first in line at work change which was nothing new for me, I was always the eager one and today was no different. I didn't want to come in last and walk into a trap which had already been manned and set. I needed to be early so I could see where certain people placed themselves. I knew I'd be dealing with three or four guys so I needed every advantage I could get.

As the skrews strip-searched us my eyes constantly roamed. I recognized most of the cons from my yard and they me. What was to happen today was common knowledge and I noticed those around me sidling away; no one wanted to be close when the business started. The cons from the other yard hadn't arrived yet.

I quickly dressed and stepped through the metal detector; I felt eyes on me, I scanned from left to right and found them. He was sitting behind a desk with his hands folded and resting on its surface, his eyes locked on me as if I were prey. His pose was one of uncompromising rigidity, yet, fear played over his features and shone in his eyes, only to be outdone by a stronger emotion, Hate. As we stared at each other I sifted through the ashes of past years trying to find the hidden truth, to uncover what I'd done to incur this hatred. Once, I had thought that we were on the verge of becoming friends or as close to it as possible for a guard and convict, but now we were clearly enemies. For all my effort

I failed to find what I was guilty of. Not that it mattered any longer, he'd chosen a path that through all my years I'd never seen taken; he'd become more criminal than any criminal and more convict than any convict I'd ever known. He betrayed everything he once stood for and everybody he'd ever known; he'd become an enemy to his friends and a friend to his enemies; he'd grown Janus-faced, speaking one truth here and its opposite there; he drifted freely among people from both sides, thinking himself exempt from their rules as well as their consequences. Yet, despite all that, I believed he deserved a final warning, so I headed toward his desk.

When I woke up that morning it felt like any other morning. There were no signs that this day bore any more significance than the endlessly repetitive days which preceded it. I didn't feel any different. There were no premonitions of great or terrible happenings. It felt as plain and empty as all its siblings. Yet, today was the day, someone I knew would not see tomorrow, maybe more than one, but still, this knowledge added no urgency or importance to the day and once again I was disappointed. Maybe I was one of those rare few who are excused from the rolling tides which plague mankind.

When I arrived at work everything was the same there, too. The cons hadn't shown up yet, so I walked around the work areas looking for hidden things in the shadows. Everything looked strange, foreign, without man the machines had no meaning at all. There were machines that made eyeglasses, license plates, boots, and any number of other mundane things. They stood as unknown and unknowing as any great monument from a lost past, relevant and useful only to their builders, a meaningless mystery to all others.

I had things to do before the cons showed up for work. I went to my locker and took out four knives, leaving the other two behind along with a few bottles of vodka and over forty thousand dollars cash. I should've moved the money and liquor before but it was too late to worry about that now.

I placed the knives in the work areas where Snake, Buzz, and Jimmy V. could quickly arm themselves. The fourth I took to where Doolittle was supposed to keep watch. He had come to me on the sly and asked for a weapon, "just in case", he'd said, but the look in his eyes told another story. I unlocked two of the connecting gates between work areas, this would be the escape route that they could lock behind them as they flew. As I was going through these motions I felt as if it were someone else doing them and I was just along for the ride. I watched as my hands manipulated locks and hid weapons with a brisk efficiency that had never been their own. They moved without being told and did things beyond my knowledge. I felt as though I were two, one always in control while the other watched and they took turns according to the given situation; in this fashion I could always justify my actions or at least blame it on the 'other guy'.

I was sitting at my desk when the first of the cons started pouring in, he was among them. He walked through the metal detector like an animal on the hunt and stared directly at me; I had forgotten how big he was. Gone was the look of past friendship, gone was pretense, he had known my part all along and had read me as easily as if I were a child, and now he wanted me to know it. I should've been terrified that I'd been unmasked, instead I felt a strange sense of security, I knew what and who he was here for and yet, as he approached, my heart, fueled by trepidation, picked up its pace.

He came to a stop in front of my desk and gave me a sympathetic look, my heart nearly burst out of my chest.

"Sometimes we get caught up in things not of our making, but the trick is to get out when we recognize them."

Without another word he walked away. I was too stunned for speech. He felt sympathy for me! He was the one who wouldn't see the end of the day and he had the nerve to feel sorry for me! A stinking criminal who society had thrown out like yesterday's garbage; a lowly convict who had nothing and no one, who existed by the charity of the state; yet, he believed he was better than me, he felt the right to give me advice!

Anger coursed through my body, rapidly running from the top of my head to the tips of my fingers and places beyond. It was leaking from my pores, emanating in waves which devoured all thought. I could not contain it and I didn't want to, as its heat was unbearable. My vision, rippled in red, caused a disconnect with reality. This was a killing anger, I could commit any act while in its throes and not be conscious of it. He had just erased any doubt I might've had.

Someone was speaking, but I couldn't understand the words. I wasn't sure if they were even meant for me.

"I said, are you having a stroke ol' man or have you just gone stupid?"

I squinted my eyes and blinked them a few times to clear the image which stood before me. It was Doolittle with his hands shoved into his pockets and an I-don't-give-a-shit grin plastered across his face. I had the insane urge to jump up and strangle him to death. It was a nice daydream, but I choked it down and instead, said, "he's here." The words came out in a white-hot whisper.

"Who's here?"

I looked at him angrily, was he really that dumb or did he just want me to say the name?

"Teacher." I muttered between clenched teeth.

His grin grew wider. "Looks like we'll be having some fun today."

"What happened with Bull?" I asked, already knowing he answer. Doolittle was always in a good mood, but today he had an extra something in his step.

"Ah, our friend's lain down his troubles and worries and is sleeping the sleep of the peaceful. Did you have a chance to place things?"

Typical Doolittle, he never said anything straight out, instead he beat around the bush and expected you to follow.

"Yeah, everything's taken care of."

"Good. See ya when the curtain rises." With that he sauntered off whistling without a care in the world.

A dim idea was taking shape. Maybe Teacher's advice wasn't so bad after all, it's a shame he didn't take it himself.

I looked back to the entrance and saw Snake and Buzz standing together, waiting to take their turn through the metal detector. They both looked extremely serious, but then they always looked that way till the drinking started. They made their way through and headed in my direction. I hoped they were smart enough not to stop at my desk as there were too many eyes around for my liking. I didn't want it said later that I'd been seen whispering with them.

The idea was beginning to grow clearer; I'd have to distance myself, legally that is. Somehow I'd have to have an alibi that would explain away my behavior, if worse came to worse I could easily give up Snake's whole operation.

Like a bad dream Snake stood staring down at me, Buzz had continued on to his work area. My last thought was still fresh and the guilt must have shown because Snake quickly picked up on it. He leaned toward me with a nasty smile and said, "You wouldn't be having second thoughts now would you?"

"I'm sitting here, ain't I? I'm in too deep to have a change of heart now. Besides, it isn't my ass on the line."

"Not yet. It's easy to hang tough when there's no heat, Stogie, we'll see what happens when the screws tighten."

"You don't have to worry about me." I didn't like the accusation, even though it had hit very near the mark.

"That's good to hear." He glanced at the locker and smiled, "There are plenty of reasons in there for you to toe the line, right? It would be a shame if it fell into the wrong hands."

I almost laughed out loud. Here he was threatening me with snitching, the very thing I was thinking. Maybe we were more alike than I'd thought. One thing was obvious, I was better at this game than anyone thought, myself included, and the possibility of snitching was one more weapon in the arsenal.

"That's no way to speak to one of your brothers." I said smiling. "Oh, and in case you didn't know, he's already here."

"You seem to keep forgetting, brother, I know everything that happens around here... You didn't think you were my only friend on that side, did you?" He let that bombshell sink in for a few heartbeats, then went on in a hushed, almost reverent voice, "I stood in front of Bull's cell speaking to him when Doolittle did him. You should have seen it, it was a thing of beauty. He didn't cry out or struggle at all, but slid softly to the floor cradled in Doolittle's arms staring into my eyes, my grin was the last thing he saw as he died... I hope I never get that little fucker mad at me, he's a dangerous man, friend or enemy. Well, I better head out. Wouldn't want to miss the festivities. Till then, brother."

I watched him walk away, as confident as ever, he and Teacher had that in common and it's the one that I really envied them. No matter what it was, work or home, something big or trivial, I went into everything expecting the worst and more often than not those expectations were met.

Jimmy V. was just stepping through the metal detector, the last to arrive, as usual. He always played the game close to the vest, not so close so to be suspect, but close enough to get out of having to do most things; although, he had committed one murder that I knew of. There are a lot of cons like him, who pretend to be gung-ho, but are always showing up a split-second too late to be involved, no such luck for him today. As he passed my desk he nodded and winked with what I knew was a fake confidence, as I could see his hand shaking where it hung ineffectually at his side. He was no Snake or Teacher, but I knew he was a pro, after all, he'd done this sort of work on the outside. It was disquieting to see him so openly nervous while the others showed nothing, maybe he was the smart one or maybe this would be the one time too many, where his past finally caught up, with bill in hand.

The free staff showed me to my work area, it was square-shaped and enclosed by chain link fencing, while the space where a roof should've been was open to the sky. When I asked, he said that in winter a domelike plexiglas structure was placed over the opening, but due to the heat it remained open during the summer. I looked up as he spoke and saw the blue sky stretch infinitely overhead, not bad, I thought. The area was big enough for 15 to 20 guys to work comfortably, but any more than that and it would quickly become crowded. I saw similar areas on both sides which were connected by gates in the chainlink, these gates were wide open and people were passing freely between areas; I would have to keep an eye on that.

All three areas were full of cons going about their business, cutting it up with friends while firing the machines up for the day's work. There were faces I recognized and a few nods in my direction, but everyone was doing a good job of staying away from me and I couldn't blame them. The only person who had spoken to me so far was my new boss, William Jones, who insisted I call him Billy even though he was close to sixty years old. He was a small man who wore workboots about the same age as he was and an old flannel shirt which had seen better days, and the entire time he spoke he never once looked at me. For the last ten minutes he'd shown me around and explained how the soling machine works. It was a large machine which resoled worn-out boots; the machine did all the work, all I had to do was stand there and push buttons. It was one of those technological wonders that makes life easier; I could feel myself growing dumber just looking at it.

I only gave him a small piece of my attention, just enough to pick up the workings of the machine, as I wouldn't be here long enough to become a fully functioning automaton; that was one bright spot in an otherwise dreary day, the rest was dedicated to my surroundings. Was anyone trying to creep up behind me?; were eyes lingering too long in my direction? I spotted a face I knew floating by on my right, it was dissected by the links of chain between us giving it a sinister look, but there was no mistaking a man that size, it was Buzz. There was no wave or nod of acknowledgement, he simply disappeared behind a moveable wall, I now knew one of my enemies.

"Allen, are you okay?"

My boss was scrutinizing me closely, a look of concern etching his already lined face. "Yes sir, I'm fine, just checked out for a minute. Sorry 'bout that."

"No worries, and don't call me sir, Billy's fine," he said, looking at me for the first time. There was a sadness which gave his eyes an unnatural depth and if I was not mistaken, some of it was meant for me. He glanced around in a hurried manner, then leaned close and whispered in a voice tinged with raw emotion, "Heather Lowe is a friend of mine and so is her husband. She told my wife and me what you did and I'd like to thank you." He grabbed my hand and shook it vigorously. His hand was warm, dry, and honest, lacking the sweat that is second nature to the convict.

"You're welcome, Billy. It was my pleasure to help, I only wish I could have stopped it before it began."

I shook his hand back and for a moment felt a twinge of guilt, he thinks I'm a better man than I truly am and I've aided that perception. After today he'd have no illusions and I'd have no guilt. As he walked away I stood there feeling like a complete fraud. I was an integral part of the violence that had touched Officer Lowe, I picked and chose the acts I was involved in thinking the reasoning behind them exempted me from their guilt, but violence is violence, it offers no exemptions, and here I was ready to commit yet another act, but I now know, there is no changing who you truly are.

A bell rang and the work hour began. Everyone was strapped to a machine in some strange symbiotic pairing; one brain, one muscle, two becoming one. I pushed a button on my machine and fell into rhythm with the mass and knew instantly that this would be mind-numbing work.

I glanced around and saw that all the connecting gates had been shut and locked, all except the two nearest my area, they'd only been closed, the locks were missing. I wondered when it would come and how many there'd be. I had no option but to wait as I didn't know where any of them worked, it would be ideal if I could catch Snake alone, but I knew better than to dwell on fantasy, he was too savvy for that. Better to be prepared for the worst.

9 o'clock, one hour into the workday and Snake is coming toward my desk. It was too early, the move wasn't supposed to go down till the lunch break, maybe something had gone wrong. He was walking fast, taking short, choppy steps which sang with anxiety.

"I need you to do something," he said, coming to an abrupt step.

I'd already done my part and I didn't like the sound of this. Nothing had happened yet and he was already deviating from the plan.

"What is it?" I asked cautiously.

"I need you to get the free staff out of there, we're gonna do it right now."

"How in the hell am I supposed to do that? I don't have any reason to call him out here, and besides, it would be too obvious. After it's done and questions start flying about why he wasn't at his work area, he's going to point the finger straight at me!"

He stared at me with cold, hard eyes. I could almost taste the contempt he felt for me, it clung to the back of my throat, threatening to suffocate me. In a voice as soft as silk he said, "I don't care how you do it, but you get him out of there or you're next. You can die alongside your hero." He turned to leave, then added. "You have half an hour," and he was gone as quickly as he'd come.

I was panting, my breath coming in little gulps which I could barely swallow; my heart was taking turns beating then skipping, hammering wildly against my ribcage, causing vibrations to travel through my body; my pulse beat so loud I could mark its time by the thumping in my ears. I desperately needed to get control of myself, to calm down and think. It was just a threat, he needed me too much to get rid of me, but playing it cautious was probably the wise course. I had a lot to lose and little to gain by defying his orders, but there would come a day when I'd turn the tables on him, I simply had to bide my time and find a way out of this current situation. How was I to get Billy out of the way without placing myself in it?

I went to Billy's work area and I could feel all eyes on me. I saw Doolittle peeking through the far fence wearing his usual grin, this was a hell of a time to be grinning. I also saw the others, they were in a corner lost in shadow, but there was no mistaking the look on their faces, they were ready. They were bouncing around on the balls of their feet like cage fighters waiting to be unleashed.

I knocked on the door of Billy's office as I entered, he was reclining in his chair with his feet propped up on the desk. His chin rested on his chest and his eyes were closed. He scrambled into an upright position and shuffled his papers around on his desk. I had to smile as I'd been caught in the same act many times.

"Take it easy, Billy, I ain't here to catch ya. In fact, I'm sorry to disturb you at all, but I need a favor." I said easily, hoping to allay his fears and engender a little gratitude.

"Hey Mike, how's things?" he asked sheepishly.

"Same shit, different day, you know the routine. I'd like to pull up a chair and kick my feet up on that desk right along-side you."

"Look, Mike, I don't do that often, it's not a habit or anything, I'm just wiped out today is all. I'd appreciate you keeping this between us... You mentioned a favor, what do ya need?"

And just like that I had my solution. I was surprised at how calm I'd suddenly become, at how I was enjoying this, the intrigue and duplicity were like a high. He didn't want me to report him, so no matter what took place he'd keep his mouth shut; somebody or something wanted this to happen.

"I'm expecting a phone call, but I need to use the restroom something fierce. Can you cover my desk and if the call comes through take a number and tell them I'll call right back?"

He was mulling it over too long, so I added, "and whatever you do in your office is none of my business."

That clinched it.

"Okay. Let's get this done fast, I don't like to leave my area unattended, you know?"

I almost laughed, "of course, there's no telling what these animals might do. I'll be in the restroom down by the main kitchen, it's the only one that works properly." I'd chosen the restroom which was farthest away so he wouldn't be tempted to check on me.

We walked to my desk together leaving the gates open behind us, and I headed for the restroom. I hadn't gone far when I flipped a U-turn and slowly headed back, I wanted to watch. Finally I came to Snake's area, as soon as he spotted me I nodded, and he, Buzz, and Jimmy V. went through the gate into Teacher's area like bats out of hell; their hands and hearts filled with hate.

I saw them coming and was surprised and a little dismayed at the sense of euphoria that swept through me. This was personal and the long delay would make it that much more satisfying, but I hadn't anticipated feeling so happy; maybe I hadn't changed at all.

There were three of them, I knew two but the third was a stranger. As they squeezed through the gate it was no surprise to see Snake bringing up the rear; ever true to his nature he was looking out for number one. Second was Buzz, he towered over the other two and wore a mask like grim death. I had an old score to settle with him and from his look he had one too. In the lead was the unknown and the unknown is dangerous. He was short and stocky with long hair pulled back into a ponytail, which hung down his back nearly to his waist. He wasn't scared or overly excited as most youngsters are, this wasn't his first rodeo. I decided to deal with him first.

I quickly glanced around to make sure no one was creeping up behind me. All the cons had left their machines and were lined up along the fence, hungry looks on their faces, bodies twitching in anticipation. I saw neither friend nor foe, which is all I could ask. To them I was nothing more than the day's entertainment and best of all it was free, or so they thought; but there is always a price, isn't there?

After passing through the gate they immediately fanned out with a military-like precision, even though they were coming for me I found myself admiring their movements. The wings moved in as the center lagged, forming a half circle; I was struck by the thought that we'd come full circle and were once again at the beginning, now was my chance to do what I should've done then. It was time, no more thinking, I darted to my right to confront the unknown.

He didn't move. They were moving toward him, encircling him, and still he didn't move. He stood still watching their advance, eyes scanning all about him. I couldn't understand what he was doing, had fear frozen his heart, turning his limbs to stone? Was he just going to stand there and let this happen, take his medicine?

I'd seen him in action many times and although he was outnumbered I felt he could contend with the odds, if not win outright. At least the competition should be even. But still he didn't move.

My feet began to carry me forward one heavy step after another. Unconsciously I had moved through the first work area and was standing framed in the gate, before I knew what I was doing I had pushed through and was standing against the fence mingled among the convicts. I felt vague and shapeless, yet, a part of something. I had an alarm belted at my waist, but I didn't want to stop this spectacle; I couldn't have in any event as my body was following its own commands. Besides, I knew it was going to be one hell of a show, the only thing that could make this better is if Teacher had D-Man with him, then I would see things only whispered about.

As I watched with mounting disappointment the look on Teacher's face changed, gone was the studious stillness of the observer, in its place bloomed the eagerness of the participant. The excitement was growing in the air around me, and though I wasn't to be involved I felt as if I already were.

Without warning Teacher lunged at Jimmy V. It wasn't a move of desperation, unwieldy and born of panic, but graceful, almost as if he were performing a dance move. The attack was so sudden Jimmy didn't even move to defend himself, Teacher's fist crashed into his face with the force of a head-on collision, Jimmy's head snapped back in a whiplashing motion as he crumpled to the floor. Teacher's follow-through pulled him to his left and he took two quick steps and was face-to-face with Snake, but before he could act Buzz hit him in the side of the head and sent him reeling into one of the machines. The two closed on him quickly.

I glanced to where Jimmy V lay, he was shaking his head from side to side in an attempt to get rid of the cobwebs. He still had his knife clutched tightly in his right hand. He climbed groggily to his feet, regaining strength by the second. My eyes went back to the action.

It was difficult to distinguish who was doing what, arms and legs were flailing at each other with such speed they seemed to be a separate entity, ownerless. Snake's back was facing me and I could see his right arm moving piston-like while his left held onto Teacher's shirt. Huge fists, that looked more like clumps of rock than flesh, were swinging over Snake's left shoulder and landing with punishing force against the side of his face and head, every blow sent him staggering drunkenly into Buzz, momentarily halting their attack.

Buzz was gripping a knife in his left hand, but instead of using it he continued to club away with his right, fighting in the same manner as Teacher; I wondered if that was on purpose.

Snake slipped and fell to one knee, Teacher's leg instantly lashed out, his boot catching Snake under the jaw sending him motionless to the ground. Jimmy V picked that exact moment to reenter the melee. As Teacher was trying to regain his balance, Jimmy's knife plunged into his ribcage just beneath his right arm. All motion stopped as if by prior agreement, they looked like posed objects in a still life, then Teacher broke the spell. With the knife still in him he spun around Jimmy's extended arm breaking his grip on its handle and ending up behind him. He reached awkwardly up and ripped it from his side, he was now armed. His left arm shot over Jimmy's shoulder, his hand clamping onto the jaw, he wrenched back savagely making Jimmy's whole body contort and arch in an effort to ease the pressure. The knife came flashing down and buried itself behind his right collarbone, Teacher yanked it back and forth in a sawing motion, then tore it free. He retreated a few steps and settled into a crouch surveying his opponents.

Jimmy stood still for a moment, uncertain, then took a few tentative steps as ungainly as a newborn colt, then collapsed. A fountain of red shot from his neck, his jugular and carotid severed, his life quickly coming to an end.

I saw movement out of the corner of my eye and turned in its direction, it was Doolittle coming to join the party. He was supposed to stand guard on the gate that covered their escape route, but the temptation had proved too much. The closer he came the wider his grin, he looked like a child on Christmas who had received everything he asked for, yet had designs on still more. He moved like fluid, flowing unconcernedly around and over objects in his path, without breaking his stride or taking his eyes off the prize.

Snake was back on his feet and he and Buzz were warily weaving their way toward the target. Blood dripped from his chin and left eye, but he looked none the worse for wear. Again Teacher moved first, he charged at Snake, then at the last second veered into Buzz with his shoulder, sending him skidding across the floor. Instantly he rounded on Snake and said something which I couldn't hear, but they were both grinning as they closed. It looked like a hockey fight straight out of a nightmare, they had their left hands tangled up in the others shirt front trying to jerk the guy off balance, and all the while their right arms were driving the steel home over and over. They were clutching each other almost in an embrace, moving in a circle of seeming choreography; a danse macabre.

Snake broke loose and staggered away, his shirt hanging off of him in shreds. He was bleeding from over a dozen wounds in his chest and side. Teacher looked no better, his breathing was labored and frothy red bubbles were popping at the corners of his mouth, but he wouldn't relent, he surged forward only to be tackled from behind by Buzz. Immediately Snake and Doolittle piled on. The bodies, like the ocean's face, rolled and heaved with an undulating rhythm, only hinting at the turmoil beneath.

It was reminiscent of a pride of lions taking down a water buffalo. Although he is one against many, his sheer size gives hope to the chance of escape. But with a practiced patience they are soon hanging from his front and back, dangling from his sides, perched atop him anchored with claws and teeth. Now it's only a matter of time, his strength will ebb and his burden become too much. Patience and weight; great weight. He will be subdued never to rise again.

I can't breathe. I struggle with the weight holding me down, but that's not it. Something's wrong. I suck in mouthfuls of air and it isn't enough, it's as though it has become lost on its way to my lungs. I feel as if I've just finished a sprint and my breathing will not steady, will not return to normal. How long can I go on in this shape? I know what's happened, one of my lungs has been punctured and has quit on me. I need to end this, because I won't last much longer in this condition. But all my efforts are futile, no matter how I push or shove, wrench or contort, it's all for naught, the weight is too much.

I can feel punches and kicks landing, knees digging in trying to separate ribs, the soft popping sound of a knife breaking skin; yet, all these were a mere annoyance to be brushed or swatted away; I must get up! For a split second I thought of D-Man, he would laugh to see the predicament I've got myself into, but things would be a lot different if he were here.

I renewed my efforts, I had to get up while I still had the strength or I wouldn't be getting up at all.

It would be over soon now. His efforts were weakening and only coming in short bursts. They looked like swimmers in a sea of blood. I'd never seen so much blood in my life, I didn't know one could bleed so much and still be alive, even if only.

I looked to where Jimmy V lay. The blood flowing out of his neck had all but stopped, maybe there was none left. He lay in a pool roughly twice the size of his body and the others were rolling around in it adding their own to the mixture. His skin had gone waxy and pale, he no longer looked real. Besides the ticking of the index finger on his right hand, he lay as still and heavy as guilt.

A sudden movement drew my eyes back to the 'main stage.' Buzz was standing over the piled limbs with an odd look on his face. The remaining three continued their struggle while he stood staring down impassively. They were bumping against his legs and folding around them only to roll away once again; like waves hurling themselves against rocks in a seemingly futile task, yet, over time, the rock will erode and tumble into the sea, and so it was here. The look on his face changed, red splotches bloomed on his pale cheeks and forehead while his eyes narrowed. He reared back one of his legs and sent a kick slamming into the side of Snake's head, which sent him reeling into Doolittle. He instantly followed up on his attack, crouching over Snake, indiscriminately raining blows down. Doolittle scrambled away on all fours, looking over his shoulder in confusion at the turn of events. Teacher was struggling to his feet, swaying like an oak in a thunderstorm, battling to remain upright and rooted. His shirt was missing and blood ran in rivulets down his body, he was grotesque and inspiring at the same time. He still had Jimmy's knife gripped in his right fist and he was looking for his enemies. He glanced at Buzz's assault on Snake and seemed to take it for granted. Then his eyes found me.

My head was swimming. My arms were so heavy I could scarcely raise them. As I stood my weight felt immense, I'd never been this weak in my entire life. I took in the scene before me and it came as no surprise, Buzz had saved me. I knew that he'd always hated Snake, he'd just never had a reason to act on it, till now. I'd felt him pulling his punches and I did the same, message sent and received. Whoever else had been involved must've took off, because it was just the three of us. What had started out as four on one was now two on one in my favor, I marveled at how quickly things can change.

At any other time a moment's respite would've been welcome, and even though I was gathering my legs back under me, I knew I didn't have much time left as I was possibly hurt beyond repair. For the first time I noticed Stogie standing on the fringes which encircled the area, if it wasn't for his uniform he would've been indistinguishable from the mob. He wore the same look, the same lust for violence as the rest; those who enjoy violence at another's expense and from a safe distance, who, when it came to their doorstep, were appalled. This moment had been twenty years in the making and it had taken a dirty skrew to make it possible, it was past time for him to be more intimately involved.

He was coming toward me, I had to get out of here, but as hard as I tried I couldn't move. My body and brain were no longer one, my brain was frantically sending the flight signal but my body betrayed me;

standing still in the face of certain death, it seemed to have switched sides, going over to the enemy. He was only ten feet away, but it might as well have been a hundred, a thousand, for the time it took him to cover it. But finally he stood before me, knife and jaw clenched alike.

"Why didn't you push your alarm, Stogie?" he said in a hoarse whisper, which sounded like two stones being scrapped together.

I wasn't supposed to push the alarm till Snake and the others made their escape, but that plan had not worked, had it? I could've pushed it to save Snake, but... I should've pushed it immediately, I am after all still a guard, or am I? I couldn't answer the question as I didn't know the answer.

"You want me to end it for you, don't you? No matter what side you were on, you've never been man enough to make your own decisions, and I'm not gonna do you any favors now."

He let the knife slip from his hand, it fell noiselessly to the floor; absent the hand which wields it, it lay harmless.

"You better get out of here before -"

His words were cut off as Doolittle's knife bit deeply into his neck, sawing back leaving an ever-widening wound. Like a volcano's eruption, the blood shot out as if in anger, and like lava, when it splashed my face and neck it scalded. Doolittle was gone as quick as he'd come, he shot through the gate and padlocked it behind him, then disappeared.

I stared at Teacher's neck in fascination and horror. This is it, this was a man dying and I had done it. He slowly knelt to the ground and lay on his back. He didn't look in pain and he seemed somehow younger as the wrinkles left his brow.

Buzz came to stand over him, leaving Snake motionless on the floor. I had to get out of here, there was no telling what would happen next. I started toward the gate I'd entered only to find it locked. I was supposed to be the one who locked it. I couldn't understand what had happened. I looked up and saw angry faces staring at me through the chainlink. The convicts had found the padlock and locked me in. I had the key, but I also had the distinct feeling that they wouldn't let me pass. I only had one option, I reached down and pushed the alarm.

I lie on the cold ground, it feels good. It takes the heat and aches away. My eyes are filled with a brilliant blue sky staring serenely down on me, it's the stuff of which poems are made. I see a red-tailed hawk circling, riding the warm air in an ever higher arc. He's straining with every beat of his wings to sever the last thread which keeps him earthbound. He reaches a spot where all resistance ceases and he is free. No longer struggling he soars unencumbered, he has done it, he's made good his escape.

He looks down for a final time as if in remembrance, then points his head to the heaven's and disappears.

I smile and think I'll follow.

EPILOGUE

The concrete walls are pre-fabricated, they're poured into forms on the ground and raised into place by giant cranes. I was there when they were raised and puzzled together, standing with friends watching the place in which we'd soon be working, built. All the surfaces are unworked, leaving the final product looking as if it had been abandoned in the midst of construction or if a step in the process had been overlooked. As you lie on the bunk and stare at the ceiling, you can see the boot prints of workers, it gives a dizzying effect confusing up from down; in this world where possibility is snuffed out in its infancy is hidden the beginnings of a new one.

The rough hewn texture holds many surprises, if looked at long enough. Faces appear out of the blotchy, swirling concrete, they come forth as if summoned and wear the screams that are trapped inside everyone. There's a hint of connection, of relation, a shared bond which is not grasped through understanding but through suffering.

"Mr. Walker, you know your associate is still alive, don't you? And he is cooperating with the District Attorney. He has given a videotaped confession implicating you and many others. He says you're the mastermind behind the organization; that you planned and effected all the crimes; that you gave orders to subordinate members throughout the prison system and on the streets resulting in over thirty murders. Would you like to refute any of those charges?"

I knew all about Snake. His injuries had been so extensive that he'd barely pulled through. He'd been stabbed over thirty times, his skull had been fractured, he lost an eye and now wore prescription sunglasses to hide the crater in his face. The prison grapevine was remarkable in the amount and accuracy of its information and the big news racing along its branches these days was that Snake had turned snitch. He had become the very thing he hated most in this world, but it didn't surprise me; he always spoke of doing everything and more, so it only made sense that the one line he'd drawn he'd eventually cross.

On the bench beside me was a stack of paper about two inches thick, I reached down and took hold of it, placing it on the table between us, she had asked me to write and I had. I found it wiser to speak through my pen, it was easier to control the message.

Her eyes widened with sudden insight, but she asked anyway, "What is this?"

"It's what you've been asking for," I said, standing to leave. "Come back when you've read it and maybe we can have a conversation."

As I was escorted from the room I saw her hands fly to the stack and start leafing through its pages. I didn't give her everything, but what I did would be enough to thrill her. Of course, I kept the most damning for myself. With it in her hands the District Attorney wouldn't need Snake, so him and his testimony would be thrown back to the wolves. He'd been protected, housed at a federal prison on a soft yard for rats, but now they would cut him loose, sending him back home to us, and we had a wonderful welcome in store for our prodigal brother.

I tried to hang myself last night. It's what they'd expect from a remorseful man and I like to give the audience what they want, and my Lawyer ate it up. Now I had only to see how Dr. Adams reacted, after all, it was mainly for her benefit.

It had been a week since I'd given her my writings and I started to think she wasn't coming back, but here she was. We've been sitting in the interview room for ten minutes and not a single word has been spoken, this is unlike her, she's changed just like the rest of us. I knew she was shocked by what I'd written, maybe enough to have shaken some of her values and belief in the good of all mankind.

"Truth is offensive, isn't it Doctor? All sing its praises and long for its clarity, but that's just a dream woven of pretty words."

She didn't respond.

"Do you still not understand? There is no one truth, only variations on the lie; and everyone prefers their own, don't they?" I prompted.

"How could you do that to someone who had saved your life?" she asked naively. "Easy. I tell myself he went too far; that he crossed the line between convict and guard; that he broke his own rules; all of which brought his end, I was only the instrument he himself chose. I have to tell myself this because I cannot believe the opposite. Do you understand? Please, tell me you understand!"

She only stared uncomprehendingly, her eyes roaming over my face and bandaged neck. Her face, a mixture of pity and revulsion warring for dominance; war never was pitys' forte. Disbelief was plain upon her face, she wasn't burying it.

I spoke again. "I didn't tell you everything I read in Teacher's C-file. You'll remember that he was attacked and had his face cut open by one of Snake's friends -"

"You mean by one of your friends!"

"If you'd like... When I read of the incident in his file I discovered that Internal Affairs had me under investigation. They thought I had played a hand in it, you see, and my going to the sergeant was only subterfuge, which it wasn't."

"I don't see how that has anything to do with later events or how it justifies your actions."

"You will have a little patience. I.A. interviewed Teacher and as usual, he was uncooperative, until they mentioned me. That's when he uttered the words that changed everything - "Stogie's an alright guy, he was just scared." - he thought he was helping me, but his truth is not mine. What he did was to hang a placard about my neck, reading coward in bold letters. He effectively changed my entire life. With a single sentence he not only redirected my future, but he rewrote my past, and no man has the right to do that. Now do you understand when I tell you I was only the instrument? He called the shots, he headed down that particular road to that particular confrontation of his own accord. If you want to find me guilty of being a pawn, go ahead, but don't misplace your sympathy on the agent of all that occurred."

She uncoiled from her chair with a serpentine languidity, the kind that lulls you into a false sense of security just before you feel the fangs strike. Her hand came down on the table in a blur, making a sharp crack. I jumped back. She leaned forward and said, "I understand you better than you think, you're speaking of yourself." Then a vicious smile appeared, one which marred her beauty and contradicted her humanity. "Do you know that when you're convicted, and you will be, you'll be housed right here at this prison? And there are a few of Mr. Allen's friends who are dying to see you."

I knew that, but I also knew that I had finally found what I was good at in this life.

You may even say I've found my calling.

We draw hard lines early in life. Never intending to cross them and scorning these on the other side. But much later, after having been wrung out, these lines blur and smudge with an appalling ease and then we wake one day and are no longer who we thought we were; what then?

www.ingramcontent.com/pod-product-compliance
Lightning Source LLC
Chambersburg PA
CBHW030816160125
20420CB00018B/303/J

North Providence Union Free Library
1810 Mineral Spring Avenue
North Providence, RI 02904
(401) 353-5600

NO LONGER PROPERTY OF THE
NORTH PROVIDENCE UNION FREE LIBRARY